Bond

Lark sighed. Nothing wou̶̶̶̶̶̶̶̶̶̶̶̶̶̶̶̶̶̶ had his way. She had no doubt he meant to stop her from winning her silver wings.

She ran her hand over Tup's back and found it dry. She put the blanket back on and swung the saddle up and over. As she buckled the straps, she said, "This is it now, my Tup. We go on to Arlton and hope we can find the Palace, and Baron Rys, without difficulty. After that . . . I can't tell you."

Tup turned his head, and his shining black eye regarded her for a long moment. She stroked his cheek. "Aye," she said softly. "Aye, my lovely, fine boy. Whatever happens, at least we're together."

She leaped into the saddle, adjusted her boots in the stirrups, and they were off . . .

AIRS
OF NIGHT
AND SEA

TOBY BISHOP

ACE BOOKS, NEW YORK

THE BERKLEY PUBLISHING GROUP
Published by the Penguin Group
Penguin Group (USA) Inc.
375 Hudson Street, New York, New York 10014, USA
Penguin Group (Canada), 90 Eglinton Avenue East, Suite 700, Toronto, Ontario M4P 2Y3, Canada
(a division of Pearson Penguin Canada Inc.)
Penguin Books Ltd., 80 Strand, London WC2R 0RL, England
Penguin Group Ireland, 25 St. Stephen's Green, Dublin 2, Ireland (a division of Penguin Books Ltd.)
Penguin Group (Australia), 250 Camberwell Road, Camberwell, Victoria 3124, Australia
(a division of Pearson Australia Group Pty. Ltd.)
Penguin Books India Pvt. Ltd., 11 Community Centre, Panchsheel Park, New Delhi—110 017, India
Penguin Group (NZ), 67 Apollo Drive, Rosedale, North Shore 0632, New Zealand
(a division of Pearson New Zealand Ltd.)
Penguin Books (South Africa) (Pty.) Ltd., 24 Sturdee Avenue, Rosebank, Johannesburg 2196,
South Africa

Penguin Books Ltd., Registered Offices: 80 Strand, London WC2R 0RL, England

AIRS OF NIGHT AND SEA

An Ace Book / published by arrangement with the author

PRINTING HISTORY
Ace mass-market edition / January 2009

Copyright © 2009 by Louise Marley.
Cover art by Allen Douglas.
Cover design by Judith Lagerman.
Interior text design by Kristin del Rosario.

ISBN: 978-0-441-01669-3

ACE
Ace Books are published by The Berkley Publishing Group,
a division of Penguin Group (USA) Inc.,
375 Hudson Street, New York, New York 10014.
ACE and the "A" design are trademarks of Penguin Group (USA) Inc.

PRINTED IN THE UNITED STATES OF AMERICA

10 9 8 7 6 5 4 3 2 1

PROLOGUE

DIAMOND'S silver wings beat against the hot summer air, lifting the dapple gray filly above the park, beyond the beech grove, and on toward the hills, where the first autumn chill gilded the grasses and bronzed the leaves of ash and oak. Her ears flickered as she flew faster, invigorated by the taste of freedom. The saddle and sand weights, though she carried them for the first time, were no hindrance. Her monitor, a Foundation gelding, flew slowly and steadily beside her, both he and his horsemistress keeping watch over the young horse.

William of Oc and his Master Breeder watched from the paddock as Diamond darted above her monitor with an exuberant flick of her tail. Her coat caught the sun in brilliant spangles as she carved dazzling spirals above and below the old gelding. From the ground, William heard the horsemistress calling to her, trying to settle her.

Jinson groaned, "Your Grace! She's so hard to control!"

William laughed and tapped his thigh with his quirt. "Nonsense!" he said. "She's just spirited. Flying with a monitor bores her. I'm bored with it myself! I'll fly her before winter."

"Duke William, I can't recommend it," Jinson protested. "She's so young, and you're too heavy—"

"I'm not too heavy," the Duke said. "I've not eaten more than one meal a day for weeks now." He held his hand up in the sunlight. The fingers were so thin his bones showed beneath the skin. He liked the effect. He liked looking gaunt and hollow-cheeked, and besides, the paucity of food diminished the swelling of his chest, as well. "You see, Jinson?" he said. "I'm ready. And so is she."

"But—Your Grace—you've never flown, and if you can't control her—" Jinson began.

William slapped his quirt across his palm. "Enough of your whinging, man! If I can't control her, I'll fall and die. Then you'll have something else to complain about."

"My lord, I didn't mean . . . It's not as if I want you to . . ."

William caressed the quirt in his fingers, and eyed Jinson. He said in his silkiest tone, "I don't doubt your loyalty, man. Why, if something should happen to me, the Council Lords would probably banish you to Aeskland."

Jinson paled at that, and William chuckled. The winged horses turned back toward the paddock, the gelding trying to hold the lead, Diamond swerving this way and that, sparkling in the sunlight like her namesake stone. William's heart beat faster at the sight of her. She delighted him in ways he had never expected, and the affection he felt surprised him.

Jinson said, "My lord, if you're not successful—that is, I'm worried the Council might—" He broke off when William threw up his hand.

"Damn it, Jinson! And damn the Council." His mood darkened instantly. "That lot of foolish old men can't see past their own great noses. I'll pass the tax without them."

Jinson subsided with an obvious sagging of his shoulders and mouth. "Come now, Jinson," William chided. "They can't have it both ways. They're always quoting my great-great-great-grandfather at me, and he did exactly what I'm trying to do. He levied a tax to build a flying school. It's precedent, and the Lords of the Council love precedent."

Jinson kept his eyes on his boots as he said, "Yes, Your Grace."

William turned away from him, knowing his unvoiced thought, irritated by it. It was true that his ancestor, that long-ago Duke, had faced little opposition to his tax. The Academy of the Air had been a popular undertaking. The people of Oc had been convinced that training girls properly to become horsemistresses, protecting and preserving the bloodlines of the winged horses, would strengthen their little Duchy, both in its own principality of Isamar and in the larger world. They had been right. His ancestor had been a wildly popular leader.

William switched his quirt impatiently against his trouser leg. Why could no one see? It was time for something new, a new day, a new bloodline. These damned weaklings in the Council, so married to the past, to the old ways . . . Wait until they saw him fly Diamond! That would bring them to heel. Even that damned Philippa Winter—wherever she had fled to—would have to bow to his will. In fact, he had a good idea how to force her to come back. He could kill two birds with one stone—deal with that Hamley brat, who managed to stand in his way at every turn, and bring Philippa back to pay for her crimes.

He looked up into the hard blue sky. The gelding, a black called Sky Baron, flew with deliberate wingbeats. His rider, Felicity Baron, had protested this assignment, but William had cared nothing for that. Mistress Baron was getting a bit long in the tooth, in any case, and surely her mount was past his service at the South Tower. Both of them should be damned grateful to be living at their ease in Fleckham House, nothing expected of them except teaching a beautiful filly to fly.

He hated Mistress Baron's doubtful glances, but at least she did what he told her to do. He had some very persuasive ways to remind her who was master in the Duchy of Oc.

These cursed horsemistresses! The thought of their insolence made his heart pound beneath his embroidered vest. Sometimes at night he could calm himself only by picturing them, a whole line of them, bending the knee to him as he rode past. When his own Fleckham Academy was built, they would curtsy properly to their Duke. None of this insulting nodding of the head, as if that showed sufficient respect.

He thrust his irritation away as he watched Diamond come to ground, her wings fluttering as she glided, forefeet flashing silver as they reached for the grass of the park. Her hindquarters collected, then settled as she found her balance. She cantered toward the paddock, wings still spread wide. Baron's canter was too slow for her, and she dashed past him. She galloped, head high, white mane and tail streaming, toward William, leaving the old gelding to trot behind.

Diamond skidded to a stop a few feet from William and stood, tossing her head and stamping her pretty forefeet. "Get back, Jinson," William said. Jinson backed away so that Diamond could come close to William, blowing through her delicate nostrils. William put his hand on the cheek strap of her halter, murmuring, "Beautifully done, my girl, beautifully done! We'll show them, won't we? We'll be flying before you know it!"

She threw up her head, pulling away from him. She side-stepped, shaking her head so her bridle jangled, then came close again. It was, William thought, like a little dance, a flirtation. It had become a habit with her, as if she couldn't quite make up her mind.

He worried about it sometimes. She didn't press her nose against him the way the other winged horses did with their bondmates. He wished she would nuzzle him, nose at his pockets for treats, simply stand close to him, as he wanted to stand close to her. She was so restless, pawing at the ground, sometimes showing her teeth when he tried to stroke her.

They needed to fly, he thought. They needed to rise above the ground, leave all distractions below. In the air there would be no problem. In the air they would be utterly alone, just the two of them.

Diamond could hardly pull away from him when they were aloft.

ONE

PHILIPPA Winter stood beside Winter Sunset in a high pasture of southern Klee, letting the mountain breeze cool her hot cheeks and dry the sweat from Sunny's wings. Fields of lavender spilled down the steep hillside at their feet. On the opposite hill, black-faced sheep grazed in the sunshine, so close Philippa could have tossed a stone among them. Their occasional bleating was the only sound except for the whisper of the wind blowing up from the sea. Sunny stood still, listening to the peaceful quiet.

Philippa encircled her bondmate's neck with her arm. "Sunny, my girl," she said. "It may not be home, but it could be worse."

Sunny arched her neck to touch Philippa's face with her velvet muzzle. Philippa laughed and stroked her. "A little lonely, yes. But it's a beautiful spot."

A shepherd raised an arm in silent greeting, and Philippa inclined her head in response. They had become friends of a sort, she and the odd assortment of people who maintained this remote estate. When she had first arrived, weary from the long flight, weighed down with sadness, she had hardly spoken to anyone. Her silence had made no impression. The staff at Marinan were a silent lot themselves and used to solitude. But that had been more than a year ago. Since Baron Rys's captain had brought her to this mountain estate, she had grown familiar with its denizens, human and animal, and she had come to know every hill and valley of Marinan, the Ryses' ancestral home.

The family rarely came here now, having a bigger and better house in the capital city and another on the northern coast.

They left Marinan in the care of an elderly housekeeper named Lyssett, two taciturn shepherds, and two narders to till and harvest the lavender. The sweet scent of lavender permeated every corner of the old house. Even the sheep's oily wool, brushing against stray branches in the lavender fields, picked up and held the scent.

These people had lived at Marinan all their lives. The young people had long since moved to livelier places, but these faithful retainers would never part from Marinan until death did it for them. The narders carried the lavender oil and seeds to the capital for sale and returned home immediately afterward. The shepherds left the hills only for the occasional festival, or to carry wool to market. Lyssett, to Philippa's knowledge, never traveled at all except to the bottom of the long, precipitous lane to meet the mail coach. It was a circumscribed life, serenely undisturbed by the outside world. It was, in fact, the perfect place for a hunted person—and her winged horse—to hide.

A stall had been cleaned and provisioned for Winter Sunset before they arrived. The narder who showed Philippa to the barn and the stall would say only, "M'lord's orders," when she asked him any questions. Her first few days at Marinan, she was afraid to leave Sunny alone, even to sleep, but by the time they had been there a week, she understood that no stranger or random visitor ever climbed the lane to the house, and that no one except the narders and the shepherds and Lyssett occupied Marinan. When she mentioned Baron Rys, the look of respect on every face convinced her that these good country people would never betray her. All that had been needed to transfer their loyalty to her was the word of Rys's captain, given to Lyssett when he delivered Philippa and Sunny over to her care.

Soon Philippa and Sunny were flying every day without fear of discovery. They avoided the lowland villages, where people's tongues might be set a-rattle at the sight of a winged horse, and flew instead into the mountains, where they could come to ground on steep hillsides, in secluded meadows, in hidden valleys lush with oak trees and linden and tall, sweet-smelling pines. When they had set a pattern of being gone for many hours each day, Lyssett began to prepare a packet of bread and cheese and fruit, and lay it on the table next to Philippa's place at breakfast.

For that entire summer, and into the swiftly falling mountain autumn, Philippa and her mare reveled in the peace of Marinan. Sometimes Philippa, lying in her solitary bed at night, longed for news of the Academy of the Air. But she had come perilously close to losing her bondmate, and if isolation was the price she paid to avoid that tragedy, she willingly accepted it.

The occasional betraying dream of Deeping Farm, of violet-eyed Larkyn Hamley—and, foolishly, of her brother Brye—disturbed her sleep from time to time. She would wake then, and shake herself in remonstrance. It was merely weakness, the sort of nonsense possible only in sleep. She would close her eyes again, comforting herself with the knowledge that Sunny was safe in the barn just across the yard.

When winter closed in, with its snow and ice and long hours of darkness, she and Sunny rested, venturing out on only the clearest days. Spring found them both feeling as sprightly and restless as fledglings. And now, as a second summer wound down, Philippa began to feel as if she were thirty years of age instead of forty. She felt strong, relaxed, and refreshed. She also felt idle, as the days slipped away, one after another, and for this she experienced a twinge of remorse. She tried to help in the barn, and in the fields when she could, but not one of the Marinan retainers encouraged this industry.

Esmond Rys's appearance came as a surprise, the first visitor Philippa had seen in all her time at Marinan. She had noticed the elaborate meal preparations Lyssett was making, and the extra effort being expended on clipping hedges and raking gravel walks, but it didn't occur to her that the staff was expecting their lord.

The season was perhaps midway between Estian and Erdlin. It was hard to judge, as the Klee had different holidays. They didn't worship the entwined gods of the Isamarians, but had some singular deity whose festival was held at midwinter. Philippa, an avowed skeptic, had never paid much attention to such things. She had lost track of the calendar, taking each day as it came, sun or rain or wind or snow.

The sky on this day was a clear blue, the sun just beginning its descent into the west. Philippa was sweeping the aisles of the barn, sprinkling fresh sawdust from a wheelbarrow. She and Sunny had flown to one of their favorite spots that morning, a long flight to one of the high mountain pastures where a shepherd's hut stood near a tiny, sparkling pond, and the lush grass reached Sunny's knees. Philippa let Sunny graze while she dabbled her bare feet in the clear water and let the mountain sun toast her cheeks. She even dozed a little, there in the grass, before taking wing again for Marinan.

They had been back about an hour when she was startled to hear hoofbeats in the lane that wound up the mountain. She dropped her broom and hurried to the barn door. She kept her face in shadow, but leaned forward just enough to see that two horses had come into the yard.

The familiar sight of Rys's slight figure gave her a rush of pleasure. It had been so long since she had spoken to anyone except Lyssett or the narders. She stepped out into the yard, smoothing her hair with her palms as she went, hoping her habit was not too grimy with sawdust and specks of hay. "My lord!" she called. "How good to see you!"

He turned and gave her his usual restrained smile. It looked even more familiar to her since she had gotten to know his daughter, Amelia, who was very like him. Everything about these Ryses seemed understated, and yet spoke of strength and competence.

"And you, Mistress Winter," Rys said. "It's easy to see that you're well. And Sunny?"

"She's fine." She reached him as he dismounted, and on an impulse, put out her hand.

He took it, bowed over it, and said, "Philippa. You look wonderfully rested."

"We could hardly be otherwise, Esmond," she said, and chuckled. "Sunny and I are as lazy and fat as two cats in the sun. I'm surprised to see you, though I suppose I should have suspected. Lyssett has been cooking for two days, and the narders took time from the fields to rake the paths."

He smiled. "I sent a note with the mail coach." Rys's companion slid down from his own saddle, and Rys nodded in his direction. "This is my nephew, Philippa. My brother's son, Niven Rys. Niven, Philippa Winter."

The young man bowed, and said gravely, "Horsemistress. An honor."

She inclined her head to him. "My lord Niven."

"Just Niven, Mistress Winter. Please."

"As you wish. Then I am Philippa, and I propose to stable your horses there while you go in and refresh yourselves."

The young prince's brows rose at this. "Where's the staff?"

"The narders are weeding in the lavender fields this afternoon, down below the storage sheds. The shepherds—" She pointed to the west. "They're grazing the sheep in the small meadow. And Lyssett, of course, will be at work on our evening meal."

Esmond chuckled. "I see you've become one of my household, Philippa."

Her lips curved. "I've been supremely comfortable. I'm so grateful, Esmond."

"Go, then, if you would, Philippa, and stable our horses. We appreciate your help. We'll have a bit of a wash, then we can sit down over a cup of tea and talk."

LYSSETT laid on a full tea, with sandwiches and cakes, though an even more complete supper was clearly under way. The scents of roasting lamb and mint sauce filled the house.

Philippa sat at the long dining room table, toying with her teacup. Niven had the healthy appetite of a young man who had been riding all day, and he cleared every crumb from his plate. Even Esmond ate well, with compliments to Lyssett that brought a blush to the housekeeper's wrinkled cheeks.

When Esmond pushed away his plate and picked up his teacup, Philippa said, "What news of your daughter?"

"Amelia says she will begin riding soon," he said. "Her colt—she says they haven't named him yet—but she writes that he is perfect in every way." He made a deprecating gesture. "Actually, she writes at rather astonishing length about his perfections, from his glossy coat to his beautiful hooves and his spectacular wings!"

Philippa chuckled. "Every girl feels the same about her bondmate, Esmond."

"So I gather. But she sounds happy, and she says she's working him on a longue line in the dry paddock, whatever that is."

"That sounds right. Her colt should be coming two in the spring. The winged horses mature early." She sipped tea and set the cup down. "What other news? Have you just come from Arlton?"

"Yes, I had business for Prince Nicolas, and a meeting with my lord brother in the capital. I wanted to pay you a visit, and Niven offered to ride with me." He steepled his fingers, and his eyes were somber. "I preferred not to involve any of my servants. Too much talk."

"I appreciate that, Esmond," Philippa said. "And thank you, Niven, for taking the time. It's lovely to have company."

The boy nodded. "Makes a nice change from court," he said. "Too much standing around, talking!"

Rys pursed his lips. "It's the way governing gets done, Niven. You'll have to accept that if you're going to be viscount one day."

Niven grimaced. "I wish I were the younger son!" he exclaimed.

"Either way," Rys said, lifting an admonishing forefinger. "Diplomacy is at the heart of good government."

"Speaking of which . . ." Philippa said, and raised her brows at Rys.

He gave her a level look. "Are you asking about Arlton, or Oc?"

"It is Oc, of course, that interests me most," she said. "But I expect the two are related."

"Indeed," Rys said. "Horsemistresses are kept busy flying messages back and forth."

"Has William visited Arlton?"

At this, Rys shook his head, a wry twist to his lips. "Philippa, he hasn't left the Ducal Palace in more than a year. He hasn't attended a Council meeting, not even once. No one sees him except his staff and, upon occasion, Francis."

Philippa frowned. "Is this a good thing? If he doesn't leave the Palace . . ."

"It hasn't helped, apparently," Rys answered her. "William has levied an extraordinary tax on the people of Oc."

"What's an extraordinary tax?" Philippa asked.

"It means a tax on top of the normal tithes, as I understand it," Esmond said. "Not something we've had in Klee. According to Prince Nicolas, it's merely an item of interest. He isn't worried about it, so long as his own revenues aren't diminished. But it must be a hardship on your people."

Philippa frowned again. "Why is William doing this? Surely his popularity is already waning."

"More so now, I'm told. But you know his obsession, Philippa."

She sighed. "Of course. The winged horses."

"Exactly so. He has plans drawn up for a new academy—the Fleckham School."

"A new academy!" Philippa sat up very straight, and her teacup clattered in its saucer. "Why would he need such a thing?"

"The Fleckham School," Esmond said deliberately, "is to be a school for men. A school for men to learn to fly winged horses."

Philippa gaped at him. "Madness! Surely the Council won't tolerate this?"

"Some of them believe he has been successful in creating a new bloodline, Philippa. One that will tolerate men."

"But he hasn't!" she cried. She jumped up and began to pace. The heels of her riding boots clicked on the polished pine floor. "It's not the bloodline he changed, but himself!"

"Perhaps," Esmond said mildly, "there will be men willing to change as he has."

Philippa reached the big window that filled the end of the dining room. Beyond the glass, the lavender fields stretched down the mountainside, their ripe blossoms bluer than the sky.

Philippa drew a deep breath and forced herself to be still. "I don't think it will work." She turned her back on the vista of mountains and flowers to face Esmond and his nephew. "It's not that there won't be men willing to alter their bodies. Flying is worth any sacrifice. But breasts and a beardless chin don't make a woman, do they? William may have changed enough to disguise his true scent, but he's still a man. I don't presume to know why Kalla designed the winged horses as she did, but winged horses are meant to fly with women. I'm not convinced about this bonding between William and the filly."

"He's been seen with her."

"Not aloft, surely? Not yet!"

"No, not flying. He's been seen stroking her, though, they say. As to flying, Amelia writes to me that he called a horse-mistress from the South Tower of Isamar to serve as monitor. They can see her flying with the filly above the park at the Ducal Palace."

An old, half-forgotten pain flared at the back of Philippa's neck, and she rubbed at it with her fingers. "But will she fly with William? That will be the real test."

"He carries on as if it's a foregone conclusion."

Philippa dropped her hand. "I feel as if the whole world has gone mad."

Esmond Rys pushed aside his cup and plate and leaned back in his chair. "It will pass, Philippa. Be patient."

"Patient!" she snapped.

Without answering, he rose, a little stiffly, and walked to the window to stand beside her, looking past her shoulder onto the fields of lavender. "It's peaceful here," he mused.

She drew a steadying breath. "Indeed it is, Esmond. I wonder you and your family don't come here more often."

"We should," he said. "But it's a long drive from the capital."

Philippa turned again to follow Esmond's gaze out the window. Shadows stretched into the west, reaching long blue fingers from the house toward the barn. On the horizon, the first star began to glitter faintly from the fading sky. "How is William enforcing his tax?"

"He impresses young men into his militia when their families can't pay."

"Kalla's teeth," Philippa said bitterly. "He'll stop at nothing."

"Prince Nicolas has loaned him a substantial number of men, as well."

Philippa frowned. "Why would the Prince do that?"

Esmond lifted one shoulder. "I suspect he is intrigued by the idea of men flying."

"Nicolas is far too fat even to dream of such a thing!"

"His Highness is indolent by nature, it's true," Esmond said.

Behind them Niven laughed. "A fat, lazy prince," he said with satisfaction. "Utterly unlike my father."

Esmond turned and faced his nephew. "Your father is Nicolas's opposite, I think."

"In every way," Niven said with youthful pride.

"Don't underestimate Prince Nicolas," Philippa warned. "I know him. He may be indolent, and he's certainly greedy, but he's no fool. He smells profit."

Niven said, with surprising acuity, "Of course he does. He will set a high price for the right to bond with a winged horse, and many a young man's family will pay."

A little silence stretched in the pleasant room as the darkness thickened beyond the window. Philippa drew a deep breath, striving for calm. "I must go and settle Sunny for the night," she said. Her voice shook only a little. "Do your horses have any special requirements?"

"I'll do it," Niven said. "You've done enough today, Mistress Winter."

His uncle nodded approval at him. "Yes, you take care of our horses, Niven. That's good. But you can't help Philippa with Winter Sunset. A winged mare won't let you near her."

"Of course. I forgot."

"You're not used to winged horses in Klee," Philippa said. "Come, we can go out to the barn together. I'll show you where things are." They left Esmond clearing the plates and carrying them to the kitchen, and went out through the front door of the house and across the graveled yard to the barn. As they walked, Philippa said, "I'm surprised you didn't bring a groom with you."

"Uncle Esmond said no one must know you're here," Niven said. "Not even my father."

Philippa arched her eyebrows. "Does Esmond ask you to keep secrets from your father?"

The familiar Rys smile, brief and constrained, flickered across his face. "We all keep secrets," he said. "We are nothing if not a political family. We'll return to the capital tomorrow, and no one will even know we were gone."

Philippa nodded to herself as they went into the shadowed barn. It was what she hated most about politics: secrets and maneuverings and manipulation.

She let herself into Sunny's stall, and stood for a moment, stroking the mare's neck. She thought of William, with his altered body, his high voice and smooth cheeks, stroking a winged filly in the same way, and her thoughts clouded with doubt. What if she were wrong? What if—as William so devoutly hoped—he was successful in his attempt to fly?

Philippa tried to imagine a world in which men and women could both fly winged horses, but she couldn't do it. Perhaps her failure signified a lack of imagination, or even of vision. But for centuries, this had been the way of things. She had always believed it helped to create a balance, however uneasy, in a culture otherwise dominated by the masculine.

Suppose, she asked herself as she filled Sunny's water bucket, suppose it was some other man who wanted to fly a winged horse? Suppose it were gentle Lord Francis, or even this wise Klee baron who had so unexpectedly become her ally? Would she feel differently?

She closed the stall gate and braced her elbows on it, watching Sunny dip her muzzle into the fresh water. Yes, she decided. She would feel differently about it.

But she still wouldn't believe it.

TWO

THE flight of seven student flyers wheeled above the graceful old buildings of the Academy of the Air, then banked into their gradual descent. Lark looked down with pleasure on the neat silhouette of the Domicile and the familiar square of the Dormitory. The slate roofs glowed in the rays of the lowering sun. The Hall bulked in the center, elegant in its simplicity, home to the dining hall, the Headmistress's office, the library, and the classrooms. Tup flew at a leisurely pace over the perfectly trimmed hedgerows, the raked gravel of the courtyard, the gambrel roofs of the stable. As the flight reached the end of the return paddock, each horse banked again and stilled its wings to glide toward the long, grassy field, to come to ground one after another.

Tup was the last of the flight to touch down. His hindquarters flexed, and he reached with his forefeet, placing them in the grass with a touch so soft Lark could barely feel it. He cantered easily, wings spread and fluttering, up the length of the return paddock behind the other horses. When he suddenly threw up his head and skidded on his hindquarters, Lark was so startled she nearly slipped from her saddle.

"Tup!" she cried. "What—" He had almost collided with the horse in front of him, and that horse was right on the tail of the one preceding.

All of the flight stumbled to a stop at the end of the return paddock. No one dismounted, and no one had yet opened the gate. Horses and girls stared across the white pole fence at four men, dressed in the Ducal black and silver, standing stiffly in front of each of the main buildings of the Academy.

The flyers glanced at each other wonderingly. Hester, their

flight leader, said, "Dismount, girls." They did. After the horses folded their wings, Hester, her back stiff, led Golden Morning through the gate and waited at one side for the rest to come through. When they were all in the courtyard, she stood with one hand on her palomino's neck, her plain features set in hard lines. She said in a low tone, "Mamá warned me about this. The Duke will say he's sent his militia to protect us, but in truth, they're here to spy."

"Are you sure, Morning?" This came from Anabel, a tall, pretty girl who flew a gray Noble, Take A Chance.

"Oh, aye, she's sure," Lark whispered, just loud enough so that the others could hear. Tup nosed her shoulder impatiently, and she put her hand on the cheek strap of his bridle. "I wager they're watching for Mistress Winter."

Anabel turned her round blue eyes Lark's way. "But she's gone, isn't she? For good?"

A fresh pang of loss shot through Lark, but she only shrugged, and gazed past Hester's shoulder at the militiamen.

Their uniforms had narrow trousers and heavy black boots, loose-sleeved blouses with silver piping and silver insignia to designate rank. None of the four was familiar to Lark. She suspected many of the militia she had seen in Osham, and in the Uplands, too, were not even men of Oc. They had a look of Isamar to them, their hair cut very short, their eyes hard and unfriendly. The four in the courtyard stood with their hands on the hilts of their smallswords, their caps pulled down against the westering sun.

As the girls turned their horses toward the stables, Lark took a last look across the courtyard at the man standing before the Hall. She caught a flash of white as his eyes followed the winged horses, until he dropped his chin and his eyes disappeared behind the brim of his cap.

Lark found Amelia Rys waiting for her beside Tup's stall. Amelia Master, she reminded herself. Mistress Star had insisted that the Master Breeder give Amelia's colt a name at last. He was an elegant young Noble, with a coal-black mane and tail and a coat of rich reddish brown. With the other colts of his flight, he had recently begun flying with a monitor, as his bondmate watched anxiously from below.

The name settled upon for him, after lengthy consultation of the genealogies, had been Master Mahogany.

Amelia had said nothing when Mistress Star told her the name chosen for her bondmate. It was like Amelia to be silent about her feelings, but Lark read disapproval in the set of her mouth.

Hester teased her, saying, "We never like the names at first. You'll get used to it."

"I guess we can call you Master," Lark told her.

"Really," Amelia said in a colorless tone. "And I suppose I'm to call him Mahogany."

Lark chuckled. "Oh, aye," she said. "It's a lot of name for a wee bit of a horse. And I know just how you feel. Black Seraph is a lovely mouthful, if you ask me!"

Hester elbowed her. "You never say it anyway, Black, so why complain?"

Lark grinned. "Tup I named him, and Tup he'll always be to me."

"And I," Amelia said with a tiny purse of her lips, "would have chosen another name."

Lark said, "Would you, Amelia? What name?"

Amelia shrugged. "I don't know. Something simpler."

"Like what?"

Amelia's face softened. "It doesn't matter now," she said. "His dam was Miss Mahogany, and his sire was Able Master. I guess I should be grateful I won't be called Able! Amelia Able would be horrifying. But how do you shorten Mahogany?"

"I think you're stuck with it," Hester said. "We'll all get used to it, and so will he. It suits him, in any case. He's like you—quiet, but strong. He always seems to know more than he should, and to keep his own counsel." She smiled at Amelia. "And he's as red as the wood of a mahogany tree! So lovely, with those long legs and that arching neck."

The restraint of Amelia's smile gave way at that, and her face brightened as if the sun had risen behind it. "Oh, yes, he is," she said. "And so clever, too. Yesterday he unlatched his stall gate all by himself, and when I scolded him, I could swear he was laughing—" She broke off as Hester and Lark began to grin. Her thin cheeks flushed.

"Never mind, Klee," Hester said.

Amelia's blush faded, and she regarded Hester with her usual aplomb. "I thought you were now to call me Master."

Hester nodded. "True enough, though Klee suits you better. But I meant to say that we understand how you feel."

"Oh, aye," Lark said. "'Tis the bonding. It must be how it feels to fall in love."

"Not that we'll ever know about that," Hester said.

Lark smiled at her. "We might know how it feels to fall in love even though we must keep it to ourselves."

Amelia only raised one eyebrow, took a hoof pick from its shelf, and went off to her colt's stall.

Now Lark was glad to escape the eyes of the militiamen as she led Tup down the sawdust-strewn aisle of the stables. Amelia held the stall gate open, and Lark put Tup inside and began unbuckling his cinches. When she lifted the saddle and blanket off, Amelia handed her a currycomb. Lark started on Tup's near side, and Amelia, with a brush in her hand, began on the other. Tup dropped his head and groaned with pleasure as the girls worked.

When the job was well under way, Amelia said, "You saw the soldiers."

"Aye," Lark said. "Spies, Hester says. Duke William must think Mistress Winter will return."

"After an entire year?" Amelia said. "I wouldn't think so."

"Nay, nor would I." Lark sighed. "Although I miss her. 'Tisn't the same at the Academy without her and Winter Sunset."

"I don't understand your Duke. He can't really expect her to turn up here, after all that happened."

Lark said, "I doubt the Duke thinks clearly anymore. In the Uplands, we would say he's gone hinky."

Hester snickered from Goldie's stall. "I hope you're going to tell us what that little bit of dialect means, Black."

"It's what we say when a wagon's wheels come off, or maybe a gate's hinges come apart. It means he's . . . sort of in pieces. A little crazy. He's so changed, isn't he, and whatever changed him has altered his mind."

"I've never heard of anything like it," Amelia said. "Our

own Viscount Richard, in Klee—my uncle, that is—is the most serious man I've ever seen. He cares for nothing but the government, and the laws. He settles every dispute himself, and hardly ever leaves the Palace." She gave Tup's hindquarter a last sweep with the brush, and then straightened. "Yet Duke William has not stepped foot in the Rotunda since last year."

Lark stepped around to Tup's tail, keeping a hand on his hip so he would know where she was. "'Tis the oddest thing," she said. "I think Duke William doesn't like the way his body is now. I—I touched him once."

"Did you?" Amelia glanced at her, but there was no expression or reaction on her narrow features. She always looked to Lark as if she were adding things up, filing them away. Lark felt certain that if she were to tell Amelia something useful, it would fly straight to the Baron, to be employed in whatever way he saw fit.

Lark shrugged. "He swells at the chest," she said, gesturing at her own small bosom. "But when I touched him—and you can trust me, Amelia, I didn't want to—he was furious. I suppose he thinks he can hide it."

"So," Amelia said. She came to Tup's head, and began braiding his silky mane. "His purpose was to change his scent so he could fly."

"Aye. I would wager the rest was a surprise."

"Do you think it will work? That he'll fly his little Diamond?"

Lark let the black strands of Tup's tail fall through her fingers, flowing ribbons that shone in the lamplight. "I think," she said, "that a rooster may cover an egg, but he's still a rooster."

Amelia laughed, making Lark look up at her in surprise. She didn't think she had heard Amelia Rys laugh before. Amelia Master, she reminded herself.

"You're a funny thing," Amelia said, her laugh subsiding. "A true country girl."

"Aye, I am that," Lark said. "I understand the beasts and the land. And I know something of potions and simples, too. I will be surprised if the Duke flies his little Diamond without great difficulty. He's not really a woman, after all, despite breasts and a beardless chin. The dogs know him for what he

is, and Tup does, too. Poor little Diamond simply doesn't
know any better."

Amelia finished a braid, and tied it off with a bit of silk.
"Diamond might have been my bondmate," she said.

"Aye. 'Tis strange to think about it now," Lark said. "Mahogany might have gone to some other girl."

"I would hate that," Amelia said. "But I worry about the
filly. She must be terribly lonely."

"Aye, we're all worried," Lark said. "All of us who care
about the winged horses."

They finished Tup's grooming in silence. As they left the
stable, Amelia gave Lark a sidelong glance. "Tell me, Lark.
Do you not think the Duke cares about the winged horses?"

Lark didn't answer for several steps, and then she said, "I
think, Amelia, that yon Duke cares most about himself."

THERE was a militiaman posted in the dining hall, watching
the girls and the horsemistresses as they filed in. His presence
subdued the usual mealtime chatter. Lark, passing the soldier,
glanced up at him briefly. He was rather young, and neither
particularly tall nor strong-looking. He caught her glance, and
his eyes shifted quickly away, his cheeks flushing.

When Lark reached her place at the table, she was startled to
see a small, sealed square of plain beige paper propped against
her water glass. She picked it up, and gazed at it with unease.

The girls were all standing, waiting for Headmistress Star
to take her seat, but Hester leaned close. "Who's it from?" she
whispered.

Lark held it out to show her. "This is Brye's handwriting."

"Open it!" Hester said.

"I'm afraid to." Lark slipped her finger under the seal but
didn't break it.

Now Anabel and Amelia were also gazing at her curiously.
There was a rustle and scrape of chairs as the Headmistress
sat, then the horsemistresses, and finally the girls. Lark sank
into her chair, staring at the envelope. "I know it's bad," she
said. "Five years and more I've been at the Academy, and I've
never had a letter."

Hester's strong hand pressed her arm. "Get it over with, Black," she said. "Postponing it won't make it easier. If it were really bad news, anyway, it would have come from the Head."

Lark closed her eyes briefly, thinking of her brothers. Brye, the eldest, had been both brother and father to her. Silent Edmar was married now, still working in the quarry. Laughing Nick was only a few years older than she and still breaking maidens' hearts in Willakeep.

Hester was right. One of the girls' fathers had died in the winter, and she had received the news directly from Mistress Star. It couldn't be all that bad, surely.

She opened her eyes, slid her finger under the seal, and opened the letter. When she had read it, she laid it down beside her salad plate.

"Well?" Hester demanded. "What is it?"

Lark took a shaky breath, then turned her eyes up to Hester's. "It's Nick," she said. "My brother."

Hester grinned. "The handsome one?"

"Aye." Lark couldn't smile in return. Her lips trembled.

"What is it, Black? Is your brother all right?"

"He's in the militia. The Palace set the tithe so high, Deeping Farm couldn't pay it. It was Nick or Edmar, and now Edmar is married to Pamella . . . so Nick went. He's off already, and no one knows where he's been posted."

SUZANNE Star, the Headmistress, said nothing to the girls at dinner. Usually there were announcements, or advice, or news from Osham or elsewhere in the Duchy, always delivered in the dining hall. But on this night, Mistress Star waited until dinner was over. Then she came to the Dormitory and climbed the stairs to the sleeping porch as the girls readied for bed.

Lark was already in her nightdress when someone said, "Mistress Star!" Everyone stopped what she was doing and looked up. They had never seen Mistress Star on the sleeping porch before. Only Matron, or occasionally one of the junior horsemistresses, came here.

Hester stepped forward, inclining her head. "Good evening,

Mistress Star," she said. Lark had the impression Hester had been expecting this visit.

Mistress Star nodded. "Hester," she said, "and everyone. Will you come close, please?"

The girls, barefoot and in various stages of undress, came forward from their cots and arranged themselves around her. Lark had Brye's letter in her hand, already creased and crumpled from several readings. She smoothed it between her fingers as she went to stand beside Hester.

Mistress Star still wore her riding habit and boots, her gloves and cap tucked into her belt. Her lips were tight with strain, and a furrow showed between her eyes. "This," she said quietly, "was the only place I could talk to you away from those soldiers."

The girls nodded. No one spoke, but they moved closer to each other until they stood in a double circle, shoulder to shoulder.

Mistress Star nodded grim approval of this instinctive movement. "Our position, I'm afraid," she said, "is precarious. I have been warned that the—" She hesitated, and her eyes scanned the girls' faces. "The Palace wants to close the Academy of the Air."

There was a general intake of breath, and several girls put their hands to their mouths. Only Hester was unsurprised. "Mamá says it's about the Fleckham School."

"So I am told," Mistress Star said.

One of the younger girls said, "What's that? The Fleckham School?"

Another cried softly, "They can't close the Academy, can they? My papá would never allow it, now that I'm here at last, after I waited so long—"

Mistress Star put up her hand. "We must remain calm," she said. "I'm sure, Allison, that your father would object in the strongest way to the closing of the Academy. But the Council is not of one mind on this issue. And the Fleckham School, for those of you who haven't heard, is meant to be a flying school for men."

A stunned silence met this announcement. The girls knew, of course, that Duke William had a winged filly, because she had appeared in the sky last Ribbon Day, and only quick action by Lark and Tup, risking their own graduation to the third level, had helped her come safely to ground. But no one truly expected that the Duke would be able to fly with her.

Lark crumpled her brother's letter against her chest and stepped back, out of the circle. Mistress Star spoke a little longer, warning the girls to be silent in the presence of the militiamen, and to say nothing that might be used against them or the Academy in anyone's hearing. Lark went to her cot and folded Brye's letter as carefully as she could to tuck it in the drawer of her bedstand. Worry tightened her throat.

Nick, she knew, was being punished because of her. Mistress Winter had been driven away from Oc for the same reason. Neither of them would blame Lark, and they would deny that any of this was her fault, but she knew that it was.

The horse goddess had brought Tup to Lark, and he was the greatest gift she could possibly have received. But his coming had carried a heavy price for Deeping Farm and all the Hamleys. If anything happened to Nick . . .

Lark stood beside her cot, staring at her bare feet, wondering what she could do to set things right. She didn't realize Mistress Star had left and that the girls were padding back to their beds until Amelia and Hester came up beside her.

"What is it, Black?" Hester said quietly.

Lark lifted her head, and looked at her tall, plain friend through a haze of tears. "Nick—and Mistress Winter—'tis all because of me!"

"No," Amelia said. "It is because your Duke—"

Hester elbowed her. "*Our* Duke, Klee, remember? You're Isamarian now."

Amelia nodded. "You're quite right, Morning. I am." She sat on Lark's cot, and drew Lark down beside her. "This is happening, Black, because the Duke is obsessed with the winged horses. You could do nothing to change that."

"He's mad," Hester said with a touch of impatience. "Anyone can see it. How can that be your fault?"

"If anyone can see it—" Lark began, then stopped.

Amelia put a slender arm around her shoulders. "You're wondering why he gets away with it," she said. Lark nodded, miserably, wordlessly. "Powerful people are invested in protecting their power," Amelia said. "My father taught me that when I was a tiny girl. It is a rare man—"

"Or woman," Hester growled.

Amelia nodded again. "It's a rare man or woman," she amended, "whose integrity is greater than the lust for power."

"True," Hester said. She crossed her arms, tapping her fingers on her elbows. "Too many of our Council Lords think the Duke may add to their power, and they also don't want anyone questioning their authority. If the Duke is challenged, they feel they are, too."

"But then what will happen?" Lark said. "To Nick—and Mistress Winter—"

"Mistress Winter, at least, is safe," Amelia said. When Lark looked at her curiously, she added hastily, "She must be. No one's seen or heard from her in more than a year."

"I'm sure she's fine," Hester said. "But Mamá says there's more trouble coming."

"Aye," Lark said. "I wish my brother were not in the middle of it."

"We're all in the middle of it," Hester said. "Every one of us."

THREE

"My lord husband," Constance said in her breathy voice. "Are you not due at the Rotunda this morning?"

William snapped, "Ye gods, Constance, speak up, can't you? Stop whispering at me!"

"I—I'm sorry, William. I just—I had my maid lay out my things and do my hair, because I thought—"

He leaned back in his chair and reached for the quirt he kept near at hand on his desk. He turned its braided leather in his fingers and laughed when Constance flinched. "What do you think?" he smirked. "That I would strike you?"

"No—oh, no, William, of course I don't—" Her voice trailed off, and her eyes dropped.

He pointed the quirt at her and chuckled. "Maybe you'd like that, if I hit you. Like one of the horses, or a dog . . ." He stretched his arm so he could touch her cheek with the end of the quirt. She gasped, and trembled away from it.

He laughed and slapped the quirt back onto the desk. "What do you want, Constance? You can see I'm working here."

Her eyes slid nervously across the surface of his empty desk. "Are you?" she breathed. "I'm sorry. I thought you were . . ." She took another step backward, toward the door. "I thought we were going to the Council today. I'll go and change, and order . . . Perhaps you'd like . . ." She turned away, her voice growing softer and softer until he couldn't hear the end of her sentence.

He looked away from her and waited for the click of the door. Instead, he heard her say, almost inaudibly, "William?"

"What!" he snapped. "Aren't you gone yet? You can see I'm not going anywhere. I'm in my riding clothes." In fact, he had been sitting at his desk debating whether today was the day.

Her eyes flickered again. "I just wondered—won't there be trouble? You haven't been to the Council in more than a year. I was certain that you meant to attend today."

He turned his head to face her again and gazed fixedly at her until she dropped her eyes. "Since when," he said in his silkiest tone, "does my lady wife take an interest in government?"

Harsh red stained her cheeks, but she held her ground. "William—you *are* the Duke."

"How nice, Constance, that you remember that."

"It just seems that . . . since you quarreled with Philippa Winter . . ."

"Philippa has been dealt with."

Constance's eyes flicked up to his again. There was a flash of something in them, something he couldn't identify. She said, still softly, but quite clearly, "But Philippa got away, didn't she." It was not a question.

William's neck stiffened with surprise, and a spurt of anger made his voice shrill. "Have no fear, Constance! We're watching for her, and we'll have her. She'll take her punishment as she was meant to."

Constance reached for the door and opened it. From the doorway, she glanced back at him, and this time, he knew what the curl of her lips meant, and the faint widening of her eyes. She was amused. She was laughing at him, wispy Constance who cowered whenever he so much as frowned at her!

She closed the door behind her before he could grasp what had just happened. He stared at the blankness of the wood, his jaw aching with tension. If even self-absorbed Constance thought that Philippa Winter had bested him, all of Oc could be laughing behind his back.

He picked up the quirt again and banged it on the desk. He had to get her. He had wasted enough time. He knew how to lure Philippa back, and when he did, he would bring her to justice. He would show all those damned horsemistresses who wielded power in Oc.

Constance, nuisance though she was, was right about one thing. It had been more than a year since he had gone to the

Rotunda. Of course, he had his people—Philippa's brother Meredith, for one—to tell him what happened there. And Meredith, sycophant that he was, was more than happy to carry his wishes to the Council Lords. Perhaps Constance worried about losing her position as Duchess, although that seemed unlikely. It had never caused her overmuch joy, so far as he knew.

He stood and went to the window to look out into the court-yard of the Ducal Palace. He had moved Diamond to the Palace stables, in a stall far away from the other horses, where she had the run of a long, well-groomed paddock and the airiest space Jinson could provide. Even now, he felt the pull of her, that yearning to run his hands over her glossy hide, to touch the points of her silver wings, to comb her fluff of white mane. To smell her clean scent of straw and oats and sunshine.

Odd, this compulsion. He wondered if, once he had flown her, it would subside, as desire for a woman often faded away once he had possessed her.

And William wondered, running a hand over his pale hair, if he would ever desire a woman again. The potion that made it possible for him to bond with Diamond had erased that urge. It was a necessary sacrifice, and he couldn't regret it. But it was an uncomfortable circumstance. It made him feel unlike himself, at odds with his own nature.

He blew out a breath. It didn't matter. It would all be worth it.

And he would not, he decided with a final slap of the quirt against his leg, go back to the Council until he had flown her. Not much longer, surely. She was flying with sand weights and the saddle, working with the longue line, building her strength and learning the bit and the bridle. Soon he would sit in that saddle, and not long after that they would take to the air. Together.

In the meantime, he would see to bringing Philippa Winter back to Oc. It was time she paid the price for defying him.

FOUR

PHILIPPA and Sunny, returning from a flight to their favorite mountain lake, swooped low over the lavender fields. The delicate scent of the lavender blossoms rose to meet them. The sheep had grown used to the winged horse and lifted their heads from their grazing for only a moment. The shepherds waved. The narders, thigh deep in purple flowers, tipped their hats.

Autumn had passed its zenith. The snowcaps on the peaks to the east stretched lower each day. As Sunny glided to her landing in the lane below the barn, Philippa noticed how strong and tall the spring lambs had grown. They dashed among the ewes, their tails flicking merrily. They made her think of the yearlings frolicking in their paddock at the Academy, sorrels and blacks and bays and palominos galloping together, tails arching, feet twinkling in the grass, and her breast ached with a sudden, helpless longing.

There wouldn't be many yearlings in that paddock this year. The winged foals were born in two-year cycles, and the last spring crop had been pitifully small. Too many winged mares had thrown wingless foals, thanks to William's disastrous breeding program. Philippa had feared for the future of the bloodlines even then, and now that things had grown so much worse, she was helpless to do anything about it.

She dismounted and led Sunny into the barn to untack her. She had filled her water bucket and was ladling a measure of oats when she heard a whinny from beyond the yard. She left Sunny munching a leaf of alfalfa, and hurried to the door. She shaded her eyes to look down the steep lane.

A black horse was making its way up through the lavender

fields at a steady running walk. At first Philippa couldn't see who the rider was, but when he took off his hat to run his fingers through his white-blond hair, she knew.

She dusted her hands against her divided skirt, and stepped out into the yard. When he drew close enough, she raised her hand, and called, "Francis! Welcome to Marinan!"

Francis smiled down at her as he reined in his horse. "Philippa," he said. "I'm glad to have found you at last." He threw his leg over the saddle and slid easily to the ground.

"I'm always glad to see you, Francis," she answered. "And especially now. Esmond has been my only visitor all these months. What brings you to Klee?"

He looped his mare's reins over his arm. "I had a mission for Prince Nicolas in the capital, and I met a young Klee lord there, Esmond's nephew."

"That must have been Niven," she said. "The Viscount's son." She took his horse's rein, and led the way toward the barn. "A great favorite of Esmond's."

"That's the one. He knew of our adventure in Aeskland, apparently, and confided to me that you were here. Rys had given him permission."

"It was good of you to make time to visit." Philippa led the black mare into a stall, and Francis began to unbuckle her cinches. "How long can you stay?"

He glanced at her over his shoulder. "I have to get back to Osham soon," he said. "This trip was a special favor for the Prince, but I've been working in the White City since last winter. My lord brother—" He lifted the saddle and hoisted it up onto the stall gate. He leaned on it a moment, his elbows against the smooth leather seat. His tone was wry. "My brother, Philippa, has stopped attending Council meetings. It falls to me to represent the Ducal Palace."

Philippa handed Francis a towel. "I'm surprised William allows that," she said, as he turned to begin rubbing the mare's sweat-stained back.

He gave a humorless laugh. "Oh, William doesn't mind," he said. "As long as I make no decisions. Or the Council Lords either, for that matter. He refuses to sign any ruling of any significance."

"That's not government, is it?" Philippa said.

"Indeed not."

They worked in silence for a time, laying out hay and oats for the mare, spreading fresh straw beneath her feet. Sunny whickered from her stall, and Philippa went to pat her before she and Francis walked back out into the cool sunshine.

"A beautiful place," he said, tipping his head back to admire the old house.

"It is indeed," Philippa said. "You see how steep that roof is? It's because of the snow. We had drifts higher than my head last winter. We were snowbound. No one stirred from the place for entire weeks."

Francis gave her a sympathetic look. "That must have been lonely."

She shrugged. "I confess, Francis, I enjoyed it. Something of a holiday."

"Marinan reminds me of Deeping Farm," he mused, as they walked in through Lyssett's fragrant kitchen and on into the dining room. "Bigger, of course, and more elegant. But that same air of age and—I don't know—reverence."

Philippa smiled. "The Ryses are noble, and the Hamleys are farmers, but the families are not so different. They respect their heritage. And each other, too, which is no small thing."

He gave her a lopsided smile. "I think you rather liked Brye Hamley."

She turned her back on him to straighten a crooked curtain and to hide the heat in her cheeks. "Larkyn is the most fortunate of girls to have such a brother."

"You and I were not so lucky in our brothers."

"No." She composed her features and turned back to him. "Quite the opposite."

Lyssett bustled in with a teapot and a platter of tea sandwiches, eyeing Francis as she set them down.

"Lyssett," Philippa said. "This is Lord Francis Fleckham, of the Duchy of Oc in Isamar. He's a friend of the Baron's. Francis, Lyssett has been cook and housekeeper here since before Esmond was born."

Lyssett curtsied. "My lord," she said.

Francis, who had taken a chair, rose and bowed to her before sitting down again. Lyssett colored and smiled as she poured out the tea and set the plates, then disappeared into the kitchen. Francis took a sandwich and devoured it in three bites.

"It's so gratifying, Francis," Philippa said, "to see you completely restored to health."

He gave her a boyish grin. "I didn't dare die of that woman's blade," he said. "William would never have let me forget it!"

She chuckled, but the memory still pained her. Francis had come perilously close to dying of his wound. Only the country air and good food of Deeping Farm had wrought the miracle of his healing, and she would always be grateful, for the Duchy and for herself, that the friend of her childhood had survived.

"So," she said, picking up her cup and shaking off her brief nostalgia. "What news do you bring? I've heard nothing but rumors all these months, passed to Lyssett by the grocer or the fruit-vendor."

"What rumors?"

She shrugged. "Some are wild—Nicolas threatening to invade, or even William disbanding the Council. I couldn't believe those."

"No, there's no truth in those stories." Francis took another sandwich and ate this one more slowly. He cradled the teacup in his sun-browned hands and let his eyes stray to the hills beyond the window. "But I'm afraid it's true that William and Nicolas are in collusion."

Philippa put her own cup down. "Why do you think so?"

"Nicolas sent a thousand militiamen to Oc."

"Kalla's teeth! What are they for?"

"William has posted militia in every town," Francis said. He drank his tea and set the cup in its saucer with a click of porcelain. "To enforce his extraordinary tax."

"But, Francis—that's martial law!"

"It is very like."

"Surely the Council Lords will not stand for this!"

"You would think not." He turned in his chair, and leaned toward her. "The temptation is too much for them," he said in a low tone. "For some of them, in any case. They want to see their Duke as a visionary, someone who will usher in a new day for Oc."

"In which men fly winged horses," Philippa said in a flat voice.

"Precisely so."

"And we horsemistresses? The Academy of the Air?"

Francis hesitated, then said, "I can't pretend there's no risk. Some have said—openly, in the Rotunda—that closing the Academy would go further toward building the Fleckham School than levying the extraordinary tax."

She closed her eyes briefly, assailed by a wave of the fatigue she thought she had banished months ago. "Why does it make Oc stronger to take the winged horses away from women?" she asked.

"It doesn't," Francis answered. "It makes William stronger."

She opened her eyes again, and looked into his gentle face, so like and yet so unlike his elder brother's. "It shocks me, Francis. I've always placed my faith in the wisdom of the Council. And now . . . this is misogyny, is it not? A resentment that women hold any power."

"I doubt they think of themselves as misogynists."

She snorted. "Do you know another word for it?"

"No." He leaned back, his eyes on her face. "Is it possible, Philippa? For men to fly?"

She shook her head. "No. I believe it is not."

"But if William succeeds in flying this filly of his," Francis said, "there are young men waiting to be bonded. There is already a list, being kept by—" He broke off, coloring faintly. He cleared his throat. "Well. Let's just say by one of the lords."

"Oh, do let me guess," Philippa said. "My brother Meredith."

He gave her a gentle, rueful smile. "Yes. Sorry."

"Do these young men know what they will be asked to do?"

"There is talk of a potion. But no one seems too worried about it. Some feel that because men don't conceive in any case, there is less risk to the winged horses to bond with men."

"Then they haven't seen their Duke's swelling bosom or noted his beardless chin."

"He has managed to stay out of sight." Francis shrugged. "But he can't hide forever."

"If he is to fly," Philippa said, "it could be soon. She was a winter foal. She'll be coming two before long."

A little silence fell. Lyssett came in to take the empty teapot, and Philippa looked up to see with some surprise that evening had fallen around Marinan while they talked. There were voices in the kitchen, the shepherds and the narders gathering for their supper.

"You're staying, of course, Francis," Philippa said.

"If that's acceptable. It was a long ride up from the capital."

"I'm sure Lyssett has already prepared a room for you, and no doubt is cooking up one of her wonderful meals." Philippa stood up. "I'll go and ask."

Francis stood up, too. "I should see to my mare. Should I blanket her?"

"The nights are cool here," she said, "but she won't need a blanket. The barn is as well built as the house, and the shepherds keep a little close stove going in the feed room."

She turned toward the kitchen, and Francis followed. After a brief conference with the excellent Lyssett, Philippa led the way to the barn.

Francis sniffed the air. "Everything smells of lavender," he said, and smiled. "Although perhaps you can longer smell it? You must be used to it by now."

"I can smell it, and I like it." She stopped just outside the feed room and stood for a moment, tracing the pattern in the wooden wall with her fingers. "Francis—if William fails— could all these troubles just go away?"

"He has gambled everything on his success," Francis answered gravely. "It's my belief that my brother will either fly this filly—Diamond, he calls her—or die in the attempt."

PHILIPPA slept poorly that night, plagued by nightmares as she had been when she first came to Marinan. She dreamed of that awful day in the Rotunda when William had ordered her into confinement at Islington House, parting her from Winter Sunset and condemning her mare to a certain death, from heartbreak or madness. She dreamed of soldiers at the Academy, her students fleeing, their horses screaming alarm in the stables. In one of these dreams, the frantic neighing seemed so real that it shocked her out of sleep, and she sat bolt upright in her comfortable bed, stunned and relieved to find that Marinan was quiet as always. Not even the rooster had yet announced the morning. The first streaks of light had just begun to paint the eastern sky in shades of blue and gold and pink. She got up to splash water on her face, brush her hair, clean her teeth, and dress.

She crept downstairs, hoping not to wake anyone else, and was startled to find Francis already in the kitchen. He was measuring tea leaves into a pot, and the kettle had begun to steam.

"Good morning," Philippa said.

He looked up. "You couldn't sleep, either."

She crossed to the big stone sink and looked out the kitchen window toward the barn. "And you? I'm sure your bed was comfortable."

"I have worries enough to make any bed hard."

"It's a shame." Philippa propped one lean hip against the edge of the sink and watched him pour boiling water into the teapot and wrap a cozy around it. "You seem to have acquired some domestic skills," she said.

He smiled at that and pushed his pale hair back from his face. He had cut it very short, in the Isamarian style, and it made him look boyish and rather dashing. Half-consciously, Philippa smoothed her own graying red hair, wound as always into the rider's knot.

"I learned a few things at Deeping Farm," he said as he reached into a cupboard for teacups. "I can cook a bit, and I can till a field and chop a cord of wood."

Philippa allowed herself to ask, "Do you know how they are? The Hamleys?"

His face hardened. "It's the extraordinary tax," he said. "William saw to it that the tax on Deeping Farm was much too high to pay. And so Nick—the youngest brother—has been impressed into the militia."

"And Brye?" she asked.

"Brye is well," Francis said. "But he's furious."

"Of course he would be," Philippa said. She toyed with the

end of a tea towel. "If he knew that William had tried to hurt his sister, there would be no controlling him."

"I know. I worry that—" Francis broke off as he poured out the tea.

"What, Francis?"

He picked up his teacup. "William would love any excuse to confiscate Deeping Farm," he said. "And not just because of Larkyn."

"Because of your sister," Philippa said wearily. "Because he's afraid she'll expose him."

"Precisely so." He sipped his tea and gazed past her to the day brightening over the lavender fields. "I've thought of exposing him myself, except that such a scandal would only further divide the Council, to say nothing of ruining what's left of our house's reputation. Whether William forced Pamella or not, if I tried to accuse him, half of the Council would refuse to believe me, and the other half would take up arms against him. Such a disgrace would leave the Duchy with no leadership at all. Oc would fall apart."

They drank their tea in silence after that until Lyssett came down. She shooed them out of her kitchen, tutting over their having had to make their own tea. They went out to stand on the gravel walk, breathing the chilly air of the autumn morning.

Francis said, "Even my pillow smelled of lavender."

"It's lovely, isn't it?"

"It is."

"I will be sorry to leave it."

"You mustn't leave, Philippa. It's not safe for you to come back to Oc. You have to stay here, where you're safe."

She turned to face him, lifting her chin so that she could look straight into his face. "Francis, you're like a brother to me—better than a brother, in my case. You know I can't languish here, doing nothing, if the Academy is at risk."

"I'll do all I can to protect it," he said.

"But how can you stop him?"

"I don't know," Francis said heavily, "I wish I did."

"There must be something I can do."

He sighed and ran his hand through his hair. "I don't know what it would be."

She looked away, out over the lavender fields dripping with dew. "Protect our girls, Francis. And our horses. Promise me."

He patted her shoulder. "I'll do my best, Philippa."

She sighed. "That's all you can do. All any of us can do."

FIVE

WILLIAM rode toward the Academy on as direct a route as he could find. He knew what he had to do. He had tried it before, but a wise man learned from his mistakes. This time he would do it right. This time he would take them both. And when Philippa found out they were missing, she would hasten back to Oc from wherever she had gone to ground. She had foolishly allowed herself to become too attached to one of her students. He would hold her weakness up as an example, yet another reason that men should take charge of Oc's most precious resource.

Before riding out, he had spent an hour with Diamond, working her in the dry paddock with a longue line, picking up her feet and brushing the saddle blanket over her back as the horsemistress had taught him. It was boring, stultifying. He couldn't think what such dry exercises had to do with flying. But the horsemistress swore these were necessary steps to prepare for riding, then for flight.

The horsemistress, Felicity Baron, was boring, too, a plain, middle-aged woman. She did what she was told, but with ill grace. She didn't even try to hide her objections to his bonding. He would have punished her for her bad humor, except he didn't want to have to find another monitor for Diamond. Sometimes he eyed Mistress Baron's bony back as she walked away from him and wished he could deal with her as she deserved. She didn't know how lucky she was, for the moment. Once he had flown, he would put her and her old gelding, Sky Baron, out to pasture, as far from the Ducal Palace as he could manage.

After restoring Diamond to her stall, with a promise to be

back before evening, he walked down the aisle to where his new saddle horse, a good-looking chestnut mare, waited in her stall. He missed his old brown gelding, but the horse had broken down, and Jinson had carted him off to some farmer's field to rest. Had it been any other horse, William would have had him put down without a thought. The gelding, though, had served him well, and he knew he had been a demanding rider. He refused any feelings of guilt over it—everything he did was, after all, for the Duchy and for his people. The chestnut mare was not nearly as fast, nor as spirited, as the gelding had once been. Nicolas had promised to send a horse from his own stables, some tall, strong stallion who could tolerate William's riding style. But William hoped, before such an animal arrived, that he would have no need of an earthbound horse. He hoped he would be flying.

William put a bridle on the mare and led her down the aisle to the tack room. "I expect you to hold up better than my last mount," he told her as he threw the saddle on her back and began to tighten the cinches. "I ride fast and hard, and I'm not going to change."

She didn't respond, and he glanced longingly at the other side of the stables, where Diamond's stall was. Wingless horses were infintely less interesting than winged ones.

William swung himself up into the saddle and rode out of the stables and around to the back, where a grassy ride, browning now beneath the clear autumn sun, led through the park that surrounded the Palace. His stable-man came hurrying out to ask, "My lord? Don't you want a groomsman to go with you? Or your valet?"

"No, Perkins," William said. "I'm going to have a few hours to myself."

Perkins stood where he was, wiping his hands on a rag. "Aye, m'lord. As you wish."

William looked down at him. "Tell Mistress Baron to look in on Diamond for me."

"Aye, m'lord." Perkins gave a small bow and turned back into the stables. Did he, too, have an odd look on his face?

It was infuriating to think that he could no longer trust even his stable-man. He didn't trust his wife, but she hardly mattered. He had never known a woman he could trust, in any case. He felt uncertain about Jinson, with his lamentably soft heart and odd flashes of doubt about their purpose. And those clodheads in the Council! Only a fool would put faith in the wisdom of those doddering old men.

In fact, now that he came to think on it, it was only his old Slater, who made no bones about where his loyalties lay, whom he could trust. He would rather rely on honest greed than on simpering and fine words.

William reined the mare toward the ride and dug his spurs into her ribs, making her burst into a stiff trot. He spurred her again, and she began to gallop, a little raggedly. He knew he should give her a chance to warm up, but fury made him impatient. Just wait until he flew. Then they would all see, including that fat Nicolas, with his warning letters and contracts and constant queries. As if the Prince of Isamar couldn't afford a thousand militiamen without the slightest strain! It was all preposterous. None of them had any vision at all, and worse, they couldn't recognize the vision of someone else.

He wrenched the mare's reins as he turned her into the woods. She tossed her head and sidestepped, but he persisted, making her push through a close stand of cottonwoods. William ducked to avoid the branches and urged the mare on. He intended to ride straight cross-country and cut two hours off his time. The days were growing short, and the light would have faded by the time he reached the Academy. The brat spent far too much time in the stables, all hours of the day and night. He had watched her, and he knew. He would simply go in and get her. If anyone objected—that fool stable-man, or anyone else— he had militia there to deal with them. Soldiers, regular or impressed, followed orders.

Thinking of the militia reminded him of the brat's brother, the younger one. Nick, he was called, and now in the uniform of his Duke's service. He would make certain Nick Hamley was posted someplace hard, not some cushy position like the Academy of the Air or the Rotunda. The port, perhaps—things could get rough down there even at the best of times. It had gotten worse since the levy of the extraordinary tax. Tension was growing between the nobility and the working classes.

William cursed softly to himself. It was yet another reason the damned Council Lords should be grateful to him. There had been more than one instance of the militia stepping in to stop angry laborers from interfering with their betters as they tried to move about the city, and yet still Beeth and Daysmith and those others whined on in the Council about unfair taxation and soldiers on every corner. Of course they were on every corner! How else could order be maintained?

William loosened the reins, now that they were on the right path, and let the mare find her own way through the wood. He took deep breaths of the pine-scented air, and tried to calm himself. One day soon it would all come right. The tensions would be forgotten, the confusion and the questions. Once he closed the Academy, he could lift the extraordinary tax. Even the slowest of the Council Lords, the most resistant, would recognize the new direction for the Duchy, one that would lead to more profit and a greater name in Isamar. Then they could all bend the knee to him and apologize, Daysmith, Beeth, Chatham, and the rest.

And, of course, every horsemistress. The thought made him want to whip up the mare, but he resisted. It would do no good to arrive in daylight, anyway. He had to be patient, take it one step at a time. It would all come right soon enough.

He adjusted the smallsword at his belt and tried to fill his mind with thoughts of Diamond and what it would be like when he flew her at last. When he spotted the gambrel roofs of the Academy stables beyond the wood, he dismounted and left the mare cropping sparse grass in a little clearing. He could send Jinson for her later. His quarry was at hand.

SIX

LARK bent over the hedgerow and pointed to the pile of chestnuts under the lowest branch. "Have a blink at that," she said, straightening. "The squirrels know what we don't."

"And what would that be, Black?" Hester squatted down, gently moving the leaves aside with her fingers to look at the cache. "What do they know?"

" 'Twill be an early winter," Lark said. "Early and hard."

Hester laughed. "If you say so," she said. "But I don't see why squirrels should be better able to predict the weather than we are. It was such a hot summer."

Lark grinned up at her tall friend. "Just you remember, Morning. The beasts understand all kinds of things. Mark you, snow will fly before the month has passed."

Hester stood up again and shaded her eyes to look back across the rolling parkland of Beeth House. "There she is," she said. She lifted her arm to wave. "Mamá will be here in a moment."

" 'Tis so different, being third-level girls," Lark said, as they waited for Lady Beeth to reach them. "I thought I would love having more freedom, flying on my own, all of that. But now it just seems there are more things to worry about."

"These are not normal times," Hester said grimly. "With militia everywhere, it's like having the Duke himself watching over our shoulders. Don't dare wiggle a finger without fear of someone hying off to the Palace to tattle."

Lady Beeth's expression was as dark as her daughter's as she approached, striding down the park with a purposeful step.

The girls had come at the request of Mistress Star. They

delivered the Headmistress's note to Lady Beeth, who fed them biscuits and tea and sent them out to walk for a bit. She didn't read the letter to them, but they had already guessed its contents.

Times were indeed difficult, even at the Academy. Mistress Star had been forced to make little economies. There was a shortage of the coffee that had to be imported from the south, and of the fruit brought in by ship from Klee and from Isamar. Two maids had been let go. Even supplies for the winged horses suffered. There had been no hay deliveries in weeks. They could see, scanning the fields they overflew, that the second cutting was due soon, and the farmers would want to clear out their silos and stacks. Still, no hay wagon trundled down the lane, and the stack behind the stables would never last the winter.

Mistress Star and Mistress Dancer and the other horse-mistresses walked about with tight faces, their conversations stopping abruptly when any girls drew near. Huddled conferences interrupted classes. Tension ran through every activity at the Academy, wearing tempers thin.

Lark had thought this day would be a respite, a few hours away from the eyes of the soldiers and the dour atmosphere of the Hall, but she understood now that their errand was part of the crisis. She and Hester were certain that Mistress Star's letter asked the Beeths for money.

The girls hurried to meet Lady Beeth, their boots kicking up puffs of dirt from beneath the grass. The park around Beeth House was kept green by watering, but the hills to the west burned under the sun, grass and trees turning yellow and brown and red.

Lady Beeth wore a broad-brimmed hat and regarded them critically from its shade. "Those caps of yours do nothing to keep the sun from burning your noses," she said, as their paths converged.

Hester linked her arm through her mother's. "Mamá, no one cares if horsemistresses have freckled noses. We'll look like old shoes before we're thirty, anyway."

Lady Beeth pressed Hester's arm close. Lark smiled to see them together, both of them tall and angular, brown eyes bright with intelligence. Lady Beeth had a commanding manner, and plump little Lord Beeth was content to let her guide him. It was said in the White City that there was one woman in the Council of Lords, though she was not allowed to speak. Everyone knew that woman was Lady Amanda Beeth.

The three of them strolled slowly back toward Beeth House. Lady Beeth said, "How bad is it, dearest?"

"Bad enough, Mamá. We have had no meat at all this week, and Herbert himself caught the fish we had last night. Our haystack won't last past Erdlin, and Black says a hard winter is coming."

Lady Beeth turned her eyes to Lark, who nodded. "'Tis true," she said.

Lady Beeth gave a short nod without questioning the country wisdom. "Beeth will carry this problem to the Council, but I have little hope of them. They are divided right down the middle, half supporting the Duke's policy, half opposing."

"The girls won't mind economizing," Hester said. "But we have to feed our horses, Mamá."

"Of course you do, my heart." Lady Beeth pursed her lips. "Beeth and I will see to that, at least."

"Not all of it, surely, Lady Beeth? 'Tis a great expense, I fear!" Lark said.

"Indeed it is, Larkyn dear. We'll mortgage the summer estate in the Angles. That will get the Academy through the winter."

"Mamá! Is there no other way?" Hester cried. "Surely one of the other lords . . . You and Papá cannot carry this burden alone!"

Lady Beeth slowed her steps and turned aside to where a little stone bench rested beneath the drooping branches of a live oak. She sat down in the shade, and pulled off her hat to fan herself with it. "We are not alone in being burdened," she said. She dug with the toe of her shoe into the loam of dirt and oak leaves beneath the bench. "We grieve, Beeth and I, at the state our Duchy has come to. Our people are doing without, seeing their sons impressed into service, losing their savings and their security. And one can hardly travel even into the White City! At every turn soldiers are peering into wagons and carriages, blocking traffic, slowing commerce."

"What are they looking for?" Lark asked.

"They're watching for boys being sent away to avoid impressment, for goods slipping by without being taxed, a dozen other things. And"—she leaned back against the tree, heedless of the rough bark catching at the silk of her tabard—"they're looking for Philippa Winter. Daysmith learned there is a standing order to arrest her if she shows her face in Oc. I doubt she'd be able to slip away a second time."

THE girls took their leave very late, when the sky was already beginning to darken. The horses, untroubled by their bondmates' worries, were rested and eager. Tup raced down the park to leap into the air ahead of Goldie. Even Goldie was energized, shedding some of her customary dignity as she sped to catch up with Tup, lifting above him with powerful strokes of her white wings. Lark looked up, marveling at how graceful Hester was in the flying saddle. Aloft, all her angles softened. Her long arms and legs suited Goldie's strong conformation. They were beautiful to watch, haloed by the fading light as they banked to the west.

Tup stretched his neck, and beat his wings faster. Lark loosened the rein to let him ascend, swooping above and beyond Goldie, two of his wingbeats to every one of hers. He was smaller, and his slender body was as flexible as a swallow's. Lark felt his strength through her hands and her thighs, the great muscles of his wings flexing across his chest and up through the leather and wood of the saddle.

When they reached the Academy, Lark lifted the rein and laid it against Tup's neck. He shook his head from side to side in rebellion, and it was tempting to let him have his way, to fly on, to spend a few more minutes in the air. But it was nearly full dark. The lamps were burning in the Hall and the Residence, and Mistress Star would be waiting for Lady Beeth's response.

Lark called, "No, Tup! We have to go in." She laid the rein against his neck again and pressed with her left calf. His ears flattened, just for a moment, before he tilted sharply to the right, dropping toward the return paddock at a precipitous angle.

Lark grinned and tightened her calves around him. It was

his way of scolding her, to make her hold on tight. If she had slipped, even a little, he would have leveled out immediately. He had done it before.

One day soon, she promised herself, as he spread his wings and reached for the ground with his forefeet, they would indulge themselves, and fly without the saddle. He could do anything he wanted then, and she never slipped. She sometimes thought that as long as he wore the breast strap she and her lost friend Rosellen had constructed, they could fly upside down if they wanted to. Without the encumbrance of the flying saddle, they felt like one being, Lark molded to Tup's back, Tup sensing every shift of her weight, every pressure of her calves and thighs and hands.

But not tonight. He cantered up the return paddock toward the stables, and she reined him back to the posting trot before they reached the fence. Hester and Goldie were already there. Tup trotted up to them, and Lark swung her leg over the pommel to dismount. Just as her feet struck the ground, she heard Anabel's voice calling from the stable door. "Have either of you seen Amelia?"

Lark's arms prickled with sudden alarm. "No," she said. "Can't you find her?"

"No! Mistress Dancer wanted to speak to her, but I can't find her anywhere."

"Have you looked in Mahogany's stall?" Hester asked.

"I looked there first," Anabel said.

Hester and Lark went through the gate and closed it behind them. They led their horses toward the stable, and Anabel stepped aside to let them pass. "The thing is," she said in a fretful tone, "that Mahogany isn't there, either."

Lark stopped and looked back toward the courtyard. "The yearlings' pasture?"

"It's empty."

"Maybe she took him out for a walk," Hester offered, but she sounded doubtful.

"Without telling anyone? And where's Bramble?"

Anabel shook her head. "I don't know. It seems so strange."

Lark and Hester hurried to untack their horses and rub them down, while Anabel searched the dry paddock and the flight paddock, and dashed across the courtyard to make another round of the classrooms and the library. She came running back just as Lark and Hester finished filling the horses' water buckets and measuring out grain.

"No one's seen her," Anabel reported breathlessly. "And now Mistress Dancer is worried, too. She was up with her flight—" She stopped to catch her breath, one hand on her chest. "Everyone was out today, the first-levels doing ground drills at the end of the yearlings' pasture, by the grove, and the second-levels up with Mistress Dancer. I was in the library all afternoon, and everyone else in our flight had something to do!"

"Which means," Hester said, "that no one was in the stables. Where's Herbert?"

"He's having his supper in the kitchen. He hasn't seen her since this afternoon."

"And Mistress Star?"

"She was in her office, but now she's gone to the Dormitory to look for Amelia."

"There are militia everywhere," Hester snapped. "Didn't one of them see anything?"

"They say not. But you know, they stay away from the stables, because of the horses."

Lark put a hand to her throat, and stared at Anabel, then at Hester. "He's taken her."

Hester's mouth opened, and then closed. Anabel said, "Who? Who's taken her?"

"Don't you see, Hester?" Lark said. She spun about, and started across the courtyard to the Dormitory to find Mistress Star. Hester and Anabel trotted beside her.

Hester groaned, and Anabel said, "What is it? What are you two talking about?"

They reached the Dormitory and pressed through a little knot of first-levels huddled together on the steps, their eyes wide. When they reached the stairs, out of earshot of the others, Lark said, "It's the Duke, Anabel. He's taken Amelia, and he must have taken her colt and Bramble, too."

"Taken—but—why?" It was almost a wail.

"He wants to force Mistress Winter to come back," Hester said.

Just as they reached the top of the stairs to the sleeping porch, the Headmistress came out. "Hester," she said in a hard voice, "gather your flight, and meet me in my office."

She walked past them and started down the stairs. Lark gazed after her, biting her lip. "Oh, Kalla's heels," she breathed. "'Twas me he wanted."

Hester said, "You don't know that, Black."

"Aye, but I do. He hates me. And I wasn't here, so he took . . . Oh, poor Amelia! She must be frightened to death."

"He wouldn't dare hurt her, would he?" Anabel begged them, as they started down the stairs to find the rest of the third-level girls.

"He tried to hurt me," Lark said, making Anabel twist back to stare at her. "Aye, 'tis true. Last year. That's one of the reasons he forced Mistress Winter to flee, because she knew."

"But—he has his filly now. Isn't that what he wanted?"

They left the Dormitory and started back across the courtyard. Soldiers stood stiffly beside the doors, but Lark felt their eyes on her, as she had done these past weeks. She wondered where Nick had been posted, and she prayed it was as safe a place as the Academy of the Air.

Hester said, "Mamá says that once started, it's hard to reverse the drive for power. Duke William wants power over the winged horses, and over the horsemistresses—and Mistress Winter has become the symbol for that power."

"And me?" Lark said. Guilt dragged at her as she walked close to Hester's warmth. "Our farm is at risk because of me. My brother Nick is impressed into the militia because of me."

Hester's long arm encircled her. Lark wished she could turn her face into her friend's strong shoulder and weep out her anxiety and fear. But she was eighteen now, a child no longer. She was a third-level flyer, and would soon be a horsemistress, by Kalla's grace.

"Tied in somehow to Pamella," Hester said in a low tone. "And to Seraph, too, I expect. Someday we'll understand, Black." They reached the stables, and Hester pointed to her left. "Go that way and see if you can find Beatrice and Grace. I'll go the other way and look for Beryl and Lillian and Isobel."

It didn't take long to collect their classmates and lead them across to the Hall. They found Mistress Star waiting for them. The girls crowded into the office and stood next to the bookshelves while Mistress Star gazed up at them from her desk. Lamplight gleamed on the embossed leather of the great book of the genealogy that lay near her hand. Mistress Dancer stood behind Mistress Star, her arms folded.

Just so, Lark remembered with a pang, had she first met Headmistress Morgan, with Mistress Winter standing by her side. And now both of them were gone.

She had a sudden, vertiginous sensation of time speeding away from her, of the precious days at the Academy dwindling all too fast, and with dangers all around. She looked around at the members of her flight. Anabel was the prettiest, with her silky blond hair and white skin; Isobel and Beatrice were both sturdy girls with merry smiles; dark-haired Grace and red-haired Lillian were almost as small as Lark herself; Beryl was wiry and outspoken. They had wanted nothing to do with a farm girl from the Uplands when she first arrived at the Academy, these aristocratic young women. Yet now, through one of Kalla's mysteries, they had become her friends. They all stood together on the threshold of their careers as horsemistresses of Oc.

Unless Duke William succeeded in displacing them.

Mistress Star stood up, placing her fingertips on the genealogy. Lines of worry creased her weathered face. "No one seems to know what has become of Amelia Rys. We will all search for her again in the morning."

Mistress Dancer said, "We rely on you third-levels to help the younger girls stay calm."

"We hope there will be a reasonable explanation," Mistress Star began, then, with a helpless gesture, she sank down into her chair. She bent her head, and took a shaky breath. "Kalla's tail, I wish Philippa were here," she said.

Lark said hesitantly, "Mistress Star. Someone should get word to Amelia's father—"

Mistress Star shook her head. "No. Not yet. Let's see if we can't find her first."

"But—the Duke—"

"Have a care, Larkyn!" Mistress Dancer said. "The militia are watching and listening."

"In any case, it's just not possible that the Duke would have anything to do with Amelia's disappearance," Mistress Star said. "It makes no sense at all."

"But what will we tell the first- and second-levels?" Anabel asked.

"I can search for her now," Lark began.

Mistress Star shook her head. "Absolutely not. Not in the dark."

Mistress Dancer put a hand on her shoulder and looked around at the girls. "Do your best, girls," she said bluntly. "I have no advice for you except to rest as well as you can. We'll fly first thing in the morning."

SEVEN

AMELIA didn't know where she was.

Her previous experience of Oc consisted only of the Academy grounds and a brief view of the White City from the window of her father's carriage. She hadn't ridden her colt yet, and she didn't know the countryside, or the roads that led between plowed fields and cow pastures. When Duke William drove her and Mahogany out of the back door of the Academy stables, she had plunged away through the woods beyond the dry paddock. They ran, she and Mahogany, with Bramble at their heels. The Duke had been close behind, and Amelia had no chance to look around, to see in which direction she was fleeing.

Duke William had come into the stables, slapping his thigh with his quirt, prowling the aisles as if he were looking for someone.

It never occurred to Amelia at first to be fearful. She was just putting Mahogany's halter on to join the other first-levels for their ground drills. The second- and third-level girls were flying, and Herbert had gone off with his fishing tackle. Even the oc-hounds were off in the fields, except for Bramble. When Amelia looked up to see Duke William coming down the stable aisle, she stepped to the gate of Mahogany's stall, his lead in her hand.

"Good afternoon, Your Grace," she offered.

He scowled at her. "Where is everyone?"

Amelia stiffened at the abruptness of his tone. She said coldly, "Everyone is working."

His lip curled. "Working."

"Of course," she said. "Two flights are aloft. Mine is in the paddock, and I'm about to join them. Can I do something for you before I do?" She took a step forward, with Mahogany at her heels, expecting the Duke to move back out of her way.

Instead, he put his hands on his hips and eyed her for a long moment. She had to stop where she was. The realization crept over her, bit by bit, that she was utterly alone in the stables. There was not even a militiaman nearby. Bramble, lying just outside the stall, had come to her feet and now stood facing the Duke, her hackles up. Amelia knew the oc-hound to be sensitive, and Bramble's wary attitude added to her own growing alarm.

The Duke ignored the dog. "Miss Rys," he said coldly. "Well met."

She inclined her head briefly. "Your Grace."

Duke William's eyes narrowed, glittering slightly in the fading afternoon light. He took his quirt from under his arm and pointed it at her. "Come with me."

"Duke William, I'm not at liberty to—" Her words cut off abruptly as he sprang at her, and pressed his quirt against her throat. Mahogany whinnied, and reared away from the Duke. Amelia lost her hold on his lead, and for a moment she lost her breath, too. The Duke lifted the quirt, and she put one hand on the side of the stall, gasping. She could not have been more shocked if he had seized her by the neck with his thin white fingers.

"Now, let's make this easy," William said in a low tone that made her bones quiver. "You just lead your horse out into the aisle, Klee, and we'll go out the back. That way." He pointed the quirt at the gate that led to the dry paddock. "Go now."

Amelia choked for a moment, then forced a single word from her tight throat. "No."

For answer, he gripped her arm with iron fingers and dragged her into the aisle, pulling her right off her feet. Bramble began to snarl, and Mahogany snorted nervously, stamping, switching his tail.

Amelia stumbled, falling against the Duke's whip-thin body before she found her feet again. No one, in all her life, had ever laid hands on her in such a way. She stammered, "Your Grace—what is it you—"

"I gave you your chance!" he hissed. He yanked her to one side and pushed past her to try to seize Mahogany's halter lead.

Mahogany squealed, and one black forefoot flashed out, striking at the Duke's leg. The hoof caught the upper edge of his riding boot, tearing the fine, thin leather from the top to the toe.

William swore. Without a moment's hesitation, as if he had been waiting for an excuse, he laid into Mahogany with his quirt. Amelia shrieked the same word at him, "No!" but the Duke paid no attention. He struck the colt's neck and shoulders, one side, then the other. Mahogany tried to back away, but had no room. He flailed with his hooves, and the Duke's blows fell harder, coming dangerously near his wings. Amelia shouted, "Stop!"

As the Duke lifted his quirt one more time, Mahogany, teeth bared and eyes white, stormed past him through the open stall gate, knocking him to one side. The colt raced down the aisle at a full gallop. Bramble lunged into the stall to snap at the Duke's ankles. Amelia seized upon the distraction to race after Mahogany, calling his name. She heard the thud of the Duke's quirt across Bramble's slender skull, then the oc-hound's whine, but she couldn't turn back for her.

She ran straight back to the dry paddock. The gate was closed, and Mahogany was dashing from side to side, whinny-ing, trying to find escape. Amelia reached him and fumbled with the gate latch. When it released under her fingers, she threw the gate wide, and they dashed through it side by side, leaving it open behind them.

Together, they turned toward the woods. Bramble caught up with them and loped beside them as they made for the trees. The Duke came after, his long legs leaping across the grass, seem-ingly without effort.

Amelia could hardly think for shock. It had all happened so fast, without warning. None of it made sense, but then, Duke William himself made no sense. He was whip-thin, the sinews of his neck standing out like cords against his pale skin. His black eyes glittered, and his near-white hair hung loosely upon his shoulders, turning him into a creature of nightmare. He pursued them into the woods, dodging and turning as they did, shouting at them to stop.

Cold with fear yet sweating with effort, Amelia struggled to keep up with Mahogany. Bramble crowded her heels as they forced their way into the woods.

The forest was too thick to run through. Hazel thickets blocked the passages between stands of ash and oak, and time and again Amelia and Mahogany, with Bramble close behind, had to turn aside and find another way. And always, the black-garbed figure came behind them. After a time he stopped shouting, but he never ceased following them.

Amelia began to understand that he was herding them. It had seemed, when he first accosted her in the stables, that he had no plan at all, but now he appeared determined. When they turned a way he didn't want them to go, he hurried ahead to block them, forcing them to veer off in another direction. When their route pleased him, he kept a distance, silent except for the twigs and brush that broke beneath his boots.

Mahogany, praise Kalla, was wearing his wingclips, but still Amelia worried about him. He had only his halter, no blanket to protect him, and his hide was scratched and bleeding. She tried to guide him away from the worst of the brambles and branches, fearful for the membranes of his wings. Her own arms and face were scratched, and thorns caught at her tabard and skirt.

Her mind raced. Her gentle upbringing had not prepared her for this outrageous flight through the forest. She was lost. She didn't know whether she fled west or east, and she had no idea what to do when the Duke caught her. And why had he done this? He knew who she was, what her connections were. Surely he knew this was the sheerest folly!

She couldn't think how to evade him. After seeing him strike her colt with his quirt, without care for his safety or pain, she would give anything to keep Mahogany away from him. She had no plan, and no time to formulate one. She could only run deeper and deeper into the woods and hope some way to escape would present itself. Her desperate breathing rattled in her ears.

Bramble panted noisily beside her, and Mahogany grunted as he struggled beneath low-hanging branches and squeezed through the thickets of hazel.

When they reached a wide stream, studded with great gray boulders, Mahogany skidded to a halt on the strand. Amelia clung to his neck, sobbing for breath. Bramble turned back the way they had come, her hackles up, her tail straight out behind her. She snarled and growled, then barked furiously as Duke William emerged from the woods. His pale face had gone scarlet, and sweat darkened his hair. The torn boot flapped around his foot.

Mahogany snorted and reared. His hooves slipped on the rocky beach, and he backed into the swiftly moving water until the current swirled around his hocks.

Amelia cried, "No! Mahogany, stop!" She stumbled after him into the stream, fearful he would slip and fall, perhaps break a leg or injure one of his delicate pasterns.

Mahogany stopped, but he held his head high above her, so she couldn't reach the cheek strap of his halter. He laid his ears flat and glared at the Duke. His upper lip lifted to show his teeth. Amelia leaned against him, willing him to be still.

Bramble dashed back and forth along the shore, barking. The Duke snarled at her, and brandished his quirt. Bramble backed to the water's edge. Her hackles stood up across her shoulders, and she eyed the Duke, growling deep in her throat whenever he moved.

They stood in tableau for a long, tense moment, the winged horse up to his knees in water, Amelia's boots wet to the ankle, and Bramble crouched, ready to spring.

Duke William's lip curled. "Ah," he panted. "Klee. Brought to ground at last."

Amelia brushed hazel catkins from her tabard as she stepped out of the water. Her boots squished wetly on the gravel of the bank, but she held herself straight, gazing directly into Duke William's black eyes, gathering her dignity about her as best she could. "What, my lord Duke," she asked, "could you possibly want of me?"

He did not answer but pointed downstream with his quirt.

She looked behind her. Thick, impassable willows overhung the far bank of the stream. Going upstream was impossible, and the Duke blocked the way they had come.

"Your Grace," Amelia said. Her breath sobbed in her throat, and she cleared it. "You don't have to go on with this. It is not too late to set things right, and no need to inform my father—"

His laugh was short and shrill, interrupting her. "Go," he said. He took a step forward, the quirt lifted, and she knew he would not hesitate to strike her colt again.

There was nothing to do but move in the direction he pointed. Amelia stretched onto her tiptoes until she could just reach Mahogany's halter. She persuaded him to relax his neck and lower his head, then she started him along the gravel bank. Bramble walked at Mahogany's heels, and the Duke's boots crunched against the stones as he followed.

Before long they came to a narrow wooden bridge. When they passed over it they left the woods behind, finding themselves in rolling parkland, with the roof of a great house showing in the distance above a grove of beeches. Amelia turned toward the house, thinking they had reached their destination, but the Duke said, "No, Klee. Too obvious. Turn to your right."

He had recovered himself, it seemed. His hair was pulled back again, tied in its queue, and the color in his cheeks had subsided. He pointed again. "Go. Not much farther."

Amelia's feet hurt. Her riding boots were not made for long walks, nor for rough ground. Sweat soaked her tabard. The look in the Duke's eyes frightened her, but she refused to allow any sign of fear to reach her face or her voice. "What can you hope to gain from this?"

"Go!" he commanded, and shook the quirt.

She stumbled forward, leaning more and more on Mahogany. He lowered his head so she could hold his halter with one hand and brace the other on his withers. Bramble moved close to her opposite side. Amelia felt the strength of the two animals supporting her, and she took heart. After all, she was Klee, and the niece of the viscount. Whatever mad scheme the Duke of Oc had in mind, he would not dare harm her.

The sun dropped below the hills to the west, streaking the

sky with the red and rust of a harvest sunset. The colors were just beginning to fade when they came upon a shed sitting all by itself in the middle of a hayfield. The crop had been scythed once already, and the second growth was as high as Amelia's knees. A hay wagon with a broken axle rested half in and half out of the single door, which was a heavy panel of unpainted planks hung from an iron track.

Amelia stopped, and Mahogany stopped with her. Bramble looked up expectantly, her tail waving.

Duke William said, "Go in."

Amelia lifted her chin. "I will not," she said.

The Duke smiled at that and stepped closer, his quirt held lightly in his fingers. Mahogany began to snort and stamp, and flex his wings against his wingclips.

The Duke bowed to Amelia, and when he spoke, his gentle tone frightened her more than if he had shouted. He said, "Go in, Klee. Or I will drag you inside, and leave your colt out here by himself. He'll likely injure himself trying to get to you."

The oc-hound growled, and Amelia put a hand on her narrow head. "Never mind, Bramble," she said. She took the cheek strap of Mahogany's halter and led him forward. He walked obediently beside her, and Bramble, with a last growl in the Duke's direction, followed.

They went into the dim shed through the open door. Scythes and saw blades hung here and there on the walls. The graying boards were at least three fingers thick, and the wooden door was half that again. Amelia doubted she could shift it so much as a hand's breadth by herself.

William pushed the wagon out of the shed into the half-grown hay. He grunted with effort as he slid the door on its hinge, the wood screeching against the iron. When it closed at last, it clicked against the far jamb, blocking the last shaft of evening light. Amelia and Mahogany and Bramble stood in darkness.

Amelia called loudly, "Your Grace! My horse needs water, and so does this oc-hound!"

"Of course," he said smoothly. "Look in the corner." There was the rattle of a chain, then the snick of a padlock clicking into place.

Amelia placed her ear against the wall and listened to the Duke's footsteps rustling through the hayfield. She put her eye to a slit between boards, receiving a splinter in her forehead for her trouble, but the angle was wrong, and she couldn't see him. In fact, she couldn't see anything but a blur of trees and a bit of the green hay—timothy, she remembered, from her Academy classes. Dusk overtook the meadow as she stood there, and her heart sank. Unless he came back soon, it seemed Duke William meant her to spend the night in this lonely place.

For a moment, Amelia stood, her forehead against the weathered wood, her eyes prickling with tears. She took a deep, steadying breath, and thought of her father.

What would Esmond Rys do in her place? He certainly, she admonished herself, would not give in to the weakness of tears. He would assess his surroundings, deal with the most immediate needs of his animals, then think through his situation to the best of his ability. And he would expect his daughter to do likewise.

She turned from the lowering evening beyond the shed. It took a few moments for her eyes to adapt to the darkness within. Faint glimmers of twilight filtered through the chinks between the wallboards, revealing a dirt floor and scattered tumbles of equipment she didn't recognize. There was no window.

Mahogany stamped uneasily, and Amelia went to her colt and put her arm around his neck to reassure him. "I'm sorry," she murmured. "I couldn't think what to do, and now we're in a spot, aren't we?" In the far corner she saw an iron-staved barrel with a flat lid. "Come, Mahogany, and Bramble, you, too. That must be water. Let's have a drink."

The oc-hound whined, and licked her hand. Amelia squatted beside her and stroked her head. "I know, Bramble. But we'll stay calm. We're flyers, aren't we? Or we will be soon. And I am my father's daughter. We'll think of something."

She stood again and pressed her fingers to her temples. She had been schooled in politics since her childhood. She should be able to figure this out. "He must have a purpose in taking us. He wants something."

As Mahogany bent his head to drink from the barrel, Amelia

said, "We're hostages, aren't we, my friends? I don't know why, but that's what we are."

Mahogany lifted his head, and Bramble stood on her hind legs to reach her nose into the barrel. Amelia pressed her cheek to Mahogany's tangled mane. "My father will come for us when he knows. And I have no doubt Mistress Star will see to that without delay. I'm an Academy girl, after all." She took a deep breath and bent to cup a handful of water from the bucket.

It tasted surprisingly fresh. He must have filled the barrel recently. She drank her fill, then straightened. She could just make out a pile of blankets against one wall, and a flake of loose hay waited nearby. He had arranged this in advance, obviously, but if these were their provisions, it didn't look as if he expected to keep them long.

"Well, my friends." The steadiness of her own voice filled her with pride. "We had best find a way to get comfortable. I doubt we're leaving this place tonight."

LARK tried to do as Mistress Star had asked, to eat her supper, to see to Tup, then go to bed, but anxiety for Amelia distracted her so that she had no appetite, and her fumbling with Tup's halter and wingclips made him fretful. He backed away from her, tossing his head, whimpering in that way he had.

Hester came to lean over the stall gate. "What's bothering Seraph?"

"I think I am." Lark turned toward Hester, and water slopped out of the bucket she was holding, to soak the straw beneath her boots. "Kalla's teeth, take a blink at what I've done now!"

Hester said, "Come now, Black. I'll give you a hand cleaning that up. You should try to calm down."

Lark put down the bucket and let herself out of the stall gate. "It's just that I remember too well," she said glumly. "Duke William is capable of anything, and Amelia . . . well, Amelia is a baron's daughter. Diplomacy is what she understands, but yon Duke won't care about that."

The girls went down the aisle to the tack room to get a pitchfork and barrow, and trundled them back to the stall. Hester propped the gate open, and Lark began to fork up the wet straw.

"I don't think he'd dare hurt her," Hester said.

"But she must be terrified."

Hester shook her head. "I don't think Klee frightens all that easily."

Lark propped the pitchfork on the floor and looked at her friend. "You should really stop calling her Klee."

Hester shrugged. "I know. Calling her Master is just so awkward."

"And yet you tease me endlessly about what I call Tup," Lark said testily.

Hester put out her long arm to take the pitchfork from Lark's hand. "There, now, Black," she said. "Don't take it out on me. I feel just as badly as you do. Let's get this done and get some rest. We'll find her tomorrow."

Lark took a shaky breath, and relinquished the pitchfork. "I'm sorry, Hester," she said. "It's just that I'm so afraid for her. 'Tis a bad business."

"We all feel the same, I think," Hester said. "But you're the only one blaming yourself."

They finished Tup's stall in silence, then went to see that Goldie was settled. When they started out of the stables toward the Dormitory, they stopped, side by side, in the doorway. A new moon glowed on the tiled roofs of the Hall and the Domicile, and the windows shone with yellow lamplight. Before the Hall, a coach waited, its two fine gray horses standing hipshot and drowsy in the darkness. At the top of the steps, clearly outlined against the open door of the Hall, the Headmistress stood beside a tall, angular woman.

"Hurry, Black," Hester said. "It's Mamá!"

THE shed cooled quickly as night fell. Slivers of moonlight slanted through the cracks in the walls. Amelia had rubbed Mahogany with one of the blankets, and now she sat down on the stack, pulling a blanket around her shoulders against the chill. It smelled of hay and dust and mold, and it was a sort of raw, scratchy wool, but it was warm. Bramble pressed close against her, and Amelia put an arm around the oc-hound. Mahogany stood with his head near her shoulder, and she put up her free hand to touch him in the darkness.

Messages would already be flying from the Academy, alerting the Council that an Academy student was missing, sending word to Baron Rys that his daughter had disappeared. In the morning, the winged horses would fly over the fields and the forest, scanning the ground for them. They had only to hold on, to take care of each other, to remain calm. This would be the undoing of Duke William of Oc.

And she would not, no matter what the provocation, tell him what she knew.

"I won't do it," she whispered to Bramble and Mahogany. "No matter what he does, I won't tell him. Mistress Winter put her trust in my family. I'm honor-bound." Bramble tilted her head to one side, watching and listening, and Amelia patted her.

"I don't think he could have known we would be alone," she said softly. "Odd how someone who is mad can sometimes be lucky."

She patted Mahogany's cheek and sighed. She was almost as high in her station as William himself. In the long tradition of hostages, he might imprison her, even starve her, but she didn't think he would kill her. She would be of more use to him alive.

But would Mahogany?

Amelia lay down, at last, on the blankets. She must stop the whirling of her brain, or she would get no rest at all. Tomorrow, surely, he would come for her. She was no good to him shut up like this, no one knowing where she was, or that he had her.

As she forced her breathing to slow, she kept thinking of that dark glitter in the Duke's eyes. Bramble snuggled close to her, and Amelia pillowed her head on the oc-hound's silky fur. She would figure it out tomorrow. Things were always clearer in the morning.

EIGHT

BEATRICE overheard Sarah Runner, one of the junior horse-mistresses, whispering the news. Beatrice told Isobel, who murmured it in Grace's ear. Soon word spread through all the third-level flight that the Beeths and the Beeths alone had financed the Academy's expenses for the winter to come.

The girls clustered around Hester's cot after the first- and second-level girls were in their beds at the far end of the sleeping porch. The third-levels were in their nightdresses, and they settled onto Hester's and Lark's beds, sitting cross-legged in pools of lamplight. Beatrice recounted yet again what she had heard Mistress Runner say.

Anabel's forehead furrowed. "I'm so sorry, Morning. I begged my papá to help, but he says as the winged horses are the Duke's, their support is his responsibility."

"The problem," Grace said, "is that the money which should be set aside for hay and grain and other things has all gone to support the soldiers."

Beryl said, "My father believes Oc is wise to have a stronger militia. He thinks allowing a Klee girl to bond with a winged horse will lead to Klee attacking Oc once again."

Lark said indignantly, "You can't believe that, Beryl!"

Hester said, "Shhh, Black, let's not disturb the younger ones."

Beryl's lips tightened. "It doesn't matter what I believe, Black. We serve at the Duke's pleasure, do we not?"

Lark felt her cheeks flame with indignation. "It matters because Amelia is a lovely, fine girl with a good education—everything we want in a horsemistress—"

"Like you?" Beryl said slyly. Lark, stung, bit her lip and fell silent.

Anabel said, "Beryl! Don't talk to Lark like that!"

Lillian said, "But she's right. The trouble began when she came, didn't it? And now this Klee girl . . . Perhaps the Headmistress should have listened to our Duke on both points."

Flame-haired Isobel leaned forward, her freckles standing out on her pale cheeks. "I like her," she said stoutly. "Amelia, I mean." She glanced at Lark. "And you, too, Black, of course," she added. "Sorry."

"You like everyone," Beryl said sourly. "That doesn't prove anything."

"Nothing needs to be proved." This was from Grace, whose manner was usually as mild as her name. "Headmistress Winter accepted her—both of them—and that should be good enough. We owe them both our loyalty."

"Our first loyalty is to the Duke—" Beryl began, until Hester interrupted her, putting up a hand, and gazing around at all of them.

"Girls. If we fight among ourselves, we're no better than the Council Lords. Mamá says all they do these days is argue."

Beryl said under her breath, "Your mamá is not actually *on* the Council, Morning."

Hester's eyes flashed in the dimness. "But Papá is wise enough to consult her in everything."

"Lady Beeth is brilliant," Anabel said, making Lark look at her with approval. They exchanged a smile, and Lark felt a bit better.

They finally dispersed to go to their beds. Lark gave Beryl a last, doubtful glance as the dark-haired girl turned away. Beryl's remarks had hurt. Lark thought such objections to her own modest background had faded away, at least among the girls of her own flight.

Hester said, when the others had gone, "It's worse than they know, Black. Mamá says Lord Francis and old Lord Daysmith tried to raise a militia of their own, but they didn't have the funds. Lord Francis went to Arlton, to ask Prince Nicolas for help, and that was when he learned that the Prince has taken the other side, supplying money and men to Duke William. And now they've blocked the shipping lanes, so that no help can come into Oc."

Lark hugged herself, feeling a sudden chill. "What will happen, Hester?"

Hester lifted one shoulder. "No one knows. But it won't be good."

Lark hesitated, then said, "Hester, you must agree with me that someone should tell Amelia's father."

Hester heaved a tired sigh. "Mistress Star says the Academy is in enough trouble without bringing the Klee forces down on our heads."

"But he should know what's happened," Lark said.

Hester spread her hands. "No one knows what's happened. Not yet."

"I do," Lark said.

"You *think* you do. Not the same thing at all."

There seemed to be nothing else to say. Hester climbed into her bed, and Lark folded back her own blankets and slipped underneath them. She blew out the little lamp beside her bed, and turned on her side. Hester had already closed her eyes, but Lark felt restive and wakeful.

It was, she thought, more evidence of Duke William's failings. It was not just that he hated her for taking Tup, or that he had sent Mistress Winter down from the Academy, and she had had to leave Isamar altogether to avoid being imprisoned and losing Winter Sunset. But now the whole Duchy of Oc was being torn down the middle, people spying on each other, attacking each other. Even here, in the Academy, strife and discord were rising at just the time when they needed to pull together.

Lark wished she could talk it all over with Lady Beeth. Hester's mamá always seemed to know what to do.

Even better, she wished she could tell Brye about it. It would be such a relief to sit at the old scarred table in the high-ceilinged kitchen of Deeping Farm and hear her older brother's laconic assessment of events. A surge of longing for her home gave her a sudden chill despite her warm blankets.

She turned to the other side and curled against her pillow. Poor Amelia! Where was she tonight? Would she get any sleep at all?

At least Amelia had Kalla to protect her. Lark had given her own icon of Kalla to Amelia on the night her colt was foaled. Comforted by this small detail, Lark drifted into an uneasy sleep. Her last thought was a plea to Kalla to protect Amelia Rys, and Mahogany.

HEADMISTRESS Star roused the third-level flight very early, when only a faint gray light illumined the buildings of the Academy. They took a hasty breakfast in the Hall, and some of the girls grumbled at the chill of the air. Lark avoided everyone's eyes and said nothing. She had already been out to the stables, hurrying through the cold mist with a small pack that held a change of smallclothes and a few other oddments. She had hidden it even from Hester. She was first to the flight paddock for their launch, and she kept Tup facing the other horses, so no one would notice the pack tied behind the high cantle of her flying saddle.

They rose into the air in silence broken only by the sounds of flight. Mistress Star led. Hester came next, with the rest of the flight in their usual order. Each had a portion of ground to cover, and they were to fly for no more than one hour, then return to the Academy, even if they found nothing.

Lark and Tup flew east, toward Beeth House, and the sea. Lark leaned past Tup's shoulder, trying to spot Mahogany's red coat against the second growth of hay or the fading green of the hedgerows. The sun quickly burned away the mist, and the landscape opened beneath them. Farmers toiled in their fields, bringing in the last of the harvest. An occasional milk cart trundled along one of the lanes, and once she saw a group of militiamen marching up the main road to Osham. She dutifully scanned everything, turned back once or twice to have a second look at something that caught her eye. Both times it turned out to be a red-and-white cow grazing alone in a field.

Lark took great care not to miss anything, but she had no real hope of seeing Amelia and the missing Mahogany. Duke William would have hidden them well.

When the allotted hour had passed, she saw her flight in the distance, wheeling about, winging back toward the Academy as they had been instructed. She held Tup at Quarters for long minutes, waiting where she was until the winged horses converged above the Academy and assembled themselves to return to ground. When they had begun their descent, all of them turned away from her, she laid her rein against Tup's neck and squeezed his barrel with her right calf. He banked to the left, turning to the south, away from Osham.

His wings shivered with a surprised pleasure, and his ears turned eagerly forward. Tup was always ready for an adventure. When she knew he understood their direction, she gave him his head. He ascended past a few puffs of cloud into clear, cold sunshine. Lark pulled her cap low over her forehead and settled into the flying saddle. It was a long way to Arlton, and they had never flown it before. She must watch for signs of fatigue in Tup and keep a sharp eye for the landmarks she had carefully memorized in the Academy library. The broad road that wound through the Duchy until it reached the Arl River would guide her, and there were several large towns along the way to assure her she was going in the right direction.

Baron Rys had to know what had happened. A letter would be too slow. No one would listen to her, or believe her, but Lark knew in her bones that the longer Duke William held Amelia, the more danger she was in. Mistress Star would be furious at being disobeyed, but Lark was Amelia's monitor, and her friend. There was no one else to take action on her behalf.

When she spied the old tower that loomed above the town of Quin, she knew she was halfway to the Princely City. The tower's distinctive pattern of black and white stones had been clearly described in the atlas. She lifted Tup's rein, and urged him to the west, where a low ridge, topped by a grove of yellowing eucalyptus trees, ran between the town and the foothills of the Marin Mountains.

Tup descended, swooping low over the ridge, dropping behind the straggling line of trees into a grassy vale where a brook trickled southward toward its confluence with the Arl River. He spread his wings and glided down into the meadow, his feet reaching, his neck stretched. Lark let him choose his own place to come to ground, and he landed without incident, cantering with confidence toward the little stream. Tall, stiff grasses tickled Lark's knees through her riding skirt as Tup slowed to a trot, then stopped near the water. Lark swung her leg over the pommel and slid to the ground. She made Tup walk for a moment and took the saddle and blanket off his sweaty back so he could cool a bit before dipping his muzzle into the water.

She had pocketed a bit of toast and bacon at breakfast, wrapped in a napkin from the dining hall. She took them out and ate them, though they were cold and not particularly appetizing. Tup nibbled at the tops of the grass, but with little enthusiasm. It was some tough variety, with seeded heads and thick stalks.

"You'll eat better tonight, I hope," Lark told him.

He tossed his head, making his bridle rattle. She led him back to the stream. "One more drink now," she said. "Then we're off." He rustled his wings in agreement and dropped his head to the water. Lark paused for a moment, struck by the beauty of the sight, the late-fall sun sparkling on the brook and on her little stallion's glossy coat and silky wings. She looked up at the foothills to the west, then to the north. The broomstraw should be in at home, the bloodbeets already on their way to market, but everything would be different this year. Brye and Edmar would have extra work with Nick away in the militia. They would be shocked to know the trouble Lark was now in.

She sighed. None of it would matter if Duke William had his way. She had no doubt he meant to stop her from winning her silver wings. In fact, despite the faith Lillian and Beryl and the other loyalists placed in the Duke, it was possible none of them would become horsemistresses.

She ran her hand over Tup's back and found it dry. She put the blanket back on and swung the saddle up and over. As she buckled the breast strap and the cinches, she said, "This is it now, my Tup. We go on to Arlton and hope we can find the Palace, and Baron Rys, without difficulty. After that . . . I can't tell you. I doubt the horsemistresses there will be happy to see a third-level flyer descending upon them without permission. They'll be ordering me back to Osham within the first five minutes."

He turned his head, and his shining black eye regarded her for a long moment. She stroked his cheek. "Aye," she said softly. "Aye, my lovely, fine boy. Whatever happens, at least we're together."

She leaped into the saddle, adjusted her boots in the stirrups, and they were off again.

THERE was, as it turned out, no possibility that she could have missed the Princely Palace. It dominated the city of Arlton, with its multicolored domes and buildings and towers. Its builders had used everything, it seemed—blackstone from the Uplands quarries, gray granite ferried by sea from Eastreach, pink marble carted across the mountains from Crossmount. The avenues and squares and plazas spilled to the north and to the south of the bright swath of water that was the Arl River. The pink-and-gray turrets of the Palace towered over the city, surrounded by manicured parks and pastures and a great circular courtyard. Long, flat-roofed stables stretched west from the Palace itself. As Lark and Tup drew near, a winged horse rose from beyond those stables and circled to the south and east.

"There, Tup, did you see?" Lark called. She felt a renewed energy in his body as he tilted to the right and began to descend. They made a circle first, scanning the ground beneath. The turrets of the Palace were even higher than Lark had thought, their small windows at a dizzying height from the ground. As Tup wheeled past them, she saw his reflection, like that of an ebony-winged bird, flashing across the shining glass. He banked again, dropping toward a perfectly green, level paddock.

Lark took extra care, settling her heels deep in her stirrups, loosening Tup's rein, straightening her spine. Someone might be watching from those elegant stables, or from one of the windows. "Let's be perfect, my Tup!" she called.

She felt the flexion in his spine as he tucked his hind feet and reached with his forefeet. He struck the ground as lightly as any bird. His wings fluttered saucily as he cantered up the paddock, and as she slowed him to the trot, he pranced and arched his tail.

"Show-off!" she laughed. "Even after that long flight?"

He shook his head from side to side in answer, and a moment later they were at the paddock gate. Lark dismounted sedately, her right leg up and over the cantle instead of throwing it over the pommel as she usually did. She touched the point of Tup's wings, and he folded them quickly, rib to rib, until they lay neatly over the stirrups. Lark straightened her tabard and adjusted her cap, running her fingers briefly through her curls to settle them. Then, with a deep breath, she opened the paddock gate and started toward the stables.

At her approach, a gray-haired stable-girl emerged from the stable door. She stopped a short distance away from Lark, and stared pointedly at her collar. "Who're you, then?" she said. "Not a horsemistress yet, I see. No wings."

Lark lifted her chin and met the woman's eyes. They were as gray as her hair, and cool, nested in a web of wrinkles. "Nay," Lark said. "But soon enough."

The stable-girl sniffed. "That's as may be." She turned a curious eye on Tup. "And who's this?"

"This is Black Seraph." He arched his neck at the sound of his name and blew through his nostrils. "And I'm Larkyn Hamley, third-level girl at the Academy."

"Oh, aye?" The woman stood back a little, eyeing Tup. "Pretty little thing," she said, and her voice was a bit softer.

"Aye," Lark said. "That he is. What's your name?"

"I'm Sally," the stable-girl said. "What deviltry be you up to, Miss Hamley? I don't see a messenger pouch on your belt, neither."

"No," Lark said. "I need to find Baron Rys of Klee."

"Well. Can't help you there. But you can trust me with your Black Seraph, here. I'll cool him and give him a rubdown."

Lark relinquished the reins to her. "Thank you, Sally," she said. "I appreciate it." She looked up, past Sally's shoulder. The courtyard was vast, easily four times the size of that of the Academy. Beyond it, broad marble steps led up to the biggest doors she had ever seen. She felt a bit like a field mouse, dwarfed by the sheer magnitude of her surroundings. Even her voice seemed suddenly smaller as she said, "Is that—is that where I go?"

The stable-girl chuckled, not unkindly. "Oh, aye," she said. "Someone will find you if you just go in. You'd better hope it ain't one of them horsemistresses, though. They'll have a fit if they see an Academy girl come here without permission."

" 'Tis an emergency," Lark said.

"Aye. I thought as much. You'd best get about your business, then."

Lark stroked Tup, and murmured, "I'll be back soon," in his ear. He nosed her, and she pressed her cheek briefly against his neck. When she straightened, she saw Sally watching her with a bemused expression. Her eyes had warmed a little, and threatened to crinkle at the corners.

"He's in good hands," the stable-girl said. The edge had disappeared from her voice.

Lark said, "Aye, Sally. I can see that. I thank you." She turned on her heel, straightened her back, and set out across the pink and gray cobblestones toward the Palace of the Prince of Isamar.

NINE

AMELIA woke when the first morning light slanted between the wallboards. She stirred and sat up, surprised to find that she had slept right through the night. Bramble sat up immediately, panting, and Mahogany rustled his wings.

"Well, friends," Amelia said. "We're still here. What shall we do about all this?"

Bramble stood, waving her tail, and went to the water barrel to drink. "Good idea," Amelia said. "Let's start with that." She led Mahogany to the barrel for the same purpose. She scooped up a palmful of water for herself and drank it, then another. "I would never have thought I'd drink from the same place as an oc-hound and a horse," she said, stroking Bramble's narrow head. "But I'm glad to share with you both."

She stretched her arms and her spine, and grimaced at their stiffness. She scratched at her shoulders. She felt as filthy as a barn cat, and she needed to relieve herself.

Now that a bit of daylight illuminated the shed, she saw that some of the boards were wider than others. One or two were splintered, as if they had been broken and then mended. She stood for a moment, looking about her at the array of tools hanging on rusted nails and that heavy, padlocked door.

The scythe looked useless, but there was a sort of spade next to it, with a long, narrow blade. She had no idea what its true purpose was. It took some effort to wiggle it from its nail, and a shower of dirt and sawdust sprayed over her hair as she did it, but in a moment she had the spade in her hand. She took it to the widest slot of light she could find, and began to pry at a board, using the boards next to it for leverage.

When the board popped out of its place, falling with a

thump to the ground outside, Amelia exclaimed, startled by her own success. Mahogany shied away, and Bramble trotted over to put her head into the space she had opened up. "Look at that, Bramble," Amelia said with some pride. "I can wiggle through that opening, don't you think?"

The dog's tail waved, and she stood watching as Amelia put one leg through the narrow space. Mahogany whickered uneasily. Amelia wrapped her divided skirt as closely around her legs as she could, and wriggled her slender hips into the opening. The old wood caught at her tabard and at her hair, which had fallen out of its rider's knot to tumble down her back, but she persisted, and soon she was standing outside the shed in the half-grown timothy. She said to the animals, "Wait for me! I'll be right back." She hurried toward the trees to find a place.

Much more comfortable afterward, she came back to the shed, and circled it, speaking reassuring words to Bramble and Mahogany. Bramble thrust her nose through the opening in the wall, but didn't try to climb through. Mahogany whinnied, a loud, anxious call. Amelia came back to the open place, and worried at the boards next to it with her hands. "If I could just get one more out," she muttered. "You could get out, Bramble. But for Mahogany, I'd have to remove at least four of these cursed things. I can't risk his wings."

She reached back inside the shed, and maneuvered her spade out into the open. The sun was fully up above the trees now. She worried at the boards with the heavy tool. It was harder from the outside, and she was just thinking she would climb back in and try it from there when she heard him behind her.

"My, my, Klee," he said lightly. There was no mistaking the high pitch of his voice. She hadn't heard his footsteps. "You're very quick to dirty your hands."

She froze for only a moment, and then, slowly, propped her spade against the wall. She brushed at the muck and dust on her tabard and put her hands up to try to tidy her hair a bit before she turned, and inclined her head to him. "Good morning, Your Grace," she said. She attempted a tone as light as his own. His own clothes were immaculate, a pair of narrow trousers and a new pair of boots, intact. He wore a vest embroidered in elaborate patterns of red and purple and blue.

"What are you doing outside at this hour?" he asked.

"Surely, Duke William," she said, "you did not expect me to perform my necessaries on the ground in that noisome place?"

One corner of his mouth curved in a cold smile. "Forgive me," he said, with a slight bow. "I forgot your high breeding." His face was composed, his ice-blond hair brushed back into its queue, but something about his eyes, the not-quite-rightness of them, made her feel queasy.

She breathed the feeling away, and stood as straight as she could. She met his black gaze with her own. "I see you are an early riser yourself."

"Well," he said. "I have guests to attend to."

"Indeed," she said. Her mouth was dry, and she swallowed to moisten it, hoping he wouldn't notice. "And how do you propose to care for us?"

He took his quirt from under his arm and pointed it at her. "Stay right there," he ordered. He pulled a heavy iron key from his pocket, and worked it into the padlock that secured the hanging door. She saw that it took all his strength to slide the door open. She braced herself, thinking that when Mahogany emerged from the shed, they could make a run for it. Perhaps Bramble could keep the Duke busy while they dashed for the trees.

He anticipated her thought. When the door was open enough for the animals to come through, he stepped to Amelia's side, and seized her arm. She was acutely aware of the quirt in his other hand. "This way, Klee," he said in his silky tone. "Allow me to escort you."

As he forced her to walk back beneath the oak and ash trees that circled the hayfield, she heard the unmistakable sound of great wings beating the air. Two winged horses appeared from the east, soaring across the sky like great bright eagles. Amelia tried to pull back, to stay in the open, but Duke William forced her into the cover of the woods with the power of his greater strength. Amelia cried out, "Mahogany! Back!" But her colt threw up his head in confusion, and danced around her, stamping through the hazel thicket and flexing his wings against his wingclips. He wouldn't come close because of the Duke at her side, but he was too upset to listen or understand. The winged horses flew over the hayfield, slowly, tantalizingly, but they were gone in moments. Amelia could not even see who it was who had come looking for her.

The Duke chuckled, and she looked up at him. "I've been unable to imagine what it is you want."

"Well, my lady of Klee," he said conversationally, "it's not your diplomatic skills."

"No. I thought not, though I assure you, my lord, they are considerable." Mahogany had settled a bit, snorting, and followed them at a little distance, his ears drooping with misery. Bramble stayed at Amelia's heels. Her ears flattened every time the Duke spoke.

"I confess," the Duke said, steering her down a narrow path between two ancient oak trees, "that you were not my first choice."

Amelia looked up at him in surprise. Of course! She should have thought of that. He had come for someone else and found her and Mahogany by chance. "Who was your first choice, Your Grace?"

"You need not worry about that," he said, smiling. "I'm content with my prize."

Amelia dropped her eyes, thinking furiously. The path opened out onto a grassy meadow that sloped downward to its center, then up again to a small, neat stable. There was a grove beyond that, and the roofs of a great house just showed above the trees. The busy sounds of hammering and sawing carried on the still air.

"And so," she said. "Mahogany and I are your prisoners by mistake."

"It's true, I'm afraid." William scanned the sky, then pressed her forward, hurrying her down the slope. "But I've come to see it as an omen. A good omen. It strikes me that it can be most useful to have someone the Council Lords care about."

"An Academy student?" Amelia said.

"Better than that," he answered. "A daughter of Klee."

"For what purpose?"

His mouth twisted. "Philippa Winter defied our authority. It sets a bad precedent."

"And you think this will bring her back?"

"Oh, I do indeed, Klee. I do indeed."

Amelia said coldly, "That makes no sense at all. It isn't reasonable."

"No?" he said, sounding amused. "But I am the Duke. I have no need to be reasonable."

"My father would say precisely the opposite."

"Would he indeed?" He spoke coolly, but iron edged his voice.

"Of course, Your Grace. My lord father taught me early that with power comes responsibility. Authority must be rational and reasonable, above all."

His grip on her arm tightened, and she knew she would be bruised by tomorrow. He forced her to walk faster, and she stumbled briefly, then caught herself. "Miss Rys," he began. She interrupted him.

"Master," she said coldly. "My colt is Master Mahogany, and I am called Master."

He sneered at her. "Don't mistake my polite conversation for weakness, Klee. Soon I will fly my Diamond, then my power will be absolute. You would be wise to stay on my good side. The reign of women over the winged horses is coming to an end."

"If you think I would help you in any way toward that purpose, you are more foolish than I thought possible," Amelia said tartly.

His fingers bit more deeply into her skin, and his mouth twisted. In a near whisper, he said, "Don't push me, girl. You'll do as you're told. And I am not averse to causing a little pain." He pursed his lips, then his lips curved in a lopsided, mirthless smile. "Or a lot of pain, should it come to that."

"You wouldn't dare," Amelia said. "My father would—"

"Your father," the Duke said, "is not here."

"He will be," she said with confidence, "as soon as he knows."

"I think I can bring my Council to heel before that happens."

"And *I* think, my lord Duke, that the conclusion of this affair is by no means assured."

He laughed aloud, and they started up the far slope of the meadow toward the stable. "You're wrong," he said, "but I'm impressed by your good breeding, nonetheless. Unlike that country brat I had intended to borrow from the Academy."

"Borrow," she said.

"Of course. My original intention was to use the brat to entice Philippa Winter back to Oc. Perhaps you know something about that?"

Amelia looked away, past the little stable to the grove beyond it. "I know you drove her away," she said, as noncommittally as possible. She knew well how to lie, smoothly and without hesitation. But her father had taught her it was better, when possible, to skirt the issue at hand rather than to dissemble.

"She is," the Duke snapped, "a traitor to her Duchy."

Amelia said, "She's a horsemistress of Oc."

"Not for long," he answered. "Not for long."

AMELIA had seen Jinson before, when he came to the Academy to meet with Mistress Star to consult the genealogy and determine Mahogany's name. She was startled to see that it was he, shamefaced and slump-shouldered, who came to meet her outside the stable.

Duke William said, "Ye gods, man, stand up! You look like a pouting child."

Jinson opened the door to the stable wide, and stood back, his eyes avoiding Amelia's. She stepped forward, one hand on Mahogany's cheek strap.

The colt snorted with fear as he came near the Duke, and pulled back sharply so that she lost her grip on his halter. "Mahogany!" she said.

The Duke stepped forward, between her and the colt. He lifted his quirt. "Mahogany," he said. "Are you stupid, or merely stubborn?"

"Your Grace," Amelia said hastily, as the Duke advanced on her colt. "Please—he won't tolerate you . . ."

"Oh, but he will," Duke William said through a tight jaw. "Diamond does. Why shouldn't your little idiot be as amenable?" He strode forward. Mahogany reared, and backed away as fast as he could. His hocks bent nearly to the ground, and his tail dragged in the dirt.

Amelia ran forward, and the Duke caught sight of her from the corner of his eye. He whirled. Amelia's eyes were on Mahogany, and she didn't understand his intent until it was too late. This time he simply slashed at her, with as little restraint as he had used on the oc-hound, catching her shoulder a sharp, stinging blow. She cried out, cringing, and Bramble bounded forward with a fierce bark. Mahogany whinnied and galloped around them in a ragged circle.

Amelia straightened, ashamed of losing her composure. She faced the Duke. His features were distorted with rage, and he raised the quirt again, but this time she gave no ground. She lifted her head, glaring at him. His arm flexed, and she braced herself.

The second blow didn't come. An odd smile crept across the Duke's face, an expression that somehow made him look less sane than the rictus of fury had a moment ago. Bramble stood with her tail straight out behind her, her hackles stiff. Mahogany pranced at a safe distance, whickering; his ears flattening and lifting and flattening again.

"Now, now, Klee," William said easily. "There's no need for any of this. You'll serve me better if you're in one piece. Get into the stables, and Jinson will see to your needs and give your colt a stall. It's a pity he isn't more intelligent, but I'll deal with him. A lesson or two will put him in a better frame of mind."

Amelia's heart pounded beneath her tabard, and her own fury began to rise. "You won't touch him," she said in a tight voice. "Unless you go through me."

At this, the Duke laughed aloud. "Happily," he said. "But later." He spun around, turning his back on her. "Jinson, did you fetch the mare?"

"Aye, my lord."

"Good. Good. Watch her now, Jinson," he said. "Keep them both out of sight." As he strode away, he switched at his thigh with his quirt.

Mahogany trotted to Amelia the moment the Duke was gone. She stood with one hand on his halter, the other wound in Bramble's long fur. Her legs trembled with shock and anger. "Are you my jailer, then?" she demanded of Jinson.

"You'll be well cared for," he said, with a note of apology. "You and your colt."

"Without a stable-girl?"

"I meant—I mean, you'll have food, and a place to sleep, and—"

"Ah. And is that all you need to be content, Master Jinson?" Amelia spoke in her most aristocratic accent. "Food and a bed?"

He had the grace to flush and shuffle his feet. He had not met her eyes since she arrived. "It's—it's awkward, Miss. I know."

"It's criminal," she said.

"Nay," he said hastily. He turned away, and opened a stall gate, then stood back for her to lead Mahogany in. "Nay, never criminal, Miss. Because he's the Duke, after all."

As she led her colt past him, with Bramble close behind her, she spat, "Your master is a madman. You must see that."

He lifted his eyes to hers at last, and the bleak look in them gave her a spasm of sympathy, despite her anger. "I don't dare see that," he said. "'Twould be the end of me."

JINSON had set up a pallet in the tack room of the stable. Amelia pursed her lips, looking at it. "He means to keep me some time," she said.

"It seems so, Miss."

"For what purpose?"

Jinson shuffled his feet. "I—I thought it was about Mistress Winter. He wants her to come back."

"Why does he care so much about that?"

Jinson sighed, and went to the door. "His Grace doesn't confide in me," he said. "But his man—Slater, that is—says Mistress Winter defied him. He can't forgive that."

"And he thinks if he has a hostage, that will bring her back?"

"Aye. But—'twasn't meant to be you, Miss."

"That's no help, is it?"

"No, Miss."

Amelia touched the pallet, finding it well cushioned, the blankets soft and clean. She drew herself up and turned, her hands on her hips. "Very well, Jinson," she said. "Some breakfast, if you please. I haven't eaten since yesterday noon, nor have these animals."

He bowed, and backed away. Amelia walked to the tiny window at one end of the tack room and looked out into the pale blue sky. She caught a glimpse of something, silver wings, and a pair of black ones, too. She leaned closer to the wall, trying to see.

"Diamond and her monitor," Jinson said, from the doorway. She looked back at him. "The Duke's filly," he added. "From the Palace stables. She flies every day now."

He carried a tray with an apple and a saucer of bread, and a bowl of something that steamed. He set it down on the ledge beside the saddle rack and gestured to it. "I hope this is all right, Miss. There's only Paulina in the kitchen up there. She's not much of a cook."

She took the tray and carried it to the bench beneath the window. "Where am I, Jinson?"

"Fleckham House, Miss. That His Grace is turning into the Fleckham School."

"Wouldn't the Duke think someone will guess where he might have brought me?"

He shook his head. "I don't know, Miss. But 'twouldn't matter much. Must be two dozen militia here. No one's allowed on the grounds but the boys."

"Boys?"

His eyes skittered away from hers again. "Aye, Miss. The boys who—who want to fly."

She grimaced, but she picked up a spoon from the tray and poised it over the bowl of thin porridge. "Jinson—he hurt Larkyn Hamley, you know."

"I'm sorry about that, Miss."

"They say he's killed two other girls. Can you protect me from that?"

"He—I think, Miss, that he doesn't seem to—that lately girls don't—"

Before he could finish, a dark, great-coated figure appeared in the doorway behind him. It was one of the ugliest men Amelia had ever seen, with greasy hair and uneven teeth that he showed in an unpleasant grin. He thrust his hands into the capacious pockets of the caped greatcoat, and contemplated Amelia with small, dark eyes. "Why, Jinson," he said in a gravelly voice. "Who's this we have here?"

TEN

LARK stopped before the tall doors of the Palace to pull off her cap. She folded it neatly and tucked it into her belt next to her gloves. She combed through her short curls with her fingers and stamped her feet to clear any dirt from her boots before she put her hand on the door.

It swung open before she could touch the latch.

A silver-haired man in the purple and white of the prince's livery stood in the doorway, his eyes scanning her riding habit, her boots, her cropped hair, then alighting, as the stable-girl's had, on her unadorned collar. He lifted one narrow white eyebrow, and said, "The service entrance is around the corner and through the back garden."

Lark's cheeks burned with her ready blush, but she lifted her head and thrust out her chin. "I've come in search of Baron Rys of Klee," she said firmly. "I've flown all the way from Osham today, and I would appreciate being announced."

The old servant's other eyebrow rose at that, and his lips curled, then straightened. He made an exaggerated bow. "Very good, Miss," he drawled. "In that case. Allow me to show you into one of the parlors."

She followed him, careful not to slip on the polished wooden floor of the great foyer. Not until he had ushered her into a side room, where uncomfortable-looking chairs dotted a thick carpet, did she begin to look around her. He withdrew and left her alone. She wandered about, looking at the giant paintings on the walls, pulling aside the draperies to peer out into a back courtyard. She tried one of the hard chairs but immediately sprang to her feet and paced again.

"Like Mistress Winter," she muttered to herself, "I can't be still." It would have amused her if her situation had not been so pressing.

When the door opened again, it was not Baron Rys she saw but another servant. This was a younger man, wearing Klee blue. "Miss?" he said. He, too, looked her up and down. She was beginning to feel like an ox for sale, everyone examining her as if guessing her weight and her age. "I'm told you've asked to see his lordship?"

"I'm Larkyn Black," she said, with some impatience. "I've come all the way from Osham today, and I must—I really *must*, please—speak to Baron Rys."

"The baron is occupied with business, naturally. You can tell me your concern, and I will inform his lordship."

The fatigue and uncertainty of the day, the long hours in the air, and her very real fear for Amelia brought Lark's temper to the boiling point. She stamped her foot, and snapped at the man, "I'm a third-level girl from the Academy of the Air, and I have news of the baron's daughter, Amelia. 'Tis bad news, frightening news, and he'll want to hear it right away!"

He hesitated, and indecision furrowed his brow. She realized, belatedly, that he was not a great deal older than she. More gently, she said, "Sir, you may trust me in this. The baron knows me. I'd go to him myself if I could find my way through this great pile!"

He nodded, and said, "Come with me, then, Miss. He's in one of the meeting rooms."

He turned sharply about and went out of the parlor at a brisk pace. She followed him up a flight of broad stairs with an elegantly carved banister, down a long corridor with a runner of woven carpet that was thick but somehow hard under her booted feet, up another flight of stairs, narrower this time. They passed an enormous library, with shelves full of books stretching from floor to ceiling, and the longest table Lark had ever seen running down the middle, white oak with matching armchairs, and lamps at intervals down its length.

They walked on, past turnings and landings and doors in abundance. Lark tried to keep track of how many she passed, what floor she might be on. At last, the man stopped in front of a door. He said, "Wait here, please," before he knocked briefly and went into the room, closing the door behind him.

She had barely time to breathe before the door opened again, and Baron Esmond Rys, his face as calm and composed as if he had been expecting her, stood in the doorway.

"Miss Black, is it not?" he said courteously.

She nodded, her mouth suddenly gone dry, her eyes threatening tears. She swallowed hard. "My lord," she blurted. "He's taken Amelia!"

THINGS moved with astonishing swiftness after that. Lark managed to hold back her tears, even when Baron Rys took her hand, pressed her into a chair, and ordered refreshments to be brought to her while he gave other instructions to his secretary.

It was such a relief to be free of the weight of responsibility, at least for a time, that Lark found herself trembling with the aftermath of tension and worry. A tray came up from the Palace kitchens bearing a cup of bracing tea. She felt better when she had drunk it, and she answered a dozen questions from the secretary, from the baron, then from a representative of the Prince himself, who scribbled notes and conferred in hushed tones with Rys and his people.

When things had quieted, and the secretaries and assistants had left them alone, Baron Rys sat down opposite Lark. He rested his elbows on the arms of his chair, steepled his fingers, and gave her a level look. "What do you think Duke William wants?"

She recognized his expression, having seen it often in Amelia. "He wanted me, sir," she said bluntly. "But I wasn't there, and so he took Amelia."

"And why would he want to take you?"

"He hates me because my stallion was to be the first of his new breed of winged horses, but he came to be foaled on Deeping Farm. And he thinks—I can't prove this, but I believe it—that if he captures me, he will lure Mistress Winter back to Osham." She took a deep drink of her cooling tea. "And of course," she said matter-of-factly, "Duke William has gone hinky."

Rys looked at her quizzically, and she gestured with her free hand. "Sorry, sir. I mean, mad. The Duke takes a potion, and it has altered his mind. He tried to kill me once last year."

Rys's eyes narrowed at this, and his lips pressed into a hard line. "I have ordered my captains to ready our ship to Oc this very day."

"I thought you might, sir. 'Tisn't any other choice. Duke William's militia are everywhere, even at the Academy."

The baron hesitated for the barest moment. "Miss Black, I commend you for your initiative. Your headmistress should have sent word to me immediately."

"'Tis confusing for her," Lark said. "She had no proof— nor do I, in truth. I just have—that is, I think—"

"You have a conviction."

"Aye. That's it."

The furrow that had drawn between his brows when he first saw her had not loosened, yet his voice remained as uninflected as if they were discussing the weather. "Lord Francis needs to know we're coming," he said. And then, half to himself, "I wish we had Philippa Winter."

Lark jumped to her feet, energized by the tea, and even more by the relief of having someone else making decisions. "Which first?" she demanded.

He stood up more slowly and managed a small laugh. "You have done enough, I think. I'll get word to Francis. And I must speak to Prince Nicolas." He rubbed his eyes with his forefingers and sighed. It was the first time he had shown any emotion at all. "Well. You will rest the night here at the Palace, naturally. Your stallion is in excellent hands in the stables, and my secretary will find you a bed."

"Baron Rys—Prince Nicolas is in league with Duke William. He's supplying him with both men and money."

The baron's head came up, and he fixed her with a level gaze. "How do you know that?"

"'Tis something I heard yesterday, sir. That Lord Francis asked the Prince for help and discovered he was supporting the Duke."

Baron Rys reached for a bell and rang it. "I will go directly to His Highness to ask about this. If you need something further, ask my secretary."

"Can't I do something more?"

He paused with the bell in his hand. "I don't know," he said thoughtfully. "I think it depends on what His Highness tells me."

"I'm at your service, sir. For Amelia's sake."

The door opened at that moment, and Rys's secretary stood awaiting orders. Rys spoke to him briefly, then turned back to Lark. "You're distressingly young," he said. "I'm sorry you have to be involved in such affairs."

"I'll be a horsemistress by this time next year, by Kalla's grace." Even speaking the words made her stand taller, lift her head higher.

He bowed. "You sound a great deal like my daughter."

"I could do worse, Baron Rys."

He nodded, and she saw grim purpose mingle with pride in his expression. "Indeed. Well said, Miss Black." He turned then, and was gone without another word.

IT seemed to Lark that everything at the Palace was bigger by half than the same object would be in any other place. The chairs were carved oak, like the ones at the Academy, but the backs were taller. The elaborately dyed carpets were thicker, absorbing all sound from her riding boots, or from the polished shoes of the servant who came to lead her to the horse-mistresses' apartments. The windows were enormous, stretching from floor to ceiling, mullioned and draped and sparkling in the evening light. A long corridor threaded through the maze of the Palace and opened into a richly appointed drawing room, with a small fire burning in the grate and tea already set on a low table.

The servant bowed Lark into the drawing room. He said to the women there, "Mistress Larkyn Hamley, of the Academy of the Air," and withdrew swiftly, as if not wanting to observe the scene that was about to develop.

Only five horsemistresses were present, of the eight assigned to the Prince's service. All were dressed in their riding habits, and all five turned as one to stare at her. Her cheeks flamed, and she put a tentative hand to her curls. These women wouldn't know about her impossible hair, her improper birth, the unusual circumstances of her bonding. They would simply see an Academy student where she shouldn't be, with no rider's knot and no wings on her collar.

Warily, she inclined her head, then stood with her head high, her hands linked before her. "Horsemistresses," she said. "I'm Larkyn Black, third-level girl of the Academy, bonded to Black Seraph. I came—" She hesitated, not sure if they would take her word or not. "I had to speak with Baron Rys of Klee."

One of the horsemistresses, a weathered, rangy woman with graying brown hair, left the fire and walked toward her. She put her hands on her hips, and stared at Lark. "What are you doing here? You can't have come alone, surely."

"I did, Horsemistress," Lark said, carefully casting her eyes down.

"Whatever is Suzanne thinking of?" said one of the women still seated beside the fire. "Sending a third-level girl all the way to Arlton alone? And with winter coming on!"

Lark glanced at the speaker briefly, then brought her eyes back to the woman before her. She judged her to be senior among these flyers, both by her gray hair and by the way the others looked at her. "It was necessary, Mistress," Lark said stiffly. "I can explain—"

"You had better do that," the horsemistress said. She took a step to the side and gestured toward the tea table with one veined hand. "But you must be hungry after your long flight. Come and sit."

"Might as well eat first," one of the other women said. "We can scold you later." The flyer next to her chuckled, and the one opposite shushed them both.

The senior horsemistress held a chair for Lark and, when she was seated, sat down herself. She poured a cup of tea and handed it to Lark. "I'm Jocelyn Rose, bonded to Early Rose. That's Catherine Sky, bonded to Sky Mouse, and across from her—the one scowling at you—is Marielle Smoke, who flies Maid of Smoke. Our youngest flyer is next to you, Madelyn Storm, bonded to Sea Storm. Madelyn only left the Academy a few years ago, so you may find an ally." She folded her arms. "And it sounds as if you may need one."

Lark took a polite sip of tea and carefully set the cup down in its saucer, though she was, in truth, thirsty again, and ravenously hungry. She nodded to Mistress Rose. "'Tis good to meet you," she said. "All of you. I'm sorry to burst in on you this way."

"Never mind about that," Mistress Storm said quickly. Lark would have known she was the youngest. Her skin was still smooth, and no gray silvered her dark hair. "We've been longing for some real news from Oc."

"I think you'd better explain yourself," Mistress Smoke announced. She was indeed scowling. The lines drawn between her brows had the look of permanence.

"Marielle is right," said Mistress Rose. "You'll need to explain. But eat first." She pushed forward a plate of sandwiches and cakes. "Dinner is long in coming here at the Palace."

"And lasts forever," Mistress Storm added with a twinkle. "It will be hours before you see your bed."

"No one's invited her to dinner," Mistress Smoke said sourly.

Mistress Rose turned her head to her. "Please, Marielle," she said. Lark heard the steel in her tone. "Let the child eat. You remember what it was like to be hungry all the time."

The cheerful Madelyn laughed. "I'm still hungry all the time!" Her companion joined in her laughter, but no one else did.

Lark nodded, deciding food should definitely come first. Her stomach gurgled in anticipation, and she pressed a hand to it, embarrassed. Madelyn Storm winked at her. Mistress Rose put two sandwiches on a small china plate, then, with a sidelong glance at Lark's slender middle, added two little cakes, elaborately iced with sugar flowers. She tucked a sprig of grapes alongside this feast and handed the plate to Lark.

Lark smiled her thanks and started with the fruit. They had not seen grapes at the Academy in months.

When she had eaten enough to calm her stomach, and drunk the tea, Mistress Rose refilled the cup, then poured a cup for herself. She settled back in her chair and looked expectantly at Lark. "And now," she said. "Larkyn, is it? Perhaps you could begin at the beginning. I suspect you have a great deal to tell us."

Lark took a deep breath. Now that Baron Rys had begun to take steps, she felt she should make a clean breast of it all. "First," she said, twisting her fingers together in her lap, "I have to tell you that I am here without permission. Head-mistress Star doesn't know."

Mistress Smoke drew a sharp breath and began to speak, but Mistress Rose put up a stern hand, interrupting her. Lark kept her eyes on Mistress Rose as she told the whole tale, going back more than a year, when Duke William had very nearly killed her in his stable at Fleckham House. She told them of Philippa Winter's disappearance, of the privations and pressures at the Academy, of the difficulties of having militia everywhere they went. She tried to describe how changed Duke William was. Finally she came to Amelia's disappearance, and the fruitless search for her, and she ended with her own conviction that Amelia had been abducted by Duke William in her stead.

"And so," Mistress Rose said, "you took matters into your own hands."

Lark lifted her chin. "Aye, Mistress, I did. No one would believe me, but I know what I know. Amelia Rys is in danger, as is Master Mahogany. Baron Rys agrees."

"Rys!" Mistress Rose exclaimed. "You've already spoken with him?"

"'Tis why I came," Lark said.

"You little fool!" Marielle erupted, and this time Mistress Rose didn't stop her. "We'll be at war before you know it!"

"No doubt," Mistress Rose said dryly, "we already are. And I suspect," she added, with a tilt of her head toward Lark, "that you knew that would happen."

Madelyn Storm leaned forward. "Surely she's too young to have figured that out," she said in a conciliatory tone. "She's just a student flyer, after all, worried about her friend—"

Lark interrupted. "Excuse me, Mistress Storm. Mistress Rose has the right of it. I knew Baron Rys would act immediately, which is why I went to him first. The only ones who would believe me were Lord Francis and Mistress Winter. Lord Francis was at the Rotunda, and I could never get there without Mistress Star or one of the others stopping me."

"You shall never be allowed to receive your wings!" This pronouncement came from Mistress Smoke, with a shaken finger and a black look.

"None of us will if this goes on," Lark shot back. She was famous in the Uplands for her snappy tongue, and she couldn't restrain it now. The words sprang from her fear and her frustration. She leaped to her feet and put her fists on her hips. "The Duke is building a new school, the Fleckham School, to teach men to fly winged horses! And the cost is breaking the Duchy, so everyone has to pay his extraordinary tax; all the while, the Academy is going without hay and meat and fruit, and—"

"Men?" Mistress Rose said, her brows rising.

"Men can't fly!" Mistress Smoke sneered.

"'Tis hard to explain, because who has ever seen such a thing?" Lark said desperately. Her voice rose and thinned. "The Duke—he takes some potion or medicament, and he has bonded with a winged filly, and named her Diamond, and he believes he will fly her—"

"Bonded! Impossible!" someone exclaimed.

"You must be mistaken!" was Marielle's pronouncement.

Mistress Storm left her chair, and came to put a protective arm around Lark's shoulders. Lark found herself trembling again, with fury and frustration this time. Mistress Storm's arm was thin and hard, and steady against her own shaking form.

Mistress Rose stood up, her eyes never leaving Lark's face. "Whatever the truth is," she said slowly, "it's clear our young flyer here has acted out of conviction. One of us must escort her back to the Academy first thing tomorrow, with His Highness's leave, and get to the bottom of all this."

Lark dropped her eyes, hoping her rebellion would not show on her face. She thought Mistress Rose seemed a nice woman, if a trifle stern. No doubt she meant well. But Lark had a mission to fulfill. She could let nothing get in her way.

ELEVEN

AMELIA cringed as the man in the caped greatcoat loomed above her. He smelled of unwashed flesh and uncleaned clothes. His teeth were a horror, and the leer on his face chilled her to the bone. It was not madness, as with Duke William, but cruelty that glittered in his eyes. "Klee," he growled. "Now isn't that handy."

She drew herself up. "I am Amelia Master," she said stiffly. "And who might you be?"

"Name's Slater," he said. His lips were red and wet. "The Duke's personal man."

"Are you indeed?" she said, and took pride in the steadiness of her voice. "Then perhaps you could arrange for me to have suitable accommodations if I'm not to be allowed to return to the Academy at this moment."

"Suitable?" he said, with a hoarse laugh. "Seems fitting enough to me! You lot always live with your damned horses, don't you?"

"I am sure," Amelia said, "that His Grace would not approve of your tone."

Jinson took a step to put himself between Amelia and Slater. His face was white, and his voice shook as he spoke. "Miss Rys could use a proper bed, Slater."

Slater scowled at Jinson. "Do tell! Then why don't you get her one?"

"His Grace ordered me to stay here with her," Jinson said. His thin neck flushed, but he held his ground before Slater's glare.

"Afraid she'll scarper, ain't you?" Slater said. "Well, I'm not doing your work for you, Jinson. You want her to have a bed, you see to it." He took a step to the side in order to look Amelia up and down again. "Don't look like much, does she?"

"Fortunately, I have no need to depend on your opinion," Amelia said. "And if you don't intend to make yourself useful, I will thank you to absent yourself from this stable."

He grinned, showing his horrid teeth. "Better you should watch your tongue with me, my fine lady," he said, leaning toward her. "'Tis you could find yourself being—*useful*."

Jinson said, "Slater, leave Miss Rys alone. His Grace won't want you bothering her."

"Oh, he won't?" Slater said. He laughed. "We'll see about that, Jinson! And don't go playing high-and-mighty with me! I know all about you."

Jinson's eyes dropped to his boots. Slater laughed again. He pulled his greatcoat around him and swirled out of the stable. Jinson stepped to the door to watch him go.

"Why should the Duke have such a distasteful person to wait upon him?" Amelia asked.

Jinson avoided her eyes. "I—I can't explain it, Miss. But I don't like him."

"Most unpleasant," she agreed. She glanced at the pallet he had spread for her. "This will suffice for a bed," she said. "Although I wish I could simply return to the Academy."

"I do, too, Miss." Jinson crossed to the pallet, and twitched the blanket to smooth it. "I told His Grace—that is, I tried to say that—" His voice trailed off.

Amelia watched him curiously. "Jinson, if you object to all of this—if you are not in agreement with holding hostages— then why do you not go to the Council Lords and tell them? Tell Lord Francis! There's going to be terrible trouble when my father hears of this. Why be a part of it?"

He hung his head and shoved his hands in his pockets. He looked, she thought, as if he were no more than ten years older than she. He was thin and plain, with wispy brown hair and slender features. "Duke William made me Master Breeder."

"Do you mean you owe him for that?"

He shuffled his feet, and gazed out the open door. It faced east, and the morning sunshine poured through to glow on the sawdust-strewn floor. In the box stall, she heard Mahogany whicker, and Bramble, lying in the aisle, got to her feet. Amelia turned to go to her colt.

"I never wanted to be Master Breeder," Jinson said softly.

Amelia paused, and turned back to gaze at him curiously. "Did you not?"

"Nay," he said, still staring past her to the flood of pale sunshine. "I was happy being stable-man at the Ducal Palace, working for the old Duke. And then he died, and Duke William wanted—well, he meant to change everything. Including the Master Breeder."

"You could have said no."

Now he looked at her, and his eyes had gone round with something like horror. "Oh, no, Miss," he said hastily. "You don't say no to Duke William."

She said in an even tone, "I do. And I will."

"Oh, no, Miss," he repeated. "Best not. You just don't know. Best do what you can to keep him happy; go along with him . . . Please, Miss."

Amelia folded her arms and dropped her chin slightly, looking at Jinson through narrowed eyes. "Why continue in his service if you think so poorly of him?"

Misery dragged at the corners of Jinson's lips. "No choice, Miss," he said in a husky tone. "My choices went away some time ago."

ALTHOUGH the breakfast had gone cold, Amelia ate it all, including the cold toast and dry cheese, and she drank the now-clammy tea. Jinson had laid a flake of hay and a measure of grain in the aisle near Mahogany's stall, and she carried them in, seeing that Mahogany, at least, was comfortable. With Bramble nearby he was calm.

She found a currycomb in the tack room, and carried it back to the box stall. She spent a half hour on Mahogany's coat, soothing both of them in the process. "You don't know how to react to him, do you, my love?" she murmured as she worked. "The Duke confuses you."

Mahogany shook his mane, and whuffed in response. Amelia laid the currycomb on top of the half-gate and checked his halter with her fingers. He was still growing, and she decided to loosen the buckle so it wouldn't begin to chafe under his chin. He nibbled at her fingers as she worked the leather free, and she sighed and stroked him. "We may be here awhile, my love," she said. She leaned against him, her cheek on the black silk of his mane for a moment. "The histories tell many stories of royal hostages," she said, more to herself than to Mahogany, though his ears flickered, following the sound of her voice. "But I never thought, in this modern day, that I would become one."

She sighed and straightened. She poured the grain into his bucket and pulled the flake of hay open. The straw beneath Mahogany's hooves was fresh and clean, and his water bucket was full. He munched oats, tossing his head with pleasure. "At least," she told him, "I know how to conduct myself. And protocol also says I'm to be accorded the respect due my rank. Surely this Duke understands that."

Mahogany lifted his head and looked directly at her with a composed expression. She smiled at him. "You're quite right, Mahogany. At the slightest sign that it's not true, we will find some way to escape. But it's dangerous. That man Slater . . . I think we must be concerned about him."

Mahogany whuffed again and dipped his nose into the grain.

Amelia closed the gate, picked up the currycomb, and went back to the tack room.

The tray had disappeared, and in its place was a little packet of things: a hairbrush, a toothbrush, a towel, and a mirror. Beneath these things were folded clothes, a skirt, two tabards, and a set of smallclothes that had obviously once belonged to someone larger than she. At least they were clean, even smelling faintly of bleach. Amelia stood with her arms folded, staring down at them, then went to the door of the stable.

A grove of beeches stood between the little stable and the main house. Their leaves had fallen, making a carpet of gold and brown beneath the bare branches. She could just see the roof of the house above the trees. The noises of construction went on, almost shockingly ordinary. It hardly seemed possible that she couldn't simply walk up through the grove, climb the rocky bank she saw beyond it, and ask for help. There must be dozens of workers there, by the sound.

She stepped out of the stables.

Two soldiers, dressed in the black-and-silver uniform of the Ducal Palace, stood just beyond the gravel drive in front of the stable, facing her. She made no greeting, nor did they. Two more soldiers were posted at the edge of the beech grove, with a full view of the dry paddock, the rear door of the stable, and the meadow that stretched away to the wood above. Amelia turned and went back into the tack room. She would not humiliate herself by testing their watchfulness. Soon, she told herself, soon the Academy would see to it that she was set free. They would not allow her to languish here for long. She was due to ride Mahogany very soon, and to fly not long after that, with the other first-levels. She had training to do.

BARON Rys's secretary knocked on the door of the horse-mistresses' apartment late in the evening and asked Lark to accompany him to his master's sitting room. "His lordship apologizes for not coming himself," the man said, with a shallow bow. "He has been closeted with the Prince for some hours, and now has urgent letters to write."

Lark was already on her feet, ready to accompany him, but Mistress Rose spoke quickly. "If the baron needs a flyer," she said, "he should ask for one of us. This young lady has not yet earned her wings."

"Please, Mistress Rose," Lark began, but the secretary spoke over her.

"Baron Rys wishes to speak to Miss Black about his daughter, Amelia." Lark bit her lip, and waited. Smoothly, the secretary went on. "Lady Amelia is a first-level student at the Academy of the Air."

"Oh, aye," Lark said. "Aye, she is. And I'm her sponsor."

The secretary held the door open for Lark, and she hurried through. Behind her, she heard him assure the other horse-mistresses he would escort her back to them before long. Lark was already well down the corridor when he caught up with her.

"What is it?" she asked him, as they paced toward the center of the Palace. "What's happened?"

"I'm sure I don't know, Miss," he said, his tone just as bland as it had been with Mistress Rose. "His lordship will tell you all you need to know."

It was odd, Lark thought, to see the way Baron Rys worked. She had become accustomed to seeing Duke William on his own a great deal, riding his brown gelding, but the Baron seemed to be accompanied by a flock of assistants at every moment. Even now, as she was ushered into his sitting room, an undersecretary lifted a sheaf of papers from beneath his pen and carried them off. The man who had brought her pulled a chair into a corner beneath a standing lamp and opened another sheaf of closely written papers.

Baron Rys sighed and stood up, taking off his round spectacles to rub at his eyes with his fingers. Lark crossed to him, and inclined her head. "My lord," she said, hoping it was the proper way to address him. "What did the Prince say?"

Rys blinked a little, as if his eyes were dry. "You were correct, Larkyn," he said wearily. "His Highness has seen fit to ally himself with William, to support his goal of a new academy."

"And Amelia?" Lark said.

"Prince Nicolas asked for proof."

"But of course we have none."

"None. If the Duke had made a demand . . . a ransom letter, for example . . ."

"Baron Rys," Lark said urgently, "I know. You must believe me. He has taken her."

Rys straightened, as if his back hurt him. "I wish I did not believe you, Larkyn, but I do. And if you are right—if we are right—" He blew out a breath, and Lark thought he looked ten years older than he had when she arrived that afternoon. "I've devoted my adult life to the ideal of peace between our peoples," he said, half to himself. "The war between Klee and Isamar, when I was a boy . . . I saw what it did to the soldiers, to our lands. My father would not listen to anyone. He was determined to reunite the two principalities under one crown, and he would not give in until the battle of the South Tower went so badly. By then it was too late."

"Mistress Winter," Lark said.

"Yes. She fought at the South Tower," he answered. "There were hostages there, held by Prince Nicolas's father, and they died, all of them. They died of thirst and hunger, because neither my father nor Nicolas's would call a halt."

"We'll get Amelia back," Lark said softly. "I promise you, sir."

"We'll need Philippa for that," he said, and he gave her a level gaze. There was no emotion in his face, just as she was sure Amelia was showing none on hers, wherever she was. They were as well schooled in diplomacy as the winged horses were in the Airs.

"I'll fetch her," Lark said simply. "Just tell me where."

TWELVE

WILLIAM stroked Diamond's smooth neck, his thin fingers tracing the faint dapples that spangled her silvery coat. "You're like satin, little one," he said. "Though you're not so little now, are you? I think you're ready to carry me."

She had reached her full height of sixteen hands, a good height for a tall man. Her arched neck was sleek with muscle, her back short and straight, her croup angled smartly. Her fetlocks were as dainty as a girl's, but her legs and hocks were sturdy.

William breathed in her sweet smell. The longing to rise with her into the air, to look down on the parks and fields, was almost too much to bear. Still, he must not rush it. Nothing must go wrong when he flew Diamond the first time. It had to be perfect.

And there had to be an audience.

"You're asking for a tragedy, Your Grace."

William froze, his hand on Diamond's withers, then he stroked her deliberately, from mane to tail, forcing Felicity Baron to watch him do it. Diamond began to shift impatiently beneath his hand, her hide shivering as if to rid herself of a fly. She turned her head and flicked her ears toward Mistress Baron with a little welcoming whicker. William frowned and lifted his hand. "You should really try to open your mind, Mistress Baron. You're too set in your ways."

He turned. She inclined her head to him, and he gritted his teeth with impatience. She said, "Your bonding with Diamond is far from perfect, Your Grace. In flight, horse and rider must be in absolute accord, or—"

His lip curled. "You know nothing about our bonding."

"I have eyes," she answered. She stood, lean and worn as an old fence post, glaring at him as if he were no more than a recalcitrant Academy student.

"Use them, then." He wished he could send her back to Isamar. He was tired of her scowls and lectures. But Diamond needed a monitor, and he didn't want her to have to start all over with someone new. A little more smoothly, he said, "I'm standing right beside her. What other man could do that with a winged horse?"

"She flinches away from you." Her voice was as dull as the blade of a rusty knife.

"She's hot," he said, but his words sounded weak even in his own ears. He turned back to Diamond and deliberately looped his arm around her neck. "You see, Horsemistress," he said. "She's mine. And we're going to fly, with your help or without it."

"Devoted my life to the winged horses," she said bitingly. "I won't abandon this one."

He looked back at her, his eyes narrowing. "Or abandon your Duke?"

She hesitated for a long moment, and he felt rage rise in his breast. They were all the same, these women, bitches and harridans, every one of them! They thought they were better than anyone else, just because they were bonded, because they flew, because they thought no one else could. They were going to get a lesson they would never forget. The moment the Fleckham School was full of young men eager to fly, he would get rid of the whole lot.

"Of course," Felicity Baron said at last, "I serve the Duchy."

"And the Duke," he said, his voice sharp.

"I serve at the Duke's pleasure," she agreed, without warmth. "But the winged horses are my first concern."

William released Diamond and crossed to the stall gate. Mistress Baron stepped aside, and followed him out into the wide aisle of the Palace stables. He said, "I want to fly three days from today. Try heavier sand weights tomorrow."

"Diamond can manage more weight," Mistress Baron said. "But if you try to fly her, I can't take responsibility for what happens."

"Don't trouble yourself," William said, his throat tight with anger. His fist tightened around his quirt, and his arm itched to raise it against this maddening woman. "I take responsibility for myself."

"And for the filly?" she said.

He rounded on her. "Damn you, woman," he said. "I'm your Duke! You'll address me with respect."

Her lips thinned as she looked at him, making her look even older and craggier. A most infelicitous visage, he thought, all lines and bones and wrinkles. "I would think a lifetime of service demonstrates adequate respect, Your Grace." It seemed to him she put a little extra weight in the final words, just a slight sarcastic emphasis.

"Just remember," he said, his voice shaking with anger. "Three days. I want her ready."

"At least," she said in a dry voice, "ride the poor thing first. On the ground."

"Of course," William said. "I had always planned that."

Felicity Baron inclined her head, spun about, and walked away. William watched her go, his jaw clenched, his fingers curling and uncurling on his quirt. He would show her. He would show them all. Of course he would ride Diamond first, give her a chance to get used to him.

He followed the horsemistress out of the stables and started across the courtyard toward the Palace. Two militiamen snapped to attention as he approached, and the tall door opened for him before he reached it. He went through into the foyer and snapped at Parkson, who stood bowing behind the door, "Send Slater to me." He would double the potion again. He didn't believe for a minute that the bitch of a horsemistress was right, but he would take no chances.

HE sent Slater to the apothecary, then went into the grand study on the second floor of the Palace, with its view of the park to the south. He settled at the wide cherrywood desk that had been his father's, and rang for his secretaries. They sat across from him, two of them, to deal with some correspondence from the Council Lords and a query from Prince Nicolas. There was a stack of accounts to examine, lists of figures detailing the expense of feeding and housing and clothing the militia.

William felt snappish and impatient. He had not eaten since dinner the night before, nor did he intend to eat until tonight, but although the emptiness of his belly encouraged him, his head ached and his guts growled with hunger.

He waved the accounts aside, and dictated responses to the letters. He had just scrawled his signature—*William of Oc*—across the last of them when Parkson appeared in the doorway.

"My lord Duke," he said. "Lord Beeth of the Council."

William leaned back in his chair, gusting a sigh of annoyance. He had little choice in this matter. Any Council Lord had the right to an audience with the Duke, and already Beeth could see he was here at his desk. Both secretaries were on their feet, bowing to him.

And there—ye gods, William thought, could the man so much as take a step without her?—there behind Beeth was his wife, tall, broad of shoulder and hip, her angular face unsmiling. Though Beeth came into the room first, sketching a bow to William, Lady Beeth somehow contrived to make it look as if she were in the lead. She stepped to her husband's side, a head taller than he, and dipped a perfect, if shallow, curtsy.

"Your Grace," Beeth said.

"My lord Duke," Lady Beeth said. There was a glint in her eye and steel in her voice.

William folded his arms across his chest. He kept his seat, cocking his head to one side. "Lord and Lady Beeth," he said. "How kind of you to call."

The secretaries backed away, casting each other wary glances. William waved a hand at Parkson. "Tea, Parkson. And you two, get on about your business. I'll have a word with his lordship, then I'll call you."

When the servant and the secretaries were gone, William pointed to the chairs opposite the desk. "What an unexpected pleasure," he said, letting his impatience show in his voice, "to be called upon by a Lord of the Council."

"Thank you for seeing me, Your Grace," Beeth said mildly.

"We are always glad to see our Council Lords."

Beeth sat, and crossed his plump legs. Lady Beeth settled into the chair as if it were she and not William who was royalty in this room. He eyed her with distaste.

"Duke William," Beeth said. "There is an Academy student missing."

"And you come to me with this?" William said. He yawned, and gazed up at the ceiling. "What do you expect me to do about it?"

"There are those," Lady Beeth said, as if she had any right at all to speak to him, "who think you had a hand in her disappearance."

William dropped his gaze to look the woman up and down, and his lip curled. "Indeed," he said softly. "And what is this to do with you, my lady?"

She drew breath, but Beeth, for once, spoke for himself. "Our daughter Hester is a third-level girl," he said hastily. "She came to see us yesterday, after all the flyers had searched everywhere they could think of to find their classmate."

"It is the Klee girl, Your Grace," Lady Beeth snapped. "But I suspect you knew that."

Hastily, Beeth said, "You know, Duke William, we've had to mortgage our summer estate to fund upkeep for the Academy for the winter, as Your Grace has seen fit to cut your financial support in half."

"We have two schools to support now," William said. He smiled at them. "And we're quite certain our Council does not wish us to raise taxes again."

"A number of Council Lords have daughters at the Academy," Beeth said. "There would be a rebellion if—"

Amanda Beeth clicked her tongue, interrupting her husband. "Duke William! What about Amelia Rys?"

William let his smile fade, and he narrowed his eyes at her. "What about her?"

"Where is she?"

William straightened, suddenly, and Beeth flinched. Lady Beeth, however, only stiffened her neck. "How dare you," William purred, "come here and accuse me?"

Beeth cleared his throat and ran a finger around the inside of his collar. It did look tight, William thought. Too bad he couldn't put that collar on Amanda Beeth and draw it even tighter. "Your Grace," Beeth said, "I'm sure my lady wife had no wish to offend you. But if we can't find this girl, the Head-mistress will have to notify her father. There will be trouble with Klee."

"Klee," William said. "Oh, yes. Klee saw fit to send one of their daughters here, to fly one of *our* horses. We never sanc-tioned such a step. And Viscount Richard could never be trou-bled to ask our permission."

"But it's done now," Beeth said. "Your Grace knows well you can't undo a bonding." His eyes flickered away from William's, but Amanda Beeth held his gaze, her own like steel.

"Did you take her?" she demanded rudely.

William stood up, kicking back his chair. Beeth jumped to his feet, but Lady Beeth sat where she was, regarding him steadily. William turned his back on her, deliberately, and walked to the huge stone fireplace that dominated one wall. There was no fire in it. He put a hand on the blackstone man-telpiece, liking the way his fingers looked against the dark stone, long and white and bone-thin. They reminded him that he was, by the grace of the entwined gods, Duke of Oc. His leadership was ordained, and he must trust his own instincts. This twist of events could be turned to advantage, for himself, and for Oc. He had only to use his head.

He looked over his shoulder at the Beeths. "There is a long tradition," he said smoothly, "of holding royal hostages. Philippa Winter fled the Duchy to escape the punishment legally meted out to her by our Council. The precedent this sets threatens the authority of the Council and of the Palace, and we mean to have her return and accept her sentence. The Klee girl was not our first choice of hostage, but she was the one who was—shall we say—" He smiled as Amanda Beeth bristled, looking rather like an oc-hound bitch with her hack-les up. "She was available," he finished. "And she's perfectly safe where she is. I promise you."

"My lord Duke," Beeth sputtered.

Again, his damnable wife intervened. She stood up, and strode around the big desk to stand before William. Her gaze was nearly level with his. "You're a disgrace to your office," she said, her bony jaw jutting at him. "Two girls dead already—or is it more, Your Grace?"

He tried to answer her with his silky tone, but heat flared up his throat and cheeks. "You forget yourself, my lady," he said, his voice shrill with anger.

"Be advised by your own words," she said tightly. "Think of the damage you're doing to your people! Klee will be upon us before Mistress Winter even knows what you've done."

He dropped his hand from the mantel and reached for his quirt, realizing too late that he had left it on the floor beneath his desk. "I can't think what you mean," he said, striving to keep the upper hand.

"You took a daughter of Klee hostage!"

"She is a student at our own Academy!" he insisted. "We have every right to—"

But Amanda Beeth, outrageously, turned her back on him and walked away. "Come, Beeth," she hissed at her husband. "The Council must know about this immediately."

Beeth hesitated just long enough for William to gather his wits. "My lord Beeth," he said, forcing his voice into steadiness. "We recommend you bridle your lady wife. She does you no credit."

Little Lord Beeth loosened his tie again and straightened his jacket before he spoke. "With respect, Your Grace, you're wrong. She is a woman beyond compare." And then he, too, turned on his heel and marched after his plain wife. They went out the door and were gone without a word of farewell.

William stared after them. The audacity of it, the sheer insolence, sent a shudder of anxiety through his body. For one horrible moment, he wondered if he had overstepped himself.

Then he shook himself, cursed under his breath, and went back to his desk. He retrieved his quirt, taking comfort from its smooth, braided leather. He walked to the window and stood, watching the mismatched couple climb into their carriage and drive away.

When Parkson put his head in through the door, William said, "Never mind the tea after all, Parkson. You drink it. I'm going out to see my filly."

THIRTEEN

LARK spent her night in a room that was kept just for visitors. It was curtained in pristine white, with a plush chair and a small, skirted dressing table with a mirror above it. Lark marveled at the comfort of Palace life as she lay down in the soft, narrow bed beneath a thick comforter, resting her head on an improbably plump down pillow. Sleep tempted her after her long day, but she had to resist. She forced herself to stay awake by going over and over worrisome things. The thoughts made her heart race, but they succeeding in keeping her awake as the noises of the Palace began to die away. She thought about Duke William, and the Fleckham School, and Nick in the militia. She remembered how Mistress Star had wished for Philippa Winter. She worried about what her punishment would be for flying away from the Academy all on her own.

She kept listening for anything to warn her that people were still up and moving about. Only in the deepest part of the night, when she felt certain all the horsemistresses were sleeping, did she rise from the warmth of the bed and creep out into the long, cold corridor. She had to hold up the skirts of her borrowed nightdress, looping them over her arm. Her feet were bare on the thick, hard carpet, and she shivered. Beyond the tall, multipaned windows, she saw neither stars nor moon, only the blackness of a cloudy midnight. Her eyes adjusted quickly to the gloom. She counted the doors, and struggled to remember the turns and landings as she had been instructed. She made several wrong turns, and once almost bumped into someone slipping furtively out of a door and down the dark corridor. A secret assignation, she supposed. She flattened herself into a wall niche and waited until the person disappeared down a staircase, then went on, her ears aching with the effort to hear anyone's approach. It seemed an hour before she finally found the library, the same she had seen when she first walked through the Palace.

The library was even darker than the corridor, the lamps on the long table extinguished, the only light a faint glow of embers in the big fireplace at one end of the room. Just as he had promised, when he bent over her to speak quickly into her ear at the elaborate dinner the night before, he had left the rolled map, tied with a ribbon of Klee blue, tucked behind a portrait over the mantelpiece. Lark seized it and hurried back the way she had come.

This time she made no mistakes, but walked directly back to the horsemistresses' apartment. She let herself in, holding her breath lest someone wake at the click of the door. Luck was with her, and moments later she laid the map on her little packet of belongings and curled up under the comforter once again. She felt wide-awake, charged with nervous energy, and she feared she might lie awake the rest of the night. She forced her eyes to close, hoping for a few hours' sleep at least.

She drew one deep, slow breath, and then another. She pictured Tup, safe in a warm stall in the Palace stables, his stomach full, other wingless horses keeping him company. Her heartbeat slowed, and she sighed.

The next thing she knew, a dull morning sunlight streamed into the room, and someone was knocking on her door. She sat up, her nerves tingling. The map lay where she had left it.

"Larkyn?" It was Madelyn Storm's voice. "If you hurry, you can have a bit of breakfast with us before your flight."

"Aye, Mistress," Lark said hastily. "Thank you. I'll come right out."

She threw back the comforter and hurried to wash her face and brush her teeth, to drag a comb through her hair. She pulled on her tabard and divided skirt, and thrust her feet into her boots. She tucked the map beneath the smallclothes in her pack. As she left the room with her things under her arm, she glanced back at the rumpled bed, not knowing if she should make it or leave it.

Mistress Storm was waiting for her outside the door and caught her glance. "Oh, don't worry about the bed, Larkyn. A maid will be in to change the sheets."

Lark nodded her thanks and followed Mistress Storm back to the sitting room. A table had been rolled in, with a pot of coffee, little glasses of some red fruit juice, rashers of bacon, a dish of boiled eggs, and a basket of yeast rolls that were twice the size of the ones served at the Academy and liberally dusted with sugar. Lark eyed it all in amazement.

Mistress Storm was watching her and began to laugh. "A feast, isn't it?" she said. "You might as well eat well for once, Larkyn. One full meal won't hurt your little stallion."

Lark already had a roll in her hand. She turned her eyes up to Mistress Storm, surprised. "Have you seen him?" she said.

Mistress Storm grinned. She looked young and rather dashing to Lark's dazzled eyes. "I went out this morning," she said. She took a plate for herself, and Lark noticed she was circumspect in how much she put on it. "I wanted to see your Black Seraph. What a beauty!"

Lark smiled, too, despite the nerves that jumped in her throat and her thighs. "Aye," she said. "I know he's small, but he's strong."

"Of course," Mistress Storm said, shelling a boiled egg with her sun-browned fingers. "He's Ocmarin, like my own Sea Storm. Bred for agility and speed."

Lark bit into the crusty roll, dropping her eyes. She didn't know if Tup had been deliberately bred at all, other than for Duke William's own reasons. She suspected the Duke cared little for Tup's agility. He had tried merely to crossbreed a colt he could fly. It was only by Kalla's grace that Tup had turned out so well, or the filly Diamond, either, for that matter.

The other horsemistresses came out of their bedrooms, yawning and stretching. They sat around the table in companionable silence until Mistress Rose began outlining the day's duties. Mistress Storm had courier duty, a flight all the way into Marin. Two of the others were to escort the Prince's carriage on a ceremonial visit to one of the southern cities. "And I," Mistress Rose said with an air of resignation, "am assigned the young princesses' riding lessons for the day."

There were groans of sympathy, and Mistress Storm said to Lark, "The princesses are ten and eight. They're abominable."

"Now, now," said Mistress Smoke, with a pursing of her thin lips. "We mustn't speak so of the royal family."

"Why not?" Mistress Storm said with asperity. "It's only the truth, by Kalla's teeth! They're spoiled beyond belief."

Mistress Rose put up a hand. "I can't argue with you, Madelyn, but it's best not to say such things where people can hear."

"It's about loyalty," Mistress Smoke began.

"Blind loyalty?" Madelyn Storm snapped. "Look where that's gotten our own Duchy!"

Mistress Smoke shook her head. "Treasonous," she said, and pursed her lips.

"Treason is endangering the bloodlines," Mistress Storm responded.

Mistress Rose stood up. "Enough of that. We're only fly-ers, and we can't solve political problems. We just carry on with our duties."

"And my duty today," Mistress Smoke said gratingly, "is to fly all the way to the Academy just because of one snippet of a girl who thinks she knows more than her betters."

Mistress Storm gave Lark a look of pure sympathy. Lark tried not to show her relief that it was Marielle Smoke who was to escort her, and not the younger flyer. She would have felt awful about deceiving Mistress Storm.

LARK followed Mistress Smoke out of the Palace into a sparkling cold morning. The clouds had vanished before the rising sun. Rime glittered on the grasses and shrubs. The air stung her lungs pleasantly with the chill of winter, and the sky was a clear, pale blue. Marielle's gray Foundation mare stamped in the cold beside Tup. The stable-girl of the Palace stables had both horses tacked and ready. Mistress Smoke stepped to a mounting block and swung into her flying saddle. She moved her mare away from the block so that Lark could use it, but Lark performed a standing mount and tucked her boots into her stirrups with a feeling of relief. The map was secure in her pack behind the cantle, and her stomach was full of the substantial breakfast. She was about to take a great risk. The stakes were high, but so were her spirits.

She reined Tup, about to follow Maid of Smoke. As he cantered down the flight paddock, he shook his bridle joyously and capered once or twice, buoyant with the energy of a good night's rest and his own youthful strength.

Lark touched his neck. "Better save some of that, my lad," she said. "'Tis a long flight we have ahead of us."

A moment later he launched, lifting above the parks and paths of the Palace grounds, banking behind Maid of Smoke so quickly he almost overtook her. Lark nudged him with her knee to bring him into position and tightened the rein to slow his speed. At least for the moment she could demonstrate to Marielle Smoke that they knew how to fly in formation.

Maid of Smoke was a classic Foundation, bigger and heavier than Tup. As with Hester's Golden Morning, she flew with dignity, but without much speed. Mistress Smoke gave a twirl of her quirt to indicate that Lark should follow on the right and behind, in an Open Columns pattern. Obediently, Lark reined Tup into position. They flew above the river with its arching bridges, skirted the towers and domes of the city, then, with a peremptory glance over her shoulder to see that Lark and Tup were in position, Marielle Smoke turned her mare north, toward Oc.

It was the moment Lark had been waiting for. She was fortunate, she knew, that Maid of Smoke was not an Ocmarin like Sea Storm. She lifted Tup's rein, warning him, then pressed her left calf against his shoulder, at the same time laying the rein lightly against the left side of his neck.

Instantly willing, he banked sharply to the right, back toward the city. His ears flicked back toward her, asking what adventure they were about.

"Just fly, Tup!" Lark called above the wind. "As fast as you dare!"

His wings fluttered with energy as he drove toward the spires of Arlton. They flew for a dozen wingbeats before Mistress Smoke realized they had veered off, and wheeled about to come after them.

Lark called, "Faster, Tup!" and leaned forward in her saddle to encourage him. The towers and domes rose before them in a thicket of pink and gray and black marble, some squat and round, some tall and thin, all of them jumbled together between the Palace and the sea. Arlton was less spacious than Osham, the buildings closer together, shading the boulevards that ran between them. Lark peered ahead, looking for the tightest, narrowest path. It was the only way they would escape the experienced horsemistress behind them.

She and Baron Rys had planned this maneuver together the night before. Esmond Rys had expressed misgivings about allowing Lark to take such a chance with Tup, but she had insisted they could handle it. Only now, as the moment presented itself, did her stomach quiver with a pang of fear.

Maid of Smoke made the turn behind them and came on steadily. Lark glanced over her shoulder and saw Mistress Smoke raise her quirt above her head and circle it, the sign for a return to ground. Lark whispered an apology the older flyer couldn't possibly hear and turned her face forward again.

A great spire with a huge clock built into its height loomed before her, and a domed building nestled close behind it. She felt Tup's indecision in a slight hesitation of his wings. She urged him to the right, then sharply to the left, ascending swiftly beyond the spire to fly in a tight circle around the dome. It was made of glass and iron, laid out in diamond shapes that rose high over an inner atrium. Lark glanced down as they passed and saw faces far below, turned up in surprise at the winged horse flying so close.

Tup rose higher, banking past chimney pots and poles from which banners snapped in the wind. Lark took advantage of a clear space to glance back again.

Maid of Smoke still came on. Lark couldn't see Mistress Smoke's expression, but she could imagine the hard-jawed fury of it. "Faster, Tup!" Lark called, tightening her calves around his barrel. She felt the heat of his body as his wings drove them toward the sea with swift, powerful strokes.

But Maid of Smoke, though slower, did not falter. Foundations were known for endurance and power, and this gray mare, with her wide, pale wings, was no exception. And Tup, though faster and more nimble, would tire long before Maid of Smoke's strength would flag.

Lark looked ahead. There was a clear way through the city, skirting the highest of the towers, but they would never lose their pursuers if they took that easy route. She lifted the rein, feeling Tup's awareness, the question in the flick of his ears. With pressure from her right calf and heel, the rein on the right side of his neck, she guided him into the most crowded part of the city, where narrow buildings leaned together over streets so cramped no carriage could ever pass through them.

For a moment, Lark could see no way for Tup to pass through, either. The buildings tumbled together, so crooked and rickety it seemed they must collapse with the slightest pressure. She searched ahead for a flash of sunlight between them, any sign of a passage they could take. She felt as if she faced a solid wall of gray and brown and white-painted wood.

Tension gripped Lark's shoulders and chest so that she could hardly breathe. "Tup!" she cried. "I can't see a way through!"

Just as she was about to give in, to rein him back to hover at Quarters, and wait for Maid of Smoke to overtake them, Tup began to tilt.

His right wing lifted, and his left dropped. Lark, with a whispered prayer to Kalla, adjusted her weight and loosened the rein. She didn't know what Tup intended, but she had to trust him.

He waited to tilt farther until he sensed her find her balance. Only at the last moment did she see the opening he had spotted. It was far too narrow to admit Tup's wings. The only way to make it through would be at a precipitous angle. Lark gripped her pommel with her right hand and steadied her left foot in its stirrup.

It was the maneuver, the final Grace, that they had had such difficulty with before winning their second-level ribbon. It wasn't so hard for Tup, but it was for the rider. And Lark had struggled for weeks with her balance in the flying saddle.

Tup stilled his wings to veer sharply down into the space between two buildings, battered wood on one side, uneven stone on the other. Lark squeezed her thighs against the stirrup leathers with all her strength. She wished she didn't have to struggle against the encumbrance of leather and wood and iron, but there was nothing to be done about that. She snugged her legs under the thigh rolls, tucked her heels down, and gave all control to Tup.

He flew at a sharper and sharper angle, until the tilt of his wings was almost perpendicular to the cobbled street below. Lark heard cries of amazement below them as girl and horse soared through the cramped passage, but she didn't dare look down. She clung to the pommel, and braced her weight far to the right. Tup glided, the momentum of his flight carrying him through, only his pinions quivering to correct his angle against the rush of the wind.

Lark had to remind herself to breathe. The hardness of the ground, the unforgiving walls that surrounded them, seemed so close she could almost feel the impact if Tup were to falter, or to make the slightest mistake . . .

But he executed the difficult Grace with perfection. A few seconds later, they were through. The buildings ahead were no more widely spaced, but they were lower, and Tup could fly above them. He lowered his right wing and lifted his left. Lark settled her weight in the center of the saddle, her seat deep against the cantle. When she felt certain they were safe, she looked back the way they had come.

This must have been the poorest part of the city, with ramshackle buildings built every which way, ancient streets twisting between them in disorderly patterns. They had sliced somehow through a space so constricted it hardly seemed possible they could have made it through.

Maid of Smoke and her rider were nowhere to be seen.

"We did it, Tup!" Lark cried. She lifted the rein and squeezed his barrel through her stirrup leathers, urging him straight on toward the sea. "You did it, my lovely, fine boy!"

It wasn't until that moment of fleeting relief that she noticed how hot Tup's neck was, how much lather had built at the jointure of his wings and his chest, how his wingbeats labored. She must get him to ground as soon as possible, somewhere Marielle Smoke wouldn't see them.

They flew over the outskirts of the city. Ahead was a narrow strip of farmland, planted now in what looked like some sort of fruit trees. The sea sparkled beyond.

Tup began to struggle. Flecks of foam from his chest spattered Lark's cheeks. She urged him lower, toward the fruit orchard, searching for a level spot where they could come to ground. She looked over her shoulder twice. Maid of Smoke had not yet made her way around the city buildings, but Lark had no doubt that Marielle Smoke would not give up so easily. She and Tup needed to get out of sight, and quickly.

They were apple trees, she saw now, as Tup descended. The fruit glowed red against the green leaves. The trees grew close together, and their branches hung low, weighted with apples that should have been harvested long since. The spaces between the trees were not wide enough for Tup's wings. For long, heart-stopping moments, Lark saw no place for Tup to land.

At one end of the orchard was a cart piled high with empty baskets, its tongue resting on the ground, waiting for the ox that would pull it. At the other end, in a clearing, was a little row of beehives, their rounded tops looking like white mushrooms from the air. Beyond that were a house and barn, and she could see the corner of a kitchen garden like her own at Deeping Farm.

Tup stilled his wings above the apple orchard and began to glide.

Lark didn't dare interfere. Whatever he had in mind, she would have to leave it to him. She would have to trust him yet again.

Tup skimmed the tops of the apple trees, his tucked hooves no more than half a rod above the branches. She felt the trembling of his muscles through her calves, and she put her hand on his neck, wishing she could impart her own remaining strength to him.

He banked slightly as they passed the last row of trees, tilting toward the little meadow dotted with its plaster beehives. Lark forced the tension from her arms and shoulders, though she feared his hooves might catch on the hives. She had been fortunate never to see a bad landing, but the horsemistresses at the Academy had made all the girls listen to tales of them. They could mean a broken wing, a leg, a neck. It was why first-level flyers never, ever came to ground without a monitor, calling instructions, orders, encouragement.

Tup dropped lower, and she saw now what he intended. The beehives were laid out in rows of three, and there was just enough space between them for Tup to canter. He would have to hold his wings high as he landed, above the tops of the hives. Lark held her breath as he made his approach.

She felt him reach with his forefeet, his extended wings trembling with effort. His hind feet touched, and he cantered, still flexing his wings upward. It wasn't natural for a winged horse to have to hold his wings so high, but Tup had no choice. Lark was painfully aware of the trembling of his pinions as he strained to lift them. They skimmed the tops of the hives with no more than two hand's breadths of room to spare.

And then they were through the rows of beehives, and Tup, with a shiver of relief, relaxed his wings, letting the pinions trail to the grass. He slowed to the trot and came to a stop just short of the barn. His sides heaved, and his head sagged as he struggled for breath.

Lark leaped from the saddle, careful of his drooping wings, and went to hold his head, to caress him, then to encourage him to fold his wings and walk a little until he was cooler.

She trembled, too, her knees weak as water. "Oh, Tup," she said breathlessly, leaning against his sweat-soaked shoulder. "That was too close."

He gave his whimpering cry and nosed her cheek. She walked him back and forth, staying well away from the little clouds of bees that rose from the hives, and keeping an eye on the sky. No more than five minutes had passed before she saw the other flyers in the distance, and she hurried Tup into the shadow of the barn, where Marielle Smoke couldn't spot them. The horsemistress would be worried about her, she supposed, but she couldn't help that. She stood in tense silence, watching Maid of Smoke carving great circles over the countryside, making them wider and wider, until she must be flying right over the coast.

"'Tis true what they say about Foundations, Tup," she murmured. "Though they're slow, they can fly so far!" He whickered, and she hugged his head to her. "But you, my lovely, brave lad," she said, kissing his hot cheek, "are the swiftest, cleverest horse in all of Isamar!"

A door banged open in the farmhouse behind them, and Lark turned warily. The farmwife came out of the house and stood on her kitchen steps to stare in wonder at the winged horse come to ground in her barnyard. Lark held a finger to her lips, begging for silence. The farmwife scowled, wiped her hands on a spotless apron, and disappeared inside her kitchen with a twitch of her long cotton skirt.

FOURTEEN

AMELIA awoke on her third day of captivity to the drizzle of rain on the roof of the stable. She used the privy beyond the back door, then went to the tack room to stand looking out at the beech grove. The bare branches dripped cold rain, and clouds lowered over everything. The militiamen posted by the grove stood in wet misery, their hat brims sodden and drooping.

Still, Amelia thought, the horsemistresses would come looking for her, as they had the day before, and the day before that, when she had seen the winged horses wheeling above the fields, searching. They couldn't fly in snow, but rain wouldn't stop them. Mistress Star couldn't have given up on her so soon! She scanned the sky, but there was no sign of flyers, at least none that she could see from beneath the stable's roof.

She had just finished brushing her hair back into its rider's knot when Jinson showed up. "Good morning, Master Jinson," she said. "Don't you think those soldiers could be invited to stand under the eaves rather than out there in the wet?"

"I'll ask them, Miss. Kind of you," he said. He had a tray in his hands with a covered plate, a small pitcher, and a tumbler. "Paulina sent your breakfast. I hope it's not too cold. I had to carry it around by the road."

Amelia lifted the cover on the plate. There were two boiled eggs, a roll gone rather hard, with a pat of butter, and a dish of bloodbeets. She sighed. "All of this was cold long before you left the kitchen."

"Sorry, Miss," he said. "That Paulina is in a nasty temper most of the time, with all the hammering and sawing up there, and militia standing about in her way, she says."

"Never mind," Amelia said. "I do thank you for trying."

He ducked his head, and went out of the tack room. Amelia put the cover back on the plate. As it was all cold in any case, there was no hurry. She would ask Jinson to bring a kettle and cups so they could make hot tea right here.

She left the tray in the tack room and went down the aisle to Mahogany. He whickered as she approached and reached eagerly across the stall gate, looking for his morning treat. She stroked his velvet nose, and said, "I'm sorry, Mahogany. No carrots, nor apples, either. I don't think you'd like bloodbeets, and that's all I could have brought you."

Unconvinced, he snuffled at her pockets. She patted him. "Come now, let's get you out in the dry paddock for a bit of exercise. We'll leave the blanket on, or you'll be as wet as those poor soldiers in the grove."

The dry paddock was, naturally, not so dry this morning. The two guards stood by the pole fence, watching, as Amelia led Mahogany out for a few turns around the muddy space. Bramble sat just under the eaves. The rain had settled into a dreary mist, and Amelia's own head was soon wet, with cold raindrops sliding inside her collar. On her third pass, she paused and looked at the militiamen through the whitewashed poles. "Excuse me," she said. "I don't know the proper way to address you. But you're welcome to stand under the eaves, out of the rain. You can still see me, should I decide to make a run for it."

One of the guards looked at her as if he didn't understand her language. The other, a dark-haired man with bright blue eyes and flashing white teeth, gave her a wide grin. "Spoken like a lady," he said.

"I am one," Amelia said.

"Oh, aye?" he said. "And how do you come to be living in yon stable, then?"

The other militiaman elbowed him, but the dark-haired man stepped back, out of his reach, and smiled at Amelia again. "My lady," he said, showing his white smile, "'tis an honor to accept your kind invitation." He gave her an exaggerated bow.

Amelia almost smiled. It felt good to feel like smiling, the first time in three days she had felt that way. "Your accent is familiar to me, sir," she said.

He tilted his head, and regarded her. "Nay," he said. "I doubt it. 'Tis unlikely you've met other Uplanders here in Osham."

She pursed her lips. "You're wrong, as it happens," she said. "My sponsor at the Academy of the Air is an Uplander. And a fine flyer, too!"

His grin faded. "You're from the Academy, Miss? You're not wearing the habit."

"It was filthy," she said simply. "Someone sent me these clothes, and they're all I have to wear." She pointed to the stable, where the slanted roof extended a fair distance past the walls. "Come now, both of you. Get out of the rain."

They did, the dark-haired one walking with a slight swagger, the other one shuffling as if his boots were full of mud. Bramble stood up at their approach and fixed them with her dark gaze. When they had stepped under the shelter of the eaves and were shaking their hats free of rain, the Uplander looked up again, through the fence at Amelia. "I think," he said, "that you've had a blink at my sister. My sister, Larkyn Hamley, though they call her Black now she's bonded." His eyes were almost as vivid a blue as Lark's, but they glinted between narrowed lids. "Why are you being held here, Miss?"

"Amelia Rys," Amelia said, and added deliberately, "though some call me Klee."

"'Tis true, then," he said. His handsome face tightened, and his black eyebrows drew together. "There's a story going around that the Duke took a hostage. I don't like it."

The other militiaman elbowed him again. "Not for you to like or not," he said. "Follows orders, that's what we does."

Lark's brother put a hand on the fence that separated him from Amelia. Mahogany snorted, and pulled back, away from his nearness. "Sorry," he said. "I forgot a moment about the winged horses. I'm Nick Hamley."

She inclined her head. He grinned again, the flash of his teeth in his tanned face like the sun coming out on a cloudy day. "Just so does Lark always dip her head," he said.

"As to my being a hostage," Amelia said, allowing her lips to purse slightly, "I believe Duke William thinks using me will force Horsemistress Winter to return to Oc."

"Bastard," Nick grated.

"Hey!" the other guard grunted. "Best not talk so about your master."

Nick turned his head and gave his fellow militiaman a steady stare. "Yon Duke is not my master," he said. "Not if he's up to this sort of thing." He turned his eyes back to Amelia. "I never wanted any part of his militia. He raised our taxes, to force me."

The guard sneered. "Going to run away, then, farmer? Desert?"

Nick drew a breath. "Not now," he said softly. "Miss Rys may need protection. Lark would want me to stay near her."

Amelia's heart fluttered with a sudden wave of gratitude. She tried to hide it by stiffening her back and turning to stroke Mahogany's neck. "I thank you, Master Hamley," she said through trembling lips. She had been fighting to ignore the strain of the past three days. She took a shaking breath, trying to regain her composure. She was still Duke William's prisoner. This was no time to let her guard down.

In a few moments she felt stronger, and she turned back to Nick Hamley. "I'm going to take my colt in now," she said. "The Master Breeder and I will soon have tea and a kettle. I'll send out cups for you."

Nick smiled and nodded toward his companion. "Even this one will accept your cup of tea, I expect," he said. "We thank you."

JINSON was more than willing to fetch a kettle and a caddy of tea, and they made a pot and sent cups out to all four militiamen before they drank one themselves. They sat on barrels in the tack room and chatted as if they were having tea in a palace instead of a prison. Jinson was pitifully eager to please her, offering a little saucer of biscuits he had slipped from the kitchen when Paulina wasn't looking, asking if the tea was too strong. Amelia crumbled one of the biscuits, and slipped fragments of it to Bramble, lying at her feet.

Their moment of peace was interrupted all too soon.

They heard hoofbeats on the lane leading down from the main road, and Jinson stepped to the door of the tack room to look out. The rain had stopped, but everything dripped noisily, and water ran from the eaves of the stable to splash on the gravel of the little drive. Jinson drew a sharp breath and spun about.

"It's Slater again," he said. His nostrils went white, and his shoulders hunched. "Perhaps, Miss, you'd best go back with your colt . . . Stay out of his way."

"I'm not afraid of him, Jinson," Amelia said. She saw by the flicker of his eyelids that he did not believe her. It was true; there was something about the Duke's man that set her nerves on edge. "I will try to stay out of sight, though," she said, a bit hastily. "I'll clean Mahogany's stall, while you . . . while you deal with him."

It was so odd, she thought, to become friendly with a person who was actually her jailer. But then, her guards, Jinson, even the unsavory Slater, were not responsible for her plight. It was Duke William, and he alone, who had created this situation. She wished she could see a way out of it. She wished someone— anyone who could help—knew where she was. She was beginning to fear that no one had guessed what had happened.

She had just lifted a forkful of wet straw and turned toward the barrow in the aisle when Slater slouched around the corner, his lips slack, his greatcoat drooping wetly around him. He looked like an enormous, bedraggled crow.

Amelia swallowed and carried the pitchfork to the barrow, trying to appear as if his presence meant nothing to her. He stood in the open stall gate, eyeing her. Mahogany snorted, and backed away as far as he could. He stood with his head thrown back, the whites of his eyes showing. Bramble, standing in the aisle next to Amelia, growled.

"If you please, Slater," Amelia said, "you're too close for my colt's comfort."

"Taking no orders from you, Miss," Slater said.

Amelia emptied the pitchfork and leaned it against the barrow, then turned her back on Slater and went to stand beside Mahogany, stroking his neck, making certain to take a firm hold on the cheek strap of his halter. His nostrils were wide, tasting the air. Amelia could smell Slater's unsavory essence herself, one of dirty clothes and an unwashed body. She was worried about her own need of a wash, of course, but she doubted Slater could detect that through his own miasma.

When Mahogany had calmed a little, she turned. "What do you want?"

"First, a civil tongue in your head," he said. "You call that bumpkin in the tack room Master; you can do the same for me."

She kept her face very still. "Master Jinson has earned my respect. You have not."

He gave her his uneven grin. "I'll earn it if I have to, Miss. But you won't like it."

Amelia sniffed and patted Mahogany one more time. She crossed the stall and went into the aisle, closing the gate firmly behind her. Slater smelled even worse up close. She turned toward the tack room, willing him to follow, to get away from her colt. He did, shuffling in the sawdust and breathing noisily.

When she reached the tack room, Jinson was nowhere to be seen. Amelia sat down on one of the barrels and smoothed her skirt around her. "If you have business, state it," she said. "Otherwise, I have work to do."

He looked her up and down, and her skin crawled under his regard. "Don't look like much, do you?"

"I've never been known for my beauty," she said. She sat very straight and fixed him with her coldest gaze. "But I have other strengths. What business do you have here, Slater?"

"Just checking on my lord's affairs," he sneered. "But I might as well warn you. I'm not so patient as His Grace."

"I hadn't noticed Duke William to be a particularly patient man," she said.

He chuckled, and even his laugh had a greasy sound to it. "Right you are, lass." He leaned toward her, much too close. She stiffened her spine, refusing to lean back away from him. "You listen to me, my *lady*," he said in a throaty whisper. His breath was foul. "The Klee killed my brother in the last war, and I ain't had me revenge yet."

Amelia's mouth went dry, but she would not give him the satisfaction of seeing her lick her lips. "I was an infant during the war."

"You're Klee," he said, straightening. "That's enough to satisfy me."

"You would avenge your brother's death by harming me."

He yanked at the lapels of his coat. "It'll do."

He started to smile, revealing those awful teeth, and her hands began to quiver. She braced herself. If he came toward her, if he touched her, she would scream for the militiamen posted outside the stable. He took a step, and another, then, blessedly, Jinson appeared in the doorway. Slater stopped where he was.

Jinson said, "What are you doing here, Slater?"

"None of your damned business, Jinson," Slater said, still staring at Amelia. She held herself still.

"If you're bothering Miss Rys, Slater, I'll make sure His Grace knows all about it."

Slater spun about, and Jinson, his lips going white, stumbled back a step. Amelia could see he immediately regretted it, pulling himself up straight, setting his jaw. Slater, she thought, must be a dangerous person to inspire such fear.

"Yer a fool, Jinson," Slater said. "You think our Duke gives two pins what happens to this uncomely lass, here? If I carried her off, he'd thank me!"

"Carry her off?" Jinson said, his eyes widening. "I'd order these militiamen to shoot you if you tried! I—I'd shoot you myself!"

"Hah," Slater said, gathering the capes of his coat around him. "If you had that much courage, I'd die of surprise." He laughed, a short, phlegmy bark. "Just watch out, here. The Duke may be distracted, but I have a good idea how to make use of our little hostage."

"What are you talking about?" Amelia demanded.

He leered at her. "Never you mind. You'll know when you need to. My *lady*." He gathered his coat around him in a whirl and stamped out of the stable.

Jinson went back to the door to watch him leave and turned back to Amelia. "Are you all right, Miss? He didn't bother you?"

She stood, and shook out her too-large skirt with trembling hands. "He did bother me, as a matter of fact, Master Jinson," she said. "But only because he's a frightening sort of person. But you've sent him off now, and I'm not hurt."

"Shall I speak to the Duke about him?"

Amelia looked up at Jinson's thin, sensitive face, and she read fear in his eyes. She gave him a slight smile. "Very gallant of you," she said. "But I can take care of myself."

He shook his head. "Nasty bit of work, Slater," he said grimly. "He keeps a gun in the pocket of that filthy coat, and he's been known to use it."

"Surely he wouldn't dare. I'm the Duke's hostage, after all."

Jinson lifted one shoulder, and looked miserable. "I don't know, Miss. It worries me."

"Do you have to leave now?"

"Aye. There's business at the Academy. The breeding plan."

"There were so few foals last spring," Amelia said.

"Aye," he said again. "'Twasn't really me, Miss. I don't know much about the breeding program. The Duke has his own ideas, but he makes me put them forward as if they was mine. He wants foals for . . ." He broke off, and his eyes flickered to the door of the tack room, to where the beech grove masked their view of Fleckham House.

"For the new school," she finished for him. "For men to fly."

"Aye," he said quietly. "And he has four boys preparing to be the first."

Amelia walked to the door, and looked up past the beech grove, where she could just see the high roofs of the great house. "I wonder, Master Jinson," she mused, "if those boys know how their bodies will have to change. Or do they think that the Duke can simply breed a different line of horses, after all these centuries?"

"Don't know," he said. "I only know what His Grace tells me. And he says now he's ready to ride Diamond, though Horsemistress Baron objects."

"And when he flies . . ." Amelia said, gazing past the dripping beeches.

"There will be them willing to do anything to fly as you girls do."

"I haven't flown yet." She turned her back on the rain-soaked scene outside the stable, and faced him. "I haven't even ridden, and I don't know if Mahogany and I will have our chance, Jinson. It seems strange to me that no one has come for us yet."

He couldn't meet her eyes. "I wish I could do something for you, Miss. I don't dare."

"But Master Jinson—if you're going to the Academy, surely you could—"

"Nay," he said sadly. "The Duke can do things to hurt my family."

"Could you not tell someone on the Council, then?"

He rubbed his hands on his trousers. "You're Klee, Miss. There are them who will find no fault with this."

She sighed. "I suppose you're right. My father taught me that a nation's memory can be long."

"'Twasn't your fault, the South Tower."

"I guess that doesn't matter. And I suppose the Academy doesn't matter, either, or my bonding to a winged horse. To such people, I'll always be Klee."

FIFTEEN

LARK shrank back into the shadows of the barn roof, pressing Tup against the wall. Overhead, Maid of Smoke made a long, slow circuit of the orchard, and Lark could almost feel Marielle Smoke's eyes burning the landscape, searching for her. The farmwife had not closed her kitchen door when she went inside, and Lark watched that, too, fearful that someone might come out and force her out into the open, or even drive her and her exhausted stallion back into the air.

But when the woman returned, she was followed only by a girl of about seventeen who carried a pail in her hands. They crossed the barnyard to Lark, the farmwife still scowling in what appeared to be a habitual look. The girl was slight and small-boned, and the swell of pregnancy rounded the printed apron she wore. Her eyes stretched wide with amazement when she caught sight of the winged horse. She curtsied to Lark, which made Lark feel strange, and the farmwife said, "I thought your horse looked awful thirsty. Olive here will get some water from the pump."

"Thank you so much," Lark said. " 'Tis true—Tup could use a drink." Olive, without speaking, walked past the corner of the barn and disappeared. Lark cast an anxious glance into the sky, but Maid of Smoke had disappeared, too.

"Huh," the farmwife said, looking Lark up and down as if she were measuring her for an apron of her own. "You don't sound like the rest of them horsemistresses. And they wear their hair different."

Lark gave her a tentative smile, and the woman's scowl lightened ever so slightly. "I'm not a horsemistress yet," Lark said. "Soon, though, next year. I'm an Uplander, and I've kept my country accent. And my hair—" She pulled off her cap, and ran her fingers through her cropped black curls. "My hair won't go in the rider's knot, because of these curls, so I cut it off."

"You're running from that one, it seems," the woman said, with a jerk of her head toward the sky.

"Aye," Lark said " 'Tis not her fault, though. She's doing her duty as she sees it."

The woman's frown deepened again, but she pointed toward the barn. "No stalls in there, but you can tether your horse in the goat pen, if you want. "

Lark's smile grew. "Do you have goats?"

"Aye, Miss. We sell goat cheese when we're not selling apples. You don't mind their smell, I hope?"

"Nay, I do not. I love goats. Tup was fostered by a goat, and I had my own flock in the Uplands."

At this the farmwife's frown smoothed until it almost vanished. "You're a farm girl yourself," she said.

"Aye," Lark said.

"And a flyer. Not the usual thing."

"Nay," Lark said, with a laugh. "Not the usual thing at all."

IN a short time, Lark found herself seated at a battered kitchen table reminiscent of the one at Deeping Farm. The farmwife, whose name turned out to be Agatha, brewed a pot of tea and, Lark was pleased to see, gave it a turn with a small, plaid-skirted fetish before she served it. Lark sipped hers and nodded approval. It was lovely to taste properly made tea once again.

Olive, who turned out to be Agatha's daughter-in-law, brought a dish of sliced apples. Shyly, she said, "Just picked today, Miss."

Lark smiled at her. "Thank you."

The woman and the girl sat down with her, each with a mug of tea. Agatha said, "You can stay here if you want, Miss Hamley. There's no one here but Olive and me, since my boy was sent off to Oc."

"Oc?" Lark said.

"Oh, aye," Agatha said. "Our Prince saw fit to send our own militia off to Osham, to serve the Duke there. No matter that the apples are rotting on the trees, or that my boy's first child is coming." She nodded toward Olive's swelling belly. "What do the nobs care about us farm-folk?"

Lark said, "Some do, Mistress, I promise you. I've met them." She sipped tea, then added, "But my own brother is in the militia, and neither was it his choice."

"Believe you me," Agatha scowled, "if the nobs had to send their own children off, there'd be a sight fewer wars than there are."

"I hope there won't be a war," Lark said, but she remembered Baron Rys's set features, the hardness of his voice, and she felt a quiver of anxiety.

"What are you going to do, Miss?" whispered the shy Olive. "Why did you flee?"

Lark bit her lip, hesitating. Surely the Baron's warning to keep her movements secret did not apply to these simple folk, but she didn't want to take a chance. Still, it was good to have Tup resting in the cool barn, where no one could see him. She didn't want to seem ungrateful.

Choosing her words carefully, she said, "There's trouble in Oc. And at the Academy of the Air. We need help from—from someone. She doesn't know about it yet."

Agatha pushed the dish of apple slices closer to Lark, and said, "She must not be living in Isamar. Everyone here knows there's trouble in Oc."

Lark took an apple slice. "Everyone does? Why?"

Olive said in her breathless voice, "Because the Prince sent the militia. Like my Ronald."

"Ronald. My son," Agatha said.

"Aye," Lark said. "'Tis hardly fair." She nibbled the apple, and was distracted by the crisp flavor that flooded her mouth. "Oh! Delicious!"

Agatha nodded grimly. "Seastars," she said. "Best apples in Isamar."

"I've never had one like it," Lark said honestly.

"Don't know what we're going to do with our harvest this year." Agatha went on. "Even if Olive and me can get the crop in, Ronald usually takes the cart round the towns and sells the apples direct. And we export some to Oc by ship, but them ships aren't sailing this year."

"You have no idea where Ronald is posted?"

Agatha shook her head. "But when you get back from where you're going, Miss, if you meet up with him . . ."

Olive said softly, "Tell him we're fine."

Agatha cast her a startled look, then nodded her approval to her daughter-in-law, though her frown was as deeply engraved into her forehead as ever. "That's right, Olive," she said. "Quite right. Tell Ronald we're fine."

WHEN Lark had checked the skies a dozen times and was convinced that Marielle Smoke had given up trying to find her, she saddled Tup again and led him out into Agatha's barnyard. A dirt lane wound down from the orchard toward the sea, and she and Tup would launch from there. Agatha and Olive gave her a bag of apples, but Lark regretfully took most of them out. "They're wonderful," she said. "But they're heavy, and we have a long flight ahead of us."

"You can sleep the night here," Agatha said for the third time. " 'Tis close to darkness, and I worry for your safety."

Lark shook her head. "Thank you," she said. "But I'll be using a star to reckon my course. It should stand above my destination as soon as the sun sets behind the mountains."

The two stood in the barnyard as she jumped up into the flying saddle. She had been tempted to leave it behind, but her things were tied behind the cantle, and she would have no way to hold them if she flew the way she preferred, with nothing but a chest strap and Tup's bridle. She glanced back at the women and touched her fingers to her peaked cap.

"Good luck, Lark," Olive said, rubbing the swell of her belly with her hands.

"Aye. And good luck with the baby."

Agatha stood, frowning and waving, as Lark reined Tup about, and he began to trot down the lane.

The dirt was well packed and smooth. Tup cantered, then sped to the hand gallop, and in moments they were aloft, bank-

ing low over the fields to avoid being spotted from Arlton.
They turned east, to where the green water glittered in the afternoon sun.

Lark had studied the Baron's map until it was as clear in
her mind as if she held it unrolled in front of her. The daring
of her mission made her shiver if she thought about it, so she
forced herself to think only of her goal. She was not afraid,
not exactly, she told herself, but it was a dangerous thing they
were undertaking. There was no avoiding it, so there was no
point in worrying about it. And she had promised the Baron.

As Tup approached the sea, Lark urged him higher, remembering everything she had ever been taught about flying
over water. The air currents could be unpredictable, she recalled. The wind could slow them down, but it could just as
easily turn and help Tup to fly faster. The flight should be ap-
proximately three hours, if all went well. She knew there
would be a point of no return, where it was too late to turn
back, too late to change her mind, but she thrust that out of her
mind. In truth, she told herself, she had passed the point of no
return the moment she'd abandoned her flight and flown south
from the Academy without permission. Her path had been set
then.

Sure that by now she was out of sight of the horsemistresses
from Arlton, or even from the South Tower, she urged Tup
higher. He ascended, and they flew steadily on over the expanse
of ocean, until the farms and buildings of Isamar dropped out of
sight behind them, and the mountain peaks began to shrink. The
lowering sun shone on their backs, and the salt wind blew
sharply in Lark's face and brought tears to her eyes. Soon Lark
could not even see the western shore over her shoulder. She settled into the flying saddle, gave Tup his head, and prayed to
Kalla to guide their flight. The one thing they could not afford,
over water, was to make any error in their direction.

For perhaps an hour they flew with no land visible behind
them or ahead of them. There was nothing to see but the green
waves tossing below, and an occasional seabird in the distance. Once or twice a gust of wind buffeted Tup, but he
stilled his wings and soared until they passed it, then began to
beat his wings again when the air was steadier. He flew as

confidently as if he had crossed the sea many times. Perhaps, Lark mused, such knowledge was in his soul. Some believed the winged horses descended from the Old Ones, who left their lairs in the highest mountains to fly over ancient glaciers and long-vanished snowfields. Or perhaps it was even Seraph, the original Ocmarin, who had once flown above the sea and passed the memory along to the horses of his bloodline.

Lark judged, after a time, that they must have passed the midpoint of their crossing. She tried to keep her muscles loose, her hands confident on the reins. She sensed no undue fatigue in Tup, but the chop of the water beneath them, growing darker by the moment, seemed ominous to her. She lifted her eyes, determined not to look at it again.

She peered ahead, searching for the glimmer of the evening star. Baron Rys had told her it would stand above Marinan, that he had seen it himself from his ships at sea. If she and Tup made straight for it, they could make no mistake.

When she saw an edge of darkness on the horizon, at first she thought they had already reached Klee. But as they flew toward it, she realized with a shiver of anxiety that it was a bank of cloud, rolling along the surface of the water. She was tempted to urge Tup to fly faster, but she feared tiring him. She also feared that the clouds would cover the evening star, and they would lose their direction.

She put her hands on Tup's withers, feeling the heat of his body through her palms. He, at least, seemed to have no qualms. His muscles worked smoothly and steadily, and his ears were pricked forward as if he knew just where he was going.

She hoped he did. The cloud bank rose, roiling in shades of gray like the smoke from the autumn fires. It obscured the water and stretched admonishing fingers into the sky. For a dozen of Tup's wingbeats, she watched the clouds swell higher and higher, and still she had not found the star by which to reckon.

And then she felt, rather than saw, the sun slip behind the western horizon. The wind from the sea grew colder, and the sky darkened swiftly around them. For long moments they flew through clouds, fog beneath, fog above, and no light in sky or water to guide them. Lark felt as blind as if she had lost her sight.

And then, something pricked the darkness.

A tiny, cold flame flickered to life far ahead. It lay slightly to the north of their position, and though it was small, its steady shine pierced the edge of the fog bank, beckoning them through the night to the shores of Klee.

"There, Tup!" Lark cried. She laid the rein lightly on the right side of his neck and pressed with her right calf. He tilted, and his wings beat faster.

The clouds rose higher, and the star disappeared. But they had seen it. Tup had seen it.

Other stars began to glimmer through the dimness, faint sparks that flared and faded as the mists shifted. Lark offered one more prayer to Kalla that she and her bondmate would come safely to ground. She leaned a little forward in her saddle, and Tup flew steadily on, as straight as any bird remembering its home.

SHEAVES of lavender filled the sheds at Marinan, hung stems up so that the essence could drip into the heads. When the narders stripped the blooms, they would express the lavender oil into glass bottles, cork them, and carefully shelve them. The year before, Philippa had watched the hired oxcart trundle down the twisting mountain lane, the precious bottles packed in layers of straw to keep them from breaking, the narders walking alongside to steady the ox's pace and guard against rocks or ruts that might jostle their cargo.

Market time had come round again. Philippa had spent the afternoon helping the narders pull handcarts full of fragrant blossoms up to the processing sheds. They had not asked for her help, but she was glad to be allowed to make herself useful. She wore a borrowed pair of loose trousers and a light shirt, and Lyssett had given her a heavy canvas apron to absorb the lavender stains. She hauled the handcart down the slope into the field, where one of the narders filled it with tied sheaves, then she hauled it back up to the shed, where she deposited her load.

When the handcart was empty, she straightened, rubbing the small of her back where it had begun to ache with the effort of pulling the handcart uphill to the shed. She looked out over the lavender fields and saw that the job was nearly finished. One of the narders passed her on his way back to the fields, and nodded a greeting. He didn't speak, and neither did she. Philippa, bemused, realized she had adopted the same habit of silence that marked the Marinan retainers. The thought gave her a stab of loneliness. She felt, for a painful moment, as homesick as a first-level girl.

She turned with the handcart to go back down through the fields. It was really too dark to make another trip, but she knew the narders hoped to finish the job tonight. The sun had set behind an enormous bank of building clouds, and the sky had gone dark over the eastern mountains.

Philippa paused to look up into the sky, where a few faint stars flickered, then down into the dark valley below. A hawk, silhouetted by gray clouds, sailed above the meadow, where the shepherds were driving in the black and white sheep. Philippa started down the slope, then stopped, frowning, and looked up again.

The creature was black, but it was too big to be any bird she recognized. And it was growing bigger by the minute. Its wingspan was wide and narrow, its wingbeats slow, as if it were tired.

Philippa dropped the bars of the handcart and turned back toward the barn, leaving the cart where it lay. Her hawk was no bird at all, but a winged horse. A winged horse trying to come to ground in a strange place, on a mountainside, and in the dark.

She fairly flew herself, racing up the slope, dashing into the barn, flinging open the stall door to toss a hackamore over Sunny's head. There was no time for the saddle. She hurried Sunny out to the mounting block at a trot, leaping onto her back as swiftly as she could. She reined Sunny toward the lane and urged her forward. The winged horse was banking, turning toward Marinan. The flyers would surely see the lighted windows, and even the glow of the lamp outside the barn, but the lane, shrouded as it was by dogwood and a tangle of wild rose hedges, was hard to see from the air even in daylight. It would be impossible in darkness.

Sunny spotted the flyers herself. She whickered eagerly, and began her canter the moment she felt Philippa's legs snug beneath her wings.

She launched herself without any urging, and flew with powerful wingbeats down the mountain to intercept the flight path of the newcomers. Philippa peered into the darkness, realizing with a rush of panic just who it was flying toward Marinan in near-perfect darkness.

Only Larkyn Hamley, she thought, would dare such a journey. And she must have made it without permission, because she would never have been allowed to undertake it without a monitor. It was one thing for an experienced horsemistress to fly across the sea alone, and quite another for one who had not yet passed her final tests. To say nothing of making the flight at night, something Philippa herself would prefer not to do!

But all of that could wait until Larkyn and Black Seraph were safely on the ground. Philippa, who had not taken time to seize her quirt, signaled to Larkyn with her hand, and received a salute in return. Seraph's ears flicked forward at the sight of Winter Sunset, who had monitored all of his training flights. It seemed that even seeing her ahead of him gave him new strength. He ascended a bit, and his tiring wings seemed to steady.

Philippa, with the younger flyers falling in behind her, reined Sunny about and flew directly above the steep, narrow lane to show Larkyn and Black Seraph where it was. She guided Sunny down, leaving plenty of room behind her for the others to follow. All the while, a little bubble of happiness was growing in her breast, a swelling of pleasure and anticipation. It would be so good to talk with someone from the Academy, and most especially this someone, even if she must scold the child for her foolhardiness!

She and Sunny came to ground neatly, having practiced this same return nearly every day for more than a year. As Sunny trotted up the lane toward the barn, Philippa looked back over her shoulder, and saw Black Seraph make a competent landing, although he had to beat his wings once or twice for balance. Larkyn's white face showed the strain of their long flight, and Philippa felt certain Seraph, too, was exhausted. She would, she decided, save her reprimands for later. First, they must cool Seraph and feed and water him. Then Larkyn would need refreshment, and Lyssett could arrange a warm bath for her.

Just as the two of them reached the yard, the heavens opened, and great, chilling sheets of rain poured down on the fields and the lane, drenching the young flyers as they hurried toward shelter.

Philippa sent Sunny ahead of her into the barn with a pat on her hindquarters, while she turned to wait in the doorway for the girl to reach her. Throwing aside her customary reserve, she took the child in her arms and hugged her with all her strength. "Larkyn!" she said. "What a thing to do!"

The girl disentangled herself from Philippa's embrace and gave her a weary but triumphant smile. "I know," she said simply. "But it was Tup. Tup did it."

"Of course he did," Philippa said warmly. She put out her hand to touch the little black stallion's rain-soaked neck. "Seraph, what a splendid creature you are! You're worthy of your ancestor's name! Come now, Larkyn. Bring him in where it's dry. It's a terrible night out there."

SIXTEEN

WILLIAM, in riding clothes, was halfway across the circular courtyard of the Ducal Palace on his way to the stables. The day was crisp and cold, perfect, he understood, for flying. The thought of it, of being swept aloft by his filly's strong wings, of feeling that chilly breeze in his face, of looking down on the roofs and parks of the Palace, nearly took his breath away.

Soon he would do just that. But today was, in its own way, a great day. Today he would ride Diamond.

Felicity Baron had been drilling her with the saddle, working her on the longue line, and strengthening her with sand weights. And if all went well, William swore to himself, if all went well, within the week he would take to the air. He walked faster.

Galloping hoofbeats made him turn toward the long, finely graveled drive that wound through the park from the main road. Someone was coming toward the Palace at a great rate, a man wearing the black and silver colors, and bent over the neck of a lathered bay. A courier, no doubt, racing from Osham, from the Rotunda, and the Council. No way to tell if the message would be from those lords still loyal, or from the disgruntled ones, Beeth, Daysmith, Chatham, or that irritating Applewhite, who had conveniently forgotten all that his family owed to the Fleckhams.

"Ye gods," William muttered. "Can't they leave me alone for one day?" He hurried on, switching impatiently at his leg with his quirt. He would let Parkson send the courier on to his secretaries. They could deal with whatever it might be, earn their pay for once.

Diamond was not in her stall, and William went on through the stables to the back door, expecting to find Felicity Baron drilling her in the dry paddock. His boots made no sound in the sawdust-strewn aisle. He found the top of the half door open, and put his head out to check that his filly and the horsemistress were there.

He saw Mistress Baron leaning against the far side of the pole fence in the dry paddock, an uncharacteristic smile on her leathery face, which was tipped up as if to enjoy the pale sunshine. On her right side, her old gelding stood hipshot, wings and head drooping.

And Diamond, her long-lashed eyes nearly closed, stood on Mistress Baron's left. She was resting her chin on the horsemistress's shoulder. She wasn't fidgeting, or blowing, or any of the nervous things she always did around William. She was more relaxed than he had ever seen her, shining jewel-bright in the cold sunshine, her ears flicking lazily at something Mistress Baron was murmuring.

William's heart suddenly ached as if it had been stabbed through. He stepped back into the shadows of the stable, and tried to assess this phenomenon.

Fool, he berated himself. What are you, a lovesick boy, that seeing your filly happy without you fills you with envy?

He put his back to the wall and tilted his head against it. He closed his eyes. For one long, black moment, he was painfully aware of the swelling of his chest against his vest, of the embarrassing pull of his trousers across his hips, which had grown wider though he ate almost nothing. He put up a hand and touched his smooth chin. He had not had to shave in more than two years. And yet his filly, his perfect Diamond, would never stand still with him, never lean on him in the affectionate way she did with that blasted horsemistress.

He straightened abruptly, and the wood of the wall caught at his hair. He jerked it free, glad of the sting of it, impatient with himself.

It was her fault, of course. It was Felicity Baron, deliberately alienating him from his filly, trying to break his bond with her.

He tucked his quirt under his arm and stalked out into the

cool, bright morning. He would show her! He would ride Diamond right now and prove he could do it. And if the old horsemistress got in his way, he would deal with her as he had dealt with others, and be damned to the consequences.

When he stepped out into the dry paddock, Diamond's ears flicked toward him, and her head shot up. Sky Baron snorted and backed away. Mistress Baron released his rein and let him go, but she kept one hand on Diamond's neck.

"Good morning," she said, her voice uninflected, just as if she hadn't been plotting against him, sneaking out here, doing everything she could to spoil Diamond for him.

"Tighten her cinches," he snapped at her. "I'm going to ride this morning."

"My lord," she began, but he interrupted her.

"None of your arguments," he said. "You'll do as you're told."

"Very well," she said mildly. "But I've been a horsemistress for nearly thirty years, and I wish you would allow me to give you a word of advice."

He crossed the dry paddock and reached Diamond's rein. "What advice would that be? I ride, too, you know."

"I do know," she said, with a wry twist to her lips. "And I think if you ride Diamond the way you ride that nice chestnut mare, you're going to be sorry."

He yanked the rein away from her, and Diamond squealed as the bridle pinched her lip.

"You have the hands of a plowman," Mistress Baron said, her eyes flinty and cold.

He glared at her, hiding his regret over having hurt the filly. "How dare you?"

"You'll ruin her forever if you jerk her around like that, Your Grace," Mistress Baron said. Her weathered face set in hard lines. "She's a winged horse, not a draft animal. Winged horses are far more sensitive—and immensely more intelligent—than wingless horses."

"You don't have to tell me that," William answered. He took a steadying breath and stroked Diamond's cheek apologetically. "I don't know why you horsemistresses assume no one else knows anything about winged horses."

She opened her mouth to say something else, but Diamond suddenly shied away, flexing her wings against the wingclips, tossing her head. William turned to face her. He let the rein hang loose between them, and he held out his hands for her to smell. He had learned that sometimes calmed her, that sometimes if he moved slowly, she would stand still under his touch. Her hide quivered, though, as if flies were crawling on it. He would have given nearly anything, he admitted to himself, if she wouldn't do that.

Time, he told himself. He approached Diamond slowly, and when she didn't flinch away, he reached beneath her left wing to tighten the cinch himself. They just needed time, the two of them. He would ride her now, and though he had no intention of admitting it to Felicity Baron, he would take great care to be gentle with his hands, to keep the reins soft. And when that hurdle had been passed, he could plan their first flight.

It had to be soon. The Fleckham School was almost ready, and the first students had received their vials of medicine. He had to fly Diamond, and prove that it was all possible.

He led her to the mounting block at the side of the dry paddock and removed the sand weights from her saddle. As he prepared to mount, her ears drooped with anxiety, and she sidestepped, out of his reach.

He gritted his teeth but made himself murmur to her comfortingly. Felicity Baron's skeptical gaze burned his neck. He wanted to order her out of the paddock, out of his sight, but he thought the presence of her monitor might calm Diamond. He coaxed Diamond to the mounting block again and bent his knee to step up onto it.

"My lord?" It was one of his secretaries, Clarence, the old one.

"What!" he snapped. "You can see I'm busy!"

"Your Grace, I'm sorry to interrupt." The secretary held a rolled missive in his hands, and he held it out as if to protect himself from the Duke's wrath. "This just came from the Council, and—"

"Ye gods, man, can't it wait?" At William's sharp tone, Diamond skittered away from the mounting block again. Behind her, Felicity Baron moved as if she would step in, and William scowled at her, shaking his head.

"My lord, the—there's a ship—"

William whirled. "A ship?"

"Yes, Your Grace." The old man's voice trembled, but he held his ground, and again thrust out the document in his hands. "A Klee ship. In Osham's harbor."

"So? We have our own ships, do we not? Send out the harbor patrol!"

"They were sent out, Your Grace, immediately. The Klee fired on them."

"You betrayed me, Beeth," William snarled.

He was still in his riding clothes. He had ridden the chestnut mare at a furious speed into Osham, hurled himself from the saddle, and charged up the steps of the Rotunda to find the Council already gathered. The balcony was empty of the usual ladies and their maids, but the lords had come with their secretaries, prepared to do business. William glared at all of them, but fastened, in the end, upon Beeth.

Little Lord Beeth stood beside the carved chair that was his place in the Council of Lords. His face reddened at the Duke's tone, but his round chin was set. "It was not I, Your Grace," he said with asperity. "I had no need. Word travels on its own, you know. It's a small duchy."

"Is it true, Duke William?" This was from Meredith Islington, Philippa Winter's brother. He, too, stood up, and cast a glance around at the other lords of the Council. "My lords, did you know of this?"

Daysmith spoke without rising, his old man's voice trembling. "My lord Duke, you have placed us in a terrible position."

William shrilled, "I am trying to force Philippa Winter back to accept her punishment!"

"By kidnapping Baron Rys's daughter?" demanded Lord Chatham. He had been sitting in his chair, but he jumped to his feet, and William could have sworn there was glee in his voice. "Your Grace, what can you have been thinking?"

"Quiet!" William roared. Fury felt better than uncertainty and had always been an efficient tool. "I am your Duke, and you will show respect for my office!"

"You are the Duke," Beeth said. "But we are the Council Lords of Oc. We share responsibility for the Duchy."

"I don't need anyone to tell me how my own Duchy is run!" William snapped.

"It seems," Daysmith quavered, "that you do. You have imperiled our people with this rash—nay, I may say, foolish—abduction."

"She is a hostage!" William said, struggling against the querulousness he heard in his own voice. "There is a long tradition of royal hostages, when there is need—"

"We are not at war," Chatham said, interrupting him without a hint of apology. "We have no need of hostages!"

"We may be at war now," Beeth said. "Your Grace, produce the girl, and at once! Stop this before it goes too far!"

"It's already gone too far," someone in an upper tier said. "What if one of our sailors had been hurt?" William didn't recognize the voice, but he would not give him the satisfaction of turning his head to identify him.

Meredith Islington put up a hand. "Wait, my lords, wait! Let's at least hear what Duke William has to say about this."

Several of the other lords voiced their agreement with Islington, and the opposing voices grew louder. William, though he could wish it were not that sycophant Islington in the lead of his supporters, let the dispute go on a moment while he gathered his thoughts. He had to find a way to make them understand. After all, the girl was perfectly safe and healthy, and would certainly be returned to her father in due course. It had not been a foolish thing to do, but a daring one. Great leaders didn't tread cautiously, afraid of making mistakes or offending people. Great leaders took risks.

Like changing centuries of tradition.

He straightened, and tugged down the vest he wore under his long riding coat. The lords and their secretaries fell silent, one by one, and turned their faces to him, waiting.

"Philippa Winter defied our authority, and this situation is her fault," he proclaimed. "It would never have been necessary had she not fled her legally imposed punishment."

"You abducted an Academy student," Chatham repeated.

"She is Klee," William said flatly. "She should never have been accepted there in the first place."

"But once she was," Beeth said, "she became one of our people."

William put up his bone-thin hand. "You are too much involved with the Academy, Beeth," he said. He was relieved to hear the silky quality return to his voice. "You should turn your attention to the Fleckham School. The Academy and its interests are part of the past, and the Fleckham School is the future."

Lord Daysmith struggled to his feet, leaning on the arm of his secretary. "Have you flown yet, my lord Duke?"

William's lip curled. "I will, Daysmith," he said. "And soon. Especially if all of you cease troubling me over trifles."

Chatham said, with a derisive snort, "You think a Klee warship in our harbor is a trifle?"

William rounded on him. "You forget yourself!" he said. "Address me properly, or leave the Council!"

"Chatham's right, Your Grace," Daysmith said. His voice shook, but his eyes were sharp as they had always been. "We have a warship to deal with. I move that the Council directs you to send an envoy, assure Baron Rys that his daughter will be returned to him safely."

William had, in fact, been on the point of suggesting just such a tactic, but the way Daysmith said it, the way Beeth and Chatham and a few other rebel lords nodded and murmured assent, enraged him. He seized his quirt in his fingers, feeling its power. He lifted it, and pointed it at Daysmith. "We will not be *directed*, as you so clumsily put it, my lord. We will make our own decisions, for the good of Oc."

"Being attacked by the Klee," Chatham said in a voice dry with sarcasm, "can hardly be good for Oc."

"Fight them," William said. There were gasps around the Rotunda, and he narrowed his eyes and swept every face with a mocking gaze. "Or are you afraid, my lords? Do we address a tea party, with swooning maidens and elderly crones afraid of their own shadows?"

"Your Grace!" Beeth cried. "You would start a war?"

Several of the others shouted agreement with Beeth, but William, though he had in fact shocked himself by saying what he had, noted that perhaps half the Council were nodding, as if the idea of war were not unpalatable. There was, of course, always money to be made in war.

"Our expanded militia is in place," William said, when the hubbub subsided enough for him to be heard. "You will appreciate that we had the foresight to levy an extraordinary tax, to protect the interests of Oc."

"I thought that was all about the winged horses," Beeth protested. "About the Fleckham School and closing the Academy!"

"Indeed, I believe you said that very thing," Chatham said. His stare was as insolent as any roughneck's, and William wished he were close enough to slash him with his quirt, to drive that look from his face. He could hardly argue the point.

"Islington," William said, pointing at Meredith. "Give the order. Our captains are waiting in the outer room of the Rotunda."

Even Islington, it seemed, had misgivings, for though he came to his feet, he did not immediately leave. "Yes, Your Grace, the order . . . What order, exactly?"

William eyed him, letting his lips curl. "Why," he said, softly, but clearly. "To return fire, of course."

Slater would be pleased. He had been pushing for this for a long time.

SEVENTEEN

As evening closed around the little stable, the sounds of hammering and sawing beyond the beech grove ceased. Amelia searched for a horse blanket in the tack room, and found one that seemed to be nearly new. She buckled it around Mahogany and wrapped herself in a long coat Jinson had provided for her. It was much too large, but it was warm and clean. She stood in the door of the tack room and looked out into the darkness. It was odd, she thought, how quickly one became used to things. She had been a prisoner only a few days, yet she had established a routine, of sorts, and managed to find comfort in small things like a cup of hot tea and a friendly conversation.

Two militiamen lounged against the trunks of the beech trees, scuffing at the dead leaves beneath their boots and talking. They straightened when they saw Amelia, then at her nod, they grinned and relaxed again.

She was on the point of turning back, to make up her cot and tidy the tack room before going to bed, when the guns started.

Amelia knew the sound from ceremonies in the Klee capital. To announce a royal progress of her uncle, the Viscount, the ships in the harbor often fired their short cannons. Amelia froze in the doorway, remembering the noise of those guns, the flame and gray smoke that swirled over the water, the smack of cast-iron balls striking empty sand beaches. But Osham's harbor had no vacant, sandy shore. The buildings went right down to the piers, and the docks were lined with boats of every size, peopled with workers and their families.

The militiamen straightened in alarm, exclaiming, looking

around as if for someone to explain what they were hearing. A moment later Jinson appeared on his small bay mare, galloping down the lane from the main road. He leaped from the saddle and tossed the mare's reins over a post.

He stopped briefly to confer with the guards, then crossed the little drive, his hasty footsteps throwing up bits of gravel. Amelia waited for him in the doorway. He went past her with a nod and went to the woodstove to begin laying a small fire.

"Sorry it's gotten so cold in here," he said.

"Master Jinson?" Amelia said. "You must have heard the guns."

"Aye," he said. His face was tight. "There's a Klee ship in Osham harbor."

"Is it the *Marinan*?"

"I don't know the name."

"It must be! The *Marinan* is my father's ship!"

"I wouldn't know, Miss. But the carronades—" He gave her an unhappy glance. "Those guns are our own."

"Our ships carry them, too," she said faintly. She felt as if she couldn't draw a proper breath. "Jinson, what's happening?"

"His Grace was called to the Rotunda today," Jinson said. "When the Klee ship sailed in. I was at the Palace, and you can see the bay there, just past the city buildings. A while later our boats went out, the ones that patrol the harbor. I was on my way here when I heard the guns."

Amelia rubbed her arms against a sudden chill, and her stomach quivered. What would they say at the Academy? It had been so hard to persuade them to accept her in the first place, and there were still those who thought she should never have been bonded, who thought of her as Klee first and an Academy girl second.

"Oh, no," she murmured. "I can't have this. There mustn't be a war over me."

Jinson put a match to the tinder in the close stove and replaced the lid. He turned to face her. "Miss, you need to stay out of sight."

"Why?" she said.

"People think—too many people, that is—they'll think . . ."

His words stumbled to a stop, and he shook his head, looking as miserable as she had so far seen him.

"They think it's my fault."

"Aye, Miss. I'm afraid so."

"But, Jinson—am I safe here, then? Who knows where he's put me?"

"No one," Jinson said. "I'll tell the guards to keep mum about you when they go off duty. And then there's only Slater."

Amelia gripped her elbows, and tried to stiffen her spine. She said, "I can't see why the Duke let it come to this. It would make more sense, surely, simply to let me go."

"Makes sense to me, Miss. Not the Duke, it seems."

Amelia pressed her hands together, trying to think. What was the right thing to do? How could she stop this? She bit her lip, hard, then she said hurriedly, half under breath, "Jinson! Let me just slip away, with Mahogany, out the back of the stable. It's dark now, and no one will see. We'll find our way back to the Academy, and I'll get word to the ship. When my father knows I'm safe, he'll withdraw."

"I'd have to persuade all these soldiers," Jinson said. "I don't think I can do that. I would have let you go before this, myself. But now—we'd best leave it to the Duke. 'Tis a time for diplomacy, I think."

"Diplomacy!" Amelia said bitterly.

Jinson looked at her, and she could see awareness in his face that he knew diplomacy was not an art Duke William practiced. With a resigned shake of the head, he said, "I'm so sorry, Miss. His Grace will have to manage it." He walked toward the door, rubbing his palms together as if he could rub away his anxiety. "Just wait here, please. I need to get my mare in, get her unsaddled."

Through the darkness, they heard the carronade again, then an answering shot, a different pitch, a higher resonance. Ships, Amelia understood with a sinking heart, firing at one another. The guardsmen at the edge of the beech grove swore, and the ones at the back called out. Lark's brother wasn't there tonight, but some other man.

Amelia stared helplessly out into the darkness. She didn't know whether to hope that her father was on the *Marinan*, or to pray that he was not. She clutched Lark's icon of Kalla, and wished protection on all ships, Klee and Oc.

Mahogany whinnied nervously from his stall. Amelia hurried back to him, with Bramble at her heels. She went into the stall and busied herself with unnecessary tasks, combing Mahogany's tail, fussing with his water bucket and hay bin, making as much noise as possible to try to block the sound of carronades from Osham's harbor.

AMELIA slept little that night. She laid her head on her pillow and closed her eyes, trying to summon up the discipline she had been taught, but sleep eluded her for many hours. Beyond the tiny window of the tack room, stars blinked in and out of a heavy cover of cloud. The guns had stopped at last, for which she was grateful. But the idea that there might be a new war between her two lands tortured her. In a real war, horsemistresses could be called upon to fight.

A horse and her horsemistress had died in the last war, at the South Tower of Isamar. Her uncle, upon his succession, had sworn never to start a war in his lifetime. But even her uncle could not oppose her father's coming after her.

She drowsed, waking often, turning restlessly on her pallet. Each time she woke she heard Mahogany shifting his feet, nickering uneasily. Only the little bay mare was quiet in her stall. Jinson had gone up to Fleckham House to sleep, and the soldiers were silent at their posts. Bramble lay beside Amelia's pallet, her eyes open, her ears twitching at every small sound.

Toward morning, Amelia at last fell into the kind of heavy sleep that made her head feel thick and her eyelids sticky. She woke from this unrefreshing slumber when she heard the guards changing outside the stable, two in front, two in back. She struggled up, rubbing at her eyes, feeling exhausted.

She splashed water on her face, and used the privy, then brushed her hair into the rider's knot. She stirred up the banked fire in the close stove and put the kettle on to boil before she went to fetch Mahogany and release him into the dry paddock. There she saw, with a little spurt of hope, that Nick Hamley had returned.

Mahogany trotted out into the dry paddock, shaking his head, rustling his wings against their clips. Amelia followed and climbed onto the bottom pole of the fence. "Master Hamley," she called.

He looked up, and when he saw her, he smiled and bowed to her, as if he were meeting her at some ceremonial function. "Good morning, Miss."

His fellow guard peered at her from beneath the eaves of the stable, but he didn't speak. Nick said something to him, then stepped out into the cold gray light. "Bit chilly, isn't it, Miss Rys?" Nick called.

Amelia climbed another pole, so that she could see over the top of the fence. "What news this morning, Master Hamley?"

He said, "Yon ships are doing a great dance in the bay. They missed each other with their guns in the darkness last night, and we can thank the entwined gods for that! But the Klee ship is blocking the mouth of the harbor."

"Then no one's been hurt?" she asked hopefully.

"Nay," he said, "not yet." There was a grimness about his face, darkening the blue of his eyes. Amelia knew those eyes, the Hamley eyes, and they made her long for the sight of Lark's pretty face and short black curls.

"Do people—do people know what it's about?" she said.

He came close enough to look up at her. He said quietly, "'Tis about you, they say, Miss. Because the Duke took you and won't give you back."

"How do they know?"

"Lady Beeth, they say. Her daughter is at the Academy, and told Lady Beeth, and Lady Beeth told Lord Beeth, and he told the Council."

"Then why doesn't someone come for me?" Amelia said.

"They don't know where you are, Miss. Lark would if she knew."

"I wouldn't want her to be in danger, too!"

"You don't seem frightened for yourself."

"I'm worried about a war."

"Aye. 'Tis a bad situation." He glanced over his shoulder, but his fellow militiaman was busy prying a rock from the tread of his boot. Nick looked up at Amelia again. "There are those who think the Duke is a visionary, and those who think he's a nutter."

She tilted her head to one side. "A—a nutter? What is that?"

Nick Hamley said, "Crazy. Mad. Out of his mind."

"Ah. That's what your sister believes, Master Hamley. Only she said 'hinky.' "

Nick gave a wry smile at that. "If my sister says 'tis so, then I expect it is." He shook his head. "Bad news for Oc. A mad Duke, and a Klee ship bearing down on Osham."

Amelia was about to answer, but Nick raised a warning finger. He was staring past her, to the half door leading from the stable to the dry paddock. Mahogany, who had been peacefully exploring the corners of the paddock, suddenly snorted in alarm and backed to the fence. Amelia heard his hocks hit the poles.

From behind her, a voice said, "Clamber down from there, my girl. We're going to show you to the Klee."

WHEN Slater's sharp-nailed hand seized Amelia's arm to force her onto his chicken-necked pinto, she tried to pull away, but his grip was too strong. He pushed her up into the saddle, thrusting carelessly at her leg and hip, and refused to release her until she had swung her leg over the stiff cantle. She drew back from him the moment he took his hands away, curling her lip with distaste at his touch, at his odor, at his repellent appearance.

"Ha!" he said, sneering up at her. He still wore his many-caped greatcoat, and a three-cornered hat with a greasy brim. "You think you're too good to be touched by the likes of me? You might learn a thing or two today, Klee."

The guards stepped forward, frowning, but they knew Slater as the Duke's man and were afraid to intervene. Bramble raced back and forth between the grove and the tack room, barking wildly. Nick Hamley tried to put himself between Slater and Amelia, but he was armed with only a smallsword, and Slater pulled a long pistol from the layers of his coat and pointed it at the Uplander. Its barrel gleamed dull and black in the gray light.

Amelia said, "Get back, Master Hamley, please." Her voice shook, and she tried to steady it as she added, "I can manage."

She saw, for one terrible moment, that Nick Hamley considered plying his smallsword against the pistol. The flintlock pistol had only one shot, she knew, and it took time to load another, but a single such shot could do a great deal of damage.

She leaned down, trying to distract Slater by grabbing at the pinto's reins. He took a step back to keep the reins from her reach, and Nick Hamley poised, his sword lifted and ready.

Slater changed the aim of his pistol, pointing it directly at Amelia's breast. He gave his snaggletoothed grin. "Put it away, man. You can't stop me."

"You're making a terrible mistake, Master Slater!" Amelia cried. She seized the pommel of the saddle as the pinto stamped his feet. Her boots could not reach the stirrups, and the pommel and cantle were both high and hard, trapping her between them. "His Grace knows better than to mistreat a royal hostage."

"You mean, as the Klee mistreated my brother?" Slater said. He yanked on the pinto's reins, and the horse skidded away from him, throwing his head and jarring Amelia half out of the saddle. Slater turned toward the lane then, and started walking, pulling the pinto along behind him. Bramble followed a few steps, then ran back toward the stables to pace again, growling and barking in confusion.

Mahogany gave a long, desperate whinny. Amelia twisted to look back, but she couldn't see him. Slater had forced her to leave him in the dry paddock, and there was no one to take care of him. Her rush of temper subsided under a flood of anxiety.

"Master Slater," Amelia said. "Please, can we not at least take my colt? He's never been separated from me, and the winged horses—"

He snarled over his shoulder, "Oh, aye? The winged horses?"

"They panic," she said, struggling to keep her own panic out of her voice and out of her face. She felt her composure cracking like thin ice on a pond. "Please . . . sir."

His grin vanished as if it had never been. "Speaking out of the other side of your mouth now, aren't you, Klee? Don't 'sir' me. I'm a workingman. Not that you'd understand what it is to work for your living."

He jerked the pinto's reins to make it move faster, and the cantle jarred the small of Amelia's back. She gasped, "You're mistaken, Slater. All of us at the Academy work hard, from early morning until late at night."

"Books," he sneered. "Flying. That's not work."

Desperately, she said, "How can I persuade you?"

He stopped, and spun in a whirl of dark fabric. "You want to persuade me?"

She swallowed, her stomach clenching. "Of course."

"Will you lift your skirts for me, then, my fine lady?"

Amelia stared at him in horror, realizing after a moment that her mouth was open, her lips gone dry. "I—surely you can't mean for me to—"

He took a step back toward her, and the pinto shied nervously. "You asked," he said.

"I meant money, or some favor from my father—some reasonable thing."

"I think," Slater said, "that girls who never bed men are unreasonable."

"We have no choice, Mr. Slater. You know that. Our horses . . ."

"Just another reason men should do the flying," he growled, and turned away. He began walking again, yanking the pinto along after him. The guards stood gazing after them, muttering to each other, made helpless by Slater's pistol.

"Where are we going?" Amelia asked. Mahogany whinnied again, then again. Her heart thudded with the same anxiety and need. When Slater didn't answer, she said, "There are rules about the treatment of hostages! Agreements reached between principalities—"

"For weaklings," he said, just loud enough for her to hear over the creaking of saddle leather and the clop of the pinto's hooves. "Too gutless for war."

"There's no war yet!"

He gave a short, terrible laugh. "When they see you, there will be."

Amelia, for an instant, feared she might burst into tears. She gritted her teeth, thinking of her father, of the years of his painstaking training. She drew a shuddering breath and pulled herself up straight in the saddle. Better he should shoot her than that war should break out.

"I demand that you stop, Master Slater," she said, with all the dignity she could muster. "This is an immoral and unjust thing to do."

He stopped, and turned about deliberately. "And just what, Miss," he said with a fearsome scowl, "do you think you can do about it?"

Amelia, suddenly flooded with disgust at his arrogance, sucked moisture into her mouth, and spat it directly into his face.

As the spittle dripped down his seamed cheek, she squared her shoulders and forced her features into immobility.

He wiped the drops from his cheek with a dirty finger and shook them off onto the ground. His leer was that of a death's head. "Do that again, Klee, and you'll pay," he said.

For answer, Amelia threw her leg over the pommel of the saddle, leaped to the ground, and started back toward the stable at a dead run. Even as her feet pounded the dirt of the lane, her back prickled with awareness of that awful long pistol. Bramble came bounding to meet her, barking furiously.

EIGHTEEN

PHILIPPA gazed across the breakfast table at Larkyn. The girl's eyes sparkled like the water of the mountain lakes, and her cheeks, now that she had rested, were pink with health and youth. Even though the news was so grim, and there was trouble ahead, Philippa could not suppress her pleasure in Larkyn's presence, at seeing Seraph grown into the strong, spirited stallion she had known he would become, and at the prospect of going home. All this she kept hidden behind as calm a countenance as she could manage, but she felt her eyes must shine almost as brightly as Larkyn's. In truth, she thought, she hadn't known how lonely she was until Larkyn and Seraph appeared above Marinan.

Lyssett had taken one look at the girl, the evening before, and set about making a substantial meal of roasted lamb chops and root vegetables, setting water to heat for a bath, ordering the narders about so that a room was aired and made ready, a stall laid with fresh straw for Black Seraph, water and hay and oats put out for the two flyers to take in to their horses.

Larkyn, despite her exhaustion, had talked all through the late dinner, talked as she soaked in the big tin tub Lyssett had filled for her, answered questions as the two of them settled their horses for the night. She explained why she had come, how she had spoken to Baron Rys and obtained his map leading her to Marinan, how she had eluded her escort from the Palace. Philippa's lips tightened as she heard the news of Amelia's disappearance, and she only nodded as Larkyn told her of her conviction that Duke William had taken the girl.

Philippa had answered, "Would that the Council Lords were as perceptive as you are."

"Lady Beeth says they are divided, half on either side."

Philippa thought about this now, as she and Larkyn ate Lyssett's fresh yeast rolls with good sheep's milk cheese and sliced winter pears. Her eyes strayed down the mountain toward the distant gleam of the ocean. "It's like a storm building at sea," she said, half to herself.

"Pardon, Mistress Winter?"

Philippa sighed. "This conflict, Larkyn. I hate to call it a war yet, but with the Prince taking sides with William, and William having offended the Klee . . ."

"But perhaps Baron Rys can get Amelia back without a real war," Larkyn said, without much conviction.

"Perhaps," Philippa said. She toyed with the cheese knife. The blade caught the sun, and light coruscated from its polished silver surface. "You said even the horsemistresses at the Academy are divided."

"Not over the issue of men flying!" Larkyn said hastily. "But some of them—and some of the students, too—feel they owe the Duke their loyalty no matter what he does."

"I wish they would put their horses before any other consideration."

"Aye."

Lyssett bustled into the dining room with a fresh pot of tea. "I hope you slept well, Miss?" she asked Larkyn.

Larkyn gave a glorious smile that made Philippa's heart turn over. Despite all the girl had done in these past few days, she was so very young, and so innocent. They all were, all the girls still yearning for their silver wings. They didn't know what it could be like, and Philippa wished with all her heart they wouldn't have to find out.

"I slept wonderfully," Larkyn said. "The bed is so soft, and the sheets smell delicious!"

"Everything here smells like lavender, I'm told," Lyssett said. "Though we can't smell it anymore, ourselves. Too many years with the scent in our noses!"

"'Tis delightful," Larkyn said, and added, "At my own

home, everything smells of broomstraw from midsummer till harvest."

Lyssett set the teapot down and looked at her curiously. "Your own home? You're not from the White City, then?"

"Nay," Larkyn answered, with pride in her young face. "Nay, I come from the Uplands of Oc, and my family grow bloodbeets and broomstraw, and keep goats and chickens."

Lyssett tilted her head to one side, regarding the girl. "I understood the girls of the Academy were always . . . That is, they're meant to be . . ." Her cheeks colored, and she stepped back from the table. "I'm sorry, Miss. I was surprised, and I spoke without thinking."

"Nay, Mistress, I'm not offended. You're right. The Academy bonds winged horses only to girls of good birth. Tup and I—Black Seraph, that is—we were a surprise!" She laughed, and Lyssett chuckled.

Philippa pressed her lips together. How much time had passed, after the battle of the South Tower, before she had been able to laugh again?

When Lyssett left the dining room, Larkyn leaned forward. "Did I say something wrong, Mistress Winter?"

Philippa busied herself pouring each of them another cup of tea. "No, Larkyn. You said nothing wrong."

"But you're upset."

"Not really." Philippa took another slice of the white cheese and laid it on her plate.

Larkyn persisted. "Something's wrong. What is it?"

Philippa lifted her eyes to Larkyn's face again. The violet eyes had darkened, and a furrow appeared between the girl's black brows. Her short curls shone like ebony. Philippa leaned back in her chair and breathed a great sigh. "It was such a good idea," she said, "for you to cut your hair."

"Aye. 'Twas the only way, just as Lady Beeth said. Though I longed for the rider's knot, when I was a first-level girl!" Larkyn smiled a little, and pushed her fingers through the curls. "Tell me what troubles you, Mistress Winter," she said. "I do know there is much to worry about. 'Tis why I'm here, after all."

"Yes, of course." Philippa sighed. "I had hoped, Larkyn,

that what happened at the South Tower would never come again. I thought we had learned something."

"You were in the battle of the South Tower," Larkyn said.

Philippa grimaced. She knew perfectly well the child was leading her. She supposed all the students whispered stories to each other in the Dormitory. Her own class had done the same. And perhaps it was better that they knew the truth rather than imagining things, getting it wrong.

Larkyn prodded gently. "A horsemistress died."

"Alana Rose, and her lovely Summer Rose, the sweetest mare. And all the hostages died, too, of hunger and cold. It was a terrible thing. A siege that went on for weeks, Klee against Isamar. When things got desperate, Duke Frederick sent us to help."

"Why did it all happen?" Larkyn asked.

"The Klee claimed that Isamar's Prince had blocked the shipping lanes, so that southern imports like coffee and some spices couldn't get through."

"Was it true?"

Philippa lifted her shoulders. "It may have been true. Or it may simply have been a struggle for power, for control of one principality over another."

"What happened then?"

"The Klee attacked the South Tower, where Prince Nicolas's father had imprisoned some of the Klee diplomats working in Arlton. Sadly, he made their families go with them. And Duke Frederick sent us out to defend the Tower, out of loyalty to the Prince, and against the advice of the Council. It was a terrible mistake, and though he never spoke of it again, I know that till the day he died, he never forgave himself."

She looked past Larkyn to the vista of meadow and sky beyond the window. "We were sent against the Klee marksmen, and Summer Rose took an arrow through her wing. She fell, screaming." Now she closed her eyes, seeing again that awful descent, the roan mare spiraling toward the ground, one wing crippled, the other flailing uselessly against the air. "Alana never made a sound."

"Kalla's heels," Larkyn breathed.

Philippa opened her eyes. "Indeed. I hope you never see

such a thing. But should it happen—it's one reason we train you all so hard."

"I know, Mistress Winter." Larkyn chewed her lip for a moment. "So this is what Duke William has done to Amelia. Taken her hostage."

"It does sound like it."

"Her father will never rest until he has her safe."

"It was a great mistake. Esmond Rys is one of the most capable men I've ever met, as I learned in Aeskland two years ago."

"What will happen?"

"I can't see a good way out of this." Philippa spread a bit of lavender jelly on a yeast roll and pushed the pot closer to the girl. "Enjoy this while you have it, Larkyn. We don't get lavender jelly in Osham. And tell me what news there is of your brother—I mean, of your brothers."

"Nick is in the militia," Larkyn said. "The extraordinary tax was more than Deeping Farm could pay."

"And the others?"

"Edmar and Pamella were married at Erdlin. You were meant to be there, of course—they do seem happy. Pamella speaks no more than a few words, still." Larkyn's eyes twinkled. "They haven't said yet, but I think she may be breeding."

"Really!" Philippa still could not get past the idea that the Lady Pamella, the Duke's sister, should actually have married silent Edmar, the quarryman. "And Brandon?"

"He thinks of Edmar as his father. We never speak of who his father might actually be—but he looks, even now, very like the Duke. Fortunately, few people from Willakeep have ever laid eyes on Duke William. If they saw Brandon in Osham, tongues would wag."

Philippa turned the yeast roll in her fingers. "And Brye?" she asked. "Without Nick, the workload must be crushing."

"He hasn't complained, but of course it must be. The harvest was hard for everyone, with so many men in the militia. Brye is mostly worried about Nick. No one knows where he was posted, and we don't know when he'll be allowed to come home."

"My holiday with your family," Philippa said, as lightly as she could, "was one of the best in my memory."

Larkyn, all innocence, said, "Brye admires you so much, Mistress Winter."

Philippa let her brows go up. "Indeed?"

"Oh, aye. I've heard him tell Nick how strong and smart you are."

"I'm flattered," Philippa said.

"Oh, aye, but I thought you knew," the girl said, dimpling. "'Tisn't easy to please him. A good man, though, and he raised me as if I were his daughter instead of his sister."

"Yes," Philippa said. She drew a deep breath, a little embarrassed to have been fishing for compliments. "Yes, your brother is a fine man. I admire him, as well. And now, finish your breakfast, Larkyn. We should be off and make use of the daylight."

THE storm of the night before had rattled the tiles of Marinan's roof, but by the time Philippa and Larkyn stepped outside to go to the barn, nothing was left of it but shreds of emptied clouds. The lavender fields sparkled with fresh moisture, and the lane was packed and damp but not muddy.

"Will we go back to Arlton?" Larkyn asked, as they went into the barn.

"No. It's closer, of course, but we should be able to make it to Oc without difficulty. We'll fly north along the coast, stop and rest, then set out for Osham." She cast the girl a wry glance. "And this time," she added, "we'll fly in daylight."

Larkyn grinned at her, acknowledging the point. She said, "Baron Rys's ship will already be there. He was gone before I left yesterday."

Philippa opened Sunny's stall gate. "We'll sleep at the Academy tonight."

"Aye. And Mistress Star will be that glad to see you," Larkyn said.

Philippa paused, one hand on Sunny's neck. "Will she, Larkyn? Are you so certain?"

"Oh, aye," Larkyn said without hesitation. "I heard her say it."

Philippa slipped Sunny's bridle over her head, and led her

out into the aisle. She paused for a moment, looking at the girl with her pretty stallion. "I'm proud of you, my dear."

"I thought you would scold me."

"No doubt I should have done so." Philippa led Sunny toward the tack room, and left her standing in the aisle as she went in for her saddle. Larkyn followed, though Philippa noticed she looped Seraph's reins through one of the iron rings set into the barn wall. She had learned, it seemed, that he could be impetuous. She lifted her own saddle and carried it back to Seraph.

Philippa followed with her own tack. "Of course you should not have left the Academy without permission, Larkyn, but—"

"Mistress Star would never have let me go if I had asked."

Philippa allowed herself a narrow smile. "I know." She spread the saddle blanket over Sunny's back, tucking it beneath her wings, then hefted the saddle up to settle it over her spine. "I'm sure Suzanne did what she thought was best, but I fear for our people."

"Aye," Larkyn said gravely. "There will be real fighting if something isn't done."

"Precisely so. And no one will be pleased that a girl of Klee is the cause."

"But she wasn't, Mistress Winter!"

Philippa held up a gloved hand. "You have no need to tell me, Larkyn. The question is whether the people of Oc can be convinced of it."

LARK understood there were dangerous times ahead, but it was so good to canter behind Winter Sunset, to launch with Philippa Winter's straight back and narrow shoulders ahead of her, that for a few precious minutes she allowed herself to revel in the moment. She could feel Tup's eagerness, too, his delight in flying with his monitor once again. He was more obedient than usual, quicker to obey the touch of her hand or her knee.

The storm of the night before had blown past, leaving the newly washed sky fresh and sparkling. Soon they would be in Osham again, in the thick of the troubles. But before that time there would be lovely hours of flying, and in the best possible company.

Lark even dared to hope that when they arrived, they might find Amelia set free, the Klee ship departing the harbor, the horsemistresses and girls of the Academy once more in accord.

Perhaps it would all blow over as swiftly as the storm had expended itself last night. Maybe when the Council Lords realized how close Duke William had brought them to war, they would all see the folly of the Fleckham School, of abolishing the Academy, of endangering the bloodlines.

Lark sighed with admiration as Philippa Winter and Winter Sunset banked above the coastline, their slender silhouette framed by the green gleam of the sea. She pulled her cap down against the glare of the morning sun. She would give it all up to Kalla. Surely, with the help of the horse goddess, anything was possible.

NINETEEN

AMELIA heard Slater shout after her, once, and then nothing. His silence was somehow the more frightening, but she dared not stop. Mahogany, sensing her fear, give a shrilling cry, and she ran faster. The hard ground jarred her ankles in her soft riding boots.

She had taken only a dozen strides when she heard the pinto's hooves behind her. Slater was coming at a gallop and would run her down in moments.

They had not gone far, not even reached the main road. She dashed toward the beech grove, striving to be within sight of the guards before Slater reached her. It was the only hope she had, that he would not actually shoot her in the presence of the soldiers. The pinto clattered up behind her, and she heard the thump of Slater's big boots as he jumped out of the saddle and skidded in the gravel. Amelia kept her eyes on the stable and the grove. Where were the guards? Had they left when their prisoner was taken away? Was there anyone to help her?

She barely had breath, but she used what she had to call, "Help! I need help!"

Mahogany neighed from the dry paddock. Bramble's barking grew frantic.

Someone came out of the stable, running. He stopped when he saw Amelia, and she saw, with a sinking heart, that it was only Jinson. His figure looked slight as a boy's, and his face was white with fear. He would be no protection against Slater's bulk. There would be nothing he could do against Slater's pistol.

Despairing, she whirled to face her pursuer.

Slater had stopped perhaps two rods away from her. He flung down the pinto's reins, and the gelding backed away, his skinny neck bobbing awkwardly. Slater reached into his pocket as he stalked toward Amelia. She backed away, too, one step, then two, until he pulled the pistol from the depths of his black coat and pointed it at her.

The muzzle looked enormous, its barrel black and thick. From her vantage point, no more than a few steps from it, it looked very like the carronades. It made her nerves jump.

"Get back in the saddle, Klee," Slater snarled.

"N-no," Amelia said. Her voice caught in her dry throat. She set her feet in the gravel, straightened her shoulders, and stiffened her back. She would not give him the satisfaction of seeing a daughter of Klee scuffling away like a frightened rabbit. "I'm staying with my colt," she said. Her voice steadied, carrying clearly through the cold air. There was, she suddenly realized, no sound of hammering or sawing coming through the grove from Fleckham House. Where had they all gone?

"You're coming," he said, "the easy way or the hard way." He started toward her.

"What do you want with her, Slater?" Jinson's voice wasn't so strong as Amelia's, and it quavered. "What's your intention?"

"Show her to the Klee," Slater said. His thick features twisted with fury, and he waved the gun in the direction of Amelia's head. "Get this damned war started."

"Not on my account," Amelia said. "I won't do it." She lifted her chin and found that she felt stronger for having defied Slater. Later—if there was a later—she supposed she would marvel at the way her training took over. She was frightened—it would be foolish not to be—but she was composed. She was a baron's daughter, after all, and she knew better than to quail before a common ruffian.

"You will, my lass," Slater said. He strode toward her with his coat flapping about him. "You'll do just as I say."

He brought the gun to her chest, no more than a hand's breadth away from her heart. "We're going," he said.

She said in a chilly voice, "No."

Jinson, behind her, stammered, "Slater—the Duke—"

The gun swung around to point at Jinson, and Jinson stumbled backward. "The Duke will thank me," Slater said. Now his ugly grin returned, and he gestured with his head at Amelia. "I'm taking the Klee problem off his hands."

"Where is His Grace?" Amelia tried to speak as if she expected an answer.

"He's riding," Slater said, with a leer. "Riding his Diamond."

"With the Klee ship in the harbor?" Jinson blurted. "War looming?"

Slater gave a phlegmy chuckle. "Our Duke cares more for flying than warfare," he said. "We'll just give him a little push."

"Not we, Master Slater," Amelia said stiffly. "I will have no part of this folly."

He stepped forward, and seized her arm with his sharp-nailed hand. "You will, lass," he said, his foul breath gusting in her face. "Because I says you will."

She drew breath to refuse again. Then, to her astonishment, Jinson jumped forward to shove at Slater, forcing him back so that his hand released her arm. Both of them, Slater and Amelia, flailed for balance. Gravel skittered from beneath his boots, and he tottered.

Slater fell hard, landing on his backside as a great whoof of air rushed from his lungs. His black coat spread around him in a layered, greasy pool. He gave a breathless grunt of pain, and his pistol clanked against the rocks.

Jinson turned his back on Slater to ask Amelia, "Are you all right, Miss? Not hurt?"

Amelia had lost her footing for only a moment. Bramble was at her knee, and she leaned on the dog as she steadied herself. She pulled at her overlarge tabard to straighten it, then looked up past Jinson's shoulder.

Slater was scrambling to his feet. His face had gone purple with rage, and his lips pulled back from his long yellow teeth so that he looked like a snarling dog.

Amelia gasped, "Master Jinson! Behind you!"

Jinson's eyes widened, and he spun about.

Slater had retrieved his pistol from the gravel, and he swung it up.

Amelia would never know if he meant to point it at her, or at Jinson. She didn't know if his choice was deliberate or random. All she knew was that he gave Jinson no time to choose whether to stand his ground and protect her, or to step aside and give her up.

The report of the long pistol came in two sounds, a heavy click as the cock struck the frizzen, then a sickening hiss as the ball left the barrel. Amelia screamed.

Jinson fell before her scream died away. He collapsed, as thoroughly as if his legs had turned to water, and he lay in a boneless heap at Amelia's feet. Blood poured from beneath his coat to spread in a dark pool that drained swiftly through the gravel to soak the ground below. Bramble whined, and backed away.

Amelia stared in dry-mouthed horror, first at Jinson, unmoving on the ground, then at Slater, who stared back at her, his mouth hanging open and his eyes stunned. For a long moment, it seemed that the echo of her scream and the echo of the shot were one sound, reverberating from the walls of the stable and through the bare trunks of the beech grove.

From the dry paddock, Mahogany whinnied again and again, and she heard the thud of his feet in the dirt as he raced from one side to the other.

Amelia was the first to break the tableau, drawing a sudden, shuddering breath. She tore her eyes from the murderer's face and dropped to her knees beside Jinson, heedless of the blood staining her skirt. Gently, she tugged at his body, trying to turn him. His shoulders were thin, his body light and warm under her hands. His body rolled, flopping back on the gravel. His arms hung limp and nerveless, and his legs twisted as one boot caught behind the opposite knee. He seemed to sigh as the last bit of air escaped his chest, but Amelia saw that it was not a breath. Jinson would breathe no more. His staring eyes were blank. His lips were parted and still, and the blood continued to spread beneath him, more blood than she would have believed possible.

She put her hands on his chest, and they came away red and sticky. She understood there was nothing she could do. Still, she couldn't leave him lying there, broken and empty, gazing into the sky. Carefully, she pulled his coat around him, as if he might be troubled by the cold. She straightened his legs, then gingerly touched his eyelids to close them. Smears of blood marked his skin when she was done, and as she stood up, trembling and sick, she scrubbed her reddened palms against her skirt.

Not until then did the militiamen return, racing and sliding down the hill from the house, dashing through the beech grove. Nick Hamley was one of them, his smallsword in his hand.

Amelia gazed up at him. She tried to say, "Dead," but nothing came from her throat.

Nick was beside her in a moment, taking in the corpse at her feet, the bulk of Slater a few paces away. He lifted his sword, and advanced on Slater. His eyes bore the glint of steel.

Slater was rummaging in his pocket with one hand, the flintlock pistol dangling from the other. Nick said, "Stop! You'll not be reloading with this blade at your throat!"

Slater, with a curse, brought out a tin ammunition box in which balls rolled, clinking together. He stepped back a little from the point of the smallsword, but the Upland farmer moved in, pressing the blade against his chest. "Don't believe me?" he said in a light, almost cheerful tone. "Drop the gun, sir, or I'll draw blood. By the entwined gods, I swear I will!"

Slater's small eyes darted up to Nick Hamley's face as if to judge his will, then slid away to Amelia, who stood trembling above Jinson's body.

Nick said, "Now, sir!" and lifted the sword till the tip was at Slater's throat, dimpling the skin with its point. Slater, with another curse, dropped the pistol onto the gravel. Still Nick Hamley didn't withdraw the blade. "And the box," he said. "I'll turn them over to your master."

At that, Slater gave his phlegmy laugh. "My master!" he said. "My master has other things on his mind."

Nick Hamley answered by letting the tip of his sword press harder on Slater's neck. A drop of blood welled around the point, not dark like the blood that stained the gravel beneath

Jinson's limp body, but scarlet and glistening. Slater sucked in a breath, and his eyes flickered from side to side.

Amelia watched in shivering revulsion as he tossed the tin box to the ground. Nick lifted the sword from his throat but kept it poised and ready in his fist. "And now, sir," he said, "as an official member of Oc's militia, it will be my privilege to escort you to the prison in Osham. 'Twill be someone there who knows what to do with you."

"I ain't going anywhere," Slater said sullenly, his bravado fading. He wiped at his throat, and his fingers came away wet. Blood still seeped from the cut in irregular droplets.

Nick brandished the smallsword. Its tip was dark with blood. "Take a blink at this," he said. "Shall I redden it more than it already is?"

Amelia drew a deep breath to drive away her nausea. She still trembled, but she spoke with a semblance of control. "You can lock him in the stable," she said to Nick. "In the tack room. And then go up to Fleckham House for help."

"Aye," Nick said. He flashed his white teeth at Slater. "Smart lass, this."

"The Duke will have your head, you fool," Slater hissed.

Amelia said, "You said the Duke has other matters on his mind, didn't you, Master Slater? I hardly think the imprisonment of a murderer is going to call him away."

Slater glared at them both for a moment. "You'll find you're wrong about that," he snapped. He turned, the heavy layers of his coat flaring around his stooped figure, and stalked into the tack room. Nick pulled the door to and set the bolt.

Amelia stood looking down at Jinson's still form. Tears burned in her throat, and she didn't dare speak for fear of releasing them. Bramble, her tail between her legs, pressed against the back of Amelia's knees. Mahogany whickered anxiously from the dry paddock.

"I'll bring someone to fetch this poor fellow," Nick said.

"Thank you, Master Hamley," Amelia choked. "I'll stay with him until you return."

"Aye," Nick said. "You look a little unsteady on your pins, Miss. I'll bring you that mounting block, right? Do you sit a bit until you feel stronger. Nasty business."

After Nick rolled the mounting block across the gravel, she sat down on it, and folded her hands in her lap. She heard Nick's boots scrambling up the slope toward Fleckham House, but she kept her eyes on Jinson's still face. The scene of his killing ran over and over in her mind. She wanted to stop it, but those awful moments kept flashing before her, Jinson's eyes widening, the sickening sound of the cock, the hiss of the ball leaving the barrel of the pistol. And then, with such shocking finality, poor Jinson going down.

He had tried to protect her. He had stepped in front of her, dared the pistol, for her sake.

Amelia knew that Jinson was not well liked, that everyone considered him unsuited for the job of Master Breeder—and he was. But he had cared for the winged horses, and he had cared about her, unjustly imprisoned and misused by his master. She whispered tearfully, "I am so sorry, Master Jinson. I don't know if you have anyone to mourn you, but I will do it. I promise."

She got up from the mounting block to pick up the pistol and the little tin of ammunition from where they had dropped onto the gravel, then she sat down again. For long moments she was nearly as still as Jinson. From the dry paddock Mahogany whickered questioningly every few minutes, but still Amelia stayed where she was. She didn't rise until Nick rumbled down the lane in the Fleckham House oxcart. The ox, used to transporting all sorts of dead things, stood stolidly as Nick and one of the other militiamen lifted Jinson into the back of the cart. There was a big sheet of rolled canvas in one side of the cart bed, and they unrolled it and stretched it over his body.

Nick went to the tack room and tried the bolt to be certain it would hold. His fellow guardsman took up a post beside the door while Nick climbed onto the bench seat of the cart and whipped up the ox.

Amelia stood uncertainly, watching the cart roll away. She had dropped the heavy pistol and the tin of bullets into her pocket, and they dragged at her, heavy as death. The militiaman left behind had apparently forgotten all about them. To his credit, she thought, he was more concerned with Slater, the murderer, than he was with her.

In the distance, with a sound like a roll of thunder, the guns began again in the harbor, a boom and an answering shot, then a silence while the guns were reloaded, and then more dull booms, diminished to mere thuds by the distance. Smashers, they called the balls fired from carronades, because they smashed wood into deadly splinters. Amelia stared in the direction of the bay, thinking of other men, innocent soldiers like Nick Hamley, lying in pools of blood like the one drying now beneath her boots.

There must be something she could do, something to stop all this madness. If she was the cause, or even the excuse, for this war, she must stop it.

She took a trembling step toward the side of the stable. The guard said nothing. His eyes were following Nick and the oxcart as they rumbled up the lane. Amelia took another step.

She glanced back at the soldier, but he seemed not to realize she could simply walk away. He, too, was listening to the sound of the guns from the sea. "They're shooting again," he said.

"I hear it," she said. She put a hand to her throat. "What do you think it means?"

"It's war, Miss. Those damned Klee—" He stopped, looking at her, as if he had suddenly realized who she was. He opened his mouth, then closed it, fishlike, confused and uncertain.

"I'm just going to fetch some water for my colt, and get away from—" She glanced pointedly at the bloodstained gravel, and gave a deliberate shudder before she turned away.

The guard stared after her, frowning. He lifted his smallsword as if to give her some order, but then lowered it, looking in confusion at the locked tack room. He looked torn between his duty to restrain a murderer and his orders from the Duke to guard the royal hostage.

Slater shouted something from the tack room, but she couldn't hear what it was. She went on around the side of the stable. When she was out of sight of the guard, she picked up her too-long skirts and ran to the dry paddock. Bramble, with one yip, followed.

Mahogany met her at the gate, whickering in relief, butting at her chest with his nose as if to reprimand her for her absence.

Amelia threw her arms around his neck and pressed her cheek against his mane for a brief moment, then pulled back. "Mahogany," she said softly. "We've never done this before, and now we have no saddle and no bridle. But you and I have no time for niceties. I'm going to ride, all right? Bareback. Lark says it's the perfect way. And you must pay close attention to me, though I have only your halter and lead. You have to know where we need to go. You have to hurry, but not be careless."

Mahogany blew through his nostrils, and stood very still as she arranged his wings and made sure the wingclips were secure. When she leaped upon his back, he turned his head and sniffed at her knee.

"Good, Mahogany, very good," Amelia said.

He turned his head forward again and seemed to gather himself, to prepare for whatever was asked of him. It was true, she thought, what Lark and Hester had said. Kalla had bonded her to a winged horse who reflected her own personality, almost as if Mahogany had been at her side as she learned diplomacy and leadership and the responsibilities that came with her birth. She touched his shoulder, and said again, "Good." There was no need to be fulsome in her praise. He sensed, she could tell, the urgency of their plight, the weight of their duty.

Amelia prayed this would not stress his tender bones nor harm the tendons of his pasterns. He had been training with the saddle and sand weights, and they would have begun riding in the paddocks before the Erdlin festival, which was only weeks away. Surely, she thought, her slight weight could hardly hurt him.

She had left the gate open, and she urged him through it with pressure from her calves and murmured commands. He started to turn toward the lane, but she pulled on the halter lead to stop him. "Not that way, my love," she whispered. "They'll see us."

His feet shifted uncertainly. She laid the lead against the left side of his neck, and said, softly so the militiaman would not hear her, "This way, Mahogany. First we'll get into the woods, then we'll find our direction. Go now, my lad. Go!"

And Mahogany, catching her determination and the need for silence and hurry, set out at a smooth running walk down the slope of the little vale, then up toward the woods through which they had come three days before. Bramble trotted beside the colt, her ears and tail high.

Amelia's body tightened as they moved out into the open, but she forced herself to relax. Any tension she felt would translate through her hands, frighten Mahogany. At every moment she expected a shout of discovery behind her. Mahogany scrambled up the far slope, far faster than she could have done on foot. When they reached the cover of the woods, Amelia slipped down, feeling weak with relief. She hugged Mahogany's neck and praised him, then led him off through the trees.

They had to crowd their way through the dry hawthorn bushes. Bramble scrambled beneath branches and over roots, while Amelia struggled to find the clearest path so Mahogany's delicate wings would not be scratched or torn. "We'll soon be out of this," she told him, hoping it was true. "And I'll ride again. We did well, Mahogany, my love. We did well."

She wished she dared turn for the Academy. She longed for the safety of the Dormitory and the stables there. At the very least, she could send Bramble home.

When they reached a little clearing, where they could rest for a moment, she knelt beside the dog and took her long-nosed face between her hands. "Bramble," she said. "Listen to me."

The oc-hound's ears came up, and her eyes fixed on Amelia's.

"Bramble. Go home. Go to the Academy."

The dog waved her tail, and whined.

"Home, Bramble!" Amelia stood, and pointed in what she thought was the right direction. "Go home!"

The oc-hound hesitated only a moment, then gave a short, sharp bark. She whirled, and sprang off into the darkness.

Amelia watched until she disappeared, wishing with all her heart she could go with her.

But her duty called her in another direction. Surely, she thought, it was what her father would want her to do.

hand held before her lips as if to stop herself from some comment.

It didn't matter. It would be worth it if Diamond would let him approach without that nervous stamping, that shying away.

He strode across the courtyard and into the stables. When his stable-man approached, he shook his head, refusing help. He took the flying saddle from its post in the tack room, and the softest saddle blanket he could find, and carried them down the aisle to Diamond's stall.

He settled the saddle over the half-gate. The filly flicked her ears toward him and trotted willingly enough to the gate to nose his palm, to nibble the bit of barley he had brought for her. The morning sun poured through the high windows of the stables, casting shadows here and there where oat bins and water buckets interrupted it. In the dappled light, Diamond glowed like her namesake stone, and her delicate silver wings flexed beneath their wingclips.

"No, darling, not today," William murmured. "Today we ride."

At the thought, his heart beat in his throat as if he were a girl in love. The thought crooked his lips in a smile. That didn't matter, either. He was the first, a pioneer. If this was what it felt like, so be it. Once he knew all of these things, he could instruct the young men who would come after him.

He supposed the horsemistresses told the girls before they were bonded what it would be like. But they could never feel exactly as he did because they didn't have his beautiful Diamond, his perfect filly. He opened the gate and slipped into the stall, his calfskin boots nearly silent in the straw.

Diamond took a step back and lifted her head high on her arching neck. Her eyes were wide, liquid black, the lashes long and dark against the silver-gray of her face. Her white mane fell over her withers in long strands of silk, like a maiden's long hair spilling over her shoulders. William stood very still, willing her to come to him. He wanted her to make the first step, today of all days.

A long moment passed. In the park, the yellowhammers called from the hedgerows. One of the wingless horses whinnied from the pasture, and Diamond turned her head briefly toward the sound.

TWENTY

WILLIAM forbade anyone, and especially Felicity Baron, to
follow him to the stables of the Ducal Palace. When the guns
started up in the harbor, his secretaries, Harold and Clarence,
frowned like cranky old women, and sputtered things about
the demands of the Council, about mustering the militia to the
docks, about needing William's presence in this time of crisis.
He waved them away. Horsemistress Baron followed him
across the courtyard, tagging after him like a hound bitch, until he ordered her away, too. Even Constance giggled something about coming to watch, and he barely restrained himself
from striking her with his quirt.

This was his day. The sun shone with cold brilliance on the
red and gold shrubberies in the park. Snow crowned the
mountain peaks, and the wind that blew from their slop
chilled his hot cheeks. In some strange way, the sounds of b
tle from beyond the spires of Osham were part of the exp
ence, the feeling of risking everything, of putting
resource on the line for his dream. He could think of lit
Diamond, and what it would feel like to ride her, and
people would look at him when he flew at last. The
bow down to his leadership and his vision! There wo
more of this constant questioning and criticism.

It was his destiny to change the course of histor

With that in mind, he had doubled, then tripled
his potion last night. It made him feel odd. He
tossing in his bed, wakened frequently by bou
sweating. His chest ached and was more swo
He tried to ignore that and dressed without lo
ror. Constance, at the breakfast table, eyed

William hardly breathed. Diamond brought her delicate muzzle back toward him. She sniffed, then, one small shining hoof at a time, she walked to him.

William stroked her forehead, and tangled his fingers in her mane. He sniffed, too, treasuring the clean, oaty smell of her, the tang of horseflesh that had never meant anything to him until he was bonded. "My perfect Diamond," he said softly. "This is a great day."

She stood very still as he draped the saddle blanket over her back and lifted the flying saddle into place. He buckled the cinches carefully beneath her wings. He slipped the breast strap around her chest and fastened it. He'd been watching Felicity Baron and her gelding, and he knew how to fit the stirrups under her wings. She accepted the bridle without demur.

When all was in order, he stood back and surveyed her. She switched her tail and blew through her nostrils, making them flare pink.

He laughed. "Impatient, are you, my little darling?" He looped her reins over his arm and opened the stall gate. "Come, then. Let's see how we do."

William was accustomed to leaping into the saddle without thought for the horse's back, and they often grunted at the sudden weight, the roughness of his mount. But with Diamond, William meant to be as gentle and steady as he could. Despite his dismissal of Felicity Baron's recommendations, and though he would never admit that she had been right about his heavy hands, he had taken her warning to heart. He led Diamond to a mounting block and stepped up on it before lowering himself carefully into the saddle. He found the stirrups with his boots and settled against the cantle of the saddle.

She threw up her head, and that shiver that so distressed him ran through her body from head to tail.

William sat still, giving no direction, letting the reins swing loose below her chin.

She breathed deeply, and he felt the expansion and contraction of her ribs beneath his calves. Her folded wings trembled over his ankles. He felt a shiver of his own, one of pure delight, and of the exquisite joy of possession. She was his. No one else could touch her. No one else would ever sit in this saddle.

He reached down and stroked the point of her right wing with his palm.

Then he lifted the reins cautiously and tightened his calves around her barrel. She shivered again, but she began to walk.

William disdained the dry paddock, though that, too, had been one of Mistress Baron's suggestions. He tugged the right rein, ever so carefully, and laid the left against Diamond's neck. When she turned to the right, toward the park, he immediately loosened the rein, letting her choose her path. Her gait was smooth and steady as she headed down the grassy slope toward the orchard. Relief and elation made William giddy.

Diamond's ears flicked forward, and back, and she broke into a trot.

William let her go, posting easily in the stirrups, and together they rode toward the far end of the park. As they passed beyond the hedgerow, Diamond broke into a fluid, rocking canter, a smoother, lighter gait than William had ever experienced. He thought his heart might burst from the sheer joy of the moment.

When womanish tears stung his eyes, he reined her in. It would never do, after all, to lose sight of who and what he was.

He turned her about and gave her his heels to make her gallop back up the park. She bucked once, her heels flying high behind him so that the high pommel jammed into his belly. "Damn you, Diamond," he cried, laughing. "I'll let that go for now—but you remember who is the rider and who the ridden!"

For answer, she shook her head, rattling her bridle, and danced a little sideways. He would have punished another horse, yanked at the bit, turned him in a tight circle to show his control. But he was beguiled by the glitter of Diamond's mane frothing in the sunlight and the saucy tilt of her pointed ears.

He chuckled and let it go. He let her choose her own pace to go back toward the stable. When they reached it, he climbed down and stood for a moment, stroking her neck, feeding her a little more barley from his palm.

"You'll fly with your monitor this afternoon," he murmured

to her. "And I'll watch. But tomorrow—" He glanced over his shoulder and found that his secretaries were both standing on the steps of the Palace, awaiting him. A militiaman in the black-and-silver uniform was with them, a smallsword slung from his belt. A cart waited in the courtyard with an ox in its traces, and something in the bed, covered with canvas.

William turned his back on them and rubbed Diamond's withers. "Tomorrow, or the next day, you fly with me, my little Diamond." He circled her neck with his arm and tried to pull her lovely head close to his chest.

She suddenly backed away from him, tossing her head and laying back her ears. He stepped back away from her, hoping no one had noticed. He dropped the reins to the ground and called for Mistress Baron to come and untack the filly.

When Felicity Baron had taken charge of Diamond, William turned to face the secretaries and the militiaman waiting for him on the steps. He sighed, irritated, his joy in the morning evaporating. He stalked across the courtyard, switching at his thigh with his quirt, and wished he could think of something that would stop Diamond pulling away from him like that.

Perhaps the horsemistress was wrong. Maybe a heavier hand would be better. He must show her, after all, that he was master.

WILLIAM stood beside the fireplace, glad of the warmth of the flames behind him. Since he had grown so thin, he hardly ever felt warm enough, and the chill of winter seeped in through the tall, mullioned windows despite the heavy curtains. The marble floors felt icy through the thin leather of his boots. Behind his back, he spread his fingers to the heat of the fire.

Across the room, his secretaries and one militiaman, dark-haired and blue-eyed, stood waiting for his response. The militiaman stood before the plush divan, his hands on his hips. The secretaries looked from him to William with worried eyes.

"I only have your word for this," William said. He smoothed his hair with his hand and thought that it was almost long enough for a rider's knot. His mind strayed immediately to Diamond, and her flinching away from him. A thread of nausea ran through his gut, and he gritted his teeth. He had to force himself to focus on the matter at hand.

"Shot your Master Breeder, sir," the militiaman said. He had a handsome face, and his teeth, when he spoke, showed white in his suntanned face. He looked as if he often smiled, but now his features were grim. "Shot him dead. Master Jinson never had a chance."

"Slater is my personal assistant. He must have had a reason," William said. Anger at this situation, at the embarrassment of it, at the need to make some decision, drove away his uneasiness over Diamond. He would deal with the filly later. "Where is he?"

The militiaman spoke again, apparently unimpressed by being in the presence of his Duke. "In the tack room at the small stable beyond the spinney," he said. "Locked him in there where he couldn't hurt anybody else."

"You *locked* him in the tack room?" William said. He turned on the militiaman, glad to have a focus for his fury.

"Oh, aye, Your Grace. Shot the bolt tight." The ghost of a smile tugged at the man's mouth. "That one won't be having a blink at the sun till someone lets him out."

William scowled. "How dare you make such a decision without my authority?"

The man gave an insouciant shrug. "Begging your pardon, sir, but you weren't there, and a man's dead by this Slater's hand. I'm supposed to be militia, though I never wanted it. I'm told I'm supposed to guard people from danger."

William glared at him. "You were set to guard someone else at that stable."

"Oh, aye," the militiaman said. The secretaries were watching him with a sort of stunned bemusement at his lack of proper deference to the Duke of Oc. "Slater might have killed the lass, too, sir, if I hadn't been there."

"You're a liar," William said flatly.

"Your Grace, he took her away on that pinto pony of his. Said he was going to 'show her to the Klee.'"

At this William drew a breath and turned his back to stare into the flames. Damn Slater! The man had gotten above him—

self and put William in a bad spot. He needed Slater, needed him to supply him with his potion, to keep his mouth shut about that—and a few other things—and to come up with enough potion to start the process with the four young men at Fleckham House. Only Slater knew which apothecaries could be persuaded to do what needed doing.

And now he would have to find a way to excuse this. Jinson dead, ye gods! What was Slater thinking?

Slowly, deliberately, William turned to face the secretaries. He ignored the militiaman, hoping to put him in his place. "Clarence, get down to Fleckham House, to the stable beyond the beech grove, and get Slater out of there. Bring him here to answer to me."

Clarence bowed and turned swiftly to leave the room.

"And you, Harold." The junior secretary straightened, eyebrows lifted. "See that Jinson's body is prepared for burial. Find out if he has family that needs to be notified."

Harold nodded. "Yes, Your Grace." He, too, left, leaving the militiaman directing his unabashed gaze at William. There was something familiar in that level blue gaze, but William couldn't quite put his finger on what it was.

"What happened to our hostage?" William asked.

The man shrugged again. "She was there when I left."

"Did you make provisions for her to be—to be guarded?"

Now the easy grin broke out on the militiaman's handsome face. "I made provisions for her to be safe, sir. There's a guard, but I doubt me he's worried about a slip of a lass. He's there to see that a murderer stays to receive his judgment."

"You have a ready tongue, do you not?" William said with feigned casualness. He was sifting through his memory, trying to think why those blue eyes, that dark, curling hair, were familiar. "Where are you from, man?"

The militiaman bent his head, and said, "I'm an Uplander. Nick Hamley, of Deeping Farm, at your service."

William stiffened, and for a moment he could think of not a single word to say. Hamley! The brat's name was Hamley, and she came from Deeping Farm . . . This militiaman was her brother; he had to be.

William's eyes narrowed. There must be a way to turn this to good use, but his mind was clouded and sluggish. "Hamley," he said cautiously.

"The same, sir."

"If our hostage is gone, we will hold you responsible."

Hamley seemed unconcerned with this threat. He raised his glossy black eyebrows, and tilted his head to one side. "Begging your pardon, sir. The murder of yon Master Breeder seemed the most pressing matter."

"You're not paid to think, man," William snapped. "You're paid to follow orders." He turned his back and stared into the fire, thinking furiously. It was too bad about Jinson—damn the man, he should have known enough to stay out of Slater's way!—but he couldn't let Slater stay imprisoned. He needed him, or someone like him.

Over his shoulder, he eyed the handsome Uplander. No, he'd never do. He was too much like the Hamley brat. He would never fetch and carry the way Slater would. And he wouldn't know the apothecaries on the outskirts of the White City, wouldn't know which were willing to perform special services for their Duke, or how to force them to do their Duke's will if they resisted. Without the potion, his dreams would crumble to nothing.

He turned to face the militiaman. "Go back to Fleckham House and guard the prisoner."

Hamley raised one eyebrow. "Which prisoner, sir?"

William suppressed the flicker of rage at his insubordinate tone. "The girl, of course," he spat. "Clarence will bring Slater to me."

With outrageous casualness, Hamley said, "Your secretary? Do you think that's wise? There's no question of his guilt. None at all."

"Do as you're told, man. Leave such decisions to your betters."

He didn't watch Hamley leave, but he could have sworn he heard the man give a sardonic chuckle before the door closed behind him. He would tell Islington to put this Nick Hamley front and center when it came to a battle. He would not have militiamen telling him what to do.

When Harold returned, William told him, "Write an order for the Academy. We want every horsemistress within an hour's flight of Osham mustered at the Rotunda in the morning. The patrol boats can drive away that Klee ship, but they'll need cover." Harold's eyes widened, but he, at least, knew better than to argue with his Duke. He bowed and sat down at the desk, drawing a piece of parchment and a quill pen toward him.

As he dipped the pen into the ink, William said, "Oh, and tell them we want the third-level girls in the air, as well. They might as well earn their very expensive keep, for once."

When the door clicked shut behind his secretary, William went to stand beside the tall windows, absently tugging at his vest. It was a good thing after all, he mused, that that bitch Philippa Winter had not shown her face in Oc. Philippa would have simply refused the order he had just given. Suzanne Star wouldn't have the courage.

TWENTY-ONE

PHILIPPA and Sunny led the younger flyers north, staying inland where the winds were steady. Their flight path took them over fields emptied of their harvest, where farmers were plowing under the stalks and vines to prepare the fields for winter. They stopped their work to gawk at the flyers passing overhead. Philippa touched Sunny's shoulder so the mare would dip her broad red wings in salute to them, and the farmers below waved their hats in response.

They passed several hamlets of flat-roofed houses with kitchen gardens stretching behind them. The gardens reminded Philippa of Deeping Farm, and she wondered if Larkyn, too, yearned for that homely place, the friendly silences of the Hamley brothers around their scarred kitchen table, and the atmosphere of honest work and animal husbandry, the concern for food and health and family overriding any political issues. It was there that she had come to realize how artificial the rule of the Duchy had become.

When they reached the shore, she found a long, level stretch of beach, and guided Sunny down. Larkyn and Seraph came close behind, trotting to a stop beside a dune covered in long, brown grass. A freshwater brook ran down from the fields to empty into the sea. They spent two pleasant hours resting, giving the horses a little grain and letting them drink from the brook. They ate Lyssett's sandwiches of crusty bread and the sheep's milk cheese Philippa had grown so fond of, with the last of the tomatoes from Marinan's garden. They drank from the same stream as the horses, then strolled, stretching their legs and shoulders in the chilly sunshine.

All too soon it was time to take to the air again. Philippa

and Sunny turned due west toward Osham, with Larkyn and Seraph close behind. Once they had crossed the point of no return, which Philippa judged by the position of the sun, the sea winds seemed to lift them, buoy them in their flight. Sunny rested her wings from time to time, gliding on the currents. Philippa glanced back often, noting with approval that Black Seraph followed her example, flying steadily, with none of his playful darting about. No doubt, having made this crossing once already, he had learned something about flying over the sea.

Philippa began to search the western horizon for her first glimpse of the spires and towers of Osham. She hoped her return would be of some help to Suzanne and not make things worse. Duke William could try to take her from the Academy by force, and if he did, she would have to give in. She couldn't allow anything to endanger the girls or their instructors.

The snowfields on the flanks of the western peaks were turning pink and gold under the lowering sun when Philippa caught sight of the familiar crenellated top of the North Tower. It was white, as befit the White City. Its tall, slender silhouette marked the entrance to Osham's harbor. Its great light flashed out over the sea at night, warning ships from the rocks when the thick fogs of winter roiled over the coast.

At the mouth of the harbor a five-masted schooner rocked gently, its sails furled, its blue pennants snapping in the breeze.

There was no fog today, but the air aloft was bitterly cold. Philippa could believe Larkyn's prediction of an early winter.

She and Larkyn swooped around the Tower and past it, to skirt the spires of Osham and circle the copper dome of the Tower of the Seasons. They flew high above the New Bridge where it spanned the Grand River, connecting the northern neighborhoods of Osham with the city center and the Rotunda of the Council of Lords. They banked above the Old Bridge, with its ancient stone pilings crumbling away under the force of the river's current, and descended directly in line with the return paddock of the Academy of the Air. When the gambrel roofs of its stables rose before her, Philippa's heart ached at the poignancy of her long-awaited homecoming.

As Sunny and Black Seraph soared down over the grove and cantered up the familiar grassy ride, girls in their black riding habits came pouring out of the Hall. By the time Sunny folded her wings and Philippa stripped off her gloves, Suzanne Star and Kathryn Dancer were hurrying across the courtyard. When they came close, Philippa saw the strain around their eyes, the lines graven in their cheeks. They said little as they embraced her. Kathryn's hug was perfunctory, but Suzanne held her a moment longer than necessary, as if loath to let her go, and Philippa, normally undemonstrative, returned her embrace with warmth. The students took Sunny's reins, and Seraph's, and Philippa and Larkyn followed the horsemistresses back to the Hall, up the wide steps, and into the shadowed foyer.

Two black-uniformed militiamen stared straight ahead as they passed. Their presence made Philippa's skin prickle with anger.

She passed beneath the portrait of Redbird, Sunny's Noble forebear, with the briefest of glances. Soon she and Larkyn were seated in the Headmistress's office, and Suzanne had begun to speak.

She was interrupted briefly by Matron with a tray of tea and biscuits, which they gladly accepted. When Matron had withdrawn, after a word of welcome to Philippa, Suzanne went on. "They fired the guns all night. No one has seen the Duke, and word from the Rotunda is that the Lords of the Council can't agree on what to do."

"Larkyn told me you had soldiers at the Academy."

"They're watching for you, Philippa," Suzanne said grimly. "Duke William will know you're here by morning. But perhaps he will be too busy to do anything about it. Our patrol boats are in the bay, and the Klee ship is blocking the mouth."

"We saw that as we flew past," Philippa said. Larkyn nodded in wide-eyed silence.

"I don't think there's any way now to avoid war with the Klee."

"Baron Rys is a reasonable man," Philippa said. "If the Duke will produce his daughter—"

"Rys may be reasonable, but our Duke isn't."

Kathryn made a sound of protest at this, but Suzanne put up a hand, and pressed on. "There's a complication, Philippa. Beeth and Daysmith and Chatham have mustered their own militia. It's small, because they have little money to pay the soldiers, but I'm given to believe the men are passionate about their cause."

"And the Duke's brother?" Philippa asked tersely.

Suzanne glanced at Kathryn, who folded her arms. "Lord Francis has taken the part of the rebel lords," Kathryn said. "He's led us to the very brink of civil war."

"It's hardly Lord Francis's fault—" Suzanne began.

"You don't approve of what Francis has done?" Philippa said sharply. She heard the old, lamented edge in her tone, a sound she had not heard in more than a year.

"No!" Kathryn began.

"But I do," Suzanne said. "The Duke has hardly set foot in the Council for months. Oc is as leaderless as one of those Aesk tribes wandering about on the glacier!"

Kathryn said, "Lord Francis pledged fealty to the Duke, and so did we. It would be treasonous to break our oath."

"But the Duke has not kept faith with his own oath," Suzanne said, a little tiredly. It struck Philippa that Suzanne and Kathryn must have had this argument many times before. "And he has committed treason by corrupting the bloodlines."

"The winged horses belong to the Duke, no matter who he is, no matter whether we like him or not," Kathryn responded. "Those are the laws that brought peace to Oc centuries ago, and those are the laws we are bound to follow."

The two women glared at each other.

"And the other horsemistresses?" Philippa asked. "How do they feel?"

"The Academy is like the Council," Suzanne said. "Divided down the middle."

"And the girls . . ."

"The same, Philippa."

Through all of this Larkyn sat wide-eyed, her slender

hands clenched in her lap. In the little silence that followed, she said, "Is it—is it all my fault?"

"You had no business going to Arlton, inciting the Klee to come with their gunship—" Kathryn began sternly, but Suzanne interrupted her.

"Your instincts were good, Larkyn," she said. "Though I resisted telling Baron Rys at first. I didn't realize then how heated things had become in the Rotunda. We've had no luck finding Amelia, and it's been days now. It's better her father was informed immediately."

Kathryn was shaking her head. "Everything has piled up, and the situation is so confusing! I can't figure it out myself!"

"It's clear enough," Suzanne said, her voice rough with a sort of restrained impatience. "Duke William wants to close the Academy, and to that end he has taxed the people beyond their endurance and called up the militia to enforce it. And then—to make matters worse—infuriated the Klee by kidnapping Amelia Rys."

Philippa said, "I gather no one knows where the Duke has been?"

"We have nothing but rumors," Suzanne said. "His school at Fleckham House is ready, and he has four young men there waiting to be bonded to winged horses."

"Do they know what that's going to require?" Philippa asked dryly.

Suzanne shrugged. Kathryn began to speak, but she was interrupted by the roar of a carronade from the harbor. She cried out, and Larkyn pressed her hands to her ears.

Philippa frowned. "Has anyone been hurt?"

Suzanne nodded. "Matron's sister is a bonesetter, and she was called from her apothecary shop to tend to two men who were wounded. Those cannons shatter the decks of the boats, if they hit, and send shards of wood everywhere. Fortunately, they're not very accurate."

"I must," Philippa said, "see Lord Francis. We need a coordinated approach."

"Can we keep our girls out of it?" Suzanne said. "Perhaps the Prince will allow the horsemistresses to return from Arlton to assist . . ."

Philippa shook her head. "We're more likely to receive help from the Klee Baron than our own Prince."

AFTER some discussion, the horsemistresses came to an uneasy agreement that they should try, for the moment, to go on with life as usual at the Academy. Accordingly, they gathered in the Hall for the evening meal, and Philippa sat in her old place at the high table.

She understood immediately that any semblance of normal life was superficial. It was not only the explosions from the harbor that made the girls and women sit in tense silence, but the conflict inside the Hall. As the soup was served, Philippa eyed the students at their long tables. They had, it seemed, divided themselves. It was subtle, not so much a rearrangement of their chairs as an attitude, a shoulder turned away here, a head averted there, bodies adjusted so that eyes would not meet.

"Kalla's teeth," Philippa muttered. "Is there civil war even within our own walls?"

"There is," Suzanne answered grimly. "Even among the first-level girls, who haven't begun riding yet. They adopt their parents' position, whatever that might be. I hear them arguing, when they don't know I'm there, debating fealty and obedience."

"Have you spoken to them?" Philippa asked.

Suzanne gave her a glance full of misery and guilt. "Philippa, I'm so glad you're here. I haven't known what to say, and Kathryn and I, as you see—I just don't know what will happen to us!" She pressed a trembling hand to her lips, and her eyes, wreathed with the lines that were the badge of every working horsemistress, glittered with unshed tears.

Philippa pressed her own lips hard together and gritted her teeth against the wave of fury that swelled and broke in her breast. When she dared speak, she said tightly, "Suzanne. My dear. May I speak to your students?"

Suzanne nodded. Past her, Philippa saw Kathryn watching the two of them, her mouth, too, pulled tight. Philippa nodded to her. "Kathryn, I think I should have your agreement, too.

This is not good for the girls or for us . . . or for our horses. They have to be our first concern."

Kathryn sat very still for a moment, then her shoulders sagged. "I know, Philippa. I keep wondering what Margareth might have said, what she would have done . . ."

"She would never allow us to split like this," Philippa said. "It goes against everything she believed in, everything she devoted her life to."

Suzanne said shakily, "I never wanted to be Headmistress, Philippa; you know that."

Philippa, in an unusual gesture for her, touched Suzanne's shoulder. "You're doing your best, and so is Kathryn." After a pause, in which she tried to breathe away her anger, to sort out her thoughts, she added softly, "And so am I."

She waited until the soup was cleared away, and the little rainbow array of lettuce and autumn vegetables had been set in front of the girls and the horsemistresses. Then she stood, smoothed her tabard, and spoke in a clear, carrying voice. "May I have your attention, please?"

The girls turned startled faces up to her. She looked at them for a painful moment, and her anger burned afresh. William had a great deal to answer for. She promised herself she would demand that answer very soon.

She thought of the beautiful horses resting now in the stables across the courtyard. She thought of the centuries of careful breeding, the husbandry of dukes, of generations of horsemistresses dedicated to the care and training of Kalla's creatures. She thought of the miracle of flight, that precious gift of Kalla, and her throat closed.

She swallowed, and straightened. She had shed no tears since her dear friend Margareth's death, and she was not about to shed them now. When the familiar pain started in the back of her neck, she welcomed it.

She spoke in a voice that cut through the weighted silence in the hall like the slash of a sword. "It is not to a duke or a lord that we owe our loyalty," she said. "It is to the winged horses. We serve our bondmates, and we protect the bloodlines." She paused, scanning the faces below her. "If we must fight, we must fight side by side."

Several of the girls stirred in their chairs, frowning. Some nodded, and Philippa heard Suzanne, beside her, release a held breath.

"I can think of nothing worse," Philippa went on, "than to see horsemistresses take flight against each other, or to ask a winged horse to oppose one of his own."

There was a pause, then a third-level girl, Beryl, stood up. She inclined her head courteously to Philippa, but she spoke harshly. "Mistress Winter, my father says we're bound to obey our Duke's orders. He says it's our duty."

Several of the students and one or two of those at the high table murmured agreement.

Philippa waited until silence fell over the room again, then she said slowly, "I think, Beryl, that it depends on what those orders are. We don't train for six years here at the Academy, and dedicate thirty or more years of our lives to the winged horses, to practice blind obedience. What duty could ask us to thrust away everything we know because someone in a high position tells us to?"

There was a stir at this, and several other girls jumped up, their chairs scraping against the tiled floor. Philippa saw that some girls whispered to each other, their heads bent together, while others began to snap at each other across their untouched salads. The servers stood uncertainly in the doorway, holding trays with the cooling fish course, as the noise rose in the hall.

Suzanne stood slowly, leaning on the table. Philippa remembered Margareth doing just the same, supporting herself with her hands, as if the weight of responsibility were a physical burden. Suzanne Star was too young to move that way. It was another thing William should answer for, although Philippa doubted he would care.

"Quiet!" Suzanne called, across the hubbub. When the noise did not die down, she slapped the table with the flat of her hand, making the flatware jump. "Silence, please!"

Gradually, the voices quieted, and the girls, though they still looked angry, took their seats. Suzanne waved to the servers, and they started to move among the tables again. She and Philippa sat down.

"I don't know what else I can say," Philippa said. "I've been no help at all."

"This conflict runs too deep," Suzanne said.

Sarah Runner, one of the junior horsemistresses, said, "I never thought to see such a thing in our own duchy."

"I don't know if we can survive it," Philippa said grimly. "Prince Nicolas would love to take over the bloodlines, and Oc would lose its only real claim to independence."

There was a movement at the far end of the hall, and someone came in through the big doors. Philippa said, "Isn't that Felicity Baron?"

Suzanne said, "Yes. The Duke assigned Sky Baron to mentor his filly. Felicity's been posted to the Ducal Palace."

The older horsemistress strode toward the high table with a purposeful step. Her weathered face was drawn, and Philippa felt a premonitory apprehension.

"Really," Suzanne said quietly, as the older horsemistress came closer, "I thought by now the Duke would have sent Felicity down. She's always been outspoken."

"I suppose he has to have someone."

They broke off their exchange as Felicity Baron stepped up on the dais and came to them. She inclined her head to Philippa, and said without preamble, "He's ridden her."

Suzanne said, "What? Who's ridden?"

Philippa said, "It's Diamond, isn't it? The Duke has ridden his filly."

"Yes," Felicity said.

There was a moment of stunned silence at the high table. "I can hardly believe it! I didn't really think . . ." Suzanne began.

Philippa said, "I had hoped she wouldn't allow it. It hardly seems possible."

"I know." Felicity nodded. "But he's done it now."

"How did it go?" Philippa asked.

Felicity shrugged her bony shoulders. "That's a confused young horse. She blows hot and cold with him."

"And how does the Duke look?"

"Very odd, Philippa. And he acts even more strange."

"What's going to happen?" Suzanne asked. The other

horsemistresses at the high table were watching and listening, and Felicity included them in her hard glance.

"He won't listen to me," she said. "He's going to try to fly. If he does, more of the lords will come over to his side, I'm afraid."

"And does anyone have the slightest idea where he's keeping Amelia Rys?" Philippa asked in an undertone.

Felicity shook her head. "I never saw her."

TWENTY-TWO

THE night air bit into Amelia's lungs, making them ache. The sleeves of her too-large tabard hung loosely around her wrists, letting in the chill. It was damp from perspiration on the chest and the back, and under the arms, and as it dried, she grew even colder. She tightened the belt around her waist and tried not to shiver. She thought she might feel warmer if she walked, but Mahogany made such good time on the road that it seemed best to ride. She could never keep pace with his ground-eating running walk.

She judged the time to be past midnight. It had taken her and Mahogany hours to work their way through the woods, sometimes having to backtrack when they came to an impenetrable thicket, at others having to crack branches and twigs to force themselves forward. She had been dripping with perspiration then. It had been a relief to break out of the trees and bushes, to see the main road twisting between the hedgerows, starlight gleaming on its smooth surface.

The sounds of guns from the harbor reverberated through the icy air, seeming louder in the darkness than they had during the day. Mahogany flinched beneath her at first, each explosion seeming to jar his nerves, but he had soon steadied. His running walk was a lovely gait, easy to ride, and it sped them steadily and swiftly on through the night. The copper dome of the Tower of the Seasons glistened with reflected stars, giving them a clear goal. For perhaps half an hour they had the road to themselves, with the wintry wind in their faces.

When Amelia heard men's voices behind her, she urged Mahogany off the road, and slipped down to hold his bridle.

She stood in the shadows of the hedgerow, hoping that the lantern the men carried would blind their eyes to the darkness.

There were only four of them, hurrying along the road on foot, urging each other to a faster speed. " 'Twill all be over if we don't get there soon," one of them said. Another answered, but Amelia couldn't understand his words.

There was a great flash of light to the east, from the bay.

The voice said again, "There! You see? 'Tis already under way. We're going to miss it!"

A different voice said, " 'Tis only the ships, you fool! We don't know what's happening on the shore."

They were almost past. Amelia cupped Mahogany's nose with her fingers and pressed his head close to her. The men wore the black uniforms of the Duke's militia, and they were so close she could smell their sweaty clothes and the stale fragrance of tobacco. She felt Mahogany's nostrils quiver beneath her hand. She willed him to tolerate the scent, just for the moment. He blew into her palm, but he stood as still as ice.

Just as the men trotted past, she heard another voice. "Just get me there in time to shoot once at the damned Klee! Just once!" And then they were past, and hurrying down the road away from her.

Amelia's knees shook with tension, and she spent a weak moment leaning on Mahogany's neck, letting her cold cheek absorb some of the warmth of his body. He turned his head to her, sniffing, and she knew he was exchanging her own familiar scent for that of the strange men. She stroked his muzzle, and whispered, "Mahogany, you are worthy of the Rys name! Kalla bless you!"

She let a few moments pass before she led him back up on the road. She led him for a while, thinking the walk would warm her, then, when she felt that the militiamen had a good lead, she jumped up onto his back again. He didn't flinch this time at her weight and resumed his steady pace. From time to time they heard the carronade, and saw the flashes, and twice Amelia thought she heard the sounds of smaller guns, but she could not be sure.

The people of Oc, evidently, were staying close to their homes. She saw no other travelers, and few lights in the houses she passed. She had just begun to shiver again when the uneven clatter of a horse's hooves sounded behind her.

This time Mahogany didn't wait to be told. His eyes were sharper than hers, and he spotted a break in the hedgerow, where a narrow lane twisted away from the road. In a flash he ducked through the open space, scraping her knees only a little on the bare branches of the hedge, and slid down into the little vale behind it. She didn't dismount this time but leaned far forward to cling to his neck, hiding herself from the eyes of the rider coming so fast toward them.

It was only one horse, but there was something familiar about the sound of those hooves, the unevenness of the gait, the creak of the saddle leather. The rider was keeping up a steady stream of curses, aimed at the horse, at life in general, and once she heard Duke William's name. Amelia thought it was strange the man would waste his breath cursing with no one to hear him, but when the horse had galloped past, grunting and panting, she sat up straight.

Above the dark silhouette of the hedgerow, outlined against the stars, she recognized the hunched shoulders and the flapping greatcoat of Slater.

She held her breath, watching him make his noisy, graceless way toward the city. He had escaped, or had been let go. Perhaps Duke William had even given the order to set him free. Jinson's death, she supposed, would be only a minor inconvenience, whereas Slater . . .

She reined Mahogany back onto the road, and as they set off again, she said softly, "Mark my words, Mahogany. It is a great weakness in a leader to be dependent. The Duke of Oc has put himself in a precarious position."

Mahogany's ears flickered back to her voice, then forward again, and his head bobbed neatly from side to side as he pressed on toward Osham.

THE stars had begun to fade by the time they crossed the New Bridge and found themselves in the inner city. The explosions had died away. When Mahogany topped a little rise, Amelia looked out toward the harbor and drew a sharp breath. The *Marinan*, its blue banners barely visible in the gray dawn, its sails neatly furled, rocked quietly at anchor in the mouth of the harbor. She pressed a hand to her heart, caught off guard by a sudden longing to see her father, to hand over the burden she carried.

"Not yet," she whispered. "Not yet. But soon!"

Around her the houses were quiet, the shops shuttered. She began to shiver again, not so much with the cold as with exhaustion. She pressed her tabard close to her neck, and a whiff of her own body offended her nostrils. She smelled little better than the militiamen who had passed her hours before.

She tightened the halter lead to rein Mahogany in, to keep his hoofbeats a little quieter on the cobbled streets of Osham. As if they had been riding together like this for months instead of just the long hours of a solitary night, and even though it was a single rope instead of two leather reins, he slowed his pace. For the hundredth time, Amelia thought what a miraculous creature he was. All the winged horses were smarter, stronger, wiser than any other beast.

At that thought, she managed a small chuckle and patted Mahogany's mane, tangled from their foray through the forest. "You're no beast, are you, Mahogany?" she said softly. "It was wrong even to think it! You're practically as human as I am."

The streets narrowed as they moved toward the bay. The Tower of the Seasons bulked against the graying sky behind them, and the buildings leaned close to each other, keeping the lanes in thick shadow even as the sky began to brighten. The Rotunda, Amelia knew, was not far from the Tower of the Seasons, and there the avenues were wide and open, but she would avoid that part of the city. She meant to find her way to the docks, and to the lighthouse.

Amelia knew a good deal about the North Tower. She had passed its slender column with her father once and had looked out the carriage window to see its great light glowing across the fishing boats tethered to long, narrow docks. The boats that patrolled the harbor docked just beneath it. Her father had pointed them out, and told her the story of the previous war between Klee and Oc, when the South Tower had become a place of misery and death. "This one," he had said, "will never be a prison for hostages. Only the lightkeeper climbs those stairs. It was part of our pact with Isamar, when we resumed exporting our goods, that the North Tower would never be used that way. Prince Nicolas's father signed that pact with your grandfather."

She slipped down from Mahogany's back when they reached a turning. The main part of the road turned left, to the north, but a cramped alley wound to the east, toward the bay. Amelia led Mahogany gingerly down the dark, narrow space. Lights were beginning to come on here and there, lamps being lit, fires stirred to life, making windows glow through the early-morning gloom. Still, the city seemed eerily quiet, the streets strangely empty. People should be stirring, fishmongers and bakers and coal men delivering their wares.

She supposed she should take it as a stroke of good luck. It was important that she reach the North Tower before the city was fully awake. A girl and a winged horse could hardly pass unnoticed through the streets, and by now she must look as if she'd been rolled in dirt. Mahogany, too, was in shameful condition, scratched and matted.

She put a hand on his shoulder. "At least," she murmured, "you don't have to worry about the Duke now."

And then she saw them. And they saw her, before she could slip back into the darkness.

The alley was too dim to see their clothes, but she knew they were men by their voices. She couldn't tell how many there were as they leaped out of an arched doorway to block her path. One of them demanded, "Which side?"

Mahogany snorted his alarm at the male scent. "Wh-what?" Amelia stammered.

"Which side? Duke or rebel?" the man asked again.

One of his companions took a step forward, making Mahogany throw his head high. "'Tis just a girl, you gammon! She don't have a side!"

"She has a horse, don't she? You ever know anyone but a nob has a horse?"

Mahogany snorted again, and scrambled back from the men, dragging Amelia with him.

The men lunged forward, seeing this, and now Amelia saw there were three of them, dressed in the sort of loose pants and jackets workingmen wore. Knitted caps were pulled down over their ears, and one of them had some sort of bludgeon in his hand.

"Please, sirs!" she said, trying to keep her voice even. "Please keep your distance."

They stopped, and one of them laughed again. "Please, sirs," he whined in imitation. And then, roughly, "Come on, lads, 'tis a girl for the taking, and a horse, too! What are we waiting for?"

The one that had asked about her side, and who carried the bludgeon, said in a low, unpleasant voice, "I'll tell you what for, idiot. If she's a nob, she's worth something."

"And we can sell the horse," the third one said.

"Or," the laughing one said, "we could just have a bit of fun, then sell 'em both." He strode forward, his hand out as if to seize Amelia's arm.

Mahogany whinnied and reared, jerking the lead from Amelia's hand. She whirled to go after him, and the man swore as his hand grasped empty air.

Amelia seized the colt's lead and whirled to face her tormentors. "Leave us alone," she said, "or I'll scream for the night watch."

At this they all snickered, and one of them said, "Night watch? None of 'em left, lassie. All gone for the militia."

"Or for the rebels," someone said.

The man with the bludgeon, obviously the leader, made a gesture with his free hand. One of the men dashed around behind Mahogany, who reared again, and sidestepped, nearly running into a wall. Amelia tugged on his lead, trying to quiet him, but his eyes rolled, showing their whites in the gloom.

Amelia cast a glance back at the leader, desperately trying to think what to do. For a second time in as many days, she lamented that her education in statecraft gave her no skills for dealing with thugs. She thought furiously. "Sir," she began, but was interrupted by the man behind her.

"Zito's ass," he said with real astonishment. "Jake, look at this! This horse has wings!"

The man with the bludgeon took a closer look at Mahogany, then, turning back toward Amelia, he began to grin. The other two men chortled, and congratulated each other on their find.

Amelia's heart sank to her boots.

TWENTY-THREE

WILLIAM set out early in the morning from the Palace. The four young men already residing at the Fleckham School should know his great news first. He would have liked to ride Diamond there, to prove it to them, but this morning she was particularly skittish. He didn't dare risk her throwing him with his boys watching. Felicity Baron might have been able to quiet her, but she was nowhere to be seen. William scowled at Sky Baron's empty stall. All the woman did was whine and criticize, then when he needed her, she disappeared.

There was no one else to help him with Diamond. He swore he would find a stable-man willing to take the potion—or one he could force to take it—so that he would not have to deal with things like shoveling muck and sawdust.

He didn't want the filly to go hungry or thirsty, though, so he did those chores himself. She came to him briefly, but when he brought out the bridle, she danced away, shaking her head and rustling her wings.

"Calm down, Diamond," he said irritably, tugging at his vest. "Nothing's different from yesterday!" His chest ached, and his gut felt tight and a little queasy, as if he had eaten something bad the night before. In truth, he had eaten nothing, and had taken only coffee this morning.

Diamond stood in the corner of the stall, her head high and her nostrils flaring. His fingers tightened on his quirt as his temper flickered. He expected the old rush of anger, but it died before it could grow into a real flame.

She was so beautiful, even when she challenged him this way. Her hide glittered in the cold sunlight, and her wings looked like folded fans, the ribs dark and delicate, the membranes like silver satin. He relaxed and leaned against the stall door.

"I suppose you miss your mentor," he said lightly. Her nose lifted, and she sniffed audibly. "Very well, my wayward girl. This afternoon, when I return from Fleckham House. Mark you, be ready then, for there will be none of this nonsense!"

Diamond snorted, and lowered her head. William checked that her water bucket was full and stirred the oats with his hand to entice her to them. He opened the gate and stepped out into the aisle, then stopped abruptly.

"Ye gods! Constance!" he exclaimed. "What the devil are you doing here?"

His wife stood looking past him into the stall. Two spots of pink stood on her cheeks, incongruous against her colorless skin. She said, "She's grown."

"Of course she's grown," William snapped, pushing past her toward the tack room. He would take the chestnut mare today, though she'd been limping the last time he rode her. Surely by now the stable-man had done something about that.

The stable-man appeared instantly when he called for him and hurried off to saddle the mare. William pulled on his gloves and buttoned his coat.

He stood in the door of the stables, waiting for his mount. Constance trailed out beside him, her skirts catching bits of straw and sawdust. She wrapped her shawl tighter around her shoulders and tilted her head to look up at him.

"William," she said.

He didn't answer.

"William, my maid says they're fighting in the city."

He gritted his teeth. "There's a Klee ship blocking the harbor, Constance. Of course they're fighting."

"No, not fighting the Klee," she said. Her voice was breathy, but he caught the insinuating tone. He looked down at her.

She had a little, kittenish face, which years before he had found mildly attractive. She had always been shy, and more than a little fearful of him, which he didn't mind at all. But now Constance regarded him with something like relish. She looked like a cat about to devour a bird. Her rosebud lips pursed, and her eyes were bright with malice. "Not the Klee, my lord husband," she said in her little-girl voice. "Each other. Your people."

She fingered her shawl and watched for his reaction.

"You shouldn't repeat stupid gossip," he snarled, and looked away again.

The stable-man led out the mare, and William frowned. The horse was still favoring her left forefoot.

"It's not gossip," Constance said. "It's news. There's a difference, William."

He pulled his quirt from his belt, and the mare whuffed nervously and stepped away. The stable-man had to grab for the reins and pull the horse forward.

William swung up into the saddle and looked down at Constance. "You shouldn't listen to such nonsense, Constance. If there were something to worry about, I would tell you."

"You don't understand," she said, moving closer to the horse and putting her small hand on his stirrup. "They're saying it's going to be civil war, William. Between those that want to fight the Klee and those who don't."

William sneered, "If I say fight, they'll fight. All of them. They'll do as they're told."

Her eyes flickered to the side, then back, more catlike than ever. In her childish voice, she said, "Not everyone will do as you tell them, my lord husband. Not anymore."

William felt a spasm of rage that made him jerk the reins in his hands, and the mare sidestepped, making Constance fall back. "How dare you speak to me this way?" William demanded of his wife. "Have you no loyalty at all?"

She shrugged. "They say you listen to no one, William." She gave a small, tight-lipped smile. "I thought perhaps you might listen to me."

And then, as he wheeled the mare and started off across the courtyard, she added, so quietly he wasn't sure he heard, "Before it's too late."

THE mare was well and truly lame by the time William reached Fleckham House, and he was in a towering temper.

Only the sight of his old home sporting a beautifully carved sign over the door that read THE FLECKHAM SCHOOL and the freshly painted stables awaiting the fillies and colts that would soon come soothed him somewhat. Still, as he leaped down from the mare and handed her off to the stable-man who rushed out to meet him, bowing and babbling obsequious nonsense, William felt irritable and tense.

It was easy to blame Constance as the bearer of bad news, but it hadn't helped that he could hear the carronades again from the bay, and the occasional shot of a long pistol or even a matchlock rifle from the city center. Those idiots of the Council couldn't even manage a war, it seemed. Couldn't they see he had more pressing things to attend to?

He should, of course, have been able to delegate this battle to his brother Francis, but he dared not. He feared Francis would simply refuse, and that was one humiliation he didn't need. The thought of more disloyalty made his gorge rise and burn in his throat.

He strode up to the entryway to the Fleckham School, trying to feel proud of this accomplishment. Soon the place would ring with the voices of students. Young men. Young men who would learn to fly winged horses.

He could have wrung Constance's skinny neck for ruining this great day. She was lucky there would be time for him to cool off before he saw her again.

He found the four boys in a large, airy room that had been the morning room of Fleckham House, and that was now furnished with floor-to-ceiling bookshelves and tables outfitted with reading lamps. The boys were gathered around a table, playing a game of cards and laughing together. When they saw him, they leaped to their feet, blushing and bowing. One of them scooped up the cards and stuffed them into his pocket, and another stepped forward, saying, "Your Grace . . . we didn't know . . . We weren't expecting you, and since Mistress Baron—"

William waved off the apologies. "It doesn't matter. I know you have little to do yet, but I came to tell you—" He stopped, uncomfortably aware that they were staring at him. He could barely resist the urge to look down at himself, to see what drew their eyes. He stiffened his neck, and said, "It will not be long now, my friends. You will soon have horses—bondmates."

One of them said wonderingly, "What's happened, my lord?"

William allowed himself a small smile. "I have ridden my filly."

That caught their attention. Their eyes widened, and they made admiring sounds. One said, "Your Grace, you've made history!"

William nodded. "Exactly so. I have made history, and you will, too, before long."

Another boy, a small lad with pale hair who William thought must be one of his second or third cousins, though he couldn't remember the name, asked, "Will you fly soon, then?"

The other boys hissed at him as if he had said something rude, but William chuckled. "No, no, it's a good question," he said. "It's the right question. You young men are giving up a great deal to come here, to prepare for this development in the history of the Duchy." He propped an elbow on top of a book-case, feeling much better than he had all morning. "I will fly my Diamond tomorrow. I'll be sure to come this way so you can see us aloft."

They exclaimed anew over this. William chatted with them for a few moments, then took his leave. The pale-haired boy stopped him just as he put his hand on the door latch. "My lord Duke? Can you tell us anything of the war?"

William frowned. "What are you talking about?" he said coldly.

The boy blanched, but he held his ground. He must surely be a Fleckham, with those black eyes and that hair. "No one will tell us anything, Your Grace, but we hear the servants talking. When they think we can't hear."

"And what are they saying?"

"Well." The boy glanced around at his comrades. "Well, Your Grace, they're saying the Klee are blocking the harbor because the Viscount's niece has been kidnapped."

"The Klee have always been our enemies," William said in a flat voice.

"But not since the South Tower," the boy said. "Since Klee and Isamar signed a treaty. But they're saying you and your brother—Lord Francis, that is—" His resolve seemed to give way, and he dropped his eyes.

"What?" William asked, in the silky tone older men knew enough to fear. He was gratified to see the last shreds of color fade from the boy's already-pale face.

Still the lad persisted, though he kept his eyes down, and spoke, evidently, to his feet. "We heard . . . we heard the horsemistress talking with Paulina."

William stood very, very still. "Are you going to tell me what she said?" he asked softly. "Or shall I take it up with the housekeeper myself and tell her you told me?"

The boy said in a rush, "They say Lord Francis, with the Council Lords Beeth and Daysmith and—I forget the rest— have their own militia. Men are going to Beeth House to enlist."

"That's treason," William said. He included the other boys with his gaze. "You all understand that."

The other three nodded, wide-eyed and silent.

"And you?" he asked the pale-haired boy.

Slowly, the boy raised his eyes—the black Fleckham eyes William and Francis both had. He said, "The horsemistress says tampering with the bloodlines is treason, Your Grace."

William's fist closed around his quirt, and he almost pulled it from his belt. He imagined, briefly, striking the boy with it, teaching him a lesson he would remember forever.

With a silent expulsion of angry breath, he released the quirt. He put his hand on the doorjamb and leaned on it in as negligent a pose as he could manage. "What's your name, lad?"

"Frederick, sir."

"I've forgotten who your parents are."

"My mother is your cousin," Frederick said. "She named me for your father."

"Ah." William straightened. "Well, Frederick, you're very like my father. He had courage, and so do you. You'll make a fine horsemaster." He tried to hide his fury behind his crooked smile. The boy bowed and stepped back to join his fellows.

William eyed them all once again, then turned sharply on the toe of his boot to leave the room. He felt their curious eyes on his back as he shut the door behind him. He stalked out through the gleaming foyer, down the broad steps, and across the courtyard to the stables. His breath came fast, puffing clouds of steam into the icy air.

The stable-man came to meet him, with some story about the mare's foreleg needing ice and rest, but William brushed him off. He wanted to get back to Diamond. He would send Slater to find out what was happening at Beeth House. And, he supposed, though he had no stomach for it, he would have to convene the Council. Constance, damn her, had been right. And if what young Frederick said was true, he needed to step in before things got out of hand.

As he mounted the mare, and she limped out of the courtyard, a carronade fired in the bay. William pulled his quirt from his belt and whipped the horse, making her break into a painful, uneven trot.

TWENTY-FOUR

THE third-level class had divided itself in half. Lark and Hester and Anabel, and quiet Grace, were on one side of the issue. Beryl, Lillian, and Beatrice were on the other. Isobel was struggling to remain neutral.

Bramble had shown up at the Academy sometime in the night. Herbert had found her waiting outside the stables when he came down that morning.

"I think she was with Amelia," Hester said, as they slipped out of their riding habits and into their nightdresses. "It worries me, but I'm worried about what's happening here, too. We've had such terrible arguments. Beryl is the worst, because her father has convinced her that the Duchy will fall apart if the Duke's authority is questioned."

Lark whispered back, "They're willing to see the Academy closed in favor of the Fleckham School?"

Hester grimaced. "One thinks the Duke won't really do it, that it's just talk; another thinks he must know better than anyone else does, just because he's the Duke. And they talk about tradition."

"Tradition!" Lark shook her head, unable to grasp the idea. "But *we're* part of the tradition, we and our bondmates!"

"And they would say obedience to the Duke is tradition."

Lark folded her tabard and divided skirt, and stowed them in her bedside cabinet. As she slipped beneath the sheets, she sighed with pleasure. "'Tis so good to be home again," she said.

Hester murmured slyly, "You always say the Uplands are your home, Black."

Lark turned on her side and gazed at Hester. "Aye, so they

are. But the Academy is my home, too, and lovely fine it looked as we flew in!" She rolled onto her back. "But if you could have a blink at Klee! Such grand mountains, and fields of lavender and mustard . . ."

"I've heard that."

There was a little silence, then Lark said softly, "Have you heard from your mamá?"

"No. I worry about them, with the fighting going on."

"Surely Lord Beeth would not be on the patrol ships."

"No, but there's other fighting. Everyone who comes from Osham is talking about it."

"'Tis a bad time for Oc."

Hester said gravely, "So it is, Black. A very bad time indeed."

"I hope Amelia is all right."

"So do I. For her own sake, and for ours. Because if she's not, years of peace with the Klee will be ruined."

AMELIA and Mahogany stood side by side, Mahogany's hindquarters hard against the shuttered window of a tiny shop. Amelia pressed her own body tight against Mahogany's left shoulder. They were both trembling, but Mahogany felt warm and solid, and Amelia willed him to steadiness. She thought of calling for help, but decided it would be useless. The buildings around her were silent, and the only light came from the gas lamp on the corner.

Besides, such a display would be beneath her dignity. She was a Rys. She could handle these ruffians on her own.

"Sirs," she said. "You're making a grave error in detaining me."

The leader of the band of ruffians growled, "You think so?"

The laughing one said, "Hoo, Jake, better watch out f' yer grave error!"

The leader chuckled. He took a step forward, and Mahogany flinched. He brandished his bludgeon in Amelia's direction. "Lass, you and yon horse are money on the hoof, and no mistake. No one around to stop us, neither. Now, just you hand over that lead rope, and we'll see what we can do about you."

He stepped forward. Mahogany squealed and lashed out with a forefoot.

The man cursed, and jumped back. "Tom, grab the girl. Them horses go wherever their girls do, I hear."

His companion circled around behind him, staying out of the reach of Mahogany's hooves. He gingerly approached Amelia, reaching for her with one dirty hand. Mahogany snorted, and tossed his head. He tried to back farther, but he had no room to move. The leader waved his bludgeon. The light was beginning to rise, and Amelia saw that the weapon was a long, heavy bit of wood carved in one piece, and studded with nails.

The one named Tom spread his fingers to seize Amelia's arm.

Amelia murmured, "Mahogany, my love. Stay calm," and she reached into her pocket.

In her shock at Jinson's death, she hadn't noticed the weight of the long pistol. Now, as she drew it from the pocket of her borrowed skirt, it nearly slipped from her fingers. She hissed a breath and gripped it more tightly as the fear of dropping it sent sparks of alarm along her nerves. She pulled it out into the dim light of early dawn, and pointed it at the man called Jake. The yellow flicker of the gas lamp shone on its oiled barrel.

Deliberately, as if she had done it a thousand times, Amelia pulled back the cock with her thumbs, then held the heavy pistol in both hands.

Tom gasped, and stepped back. "Jake! She has a—"

Jake froze where he was. The hobnailed bludgeon wavered, then lowered. "I see it," he said.

The third man, whose name Amelia had not heard, was not laughing now. "Zito's ass, Jake, them things can kill a man."

"I believe," Amelia said icily, "that's what they're for."

"Now," Jake said uncertainly. "What would a lass like you know about such things?"

"I know this," Amelia said. "This pistol is no good for shooting rabbits. It makes far too big a hole. It spoils the meat."

She felt Mahogany's warmth radiating through her. He had steadied when she had, and was standing very still, supporting her with the strength of his muscled shoulder almost as if he had an arm to put around her. His near wing flexed slightly against the wingclip, but his feet were planted firmly on the cobblestones.

Amelia smiled. "And now," she said. "You ruffians will back away, all of you."

"Ruffians!" Jake started to lift his bludgeon again. Amelia set her feet wide, lifted her arms with the elbows bent, and pointed Slater's pistol right at his midriff.

"You wouldn't dare," he said, but she heard the note of doubt in his gruff voice.

"Well, sir," she said. "It will be your privilege to find out."

"Jake," Tom began, but Jake growled some inarticulate warning and fell silent.

The third man had slipped away, around the corner and into the darkness. Tom looked longingly after him and took a step in that direction. Jake said, "Tom. Grab her arm."

Tom answered, "Not me, Jake. You wants her arm grabbed, you do it yourself!" and he, too, was gone, with a clatter of boots on stone.

Amelia hardly dared to breathe. She and the man named Jake stared at each other in the growing light, each of them breathing curls of mist that rose and dissipated in the icy air. Amelia thought, irrelevantly, that the air smelled like that at Marinan before a snowstorm.

Jake finally gave up. He clanked his bludgeon against the stones and half turned. Over his shoulder, he said, "You wouldn't shoot a poor man in the back, lass?"

She said, "I make no promises. Would you have struck me with your nasty club?"

He gave her a narrow-eyed look, then walked slowly away, the bludgeon dangling by his leg. Not until he reached the corner did he break into an awkward run, and disappear.

Amelia held herself straight for several seconds, and then let herself slump against Mahogany. Her wrists bent, and pointed the gun at the cobblestones. "Mahogany!" she breathed. "I was so frightened!" And in a mere whisper, she added, "Next time, my love, I must be certain there is a bullet in the gun before I threaten to use it!"

Mahogany blew lightly against her shoulder as if he agreed. She laughed softly, straightened, and tucked the long pistol back into her pocket. She took Mahogany's lead, and they started off once more in the direction of the bay.

With every step the smell of salt and fish grew stronger, and she could see, through the close-set buildings of the poor neighborhood, flashes of light from the North Tower.

"Soon," she said to Mahogany, as they wended their way through the tangled lanes, "soon we will put an end to all this and go back to the Academy where we belong."

TWENTY-FIVE

PHILIPPA scanned the sky as she crossed the courtyard to the stables in the early morning. It looked and smelled like snow. By the time she reached the hay-scented warmth of the tack room, her hands and nose stung with cold.

She stopped just past the tack-room door, on her way to Sunny's stall. Something was different, and it was not the weather. She shook her head, wondering what it was that had struck her. She couldn't think of it, and she went on down the aisle.

It wasn't until the girls came in, twittering excitedly, that she realized the militiamen posted beside the Hall had vanished in the night.

When she heard Larkyn's voice in the aisle, and Hester's deeper one, she left Sunny and went across to where they were both raking old straw from their horses' stalls.

Larkyn looked up. "Mistress Winter! Did you see, the militia have gone?"

"I did. Does anyone know what it means?"

Hester came out of Golden Morning's stall, and set her pitchfork carefully in the aisle, its tines turned toward the wall. "I'm afraid they went to tell the Duke you're back."

"But," Larkyn protested, "that wouldn't take all of them! They're all gone, every one, and none have come to replace them!"

Philippa looked around at the other stalls, where girls were cleaning, carrying water, measuring grain. "It seems there is peace among you girls this morning," she said.

"Nay," Larkyn said bluntly. "No more than yesterday. Everyone thinks this means something different."

Philippa arched an eyebrow. "Indeed? What do they think?"

Hester said, "On our side, we think the militia deserted the Duke's service. On the opposite side, Beryl and Lillian and the others, they think they went to fight the Klee."

"That's foolish," Philippa said with asperity. "Beryl should know better. They could only do that under orders. Did any orders come?"

Hester shrugged. "Not that we know of. Perhaps Mistress Star knows something."

"Perhaps." Philippa turned to go back to Sunny, but one of the first-level girls came running, skidding to a stop in the sawdust, and hastily inclining her head to her.

"Mistress Winter?" she asked.

"Yes. Who are you?" Philippa said.

The girl barely stopped herself from curtsying, and Philippa's lips twitched slightly. "Sorry, Mistress," she said, coloring.

Hester, always the diplomat, stepped up beside Philippa. "Mistress Winter, this is Edith Early, bonded to Early Spring."

Philippa nodded. "Hello, Edith. That's a venerable name your bondmate carries."

"Yes, Mistress, I know." The girl stared at Philippa with open-mouthed curiosity, and seemed to have forgotten her mission.

"What do you want, Edith?" Philippa prodded.

"Oh! Oh, sorry, Mistress." Edith blushed harder. "Mistress Star sent me to ask you to come to her office. There's a visitor—" The girl seemed to forget her embarrassment all at once and bounced a little on her toes as if her body could hardly contain her energy. "Mistress, it's Lord Francis. The Duke's brother. And he has someone with him." The girl's eyes flickered over Larkyn, then swiftly away.

PHILIPPA crossed the foyer of the Hall with an eager step. She knocked on Suzanne's door, then opened it to find Suzanne at her desk and Francis standing beside the window, the cool light gleaming on his white-blond hair. It struck her for the hundredth time how different the Fleckham features, the black eyes and narrow nose, could look on different men.

"My lord Francis," she said warmly, and held out her hands to him. "My friend."

He took them, pressing them in his own, and gave her a tired smile. "Philippa. I'm glad to see you home again."

His eyes went past her, and she turned to follow his gaze.

A tall, broad-shouldered man stood leaning against the opposite wall, holding a boiled-wool hat in his hands. His black hair, shot through with gray, was cut much shorter than was fashionable for Osham. His sun-browned face was just as she remembered it, strong-featured and firm-lipped.

Philippa's cheeks warmed. She forced herself to incline her head, to meet his eyes with a composed smile. She hoped her cheeks weren't flaming.

"Master Hamley," she said. "It's good to see you. It's been a long time."

He bowed. "Lord Francis is right," he said. "You look very well, Mistress Winter."

He took her hand in his, and her own fingers felt like bird bones in the crush of his strong ones. On an impulse, she put out her other hand, to hold his hand between her two palms. The contact felt indescribably warm, and she began to feel better than she had in days. "Brye, have you heard from Nick? Is he well?"

He shook his head. A lock of hair fell across his forehead. "Haven't heard a word. Hard not to worry."

"It must be. I'm sorry." She released his hand and turned back to Francis. "What news, Francis? And how did you know I was here?"

Francis left the window and sprawled in a chair opposite Suzanne, extending his long legs across the carpet. "You'll have noticed the militia posted here at the Academy have all gone," he said.

"Yes. The girls were all talking about it this morning."

"Those men came to me," he said wearily. "All but two of them."

"Francis—that must be a good thing."

"It is," he said. "But it means—almost without our planning it—that the lines have been drawn between the citizenry who support my brother and those who don't."

"We're seeing it here, too," Suzanne said quietly.

Philippa pulled her gloves out of her belt to pleat them between her fingers as she paced the office. "When you say they came to you, Francis, what does that mean?"

"They came to Beeth House, because the word is out now. Beeth and I—and Daysmith and Chatham and a few others— saw this coming. When Rys's ship showed up, we thought we'd better organize the resistance."

"You have a militia of your own?"

"I never wanted to oppose my brother, Philippa; you know that. But he's well over the line now, and I'm concerned for the future of the Duchy. Many of our people think he's dragging them into a war over one abducted girl." He rubbed his eyes with the heels of his hands. "I assume Amelia Rys is why you came back at this particular moment, Philippa."

"She's our responsibility, of course," she said. "I have no doubt William took her to force me to return. I couldn't ignore that. And since I've come back"—she glanced at Suzanne—"I find that the Academy itself, all of us who fly the winged horses, are at risk."

"If William succeeds in flying this filly, I don't know what will happen."

Philippa walked to the window and put her back to it. "And Master Hamley? Your reason for being here?"

"Heard things," he said. "The only way to find out was to come."

"And now," Suzanne said, holding out a rolled parchment with the Ducal seal blazoned on the side, "we have this."

"What is it?" Philippa asked.

"Orders from Duke William. He wants every horsemistress and third-level girl to report to the Rotunda stables. The order says they're to be ready to fly against the Klee."

Philippa folded her gloves back into her belt and linked her hands before her. "He would send students into a battle." It wasn't a question, and no one tried to answer it.

Francis stood up. "I have to get back to Beeth House," he said. "There are skirmishes already in the city between the loyalists and the resistance. People are afraid to go out in the streets, to go to their shops or their jobs. If William means to attack Rys's ship, we have to do something to stop that."

"It's a civil war," Brye Hamley said.

"That's it, isn't it?" Philippa said. "William has sparked a civil war." She shook her head and sighed. "We should pray that his filly refuses to fly with him. That could put an end to this insanity."

FRANCIS led the way out of Suzanne's office. As they all stepped out into the frosty morning, Philippa was exquisitely aware of Brye Hamley's broad shoulder beside her own, of his greater height, the sheer strength of his presence. It was a relief when Larkyn dashed up the steps to embrace her brother and begin pestering him with questions.

Philippa left them to their reunion and spoke to Francis. "What do you want us to do?"

He said, "Refuse the Duke's order. Stay where you are, out of danger."

"Of course I'll refuse the order," she said. "But I can't speak for everyone."

"I understand. And I don't have the authority to countermand it."

The women and girls of the Academy began to gather in the courtyard, coming out of the stables, of the Dormitory and Residence, standing together in the cold. The oc-hounds came, too, drawn by the intensity of feeling. They stood among the flyers like silver-gray sentinels, their tails waving slowly, their eyes, like everyone else's, fixed on Philippa and Suzanne.

No, on herself, Philippa thought. Though Suzanne was the Headmistress, somehow it was to her they were turning, seeking guidance, though she had not stood on these steps in nearly a year and a half. Even Suzanne turned to her, holding out the missive from the Ducal Palace.

"Talk to them, Philippa, please," she said in a low voice. "I don't know what to say."

Reluctantly, Philippa took the parchment. "I've never been

popular, Suzanne," she said. "I'm not quite certain why this falls to me."

"Because you should have been Head," Suzanne said simply. "We all know that."

"But you *are* Headmistress, Suzanne," Philippa began. "And a fine one—"

Suzanne interrupted her, shaking her head. "Just read it to them, Philippa. There's nothing I can say to change their minds."

Philippa hesitated. Bramble trotted up the steps to sit at her feet, facing the courtyard. Philippa touched her silky head. "Good girl," she murmured. She fumbled briefly with the stiff parchment before she could unroll it.

She scanned its text, then lifted her eyes to the faces below. Some of the girls were shivering in the chill.

Philippa said, "Good morning, everyone." No one answered. The oc-hounds stirred, moving a foot, waving a plumy tail. Bramble cocked one ear toward Philippa.

She held out the parchment. "This order came this morning from the Ducal Palace. Lord Francis and the other lords who support the Academy—who have given of their property and risked their positions for us—have asked us to refuse it." She let the silence stretch as she tried to meet every eye in the courtyard. Then she opened the parchment, and began to read it aloud.

SHE supposed, as she watched a half dozen horsemistresses and three third-level girls launch from the end of the flight paddock, that she should be grateful there weren't more. The junior horsemistress Sarah Runner stood beside her. She held her shoulders straight and her head high, but her eyes were suspiciously red. She said shakily, "It feels like the end of the world."

Philippa nodded grimly. "Precisely so, Sarah. Imagine how our girls feel."

Both horsemistresses looked across the courtyard to the students clustered in the door of the stables. Several, Philippa saw with a heavy heart, wept openly. Hester and Larkyn and

Anabel, their faces stony, stood watching their classmates flying away from them. When they were gone, those three—and Grace, whose independent spirit had come as something of a surprise—came across the cobblestones to incline their heads to Lord Francis. They looked as if the last shreds of their innocence had been torn away. Philippa would have given almost anything to put them back.

It was Hester who spoke for them. That one would always gather followers to her—if she had the chance.

"Lord Francis," Hester said. "Larkyn Black, Anabel Chance, and Grace Spring join me, Hester Morning, in offering you our services."

Francis's nod was grave, and not in the least condescending. He knew, Philippa thought, that it might indeed come to this, as the struggle with his brother intensified. "Thank you," he said. "We all understand how difficult this decision was for you to make."

Hester made a gesture with her head toward the stables. "Isobel has taken a neutral position, my lord," she said. "So you can see that we are divided right down the middle."

Philippa blew out a breath. "Come, Hester," she said, "and the rest of you. Let's get everyone into the hall, out of the cold, and hear what Lord Francis would like us to do."

Before they trooped indoors, Brye Hamley came to bow to Philippa and take his leave. "I'm going in search of Nick. I'll send him to Beeth House, if I can find him," he said with grim purpose. "Lord Francis will be expecting him."

"Has Jolinda provided you with a horse?" Philippa asked.

"She has, thanks," he said. With a touch of his fingers to the drooping brim of his hat, he was gone. She lingered on the steps to watch his tall figure cross the courtyard to the stables. If there must be conflict, she was grateful to stand on the same side as such a man.

She turned then and went with a heavy step into the foyer of the Hall. The threatened snow began to fall before she closed the doors, and she hoped her colleagues and her students were safely to ground before it grew too heavy.

She watched the horsemistresses and their students take their seats in silence. Lord Francis stepped up beside the high table. His coat and trousers were black, but the silver insignia of Oc was conspicuously missing from his belt and his collar. Philippa had the strange thought that they might have to change the signature color of the Duke's service, then pushed that away. It was hard enough to believe they were actually going to oppose William openly, without trying to guess what the future might hold.

First, she hoped to find a way to prevent winged horses from being sent into battle.

And she hoped she could find out what had happened to Amelia Rys.

TWENTY-SIX

WILLIAM wore a long, heavy wool cloak with a high mink collar. Its hem was damp by the time he crossed the plaza to the Rotunda steps. Constance trailed behind him, wrapped in ermine, with a hood pulled over her hair. The sky lowered above the dome. The colorful pennants, one for each of the thirty-eight noble families, drooped under flurries of snow. William paused at the top of the steps, looking out past the live oak to where the horsemistresses and the Academy students waited with their mounts. The paltry number of them—surely no more than ten or twelve—appalled him.

He snarled at his secretary, who was walking behind him, "I want the name of every horsemistress and student flyer there."

"Yes, my lord."

"And then I want a list of all horsemistresses who did not obey my order." William turned toward the Rotunda, but he said over his shoulder, "I want the students' names, too. The third-levels who didn't come."

He heard shock in the man's hushed tone as he repeated, "Yes, Your Grace," but he ignored it. He strode on through the great double doors, his cloak swirling over the marble floor. They would all pay, every woman and girl who had ignored his command. He would be a horsemaster before a week was out. No, before another day had passed. If the weather would only clear, he would fly Diamond tomorrow.

As he passed into the warmth of the Rotunda, he heard what sounded like a gunshot from the region of the docks. He glanced to his left and saw that the Council guards were all looking in that direction.

Well, let them look. A few skirmishes were nothing. Great

accomplishments required sacrifices. Once he had proved himself, peace would settle over the Duchy again. And it would be peace on *his* terms.

He stalked down the tiered steps to the carved chair awaiting him in the center. Constance scurried behind him. The Council Lords were already gathered, and someone, it seemed, had been speaking. All fell silent as he entered, and rose to their feet. Even the ladies and their maids in the gallery ceased their whispers and rustles.

He gave them a negligent wave and settled into his chair, letting his smallsword fall to one side. Slowly, with some scraping of chairs, murmuring to aides and secretaries, the Lords of Oc's Council sat down again. Constance's maid helped her to wriggle out of her fur cloak and readjusted the rope of pearls that wound around her neck and hung nearly to her waist. William gave her a disdainful look. He hated those pearls. He had been persuaded to give them to her as a wedding present, and he couldn't think why he had ever wasted his money on such ostentation.

Her gaze flickered up to his, then away to the ladies in the gallery. She wore no expression on her face at all, but it seemed to William she was less shy than she had been previously. She was less . . . Was it fearful? He didn't know what had given her this little burst of courage.

Well, it wasn't important. Constance mattered far less than Diamond.

He leaned back in his chair, propping his chin on his fist, and gave his Council a defiant look. "My lords of Oc," he said. "It's good to be with you again."

For an uncomfortable moment, no one answered, then Meredith Islington stood up. "We know you've been busy, Your Grace. We welcome you back to the Council."

William eyed the other men. One or two nodded agreement with Islington. Others scowled, leaning back in their chairs as if to absent themselves from the exchange. Most sat squarely, noncommittally. William smiled.

"We could hardly be unaware," he said, "that there is dissension in the Duchy. We have come today to reassure you that our ultimate goal is nearly in hand."

Old Lord Daysmith struggled to his feet, aided by a secretary who jumped up from the stool beside him. Daysmith glowered down the tiers at William, and William stared back, lifting one questioning brow.

"Duke William," Daysmith said in his quavering voice. "Your patrol boats are firing on a Klee ship in our harbor. Our citizens are imagining a war with the Klee. Gangs of brigands roam the streets because there is no guard to control them. The Council Lords would like to know just what your goal is and why you've allowed the peace of the Duchy to be so disturbed."

The old fool, William thought bitterly. He thought he had nothing to lose, that his age and infirmity protected him.

But he kept the smile on his face and spoke lightly. "The arrival of the Klee ship proves the need for an expanded militia, does it not?"

Another lord leaped to his feet. This one was Billings, who needed no assistance. He was younger even than Francis, newly come into his title. "Your Grace," he said loudly. "I demand you release the Klee Viscount's niece!"

"*You* demand?" William said in an icy tone. "You forget yourself, my lord."

Billings gave a negligent shrug that set William's teeth on edge. "It is you, Your Grace, who forgets. You've forgotten your duty to your people." He sat down amid a few murmurs of agreement and one or two exclamations of protest at his brashness.

William's smile had faded, but he kept his face impassive. "You may know, my lords," he said, "that the horse-mistress Philippa Winter—with neither my knowledge nor my permission—bartered a position at the Academy of the Air for the use of a Klee ship to go into Aeskland."

"As our own militia should have done," someone called.

William whipped his head around to see who had spoken, but he was too late. He had left his secretary outside, and he supposed it would be no good asking Constance. She lounged in her chair, playing with the cursed pearls, and gazing idly up into the balcony.

Islington countered, "The risk was too great. Indeed, the Duke's own brother was injured, almost fatally."

Someone else put in, "Two of our own citizens—children—were kidnapped!"

And another said, "They were only peasants," causing an uproar of argument.

William dropped his chin and regarded the lords from beneath his brows. He waited for the hubbub to subside. When the Rotunda was quiet again, he nodded. "Lord Islington is right," he said. "Our brother almost died in that foolhardy adventure. We're glad to say, however, that he's now fully restored to health. And we think it behooves us all to talk about the future and not the past."

"Your Grace." Another man stood. It was Chatham this time. He was a grave man, who spoke seldom, and who commanded every ear when he did decide to raise his voice.

William eyed him.

"Your Grace," Chatham said, evidently unperturbed, "there are those of us who object to your inciting this war with the Klee."

William let his lip curl. "My lord Chatham," he purred, "you are in error. We have not incited a war."

"And the girl?" Billings called, without bothering to rise. "That's incitement enough!"

William felt heat in his throat and his cheeks, and his heart pounded dangerously. It was the potion, he thought. He had never before had such difficulty keeping his nerve. Beside him, Constance turned in her chair, eyeing him with that oddly avid expression. Damn her, too. He would have a word with her later about loyalty, and appearances.

He forced his voice to an even pitch. "We understand, my lords, that feeling is high here in our Council at the moment, so we will forgive some slight discourtesy. But we wish to make it very clear that we oppose any bonding of a winged horse to a foreigner."

"A little late for that, is it not?" Daysmith called.

William glared at him. "Philippa Winter acted illegally in agreeing to this bonding. The winged horses of Oc are not for sale."

Lord Beeth stood up. No doubt, William thought sourly, his lady was sending him signals from the gallery, although

Beeth showed no sign of it. He folded his arms. "Your Grace, I believe Horsemistress Winter received your permission. After you received a letter from Lord Francis."

William's heart fluttered again, and his eyes began to sting. The thought that he might actually lose control in front of the Council filled him with rage. "They manipulated the law!" he shouted. "And upon reflection—" His voice shook, and he gripped the arm of his chair to steady himself. More calmly, he said, "Upon reflection, we have decided their action should not stand."

Lord Beeth's mouth twisted, and he sat down. Billings half rose, but Daysmith interrupted. "Duke William! Let's stop this nonsense before men begin dying!"

"My lord Daysmith," William said. "When we send our winged horses against the Klee ship, to support the patrol boats, they will leave the harbor, we have no doubt. Then we can—negotiate with them for the return of the girl." He tugged at his vest. "But not the horse," he added lightly. "The colt belongs to Oc."

"But what about this Fleckham School?" Daysmith demanded. "And what about the Academy of the Air?"

William raised one hand. "We beg your patience, my lords. Had it not been for this unseasonable snow, we should have had great news for you this very day. But soon, I promise you. Perhaps even tomorrow."

"Duke William." It was Chatham again. Every head in the Council turned to face him. Even Constance twisted in her place to look.

"Do you have something to add, my lord?" William asked.

"I do, Your Grace." Chatham looked around at the other men, and nodded as if he had counted them and found them sufficient. "We have no desire to keep secrets from you, Duke William," he said. "But we have formed a small force to prevent you from attacking the Klee."

"What!" William exclaimed. He smacked the broad, carved arm of his chair with the flat of his hand. "How dare you! Which among you dared to—"

Chatham put up a hand, just as if he himself were the Duke. William's heart beat so loudly he could hardly hear as

Chatham said, "For the good of our people, Your Grace, we intend to prevent this war."

"You forget," William cried, a little shrilly, "that they are my people, too! They will obey their Duke!"

"Or his brother."

This was Billings, lounging in his seat, one leg crossed over the other. A shocked silence fell at his pronouncement.

William stared at him, feeling as if the floor had suddenly spun beneath his feet. He only just stopped himself from repeating, "Brother?"

He should have seen it. Francis was not present, but he rarely attended Council meetings, having no real role. Francis. A traitor after all. No doubt Francis meant to steal his throne.

"No one will follow a usurper," Meredith Islington called.

William stood and lifted Constance to her feet. He propelled her ahead of him up the tiers toward the doors. At the top, he stopped, and faced the Council.

"We warn you," he said, very softly. "Those of you who dare to betray us. When we have flown—when your Duke is a true horsemaster—no one will dare defy us. You will regret your faithlessness. A new day is about to dawn in Oc."

With that, he turned in a swirl of wool and mink, and left the chamber.

NOT until they were in the carriage, with Constance tucked under a goat's-hair lap robe, did she speak. She looked up at him, with that odd, avaricious look in her eye. "I was under the impression the girl had escaped," she said softly.

"Don't be an idiot, Constance," William snapped, and turned away from her to look out the carriage window. The snow had stopped, and the streets gleamed wet and gray. "The Council doesn't need to know everything."

"No?" Constance smoothed the silken nap of the lap robe and pulled her ermine collar closer around her slender neck. "Naturally I thought they might. Since Slater tried to drag the child down to the port to show her to the Klee."

William had to fight the urge to grip that long rope of

pearls and twist it until Constance's little white face turned blue. For a moment he dared not speak. When he thought he could control his voice, he said, "My lady wife, I would advise you not to listen to gossip. If I think you need to know something"—he glanced at her over his shoulder, without turning from the window—"I will tell you."

She dropped her eyelids in her usual demure fashion, but not before he had seen the spark in them, the faint light of some other reaction he could not quite name. "Yes, my lord," she said.

"Constance—"

She pulled the ermine closer around her, hiding the pearls. "Yes, William."

"The situation in Oc is complicated at the moment. I require absolute loyalty."

Now her own eyes drifted out to the wet scenes of the city rolling by. "Of course, William," she said, a little vaguely. "Of course."

He tried to concentrate on what was to come, on what he needed to do to be ready to fly tomorrow. But once they had arrived at the Ducal Palace, and he had left the carriage to go into the stables, he still wondered. If even his Duchess hesitated . . . doubted him . . .

It didn't matter, he told himself as he gathered a scoop of oats and a brush from the tack room. He needed only one more day.

TWENTY-SEVEN

AMELIA huddled with Mahogany in a shadowy, fish-scented warehouse that seemed to have been abandoned. After escaping the three who had detained her in the street, she had led her colt as quickly as she dared through the cramped lanes down toward the docks. She soon understood that the ruffians she had already met were not the only ones abroad in the night.

It was Mahogany who had found their present hiding place. They dashed into an alley when they heard shouts nearby, and then shots. A bullet cracked a lamppost terrifyingly near Amelia's head. The two of them shrank back against a rough brick wall and waited for the sounds to die away, then, breathlessly, they crept on their way again, staying in the shadows, trying to find their way through the maze of lanes and alleys toward the North Tower. Its light, flashing on and off out over the harbor, seemed to Amelia to be alternately coaxing her and mocking her.

She knew the pattern she wanted from that light. She thought she could persuade the keeper to do it, to send the message to her father, but first, she had to find a way to arrive at the Tower in one piece.

As she and Mahogany moved slowly toward the bay, the morning light turned from gray to a frosty silver, and snowflakes began to fall in random flurries. The lampkeepers came along the streets and snuffed out the gas lamps. Amelia hid even from them. She felt she could no longer trust anyone. Everyone in the world seemed to have taken sides in this strange conflict, and it seemed to her that all she could do was eliminate at least one element of the struggle. She had to let the *Marinan* know that she was here, that she was alive, that she was free.

As they passed the warehouse, Mahogany slowed and pulled back against the lead.

"What is it?" Amelia whispered to him. He had never before resisted the lead. She looked back at him, and he tossed his head and backed a couple of steps. She glanced ahead, anxious that he had seen or heard something she had missed.

There was movement on the docks now, militiamen, she thought, walking back and forth on patrol. The fishing boats bobbed uselessly at their moorage. There could be no fishing, not with the mouth of the harbor blocked and the patrol boats firing at odd intervals on the *Marinan*. No imports, no exports, no fish . . . the Duke had done a thorough job of paralyzing Osham.

Mahogany couldn't know any of that, but he clearly sensed the danger around them. He took another step backward, then, to her astonishment, he dipped his head, and took the loop of the halter lead between his teeth.

"What, Mahogany?" she whispered. "Where do you want me to go?"

Obviously satisfied that he had her full attention, Mahogany released the lead and sidestepped neatly into the wide doorway of the warehouse. It was open. Fingers of light stretched past barrels and stacked nets, and illuminated coils of astoundingly thick ropes. When Amelia followed Mahogany inside to stand beside him on the cold plank flooring, her nose assured her this must be where fishmongers could come to collect their wares. But now, with the boats idle, there were no fish to sell. Except for the bits of abandoned equipment, the warehouse was empty.

She hugged Mahogany's warm neck. "Thank you," she said, with sincerity. It was warmer in the warehouse, and though Mahogany's hooves echoed in the emptiness, accentuating their isolation, it was good to feel safe, at least for the moment.

As a few people began to move about in the street, Amelia pondered her choices. Surely, she thought, with the warehousemen and the stevedores about, the lawless gangs would vanish to whatever den they had come from. Still, she and

Mahogany would attract attention. The only horses anyone would expect to see around the docks were the draft horses pulling carts and wagons full of goods from the ships. At the moment, there were no ships, and no goods. And, of course, winged horses should fly above the port, not clop along it like their flightless brothers. She had no way to hide Mahogany's glossy wings.

She found a barrel of mostly clean water at the back of the warehouse and moved the lid aside so Mahogany could drink his fill. When he was done, she drank some herself, cupping it in her palms. It smelled only slightly of fish. She thought it must be rainwater. After she had cleaned the worst of the brambles and stickers from Mahogany's mane and tail, she led him back to the open doorway and stood in the shadows peering out into the street.

"We'll simply walk there, Mahogany," she said. He blew through his nostrils and nudged her shoulder with his muzzle. "Yes, I believe you're right," she said. "There's no point in lurking here all day until night comes again, and the gangs come out. Are you ready?"

He blew again, and she patted him, then stepped out into the dreary, snow-spattered lane.

Two men in thick jackets and wide-legged canvas trousers were just turning the corner, walking toward her. They stopped where they were, goggling at the sight of a girl in a bedraggled riding habit and a slender-legged winged horse strolling between the warehouse loading docks. Amelia lifted her head, keeping her eyes fixed on the silhouette of the North Tower, and walked on as if her being there were the most natural thing in the world.

Her cheeks burned, though the air was icy. Occasional snowflakes drifted past the slanting roofs and unpainted walls of the warehouses and sheds she passed. When she reached the first corner, she paused, with Mahogany's nose touching the back of her neck. She peered toward the bay, where she could see the masts and furled sails of the fishing boats rocking gently in their moorage. A patrol boat, flying the black-and-silver flag of the Duke, was just sailing out into the harbor, several men in its prow, its carronades bristling on the deck. In the other direction, past a jumble of weathered buildings that spilled away from the bay, she saw the slender spire of the North Tower.

A sense of renewed urgency gripped her. She set off down the nearest street that seemed to curve in the direction of the Tower, trying to look as if she knew where she was going.

For ten minutes or so she and Mahogany walked on. Twice more, men stopped to stare at her, and once a woman in a heavy canvas apron and what looked like a filleting knife in her hand came to the door of a dilapidated shop with a sign carved into the shape of a fish. The woman stood staring, openmouthed, as Amelia and Mahogany came down her street. As they passed, Amelia inclined her head. The woman gawked at her, dropped the knife into a capacious pocket in her apron, then curtsied.

Amelia smiled at this and walked on. Mahogany matched his steps to hers. They turned down a lane here, a street there, trying to find their way to the Tower. Amelia, despite having had no rest at all during the night, felt energized by having her goal within reach. She picked up the pace, and Mahogany's hooves beat a neat pattern on the stones as they pressed forward.

They had just reached a wider street, not quite a boulevard, but at least a road where Amelia could imagine wagons passing, when a little formation of men in black uniforms came marching toward her. Someone shouted an order, and the men stopped. They, too, stared at Amelia, and at the bay horse at her shoulder.

One of them said, just loud enough for her to hear, "Zito's ass, Wallace, them's wings on that horse."

And the one who had given the order to halt said, "It's the Klee girl!" He pulled a smallsword from a scabbard at his belt, and brandished it at Amelia. "This is our lucky day, boys. Just what the Duke ordered up, and she's walked right into our arms!"

As a group, the men started across the wide street toward Amelia and Mahogany. Mahogany threw up his head and flared his nostrils, but he held his ground. Amelia froze for only an instant.

Then, with a hiss of indrawn breath, she turned toward Mahogany. "Hold very still, my love," she murmured. "We'll be faster if I ride."

Mahogany trembled as the scent of the men grew stronger. Amelia braced herself, wound her left hand in his mane, and kept the halter lead loose in her right. She leaped, and landed neatly on his back, her legs settling over his folded wings. She pressed her left calf against his pinions. "Go, Mahogany!" she cried. "Go!"

And Mahogany, as if they had done just this a thousand times, whirled on his hindquarters, his tail brushing the snow-dampened cobblestones, and dashed away from the uniformed men.

They shouted curses and commands, but Amelia never looked back. She leaned over Mahogany's neck to watch for potholes or splits in the cobblestones, frantic with anxiety that Mahogany might slip on the wet street or catch a hoof in a gap.

When the shouts faded behind them, she lifted the lead of the halter and gently pulled. "Slower, now," she said. "I don't want you to fall, Mahogany!"

Obediently, as if he understood every word, Mahogany slowed to the running walk. It was at least twice as quick a pace as Amelia could walk, so she stayed where she was.

A shot sounded from the harbor and was answered a moment later by another. People came out of their shops and leaned from the windows of houses, trying to see, calling to each other. When they saw Amelia and Mahogany, they halted to stare.

One woman, who had unshuttered her window and peered out toward the harbor, called to her. "Miss! Miss! Do you know if the Klee are coming?"

Amelia's blood ran cold at the implication. Mutely, she shook her head, and she and Mahogany were past the woman's house a moment later.

The Klee coming? Is that what the people of Oc thought?

"Kalla's heels," she muttered. "We have to hurry!"

FROM the roof of the Academy Hall, not long after the midday meal, the remaining students and horsemistresses gathered to look out toward the White City, transfixed and horrified.

They had been listening to the carronades all morning. A shot would fire across the water, to be answered a moment later by another. Everyone held their breath, or stifled groans. Lark offered wordless, helpless prayers, for Nick, for Brye, for Amelia.

The balcony ran all the way around the building, interrupted only by the facade facing the courtyard. As snow melted on the cobblestones of the courtyard, the girls and their instructors gathered to watch their colleagues and their friends take flight from the park of the Rotunda.

He had sent them all. A proper flight was seven horses, but in this case there were twelve of them, nine from the Academy and three who must have come from other posts. The formation banked to the right, and flew above the warehouses of the dock district and on toward the bay.

Lark pressed her hands over her heart. "So beautiful," she breathed.

Jolinda stood beside her, her fists on her hips, her wrinkled face set. "Oh, aye," Jolinda said. "Beautiful they are. And foolish."

"They think they're doing their duty."

"Aye," Jolinda answered dourly. "The old Duke would never have done such a thing, sending untried girls against carronades! He'd turn in his grave if he knew."

On Lark's other side, Anabel sniffled back tears. Hester was beside her, an arm over her shoulders. Anabel said brokenly, "Surely, Baron Rys has no wish to fire on winged horses."

"Nay," Lark said. " 'Tis certain he doesn't."

"The patrol boats are using the flight as cover," Hester said. Lark glanced up at her. Her face looked as if it had been carved of stone. "If the patrol boats fire on the ship, the ship has to fire back."

"But the horses . . ." Anabel said faintly.

Isobel, her face strained, had also come up the stairs to stand with them in the cold afternoon. The second- and first-level girls huddled near the wall. Mistress Star stood beside Mistress Winter, and Kathryn Dancer and the other junior instructors, chores and classes abandoned, whispered together near the door.

Everyone fell silent as the flyers coalesced into the great vee of Open Columns, then, as they flew out over the water, they closed their ranks.

Close Columns was a military formation. It was designed to break into the frightening maneuver called Arrows at a moment's notice, the horses flashing toward their target at a steep angle, recovering at the last moment to arrow back up into the sky.

Lark could hardly believe, even now, that Duke William would send these flyers against the Klee. Her heart pounded with fear, and she could feel the beat of Anabel's pulse through her arm where she gripped it. Over the Moon, leading the formation, was an arrow of silver against the heavy gray clouds that hung over the bay. A sorrel and a bay followed, and then the roan mare flown by Caroline Rambler. Beryl's chestnut Sky Heart was in the near column, his flaxen mane and tail barely visible in the dull light. Beatrice's Dark Lad, a gelding almost as dark as Tup, came after Sky Heart. The column paused, then the front horses descended sharply. A moment later the sound of a carronade reached the watchers. They could just make out the faint outline of the sails of the Klee ship. The patrol boats were too small and low for them to see, but they saw a puff of smoke rise from the water to blend with the clouds.

Lark gasped, and Anabel cried out as one of the first-levels screamed. Hester grunted something wordless.

It was the roan, in the middle of its Arrows dive, that spun backward with a sudden, terrible jerk of its body and tumbled slowly and agonizingly, toward the sea. It was too far to see the horsemistress's efforts to save it, to guide it to a splash it might survive. Before the horse struck the water, the rider was thrown free, her skirt flaring as she fell. Both horse and horsemistress disappeared behind the roofs of the city buildings.

Suzanne Star was moaning, "Oh, gods! No! It's Rambler!"

"Kalla's teeth," Philippa Winter muttered, as the rest of the flight pulled out of its formation and rose again against the gray clouds. The student flyers, at the end of the columns, banked with the leaders, flying up and out of the carronades' reach.

"Can they save him?" someone cried. Lark thought it was

Isobel, but she couldn't tear her eyes away from the awful sight of the harbor and her classmates flying above it.

"No," Mistress Winter said harshly. "He's injured, and his wings are open. They'll drag him down. Someone will save Caroline, I suppose, though she may wish they had not."

Sobs and cries of horror rose around them on the balcony. Even Sarah Runner began to weep aloud.

Mistress Winter said loudly, "No hysteria! It will upset our horses. Control yourselves." The cries were abruptly muffled, but Lark heard girls choking back tears. Her own throat ached with them, but she thrust out her chin and patted the silently weeping Anabel. She told herself she could grieve for Rambler later. She cast a glance to her left to see that Hester, too, was dry-eyed, though her face was stiff with shock.

All of them watched as the flight of winged horses hovered at Quarters. There were no more cannon shots. As the flight reassembled in Open Columns, it had one glaringly empty place. Lark could hardly bear it. The distance, and the silence, gave the entire scene the feeling of unreality. It was like a nightmare, she thought, when you know you will wake up soon, and realize none of it is real. It almost seemed that Rambler and Caroline would rise above the horizon after all, and join their fellows.

But that wasn't going to happen. A beautiful winged horse had just been lost. A horsemistress's life had been ruined in a moment, in a puff of smoke and the clap of a cannon. And for what?

A moment later, Matron hurried up the stairs and out onto the balcony, breathing hard. She had a rolled message in her hand. She carried it straight to where Mistress Winter and Mistress Star stood side by side. The two horsemistresses exchanged a glance, then Mistress Winter unrolled the letter, and they both leaned over it.

Lark was trying to think of something comforting to say to Anabel when she heard Mistress Star say, "Philippa! Don't you think—"

But Philippa Winter's straight back was already disappearing down the stairs. Mistress Star was a step behind her. Jolinda, without a word, and having received no order that Lark could see, hurried after them. Moments later Mistress Winter emerged from the double doors below the balcony, buttoning her flying coat. She pulled on her peaked cap as she strode down the steps, and by the time she had crossed the courtyard she had her gloves on and her quirt swinging at her belt. There was no sign of Mistress Star, but Jolinda came scuttling after Mistress Winter, to dash ahead of her into the stables.

Lark turned her eyes back toward the sea just in time to see the double line of horses banking beyond the Klee ship. The ship's sails were full, and it tacked across the mouth of the bay. They all heard the sounds of cannon, and saw puffs of smoke. There was an answering shot as the line of horses swept down and across the bow of the ship. Another carronade flashed, smoke rose, and the Klee ship tacked again, slowly and ponderously, like a great fat lady dancing in wide skirts.

Lark's mouth was dry with fear. She wanted to look away, but she couldn't tear her eyes from the sight. Her hand groped for her icon of Kalla, and for a moment she couldn't remember why she no longer had it.

Amelia! A shudder ran through her. In all of this, she had almost forgotten poor Amelia.

And then she forgot even that, as she and Hester and the others gaped at the sight of Mistress Winter and Winter Sunset rising from the flight paddock, Mistress Winter a straight, slender figure in black, Winter Sunset majestic in her strength and grace.

Lark gripped her elbows with her hands, shuddering with a dreadful premonition. Winter Sunset didn't bank to the east, toward the harbor. The formation of winged horses there was dissolving, each flyer performing a Half Reverse, then hovering at Quarters above the billowing sails of the Klee ship.

But Winter Sunset flew straight to the north.

"Where's she going?" Isobel said. And when no one answered her, she said again, "Where is Mistress Winter going? Don't ignore me just because I'm neutral, please! I followed my conscience, just as you did!"

Hester said, "No one minds your following your conscience, Isobel."

Isobel's eyes filled with tears. "Thank you," she said miserably. "I've been round and round it all, whether loyalty to the Duke is our duty or if we should follow Lord Francis and protect the bloodlines—I just don't know what's right."

Hester nodded. "It's difficult. There's no precedent to follow, so we have to thrash it out ourselves. Lark, don't you think—"

Lark heard these last words, but she didn't answer. She was already in the doorway, dashing headlong down the stairs, her heart pounding with fear. She thought she knew where Mistress Winter and Winter Sunset were headed, and she couldn't let them go alone.

TWENTY-EIGHT

WILLIAM had kept his father's room unchanged since his succession. The wing chair still sat beside the tall windows, angled for a good view of the stables and the paddocks. Frederick had liked sitting there, watching his winged horses drill over the park. Many and many a time, the young William had stood in the doorway to this room, waiting for his father to notice him. It had invariably been a good, long wait. Many years had passed, but those memories still carried a faint heat.

The old Duke had been irritatingly single-minded. His devotion to the traditions of the Duchy, as well as the bloodlines of the winged horses, had been maddening, but he had been a popular ruler. William knew he himself enjoyed no such affection from his people.

He leaned his hip against the curving back of the wing chair as he looked out into the courtyard. He had been forced, in the end, to call back the flyers. Not because they had lost a horse, although he knew that was the case, but because the snow had returned, drifts of it falling across the cold waters of the bay to dissolve into the waves. Winged horses, he had learned from Mistress Baron, dared not fly in a heavy snowstorm. The snow melted from the heat of their wings, she said, and pooled between the ribs so the wings were no longer efficient. Flyers caught in sudden storms had been known to fall.

The snow had not looked all that heavy to him. But those twelve—well, eleven—flyers were all he had. He hadn't dared risk them.

And, of course, he had no Master Breeder to advise him.

The *Marinan* had dropped anchor, and William recalled the patrol boats, too. It had been a gesture only, like brandishing a smallsword in an enemy's face but having no real intention of using it. He had never meant to lose a winged horse, and he supposed he should be grateful the patrol boat had recovered the horsemistress.

Damn Slater! This was really all his fault. The Rys girl would not have gotten away if Slater hadn't lost his head. And he couldn't face Baron Rys until he found the cursed girl. The people were whining about the port being closed, but they would just have to wait. He had ordered the militia out in force to find Amelia Rys. That should take no more than a few hours.

And now he didn't even have Slater to turn to. He had ordered him to disappear for a while. He had laid in a stock of the potion first, a row of dark glass bottles nestled in a bottom drawer. Slater had protested that he would be needed, but William wasn't sure he could protect him. There had been witnesses to Jinson's killing, and though he had no idea where they were now—the Klee girl and the Uplander—with the troubles brewing, and Francis doing gods-knew-what at Beeth House, he couldn't be sure. With rebellion fomenting not only in the Duchy but among the lords, he had his hands full.

He switched at his leg with his quirt. Ye gods, was loyalty so hard to come by? Even Constance, with her sideways glances and coy silences! He cursed the weather, silently and thoroughly. It could all be settled by now, Diamond and he winging over the park for all to see!

Clarence knocked and came in, saying, "Your Grace, there are some letters we should—"

William made a gesture, and said, "Not again, man! Leave us in peace." The secretary was wise enough this time to withdraw instantly, and without demur.

William pushed the heavy curtain farther back and leaned into the window. The snow had begun to fall in earnest. Any flyers caught in that would have to come to ground quickly.

Diamond was snug in her stall, of course. He thought of the letters, and of the brewing trouble in Osham, and ran his hands over his hair. Troubles hemmed him in on every side, when all he wanted, in truth, was to go across to the stables and spend an hour with his filly.

Damn it, he thought. *I'm the Duke. If that's the way I want to spend my afternoon, I will.* He straightened, dropping the curtain, then thrust it aside again.

A carriage was coming into the boulevard from the main road. He peered through the flutter of snowflakes, trying to see who it was. It was large, with some insignia on the door. Two footmen clung to the back, indistinct snow-dusted figures.

He pressed himself closer to the glass, waiting for the carriage to emerge from the shelter of the trees at the turning. If this was one of the Council Lords, he would not see him. He had had enough talk of war for one day.

The glass had grown cold with the falling snow, and his breath fogged it. He used his sleeve to wipe away the condensation, then he swore.

It was not someone from the Council. Indeed, he would have preferred one of the Council Lords—any one of them—to this visitor.

It was Philippa Winter descending from the carriage, walking across the snowy courtyard with that unfeminine stride. What a fool she was! Did she think, just because she arrived at the Palace of her own volition, that he would not take her prisoner?

Well, by the gods, she had walked right into his hands. He would see now that she took her punishment. Her mare could go to Fleckham, and Philippa could go to Islington House, where that fool Meredith would take charge of her.

And she could stay there, as far as William was concerned, until her bones shivered to dust!

TWENTY-NINE

IT was far too early for a real snowstorm, still more than two months till the Erdlin festival. But as Philippa and Sunny flew above the outskirts of the city, hard, dry flakes stung Philippa's face. The streets of the city appeared to be deserted, as if the city were closed, retired into itself until such time as it was safe to emerge. Philippa peered through a thickening veil of snow at the harbor, empty except for the Klee ship, rocking quietly at anchor. The winged horses were no longer in the air. The patrol boats must have retreated when the flight did. An eerie silence blanketed the White City, and not only because of the unseasonable snowfall. The populace of Osham had hidden itself away, to wait out the crisis in the safety of their homes. It would be months before the shopkeepers and laborers could make up their lost income.

The snow fell faster and faster. Just as Philippa saw that flakes were beginning to pool between the ribs of Sunny's wings, the broad roofs of Beeth House appeared beneath her. She pressed Sunny's shoulder with her right knee and touched her neck with the quirt to tell her to descend. Sunny banked neatly to the left, angling down through the quick glitter of crystalline snowflakes. Philippa used rein and foot to align her carefully with the road leading up to the mansion. It was frosted with snow and would be treacherous.

Sunny reached for the surface of the road with her forefeet, keeping her wings open for balance on the icy surface. Her hind feet settled gingerly onto the cobblestones, and she beat her wings to rise slightly from the surface, then settle again. She repeated this maneuver three times before she trusted her footing. When at last she had found her balance, she trotted toward the house, snorting and switching her tail.

"Good girl," Philippa told her, patting her neck with a gloved hand. She glanced ahead. The windows of Beeth House glowed a welcome through the fluttering snow. Sunny slowed to a walk as they reached its narrow courtyard. Someone within heard her hoofbeats, and the front door opened. The foyer beyond it shone with lamplight, and she heard voices through the waning afternoon light.

She was taking a risk, a measured one. She had to force William's hand before open warfare broke out. Sunny, at least, would be safe at Beeth House, no matter what happened.

Lord Beeth's letter had told of an ultimatum from the Klee, from Baron Rys himself. Either William produced Amelia, or her father would summon the full force of Viscount Richard's army to retrieve her. He threatened invasion, and he had his royal brother's support.

Philippa could hardly blame Esmond Rys. But if something wasn't done, innocent citizens would die, citizens who knew nothing of their Duke's machinations.

She slipped down from Sunny's back and looked up the steps at the open doorway of Beeth House. Some of her tension drained away when she saw the staunch Amanda Beeth awaiting her there. A stable-girl hurried around the side of the house and curtsied to Philippa.

"I'll be taking your mare, shall I, Mistress?" she said. "I'll rub her down and give her a blanket and a feed."

"Excellent," Philippa said. She handed the stable-girl Sunny's reins without hesitation. Anyone the Beeths hired was certain to be dependable. She ran lightly up the steps to Amanda Beeth, who nodded gravely and held the door wide for her.

As Philippa pulled off her cap and gloves and shook snow from the sleeves of her riding coat, Lady Beeth said, "I had no doubt you'd come. They're waiting for us in the back parlor, because most of the other rooms are full at the moment. Tea, Philippa?"

* * *

BEETH House had become a billet. Following Amanda past the dining room, the ballroom, the east-facing morning room, and the drawing room, Philippa saw men in every one of them. They wore no uniforms, but they had the grim faces and hard eyes of men with a cause, men who knew there was danger ahead.

Francis came forward to meet her when she stepped inside the back parlor. He took both her hands. "So, Philippa," he said. "Here we are again."

"Indeed, Francis. Thank you and Lord Beeth for letting me know."

"We'll need you," he said. "And you'll strengthen my resolve. It gives me no joy to fight my brother this way."

"Francis!" Philippa admonished. She squeezed his hands with her own. "You have no need even to speak the thought. All of us understand that."

"There will be some who won't believe it."

"Well. I suppose that's true. They will simply have to learn, in time."

Lord Beeth came forward and bowed to Philippa. "Mistress Winter. Is everything all right at the Academy?"

She said abruptly, "We've lost a horse. He sent a flight against the Klee ship, and Caroline Rambler and her horse have gone into the water."

Francis's lips went white. "Ye gods," he breathed.

Beeth said, "Appalling."

"Precisely so," Philippa said. She swallowed the hard lump that suddenly tightened her throat. She had been holding the awareness of the loss at arm's length, she realized, and being in the company of sympathizers threatened to destroy her composure.

"You got our message," Beeth said. He looked different, paler, harder than she had ever seen him.

"Yes, Lord Beeth. I came the moment I received it."

"We're grateful."

"I would have come in any case. We have to stop this before we lose anyone else. How did you come by Esmond's message?"

Beeth pointed toward the fireplace, and Philippa saw with

some surprise that several Council Lords had gathered there. "Lakeland saw it in the Council and changed his allegiance," Beeth said without embellishment. "He scribbled out a copy and carried it straight here."

Philippa inclined her head to the men gathered around the hearth. A serving-maid came in, balancing a vast tray with a teapot and a dozen cups, and several plates of sandwiches. Amanda Beeth went to help her and began pouring out tea and handing round the cups.

Francis said, "We have enough troubles without the Klee attacking. Order has broken down in the city. The militia is in tatters. Lakeland tells us William won't discuss his strategy—if there is one—with anyone."

"Your force here is not inconsiderable," she said.

"About a hundred. Not enough, really," Francis said, "to stop William. If we could only find this girl, and let Esmond know his daughter's safe . . ." His voice trailed off. His eyes were clouded and unhappy. He had not received any training for this role, she knew. Francis was to have been a scholar, a life he much preferred.

"I will go to the Palace, of course, Francis. You knew that I would."

"My lord, can we assure Mistress Winter's safety?"

Philippa drew a breath, and turned slowly to meet the familiar dark blue gaze. "Master Hamley," she said, looking up into his face. "It's kind of you to be concerned, but I can handle Duke William. We have a history that goes back to childhood. We understand one another."

"Yon Duke is unpredictable," he rumbled.

"Yes. He is." Philippa took a cup of tea from Amanda Beeth, and sipped. "Tell me, have you found your brother yet? Nick?"

He shook his head. The teacup he held looked ridiculously fragile in his big hands. They were broad of palm, thick-fingered. Philippa found herself staring at them, remembering how gentle they had been with the injured Bramble. She tore her eyes away when Francis took her arm. Brye scowled as Francis led her off, and it gave her a feeling of warmth, a sense that what happened to her mattered.

As she bent her head to listen to Lord Chatham, she let her gaze slip back to the doorway where Brye Hamley stood, arms folded across his chest. She hoped Francis realized how fortunate he was to have this man on his side.

THE snow was beginning to collect on the hedgerows and pastures by the time the Beeths' carriage reached the park surrounding the Ducal Palace. Philippa rested her chin on her fist and gazed out the window at the old trees along the boulevard, their bare branches frosted now with white. It felt good to be carried along by the carriage horses, to sit on a cushioned seat under a lap robe. It was a sign of age, she feared, but she couldn't deny it. Her bones were no longer so malleable as they once had been, and the flying saddle seemed to press every sensitive spot, especially in cold weather. She hoped Sunny was as warm and comfortable in the Beeths' stables as she was in their carriage.

The facade of the Palace loomed out of the snowy dusk, its multifaceted white stone profile as familiar to Philippa as that of the Academy. Lights glowed beyond the curtains and shutters, and as she watched, two serving-maids scurried up the front steps, shielding their hair with the hems of their long aprons. Philippa's gaze passed to the tall windows of the rooms that had once been Duke Frederick's, and a spasm of longing for days past twisted her heart.

A stable-man came out of the stables at the sound of her approach and crossed the courtyard to wait before the steps. Philippa threw aside her lap robe and climbed down without waiting for the footman to open her door. The stable-man gaped at her, and she nodded to him. "Blackley, isn't it?" she said.

He stammered, "Aye, Mistress, that's it. Oh, aye, Blackley, I am, His Grace's stable-man." He bit his lip, and glanced up toward the lighted windows of the Palace across the great circular courtyard. "And—and a good evening to you," he said.

An oc-hound appeared from somewhere, sensitive always to the presence of a flyer. It came to Philippa to sniff at her knees, then sat beside her, its narrow head close to her thigh. She stroked it. "Can you see to the carriage horses, Blackley?"

"Oh, aye, Mistress, I—I mean, of course. Are you—are you staying long?"

She laughed with real amusement. "I hope not! But who knows?"

He shrugged and shifted his feet uncomfortably. The two footmen were stamping in the cold and rubbing their arms. "You lot go in, for sure," Blackley said. "Someone will fetch you something to drink. And you, sir," to the driver, "bring them horses this way. We'll find a spot."

As Philippa turned to follow the footmen up the steps, the oc-hound rose and padded after her. She paused. "What's the dog's name, Blackley?"

"That's Alice, Mistress."

"Ah." Philippa touched the oc-hound's silky skull. "I suppose she's coming with me."

"Oh, aye," Blackley said. "She would do that." His gaze slid past Philippa, and she turned to see what he was looking at.

Three black-uniformed militiamen were coming down the steps. Blackley coughed, and backed away, and a moment later the carriage wheeled on around the courtyard to the carriage house beyond the stables. Philippa stood where she was, Alice pressed close to her thigh.

One of the militiamen said, "Mistress Winter? His Grace sent us to bring you to him."

"Ridiculous," Philippa said. "I don't need a military escort. Or did he think I would come here without meaning to see him?"

The guardsman, a middle-aged man with a captain's bars on his shoulder, said blandly, "I couldn't say, Horsemistress."

"No." Philippa marched past the man, Alice at her heels. "No, of course you couldn't." The other two militiamen were slow in parting for her, and she snapped, "Stand aside, you two. Let me pass."

They both stumbled backward on the icy steps, one nearly losing his footing. Philippa snorted as she strode between them.

PARKSON opened the front door to the foyer, and bowed. "Mistress Winter," he said solemnly, as if she did not have a uniformed guard on either side of her, their hands on the hilts of their smallswords. "Not a good day for flying, I should have thought."

She pulled her cap from her head and smoothed a stray strand of hair back into its rider's knot. "I came by carriage." She shook snow from her cap before she tucked it into her belt. She shrugged out of her coat, and it had already started to drip before Parkson folded it over his arm.

"I must see His Grace immediately," Philippa said.

"Yes, Horsemistress. In his office." Parkson knew the edict she was under, but no surprise or curiosity showed in his face. "I believe he's waiting for you."

"I expect he is," Philippa said. "Could you keep these men here with you, Parkson? I'm hardly going to flee into the night if they leave me alone for two moments."

He bowed, and was speaking to the militiamen when she crossed the broad foyer and started up the stairs. A serving-maid scurried out of her way as she reached the first landing, fearful as a mouse in the presence of a cat.

Philippa pursed her lips and stripped off her gloves as she walked.

She found the door standing open to the rooms where she had so often spent time with Duke Frederick, both as a girl being guided in her studies by the Duke and later as a horse-mistress, serving at the Palace. She paused in the doorway, the oc-hound beside her.

William stood beside the wing chair that had been his father's. He wore one of the embroidered vests he affected, but he could no longer close it across his chest. He was twirling his braided quirt between his thin fingers. A fire blazed in the fireplace and cast shadows through the fire screen that stretched and shrank around the low tables and the plush divan.

"Philippa," William said in his high-pitched voice. "We meet again at last."

Alice growled, and Philippa put a hand down to quiet her. "You left me no choice."

William laughed at her rudeness. "Philippa, you always have presumed upon old acquaintance. And now that you've presented yourself to fulfill your sentence, we're inclined to let you have your say before you begin your confinement."

She kicked the door closed with her boot, not taking her eyes from his face. It had grown round, though his body was so thin it seemed the firelight might illuminate his very bones.

"You've lost a horse, William, wasted one of Kalla's creatures with your recklessness."

He narrowed his eyes. "You dare speak to *me* of recklessness?"

"Did you learn nothing at all from your father?" she demanded. "He would never have ordered such a thing."

"These things happen," he said stiffly. "Naturally we regret the loss of a winged horse, but this is war."

Philippa resisted the urge to rub her neck, to relieve the pain that shot up from her shoulders. "I know Baron Rys has set an ultimatum," she said. "You must produce Amelia."

He shrugged, and the swell of his chest moved with the gesture. "We don't know where she is. The chit disappeared."

"What!" For a moment she lost control of her voice, and it shrilled in the high-ceilinged room. "Kalla's heels, William! You *lost* her?"

"She's run off. Who knows where? You know what girls are."

"Girls?" Philippa gritted. "She's an Academy student, bonded to a winged horse. And even if she weren't, she's hardly just any girl. She's the niece of the Klee Viscount."

"She should have thought of that before she took to her heels."

"You've gone too far, William. This is beyond endangering the bloodlines. You've endangered all the people of Oc. Your actions this morning—"

"You mean because we sent a flight of winged horses to distract the Klee? Nonsense. The Klee understand the gesture for just what it is."

"Which is what, William?"

"You will refer to us by our title, Philippa. You would never have called my father by his given name."

She stepped forward onto the thick hearthrug. When she took a breath to speak, she detected something odd in the air, some faint, slightly repugnant perfume. "Your father, William," she hissed, "never spoke of himself in the plural. What pretense is this?"

"Shall we stick to the subject, Philippa?" he purred. He walked around the front of the wing chair and settled himself into it, draping his long arm across the back.

"The subject is Oc's future," she said.

He smiled, the old crooked smile she had found appealing when she was sixteen. The memory turned her stomach. "The subject is your punishment, ruled upon by the very Council you put so much faith in."

"The Council is divided now," she answered. "You can't make that ruling hold."

"It won't matter," he said lightly, with a dismissive gesture of his pale hand. "We will enforce it, now that you've done your duty and presented yourself. Where is your mare? We'll see she's taken safely to the Fleckham School. She'll be put to good use."

"That would kill her, William, and you know it."

His smile held. "You should have thought of that, Philippa."

She shrugged. "As it happens, I did. She's well out of your reach."

"Nothing is out of our reach," he answered. He crossed his legs. "We're almost there, Philippa. All that's needed is one day of good weather, and everyone will know we were right."

"What do you think will happen, William? That you will fly your filly, and everyone will fall on their knees before you?" She laughed, a harsh sound in the lovely old room. "You've always been arrogant, but this is insanity."

At the word, he stiffened. He uncrossed his legs, got to his feet, and advanced toward her, his quirt in his fist. "We don't need anyone to fall on their knees, Philippa," he hissed. "But you and the rest of those bitches at the Academy will curtsy to me before the year's out!"

She lifted her chin and smiled at him. "Never."

He lifted the quirt, and his face suffused with color. "How dare you!" he cried.

She put up a hand. "William, please. A moment." He lowered the quirt, eyeing her narrowly. "Yes, I know," she said. "I do presume upon acquaintance. We've known each other all our lives, and I do think—your father—"

"Don't talk to me of my father!" he shrilled. "He had no vision!"

"He had courage," Philippa said, keeping her voice level. "And he was devoted to his people. He made great sacrifices for that."

"All he cared about were the winged horses, and the women who flew them."

Philippa sighed. "Because they are precious to Oc, William. Surely you can see that?"

"Do you think it was right for him to ignore his sons in favor of them?" He blew air between his lips and turned his face toward the fire. "And then, of course, there was Pamella."

"Pamella," Philippa said wonderingly. All at once, everything came into focus, as if an obscuring mist had suddenly cleared. Duke Frederick had indeed loved the winged horses, and by association, the horsemistresses. And now William was obsessed with them, but his preoccupation had nothing to do with affection. His allegiance was twisted, tortured into some strange, unmanageable emotion. And Pamella!

"That's why you did it, isn't it, William?" she whispered, shocked into comprehension.

He stared into the red flames. "Did what, Philippa?"

"It's why you drove Pamella away. And why you—" For a moment she couldn't push the words past her lips. She shook herself, disgusted. She was a horsemistress, for Kalla's sake, intimate with breedings and birthings and all manner of animal behavior. "It's why you raped your sister," she finally said, her voice flat and weary.

"Did she say that?" he asked, lightly, almost humorously.

"You know she doesn't speak," Philippa said.

"She could write it down. She's had a child, but I don't believe she's lost her wits."

"Your cruelty shocks me, William."

"The whole idea that Pamella's son is my child is absurd," he said.

"It's sordid, William. And I suspect Pamella won't speak

of it because, even now, she's protecting the family. The throne comes before everything, doesn't it?"

When he didn't answer, Philippa crossed the room so that she could see his profile. "Look at you. Your bosom swells, and your chin is as smooth as a girl's. You're trying to turn yourself into a woman, but you hate women. You blame that on your father, but I think, in some way, you've always hated women. It's no wonder your mind is affected."

"My mind is *not* affected!" When he turned on her, the fist with the quirt raised toward her face, he looked more like Alice the oc-hound than he did the Duke of Oc. He snarled at her, and his lip lifted away from his teeth. "You will not stand in our way, Philippa."

"It won't work, William."

He froze for a long moment, his eyes on her face. Then, forcing a laugh, he lowered the quirt. "Wait and see," he said, tugging at his vest. "Just you wait, Philippa, and you'll see."

THIRTY

"WE'RE close now, Mahogany," Amelia murmured. She kept
the lead short, his head at her shoulder. She shivered with fatigue and cold, and struggled to keep a steady hand for her
colt's sake. "See there, just around the corner of that shop.
There's the Tower!"

It rose just to the east of where they huddled between two
rickety buildings. Snow shrouded its windowed top. The
keeper's light glimmered yellow through the flicker of white
flakes. Around it the streets were deserted, the cobblestones
shimmering with a thin, unbroken film of snow. Amelia's
stomach quivered, and she tried to think when she had last
eaten. She couldn't remember, and so she forced the thought
from her mind. Just a few more steps, and they would be
there. They had only to persuade the lightkeeper, one solitary
man. Amelia thought she would appeal to his good nature, and
if that didn't work, she would promise a reward. Something
had to work out. Mahogany couldn't spend another night in the
cold.

She drew a deep breath and felt Mahogany, beside her, do
the same. Impulsively, she hugged his neck. "We're together.
That's the main thing, my love," she said. He nosed her cheek,
and she managed a shaky smile. "Come on, then. Let's go."

With his chin softly bumping her shoulder, as if they were
leaning on each other, they hurried, side by side, to the end of
the street. A sign with a painting of a boat was nailed above
the door of the corner shop, but the windows were shuttered
and the door conspicuously locked with an enormous padlock.
It seemed no one was about in the city this early evening. The
lightkeeper must feel terribly solitary.

The snowfall softened their steps as they pressed on. Mahogany's forelock and mane were white with it, reminding Amelia of a sort of cake Lyssett sometimes made at the old estate. It was flavored with cinnamon and dusted with sugar, and it always tasted of lavender. The thought made her mouth water, and she swallowed. Better not to think of food.

As they approached the corner, Mahogany's steps faltered, then stopped. He threw up his head and flattened his ears.

Amelia knew better than to ignore him. She stopped, too, her back against his warm shoulder. She leaned forward to peer cautiously past the weathered planks that formed the outer wall of the shop, then, with a swiftly indrawn breath, she pulled back.

She had had a glimpse of the bay at last, and in the distance, shrouded by the falling snow, she had seen the lanterns in the prow and the stern of the *Marinan*. So near and so far at the same time!

And between her and the Tower was another contingent of Duke William's militia.

Mahogany had caught their scent and stopped her before she plunged right out into the full view of six black-uniformed guardsmen.

Silently, she backed away, past the door with the boat sign, past the nameless building beside that, down the road again in the direction they had come. She felt a complete fool. She had simply not thought . . . but of course Duke William would set a guard at the North Tower. There were probably militiamen in the Tower itself, watching her father's ship.

With leaden feet, her hands feeling like ice, she turned Mahogany down one of the empty lanes and walked in the opposite direction. She struggled with a sense of despair. She had to reach deep within herself for some shred of hope that would keep her feet moving. She would not—she *could* not— let Duke William win. She would *not*, she promised herself for the thousandth time, be the reason for a war between their people; she simply would not!

She stumbled on a roughly placed cobblestone and felt Mahogany stumble with her. They were both too tired and too cold. They couldn't keep this up much longer, she knew. She would have to knock on someone's door, give herself up, without knowing on which side's mercy she was throwing herself.

The idea was so repugnant that she felt a brief burst of strength and managed to work her way down another road, this one broader, leading south away from the harbor and toward one of the residential neighborhoods. Outlined against the snow, she saw that the roofs here were higher, the buildings wider, separated by spaces filled now with snow, but which might be gardens.

"What would Lark do, or Hester?" she asked Mahogany. And then she remembered the icon of Kalla Lark had given her, which hung even now beneath her borrowed tabard.

She touched the little wooden figure, feeling the horse head at its top, the plume of tail that curled up and around the shoulders of the woman, the goddess. "Kalla," she whispered. "For Mahogany's sake—one of your creatures—help me!"

She knew she had no right, really, to be praying to Kalla. She had been raised to be skeptical of gods both great and small, and though she had no wish to offend Lark, she privately considered her friend's faith in such things naive.

But even as she thought that, the icon began to grow warm against her breast.

She touched it again. It was no illusion. Her fingers, cold as they were, felt the heat in the icon, just as Lark said happened often to her. It was a gentle warmth at first, then, as she and Mahogany walked beneath a snowy hill with a drive curving up it, the icon grew nearly too hot to touch.

Amelia stopped, looking about her. What could it mean?

At the top of the hill the drive led to a big house. Its windows were alight, and even from where she stood she could hear the sounds of people, men's voices calling and laughing. To her right was a wide gate, shaded by enormous holly trees. It seemed to be the sort that might be opened to let a carriage through. Beyond it, tucked beneath the hill, was some sort of smallish building. She moved around Mahogany to stand on tiptoe and look over the gate. He crowded behind her, his ears turned forward.

Tentatively, Amelia tried the latch. To her surprise, it clicked smoothly. The gate swung inward on silent hinges.

Mahogany snorted and nudged her forward with his shoulder. Amelia cast another glance around and saw a pony cart making its way up the street from the city. She went ahead of Mahogany, slipping through the gate, closing it when they were both through. They ducked behind one of the hollies, wary of the prickly leaves, and watched as the cart passed by. Two moments longer in the street, and the cart would have caught them.

The pony cart turned into the drive and started up the hill toward the big house. When it was out of their sight, Amelia led Mahogany toward the little building. Beneath the layer of snow, the drive was gravel, and there were hitching posts set in front of the building.

"It's a carriage house, Mahogany," she whispered. "If it's empty . . . we can at least get out of this cold!"

The door to the carriage house was of the sliding kind, with big hinges above it. As Amelia began to push it open, the hinges squealed, making her glance anxiously over her shoulder, but there seemed to be no one to hear. It wasn't until they were both inside, in a gloomy interior that smelled of saddle soap and leather and the faint tinge of lamp oil, that Amelia realized the icon had cooled again. Mahogany snorted, his head high and his eyes showing white. "It's all right, my love," Amelia said, and hoped she was right. She pushed the door closed again, wincing at the noise it made. When she was certain it was secure, she turned to assess their hiding place.

It was much bigger inside than she had thought it would be, extending back into a shadowed dimness. Some moments passed before her eyes adjusted to the darkness. The only light came from cracks around the door, from a space between the roof and the walls, and from what seemed to be another door leading out the back. A gig loomed in one corner, its shafts resting on the wooden floor. Amelia could make out shelves on the nearest wall, and when she felt along them with her hand, she found folded lap robes among bits of equipment and tack. The lap robes were a boon. She felt warmer already, just being indoors, and if she could wrap a blanket around her, she could manage one more night. She was awfully hungry, but she would settle, she thought, for water for Mahogany.

She shook out one of the lap robes and draped it over his back. "Now, just wait here," she said, patting his cheek. "Let me see what's out back."

She walked toward the door, careful of where she placed her feet in the darkness. The floor was reasonably smooth and clean, and she supposed that was a warning sign that the carriage house saw regular use.

Mahogany snorted again behind her, and his hooves scraped on the floor. "Wait," she told him again. "I'll be right back."

She couldn't see the latch for the door, so she put out her hand and groped along the wall to find it. When her fingers encountered warmth, the resilience of flesh beneath woolen fabric, she cried out. She snatched her hand away, stumbling backward. "What! Who's—who's there?" she faltered.

At her cry, Mahogany whickered, and came closer, then stopped, blowing uneasily.

A man, she thought. It's a man.

She took a step back, then another. Whoever it was separated himself from the wall but didn't make a sound.

Amelia spoke again, with more authority. "Who is it, please?"

She would have sworn she was answered with a sob, or a whimper.

A bit more gently she said, "I'm sorry if we've intruded. We're rather desperately cold."

Boots shuffled on the wood floor, and the person stepped forward into a dim shaft of light that slanted from the rafters. He said, "Miss, please. Don't tell them, will you?"

Now that a bit of light was shed on his features, she saw that he was not so much a man as a boy, perhaps just into his teens. He was certainly not as old as she, and he was barely taller. His face, as much as she could see of it, was a picture of misery.

"Tell whom?" she asked.

He made a small gesture with his thin shoulders. "Them soldiers at the house, Miss. I can't—I can't fight. I just can't!" His voice rose, and broke. He was indeed very young.

She held up a hand. "No, no, I won't tell anyone."

"I thought—I thought maybe you belong to that house,

with yon horse and all." His voice was as thin as his body, and full of misery.

"No, I don't. Now, you be calm, and let's decide what to do. What's your name?"

"Jimmy," he said, and ducked his head. "Well, Jim, I guess. Now that I'm a soldier."

"You're a soldier? A militiaman?" Amelia couldn't keep the surprise from her voice. Surely the lad was far too young.

He made the gesture again, a limp sort of shrug. "It's them taxes, Miss. Them extra—extra taxes, whatever you call 'em. We can't pay, and so they made me go for a soldier."

"Why are you hiding here, then, in the dark? Why aren't you up at the house with—I suppose—with your captain?"

"Them's heading out to fight in the morning," he said sadly. "And I can't shoot a pistol or use the smallsword they gave me. I can't fight at all. I'll just get killed, and my mam's heart'll break. She said it would."

Amelia bit her lip, trying to think what to do. She was so tired, and so hungry, that her mind felt thick as mud. But there must be some reason they had both come here at the same time. There must be a way they could help each other. She simply had to think what it was.

It took some time to explain to Jimmy that Mahogany was a winged horse, and that she was a fugitive, just as he was. He wasn't the brightest lad she had met, but he was eager to conspire with her to keep them all hidden.

When she had convinced him he must keep his distance from Mahogany, and that she would not under any circumstances reveal him to his captain, he relaxed a bit.

"The thing is," she said finally, "that we need water. Neither of us has eaten or slept since yesterday."

"Oh!" he said, in the brightest tone she had yet heard him use. "Oh, you should've told me, Miss! There's a water bucket just outside that there door. And—here. My mam gave this to me when I left her."

He dug into a shapeless bag resting at his feet and brought out a miracle.

Amelia took it with trembling fingers, her nose already telling her it was food. It was a substantial packet, wrapped neatly in a tea towel that smelled faintly of laundry soap. Amelia crouched on the floor to unfold it on her lap, and found a half dozen apples, a small loaf of heavy bread, some cheese and biscuits, and a little tin of tea. "Oh, Jimmy," Amelia said. "This is wonderful. Will you share with me?"

He ducked his head again. "Oh, aye," he said softly. "Eat as much as you like. I don't like them soldiers, but they eat good. I'm not hungry at all."

"Mahogany would love the apples," she said. "And if I could have a little bread and cheese . . ."

She held it up to him, but he shook his head. "Have all of it, Miss. I'm going home tomorrow, and Mam'll feed me, sure."

Mahogany, behind her, whickered hungrily. Still she hesitated, though her mouth had begun to water at the scent of the bread. "Jimmy . . . how are you going to get home? They'll be looking for you, and I'm afraid . . . I'm afraid there's going to fighting."

"Oh, aye," he said, with a flash of confidence. "And as soon as it starts, I'll be on my way home quick as my feet can carry me! I'm Osham-born and -bred, and I know the back ways."

"But won't they come for you again?"

He shook his head. "Nay, Miss. They're saying Lord Francis will be Duke next."

"Are they? Who is saying that?"

"Everyone! Well, not them up at the house, but lots of folk. My mam and my uncle. And when Lord Francis is Duke, them extra taxes will go away."

She got to her feet and went to Mahogany with the apples. As he crunched them enthusiastically, she bit a chunk from the wedge of cheese. It was sheep's cheese, soft and rich, nearly as good as that of Marinan. She could hardly restrain herself from tearing at the bread with her teeth, too. She waited until Mahogany had finished every scrap of apple, cores and stems included. She led him to the water barrel and let him drink, then she sat cross-legged on one of the lap robes and ate the unexpected gift with as much courtesy as she could manage.

Jimmy watched her, grinning. "My mam loves to see a hungry person eat," he said.

"Then I would give her joy," Amelia said, smiling back at him. She finished everything, and sighed, feeling pleasantly sleepy and nearly safe. She wrapped herself in a second lap robe, keeping the one beneath her for some cushioning against the hard planks of the floor. Jimmy did the same. They had almost drifted off to sleep, unlikely companions of the night, when Amelia had a thought.

"Jimmy," she whispered.

"Aye?"

"Do you know someone with a boat?"

THIRTY-ONE

THE sky had cleared to the hard, cold black of winter by the time Philippa marched down the steps of the Ducal Palace and across the courtyard to the stables, where William's carriage horses were being harnessed.

The Beeth driver had flatly refused to allow any of the Duke's militia to use his master's equipage. There had been an exchange between one of William's captains and the driver, but when the captain put his hand on his smallsword, Philippa intervened.

They were still in the foyer of the Palace, though the doors stood open to the icy wind. Philippa stepped between the soldier and the Beeth retainer. She put her back to the militiaman, and said quietly to the driver, "Thank you for bringing me here. Please take your horses back to Beeth House, and let Lord and Lady Beeth know I'm now in the Duke's custody."

There was a moment of tension, when she thought the man might not give in, but the militia captain rattled the scabbard of his sword, and the driver's face paled a bit.

Philippa said, "No one doubts your courage, I promise you."

He cast her a grateful glance and tossed his head at the militiamen who stood stiffly around the foyer. There were a dozen of them, and as Philippa moved toward the door, they followed her, the hard soles of their boots clicking on the marble floor. She led them at a brisk pace across the snowy cobblestones and experienced a small flicker of satisfaction when two or three of them slipped on the icy surface. Blackley was still putting the horses into their traces, and he suggested Philippa step into the tack room to stay warm while she waited.

The man who was apparently the leader of her contingent

of guards began to protest when she stepped out of his sight, waving the heavy musket he carried. Philippa heard the stable-man say, "Leave be, man. That's a horsemistress of Oc, and she deserves respect."

Philippa couldn't make out the guard's grumbled response, but Blackley snapped, "They devote their lives to the winged horses. You lot ought to know that."

There was a rattle of leather traces and the clacking of horses' hooves on the stones. The empty Beeth carriage clattered out of the courtyard, its wheels going silent when it reached the snowy boulevard. A moment later, Blackley came into the tack room and bowed to Philippa.

"Begging your pardon, Horsemistress," he said, shame-faced. "The carriage is ready to take—that is, ready for you."

"Thank you, Blackley," she said, just as if she had ordered up the carriage herself.

"I don't like it," he said. He looked as if he would like to say more, but couldn't think what. He cleared his throat, and looked over his shoulder as if the militia might have followed him into the tack room after all.

Philippa said, "I understand your feelings perfectly, Master Blackley. Don't trouble yourself. It isn't your fault."

His eyes met hers, then slid away again. He took a step closer, and she caught the scent of horseflesh and leather about him, the good, homely scents of a man who spent his life in the stables. "Mistress," he said in an undertone, "my family worked for old Duke Frederick, and we're as loyal as any—"

The captain of the guard banged on the door with his fist. "Let's go!" he said.

"Mistress," Blackley said hurriedly. "If you want, I'll keep these fools busy while you slip out the back . . ."

Philippa gave him a nod of appreciation. "You're a good man, Master Blackley. I appreciate the thought, but I'm willing to go."

"But, Mistress . . . Islington House will be . . ."

"A prison, yes. Though a velvet one!" She gave him a tight smile. "And in the bosom of my family, no less."

The captain banged again on the door. He put his head in, scowling.

"Oh, aye, we're coming," Blackley answered. He muttered to Philippa, "Bad times, Mistress. Bad times."

"Yes," Philippa said in a dry tone. "Precisely so, Master Blackley."

She walked out of the tack room and stepped up into the Duke's carriage, disdaining the proffered hand of the captain. He climbed in beside her and banged on the ceiling of the carriage with the butt of his musket. "Islington House!" he ordered. The driver shook the traces, and the carriage began to roll.

Philippa settled into a corner and folded her arms. She fixed the captain with a stony gaze, and he had the grace to flush a little and look away. They rode off in silence. Behind them came the rest of the guard, mounted on saddle horses.

They drove for twenty minutes, leaving the park of the Ducal Palace behind and wheeling swiftly out into the main road. Philippa cast a surreptitious glance through the window to assess their distance from the White City. The gas lamps of the city center glowed faintly in the distance, and squares of yellow light marked a farmhouse they were just passing. She sat up a little straighter. Her guard stared at the back wall of the carriage.

He was young, she saw, with a twinge of regret, a plump, rather short man who could hardly be older than her third-level girls. She wondered what drove a young man to the militia. Dreams of glory? Until recently, such an opportunity hardly existed in Oc. A safe job, perhaps, or perhaps such a man believed service to the Duke was its own reward. It had been easy to decide to commit herself to the winged horses, but she didn't know if committing oneself to military service would be as simple.

She looked away from the young captain, not wanting to remember his soft features, which he clearly worked hard to make as stiff and forbidding as possible. She had seen the same such effort on the faces of her students. When they were most frightened, they hardened their faces and stiffened their necks. They hid their fear from everyone, including themselves.

This young man's job was about to become much more

complicated, and possibly far more dangerous. If all went as planned, the fulcrum of the coming struggle would shift from Amelia Rys to her.

LARK watched from her hiding place as Mistress Winter, leaving Sunny behind at Beeth House, stepped up into the carriage and was driven off, alone.

Tup and Lark had hidden in the farthest empty stall of the Beeth stables. Since her second year at the Academy, Lark had summered with the Beeths and knew their estate in Marin and the one here in Osham almost as well as she knew her own home of Deeping Farm. After launching from the flight paddock at the Academy and following Mistress Winter and Sunny at a discreet distance, Lark had guided Tup down to the farthest pasture at Beeth House, where in spring and summer a little herd of brown milk cows grazed. They came to ground unseen and made their way through the thickening fall of snow to the back of the stables, where Lark remembered a pony stall. Hester's first pony had been stabled there, before being handed along to a young cousin when Hester outgrew him. The stall had been empty for years.

Lark left Tup there, admonishing him against his usual whimpering cry, and crept along the aisle to the front to watch the stable-girl take Sunny in, untack her, and settle her as if for a long stay. Lark longed to run across to Beeth House to find out what was happening, but she knew if Mistress Winter found her there, she would order her back to the Academy immediately. She would be in enough trouble as it was, but then, there had hardly been a time when she was not doing penance for one infraction or another.

Lark found a window beside a stack of straw bales, a small square of glass that looked out over the long, narrow courtyard of Beeth House. She crouched beside it and peered in wonderment. She saw Lady Beeth emerge to greet Mistress Winter. She saw men, dozens of them, moving behind the windows, or coming out through the side entrances. She thought she saw Lord Beeth once, and she was quite sure she spotted Lord Francis himself moving across the bright foyer.

She sank onto the sawdust-covered floor and tried to understand what might be happening here. She had followed Mistress Winter out of fear that her instructor would go straight to the Ducal Palace. She was relieved to find she had come here, to this welcoming place, but she couldn't guess why. Had the weather been more amenable, she and Tup could simply have circled back to the Academy, but the snow was too heavy. And now that she was here, she could hardly bear to leave without understanding what was afoot.

As the hours passed, she huddled with Tup in the pony stall. She took off his flying saddle and rubbed him down with a purloined towel, then stole a bit of water and oats from the stall of a big, wingless gelding. As she moved stealthily through the aisles, she counted the horses. Not including Winter Sunset, she found there were at least two dozen saddle horses in the stables, in addition to the eight carriage horses maintained by Lord and Lady Beeth. Only when there was a party, as at the Estian festival or one great celebration for Lord Beeth's birthday, had she seen so many horses at Beeth House. She began to wish she had persuaded Hester to come with her, but she suspected Hester would have cautioned Lark for her impulsiveness and advised restraint.

As the carriage trundled away, bearing Philippa Winter, Lark stared after it, confounded. Something was going to happen, she felt certain, something big, and she wouldn't know what it was until it was too late to help.

Hours later, when the sky had cleared, and hard, cold stars shone down on the snowy landscape, the men began to come out of Beeth House. There was a flurry of activity in the stables as they retrieved their horses, saddled and bridled them, and assembled in the courtyard. Lark kept her hand over Tup's nose to block the scent of so many men and keep him quiet. He snorted against her palm and lifted one hind leg as if to kick in protest, but she whispered, "No, Tup! Please!" and he subsided, but he pushed his head against her shoulders as if to remind her he was only doing it to please her.

There seemed to be dozens of people riding out of the courtyard a moment later. Lark left Tup and rushed back to the little window. Peering out, she saw that there were perhaps thirty men, most of them mounted, but a few marching in formation. Several of the marchers carried long, wicked-looking muskets over their shoulders. Others had smallswords swinging beside their thighs, or they had no weapon at all. At the head of the whole contingent she saw Lord Francis on a fine, tall horse, swathed in a long riding coat and with the scabbard of a smallsword laced to his pommel.

Lord Beeth rode a high-necked horse that made him look even pudgier than usual. And behind Lord Beeth, with the marchers, was a tall, broad figure that looked familiar to Lark. She looked harder, but the man wore a wide-brimmed hat and a heavy coat with its collar turned up, and she couldn't make him out. He carried no weapon, but he strode forward with purpose, his breath curling from beneath the brim of his hat.

She watched this force depart from Beeth House. Aside from a command or two, the men were silent. The rattle and creak of tack, the stamping of boots, and the clop of horses' hooves were the only sounds. Lady Beeth stood in the doorway of Beeth House, her tall figure framed in light. She neither called a farewell nor raised her hand. Lark clung to the windowsill, biting her lip, thinking furiously. Of course it all had to do with Mistress Winter, but what? And where were they going?

When the last of the men had disappeared down the lane, Lark blew one breath against the cold glass, watching the mist swell and then fade as she tried to decide what to do. She could fly back to the Academy, she supposed, and hope no one had missed her. It was a vain hope, though, and she would no doubt compound her offenses by flying alone in the dark, even though the stars were so bright. She could stay the night where she was, she and Tup huddled together in the pony stall. Or . . .

She clicked her tongue as her mind made itself up all at once. There was only one logical thing to do, though it would require some explaining.

She stood, and turned.

And found her way blocked by Hester's mamá's commanding bulk. Lady Beeth stood with her arms folded, her face stern.

"Well, Larkyn," she said. "Are you coming across to the house now?"

Lark inclined her head, out of courtesy and the faint hope of hiding the spots of color flaming in her cheeks. "Yes, Lady Beeth," she said. "I was just coming."

FIFTEEN minutes later, Lark sat across the wide kitchen table from Lady Beeth, with a feast of cold roast beef and popovers and a plate of sliced bloodbeets before her. The cook bustled around them with a pot of tea, a saucer of biscuits, and a tiny dish of plum jelly. Lark tried to eat delicately, but the beef was tender and juicy, the popovers soft as clouds. The cook winked at her from behind Lady Beeth's shoulder, and Lark, her mouth full, smiled at her.

When she had eaten half of a full plate, Lady Beeth put her elbows on the table and her chin on her open palms. "And now," she said. "You will tell me, young lady, what you were doing hiding out in our stables all the afternoon."

Lark could have protested that she was nineteen years old, after all, and truly an adult, but she didn't. Amanda Beeth always treated the motherless Lark as if she were her own daughter, and Lark returned her affection. She chewed the bite of beef in her mouth, swallowed, and answered, "I followed Mistress Winter. She left the Academy in a hurry, when the flight was over the harbor, and I was worried . . . I thought she might . . ." She waved her fork, not knowing how to say it all.

Lady Beeth only raised her eyebrows and watched her.

Lark took a sip of tea. It was light and fragrant, but it could have used, she thought, a twirl with a fetish. She lifted her eyes to Lady Beeth's and blurted, all in a rush, "Mistress Winter would sacrifice herself for the students of the Academy, for me, and for Hester, and even for Beryl and the others who are loyal to the Duke though he's making such a terrible mistake. I was afraid she would go to the Palace and turn herself in because the Council said she had to, then her horse would die and the Duke would win! And 'tisn't right; 'tis all wrong!"

"And what did you think, Larkyn? That you could stop her, all by yourself?"

Lark shook her head. "I didn't think," she admitted. "I just—Tup and I—"

"I believe Hester would say that it's up to you to do the thinking for your bondmate."

"Oh, aye." Lark looked down at her plate. Despite the scolding, the beef still looked good to her, and her fingers itched to pick up the remnants of the popover. The cook came close with the teapot to refill her cup, but Lady Beeth waved her off.

"I assume, Larkyn, that Hester doesn't know you're here."

"Nay." Lark shook her head. "She would have stopped me."

"Did you not think that she might worry about you?"

Lark's cheeks flamed again. "Nay, Lady Beeth. I didn't think about that, either."

Amanda Beeth sighed and dropped her hands into her lap. Her face softened a bit as she looked across the table, shaking her head.

"I'm sorry," Lark told her. "Truly I am. But I'm worried."

"We all are," Lady Beeth said. "Do you understand now what's happening?"

Lark shook her head. "Nay, I don't. All I know is that Mistress Winter left Sunny here and went off alone, and Amelia has been gone for days, and I'm afraid Mistress Winter is turning herself over to the Duke so he'll let Amelia go."

Lady Beeth reached across the table and touched her hand. "Larkyn, dear. We stand on the brink of civil war. Your teacher is trying to forestall that."

"Not all by herself!"

Lady Beeth smiled a bit at that. "Weren't you trying to help Philippa all by yourself?"

Lark hung her head at that. "I just—I can't bear for her to—"

The older woman squeezed her hand and released it. "She's not alone, Larkyn, trust me."

"But I saw her go off in the carriage!"

"And you saw the men ride out not half an hour ago, with Lord Francis and your brother at their head."

Lark gaped at her, and hope rose in her breast. "My . . . my brother? Nick?"

Lady Beeth looked at her oddly. "Why, no, Larkyn. It was Brye. Your elder brother."

"Brye? He's here?"

"No. He's gone with Lord Francis to rescue Philippa."

THIRTY-TWO

FROM inside the carriage, Philippa and the guard captain heard shouts before they felt the turning wheels grind to a stop on the icy road. Philippa had been leaning against the wall of the carriage. She straightened, and her stomach tightened.

The captain swore and reached for the latch of the carriage door. His musket was long and awkward, and for a moment he struggled with it, jamming it sideways in the doorway.

Philippa murmured, "Shall I help you?"

He gave her a look of pure fury that made him appear suddenly much older. He worried the musket through the doorway and slid down after it. Philippa scooted sideways on the bench seat, knocking the cushions to the floor, and looked out into the night.

She knew this road, of course. Her family home was a great pile of white stone on a hill south of the Rotunda. The best road from the Palace to Islington House led along the Grand River and across the New Bridge, constructed by Duke William's great-great-grandfather. The carriage was stopped, at the moment, in the very center of the bridge.

Stars glittered in a moonless black sky, reflecting on the moving dark water beneath the bridge and the dull metal of the muskets held by William's militia. They had them up and pointed into the darkness of the road ahead. Gas lamps flickered at the crest of the bridge and on the corner of the road beyond. Just outside of their pools of yellow light, men on horseback blocked the road. There were, Philippa supposed, about thirty of them to the mere dozen William had thought necessary to transport his captive. She couldn't see their faces, but she knew who was there.

Philippa steeled herself. With this act of rebellion, the gauntlet was cast down. She feared William would be all too eager to pick it up.

Or more likely, eager to allow others to pick it up for him.

The young captain brandished his musket. "Stand aside," he ordered. Only a slight cracking of his voice revealed his nervousness. "This party is on the Duke's business."

"We will stand aside," came Francis's calm voice, "as soon as you release the horsemistress. We will take her home."

"That's where we're taking her," the captain said. "And we mean to see it's done."

"I don't think we have quite the same destination in mind," Francis said.

William's captain stood with his legs apart. He held his musket at his hip, pointed at the rebel force. "I don't know who you are," he said.

"I'm Francis Fleckham, Captain," Francis said lightly. "We don't want a fight, and we don't want anyone to be hurt. But we *will* have the horsemistress, whether you hand her over willingly or under duress."

The captain said, "Take aim, men." Muskets were lifted to shoulders, leveled at Francis's men. Those who carried smallswords drew them.

Francis spoke with real authority. "Put down your weapons, men. There are a dozen of you, by my count, and there are thirty of us. We are all men of Oc. There is no need to splash the blood of countrymen on this bridge."

"I have my duty," the captain said.

"I know," Francis said with sympathy. "But your loyalty, I'm afraid, is misplaced."

One of the other militia, an older man with gray hair curling around his collar, growled something and pulled back the hammer on his gun.

An answering click came from the darkness, then another.

The young captain swallowed so loudly Philippa could hear it from where she sat.

She put her foot on the carriage step and braced herself with one hand on the door frame. She stood on the step, showing herself to Francis and his men.

The captain whirled to face her. The barrel of his musket looked enormous in the gaslight, but she was more wary of the panic in his eyes. "Don't move," he ordered.

"He's right, Philippa," Francis called. "Stay where you are." He clicked his tongue, and his horse took a few steps forward. Every musket rose to point at him, and Philippa sucked in her breath. Francis was fully in the light now, the pale Fleckham hair gleaming like ice.

The militia gawped as they realized who he was at last. Several of them gasped.

Francis raked them all with a glance. "Men," he said firmly, "I advise you to consider your position. Your Duke has made rash decisions and put not only you but your friends and your families at risk."

Lord Beeth called, "Have a care, Captain. We'll do what we have to."

The gray-haired man snarled something at the young captain, who hesitated, the muzzle of his musket wavering between Philippa and Francis.

Philippa said in an undertone, "Don't do it! Listen to Lord Francis, for your own sake!"

The captain's eyes narrowed, and he brought the gun to bear on her again. "Get in the carriage, Mistress," he said in a flat voice.

She held her ground. They had hoped, she and Francis and Beeth, to brazen this out without violence. Indeed, it seemed that these militiamen had no wish to take arms against a Fleckham, even if he had gone against the Duke's commands.

It was the gray-haired man who worried her. He wore the scars of some sort of fight on his face and hands, and he looked like someone who would enjoy a battle. Philippa glanced up at Francis. He, too, was assessing the older man, his eyes narrowed and his face hard.

Francis carried no weapon and had left his smallsword in its scabbard. He urged his horse forward another step, and several of the men with him did the same. The militiamen fell back a step, though the captain hissed at them, "Hold!" Only the gray-haired man did not yield. He swung his musket up to aim it directly at Francis's head.

Philippa's hand gripped the door frame of the carriage so hard the bones of her fingers hurt. The carriage driver leaped down from his seat and scurried for cover behind the frame, where the two footmen also clung, their heads down.

Francis said, "We mean business, men. This is no idle venture. You can put down your arms, let us have the horsemistress, and the incident will pass."

The gray-haired man sneered, "Why should we listen to a younger brother?" One of the other militiamen hissed something at him, and he laughed.

Someone behind Francis lifted his own musket, and another man drew his sword. Francis put up one narrow hand. "Wait," he said. "You men listen to me—"

He never had the chance to finish his thought. The gray-haired militiaman put his musket to his shoulder, and began to squeeze the trigger. The young captain cried, "No!"

And someone from Francis's side, a big man on foot with a broad-brimmed hat that flew from his head as he moved, leaped in front of Francis's horse and smacked the barrel of the musket with his hand, driving it upward.

The ball, an inch in diameter and lethal at such close range, flew above the heads of the carriage horses, whizzing past the iron balustrade that lined the New Bridge. A distant, small splash sounded when it hit the surface of the river.

There was the sound of another shot, a dull little explosion with no reverberation. The gray-haired man spun to his left, and fell. The young captain cried a command, and the men with smallswords leaped forward. Another musket fired, and from somewhere a pistol shot. At first Philippa couldn't move, frozen with horror as the situation exploded, men shouting, bodies falling, the horses snorting and shying so that the carriage jerked hard to one side.

She felt a hard arm seize her middle and yank her violently backward, just as a musket ball flew past her to smack into the cobblestones of the bridge surface. A hand, just as hard and strong as the arm, pushed her head down, wrenching her neck and banging her forehead on some spongy surface.

For a long moment it was all she could do to get a breath.

When she finally drew air into her lungs, she lifted her head and looked around wildly. She found herself inside the carriage, pressed down between the bench seats, knees and elbows on the carpet that lined the floor. Outside, men howled threats and orders, and there was a clash of metal.

The muskets, she knew, took too long to reload, so that once they were fired, the men would resort to swords and knives.

She huddled on the floor of the carriage, trying to take in the fact that Brye Hamley had not only saved Francis's life but very probably her own.

It seemed a long time, but might have been only moments, before the tumult on the bridge subsided, and someone opened the carriage door and helped Philippa out. It was not Brye this time, but Lord Beeth, his face grimy, his boots splashed with something Philippa feared was blood. She stepped down gingerly, looking about her with trepidation.

There was, she soon learned to her relief, only one death, and that was the one she had seen. The gray-haired man's body was being rolled into a blanket, and the young captain—his own captain—lifted his corpse and bundled it into the carriage once Philippa was out of it.

Order reigned on the bridge, and civility, though there were pools of blood on the cobblestones, and several of Francis's contingent stood with smallswords at the ready, as if at any moment the Duke's militiamen might change their minds about their surrender. Wounded men leaned against the balustrade while other men tended to their injuries.

None of the wounds looked serious. The carriage horses snorted alarm at the smell of blood, but their driver was at their heads, soothing them, keeping a watchful eye on the men around him. Philippa's heart missed a beat when she couldn't find Brye or Francis at first, but she found them behind the carriage, organizing William's militia to march back to the Palace.

Philippa looked into the face of the young captain. Defeat

and relief mingled on his pudgy features. His eyes and mouth looked years older than they had a short time before. Dreams of glory gone sour, she supposed. She knew from her own experience how hard death could be on the illusions of youth. Reluctant sympathy stirred in her breast, but she turned away from him. This was no time to go soft, and he would not welcome her feelings.

Francis strode around the back of the carriage. "Captain," he said.

"Yes, my lord," the young man said wearily.

"Tell my lord brother that we're sending you and your men back as a sign of good faith."

"That won't help Digby, will it, my lord?"

Francis's mouth quirked at one corner, an expression reminiscent of the crooked smile of his elder brother. "It will not, Captain. But it will help you and the rest of them."

"Aye." The young captain sighed, and his shoulders slumped. "Duke William will be very unhappy."

"It's in the Duke's power to stop all of this at any time."

The captain's brow furrowed. "Lord Francis, begging your pardon. Your lord brother says this is for a new Oc, with new connections to the Prince and men flying winged horses . . ."

"Have you seen a man fly a winged horse?" Francis said in a wry tone.

"Nay. Not yet."

"If your loyalty is placed with the Duke on that account, you may regret it," Francis said. "Now take your man back to be buried, and tell my lord brother all this will be forgotten if he will pacify the Klee and return their daughter to them."

The young captain's lips parted as if he would say something, but he hesitated. Philippa had turned back at the mention of Amelia, and saw this odd gesture. "What is it?" she asked.

The young man shook his head.

"Is it something about the Klee girl? Amelia Rys?"

The captain's round face was a picture of indecision. He touched his lips with his tongue and looked past Philippa, out into the sparkling swirl of dark water below the bridge. For a tense moment, no one moved, then he said, "I don't know the girl. Haven't seen her."

Philippa frowned and began to ask him again, but Francis moved on toward his own men, and Brye came up to offer Philippa a horse. Moments later the two groups parted, William's militia back the way they had come, Francis's contingent organizing itself for an orderly march back to Beeth House. Two of his men had received minor injuries, and they were mounted on horses for the short journey.

Philippa shook her head at Brye's offer of help and swung herself up into the saddle. The horse was a paint mare, her mane clipped close, making her spotted ears look long as a donkey's. Her neck was heavily muscled and her shoulders sturdy, and when Philippa picked up the reins, the mare took the bit in her teeth as if she was used to a heavy hand. Philippa put a hand on her neck, and said very low, "Easy, there, my friend. Let's be easy together," and the mare relaxed, chewing on the bit a little, then releasing it. Philippa patted her withers. "That's it," she said.

They had just reached the far end of the bridge when there was a small commotion behind them. Philippa twisted in her saddle and saw two men in the Duke's uniform come running across the arch of the bridge. Several of Francis's men drew their smallswords.

The two men stopped a little distance away, and a familiar voice said, "Steady there, my friends! We left our weapons with the Duke's men."

Brye Hamley stopped where he was, his fists on his hips, his face under the wide-brimmed hat in deep shadow. "Who's there?" he rumbled.

The newcomer laughed. "Take a blink, brother," he said. "'Tis that glad I am to see you!"

"Zito's ears," Brye said, and a grin spread across his face. "Nick!" He strode forward, and seized his brother by the shoulders.

"Nay, now, don't crush me!" Nick said, still laughing. "But I'm thinking Lord Francis won't turn down two more volunteers."

"No, I certainly won't," Francis said. "You're both welcome to join us. For the record, your names?"

"Nick Hamley." Nick lifted his cap to Francis, as jaunty a gesture as if he were meeting a new friend in a tavern. "Deeping Farm, the Uplands."

THIRTY-THREE

AMELIA, trembling, listened to the sounds of some sort of fracas on the bridge—the New Bridge, she thought it was called, to distinguish it from the fragile Old Bridge that could take only foot traffic. She and Mahogany and Jimmy had been asleep in their cold carriage house, and they startled awake at the noise.

"Fighting," Jimmy whispered.

"I know. It's not very close, though."

After a time the noise subsided, and Amelia curled again beneath the lap robe she was using as a blanket. Exhaustion reclaimed her before a few minutes had passed, and she didn't wake again until gray light began to show through the openings in the eaves and around the sliding door. Jimmy still slept, but Mahogany's head was up, ears turning this way and that, listening. Amelia got up and went to the back door to peer up the hill at the big house.

There were lights in the windows, and movement in the garden and in the drive leading up to it. She shrank back and pulled the door closed. She needed to relieve herself, but she didn't dare go outside with militia moving about.

After a moment, she gave in, and used the far corner of the carriage house, behind the old gig's sagging axle. Mahogany had done the same, and she supposed in time it would all take care of itself, but it was unpleasant, and she wished there were some other way. When she came back, she shook Jimmy awake, keeping a hand ready to stifle any sound he might make.

He sat up, eyes wide. "Fighting again?"

She shook her head. "No. But it looks like the soldiers up

at that house are going to leave soon. I thought we should be ready."

"Aye." He struggled free of his blankets and ran his hands through his disordered hair. He looked even younger in the daylight. His hair was more red than brown, and his nose was speckled with red freckles.

Mahogany, from his corner, snorted and stamped. Amelia hurried to shush him and stood stroking his neck, listening for the sounds of the militia in the road below the carriage house. There were voices, the sounds of boots, doors slamming. After perhaps fifteen minutes the sounds faded, the boots clomping away down the road.

"Patrol," Jimmy said. "They'll be off to the docks." He gave her a piteous look. "If them soldiers sees me there . . ."

"Just show me where your friend's boat is, and I'll do the rest," she assured him. "You can be off home to your mother."

"Aye," he said. " 'Tis my uncle's boat, actually. The *Ram's Head*. But with that horse . . . Them wings mark him, don't they?"

"They do," she said. "But with your back ways, we can slip along and no one will see us. That's why we should go now, before too many people are about." She went to the big door and slid it back a hand's breadth to look out at the road. "We'll go in the opposite direction of the patrol, all right? Are there back ways to do that?"

"Oh, aye," he said. "We'd best hurry. They says the war's going to start for real today."

She stopped with one hand on the door frame. "Today? Why today?"

He shrugged. "Don't know, Miss. They don't tell the militia nothing."

THE early snowstorm had blown to the west, where Amelia could see its gravid clouds creeping past the foothills and up the peaks of the Marins. Its passing left the sky a clear, pale blue above the city and the bay. And Jimmy, it soon developed, had not exaggerated his knowledge of the back streets.

For an hour he led her and Mahogany on a circuitous route,

dropping down toward the harbor, circling away on some cramped, crooked lane where piles of garbage rotted beside coal bins and stacks of firewood blocked doorways, then winding eastward through alleys and passages too narrow for any vehicle larger than a handcart. Amelia fussed over Mahogany, leading him cautiously through those places for fear his wings might be hurt by some jutting nail or broken board.

Amelia had never seen such neighborhoods, where people lived in cramped buildings jumbled together without apparent plan or measure. She was used to boulevards and avenues where trees and flowering shrubs created graceful landscapes. Here, the famed White City was not so much white as it was gray, and everything she saw seemed to be broken.

Jimmy peered around corners to be certain no one was about, a few times holding his arm out to keep Amelia and Mahogany hidden in an alleyway until a deliveryman or a woman with a market basket had passed. There were not many such instances. Mostly the streets were empty.

Amelia's skirt was soon damp from the melting puddles of snow, and she felt more than ever as if she would never be clean again. The smell of refuse and offal rose around her, and she saw Mahogany's nostrils twitch, as irritated as her own. She fixed her gaze on where the sea must be and was rewarded by a glimpse of cold green here and there between slanting walls and battered chimney pots.

At last the three of them crept from a final noisome alley to find themselves on the docks. A long boardwalk stretched north and south, curving around the inner edge of the harbor. Slatted docks stuck narrow fingers into the water, with boats of every size and color tied up to great iron rings. Most of the boats looked empty, sails furled, ropes and nets and barrels stowed. One or two had men working on their decks, but they showed no signs of venturing out into the bay.

Amelia looked out across the water and saw the *Marinan*, blue flags flying from its mainmast, rocking peacefully in the morning sunshine. There was no sign of preparations for war. "Are you sure they said today?" she asked Jimmy.

"Oh, aye," he said. "Today. Them Klee are itching for a fight, they said."

Amelia turned to him. "Jimmy, do you understand it's about me?"

He looked at her, his lips parted, his brow furrowed. He began to speak, stopped, and then said, "Nay, Miss, it ain't about you."

"I'm afraid it is, Jimmy."

He merely gaped at her, no light of understanding brightening his eyes.

"Didn't you wonder why I was hiding with a winged horse in that carriage house?"

"Aye. Well, nay. Not really. I was hiding, too, so . . ." His voice trailed off, and he scratched his thatch of brown hair. "But now that you say so . . . why do you want a boat, you and yon horse?"

Amelia drew a breath, and then said, as pleasantly as she could, "My name is Amelia Rys, Jimmy. I'm to become a horsemistress of Oc, but I was born in Klee."

"Klee?" he repeated.

Amelia repressed a spasm of irritation at his dullness. She said gently, "Duke William has been holding me hostage, Jimmy. That's why I need a boat. If I can reach the *Marinan*— my father's ship—in time, there need not be a war."

He bent his head, pondering this. Amelia waited, biting her lip with impatience. When he looked up again, he said, "And them extra taxes? They'd go away?"

"I don't really know about that, Jimmy. It's possible, I suppose. I only know that the *Marinan* is there in the harbor because of me, and if my father knows I'm safe, it can leave."

He nodded, slowly, and at last his face brightened a bit. "And I can go home," he said with satisfaction.

Amelia was not entirely sure this was true, but she let it pass. She said only, "Which boat belongs to your uncle?"

And Jimmy, grinning as if his cares had vanished all at once, pointed. "There it is!" he said. "The one with the ram's head painted on the front."

"The prow," Amelia said absently, peering down the moorage to find the one he meant.

"Oh, aye? Do you know about boats?"

"I know about ships," she said. "Not fishing boats. I arrived in Oc on the *Marinan*." She lifted Mahogany's lead and indicated to Jimmy that he should precede her. "Come, Jimmy, introduce me to him, will you please? And then, if I can persuade him to take me out to the ship, you can go home to your mother."

"What about yon winged horse?" he asked.

She looked at him in surprise. "Mahogany stays with me, of course," she said. "Don't you know that?"

"Know what?"

"Winged horses stay with their bondmates," she said. "Always. More than a day or two will send them mad."

His eyes widened, and he took a step backward, as if afraid Mahogany might exhibit signs of madness even now. "Come on, then," he said. "Let's see if he'll take you." He set off, then stopped abruptly. "Do you have any money, Miss? My uncle Vinny's that fond of money."

Amelia had been worrying over this all during their trek. She asked, "You don't think stopping a war is enough persuasion?"

Jimmy shook his head. "Nay," he said sadly. "'Tis money Vinny likes."

"Well, then," Amelia said with feigned conviction. "My father will pay him. When we reach the *Marinan*."

Jimmy set out again, but he gave her a doubtful glance over his shoulder. "I don't know, Miss Amelia. But Vinny's the only one I know what has a boat."

"Well, I will have to convince him." She touched the icon at her breast for reassurance.

"Aye," Jimmy said. He looked around to check that the street they were about to cross was empty, then led the way down the dock. The boat didn't look promising. Its cabin was little more than a shack stuck onto the deck, and everything was a dingy gray, except for the white ram's head with its curling horns. Poles stuck out on every side, for fishing, Amelia assumed, though her education had not run to the mechanics of that profession. Mahogany's hooves made a hollow clacking sound on the boardwalk. When they turned onto the dock where Vinny's boat was moored, he pulled back, fearful of the slatted surface. Amelia urged him forward, but slowly, fearful he might slip. Cold salt water splashed the underside and cast faint fans of spray between the boards. Everything smelled of salt and fish and oil.

But then, Amelia thought wryly, she smelled strange herself, having had neither bath nor bed for more days than she cared to count.

She followed Vinny to the end of the dock. She waited with Mahogany as he climbed aboard to knock on the cabin door. The sun glittered on the watery horizon and gleamed on the buildings of the White City. Amelia tipped her head up and closed her eyes for a moment, letting the sun warm her eyelids and her cheeks. She leaned back into Mahogany's warmth. He dropped his chin over her shoulder and blew gently through his nostrils.

"It's almost over," she said softly. "One more step, Mahogany. My father is right over there . . ."

She opened her eyes to look out across the bay at the *Marinan*. She imagined her father's composed face, his quiet demeanor, his air of calm authority as he ordered his men to their duties. A surge of longing made her throat ache. She swallowed and straightened her back. Her father would be disappointed if he saw that her eyes were swollen or her cheeks tear-stained. She would compose herself just as he always did. "One more step," she said again. Mahogany whuffed near her cheek.

Jimmy emerged from the door with its round, iron-barred window. A man came after him, a man not much taller than Jimmy himself. He must at one time have had the same red-brown hair, but it had faded to a kind of brownish pink. His unkempt straggle of beard was thin and pointed. He looked a bit like Lark's Uplands goat.

He clambered onto the dock, and stood beside Jimmy, squinting at Amelia and Mahogany. Jimmy said, "This is her," and his uncle nodded. His beard waggled, reminding Amelia even more of Molly the goat. He took a step forward, and Mahogany snorted and backed away. Jimmy said, "Them horses don't like men," and his uncle stopped where he was.

Amelia stood as straight as she could, smoothing her drooping tabard, and hoping her hair was still more or less contained in its rider's knot. "I'm Amelia Rys," she said. It seemed better not to use Master. She would need her father's name.

"Klee girl?" the man asked.

"That's right, Master—Master Vinny. I'm a daughter of Klee, now a student at the Academy of the Air. And I need to get to that ship." She pointed to the *Marinan*, and all three of them turned to it as if they hadn't seen it before.

Its white sails and neatly painted blue hull reproached the shabby boat bobbing at Amelia's feet. Longboats hung in ropes, ready to be lowered into the bay. The black shapes of the carronades faced out toward the city. There were at least a half dozen of them, dark reminders of the ship's purpose.

Vinny spat into the water beneath the dock. "Klee," he growled. "Been firing on our patrol boats for two days. We can't fish, can't take cargo in and out. The *Ram's Head* just sits here. Can't do nothing."

"I know, Master Vinny," Amelia said. "If I can get to her—to my father's ship—he will open the mouth of the harbor, and all of this will be over."

"Oh, aye? That important?" He looked her up and down, and flicked his eyes over Mahogany. His eyes were small, his lips full above the wispy beard. "'Twill be expensive," he said. "You have money?"

"You will have your reward when we reach the ship," she said. "You have my word."

"Heh. Your word," he said. "Can't spend that, can I?" His lips parted in a goatish leer. "But mayhap there's a reward due from the militia for a girl and a winged horse. Especially if the Klee wants you."

"Uncle, please," Jimmy began, weakly.

Vinny said, "Shut up, Jimmy. The *Ram's Head* is my business."

"This is about far more than business," Amelia said with asperity. "It's about war, and peace. And this war can be prevented."

Vinny said, "By a slip of a girl? Who would believe that?"

"Uncle," Jimmy said.

"Shut up," his uncle answered.

Amelia looked up and down the dock. There were two or three boats with some activity on them, though none was going out into the bay. Blessedly, Jimmy's patrol had evidently gone to another part of the docks.

She tried to imitate her father's air of dispassionate authority as she said, "There are no militia about this morning, as you can see for yourself. If you are not interested in the fee for ferrying me to the ship, I will go and ask one of those other boats. I would have expected you could use the money, as you haven't been able to fish for some days."

When he didn't answer, she said, "Decide now, if you please, sir. I want to be across the water before there's any more shooting."

She tried not to hold her breath while Vinny considered this. He scowled and tugged at a strand of his pinkish hair. Jimmy fidgeted, but Amelia stood very still. When several moments had passed, she said, "Very well, sir. Thank you for considering my request."

She turned her back, lifted Mahogany's lead, and took a step back down the dock toward the boardwalk.

"Wait," Vinny said in an uncertain tone.

Amelia stopped, but she didn't turn back. She looked over her shoulder, raised her eyebrows, and waited.

"So," Vinny said. "How much?"

She shrugged. "It will be sufficient. The Klee are known for their generosity."

"Known for making war," snapped Vinny.

Amelia looked at him for a breath, then said, very evenly, "It was not our Viscount who took a hostage and who refuses to give her up."

He eyed her. "That you, then? The Duke's hostage?"

"Of course."

"Aye. Heard something about that. Thought it was rumor put about by the rebels."

"I am she."

"And how are you going to stop that ship from firing on my poor fishing boat?"

"You may trust me on that, as well. I can let my father know it is I on your boat."

He nodded. Without another word, he stepped back and pulled something long and heavy from behind a pile of nets. He grunted with effort as he lifted it, and Jimmy leaped to his side to help him extract it and carry it across the deck. It was made of boards and cleated for traction, a walkway of some kind. He laid it across the port side of the boat, with one end on the deck and the other on the dock. He secured it with an iron bolt, then moved well away. "There you go," he said. "You and yon horse can come aboard. Let's get on with it. I'd like to get the *Ram's Head* back out to where the cod run."

THIRTY-FOUR

WILLIAM turned in his bed, his eyes still closed. The light through his eyelids seemed much brighter than it had the day before. He sat up and looked out the window to see that the weather had cleared. Beyond the slate roofs of the Palace the sky was a clear, empty blue. He threw back his covers and went to pull the curtains aside. The last of the storm clouds had retreated into the west, leaving Osham and its surrounding fields and pastures basking in cool winter sunshine.

"Diamond!" William whispered. "This is the day."

He rang for his breakfast, and while he waited for it, pulled on a full-sleeved white shirt, a pair of light trousers, and the boots he had ordered for just this purpose. They were glove soft, made with the lightest calf leather, with soft soles and low heels. He tied his hair in its queue and pulled on his vest. He forced the bone buttons into the buttonholes, straining the fabric across his chest. He paused briefly, running his hand over his swollen bosom. Perhaps, once he and Diamond had flown together, he could reduce the amount of the potion he was taking. It would be good to feel like himself again.

When the maid knocked at his door with his tray, he was just pulling on his riding coat, wondering if it would do for flying or would flap and blow about his legs and distract Diamond. He didn't realize Constance had come in behind the maid until he turned from his wardrobe to reach for his coffee cup.

"Constance! Ye gods, you gave me a start."

She was still in her dressing gown, an elaborately embroidered affair with a long, sweeping hem, and her mousy hair hung loose down her back. She looked, he thought, like a child wearing her mother's clothes. It was hard to believe she was older than Francis by at least three years. "William," she said in her breathy voice. "What are you doing?"

"I'm going to—" He stopped himself from saying "going to fly." He wouldn't say the words, not until he had actually done it. He finished, "—to ride. What did you think?"

"But, William, they're saying . . ."

"Damn it, Constance! What are they saying? Are you listening to gossip again?"

"I know we lost a winged horse the other day. It drowned in the bay."

"Blame that on the Klee."

Her eyes slid up to his, then away. "And something happened last night. On the New Bridge, someone was killed. I heard two of your—that is, two guardsmen talking about the Klee."

William blew out his lips in irritation. He wanted her out of his room, out of his sight. He wanted to go to Diamond, to have this great event done, achieved, accomplished! And here was Constance, whining and whimpering about things that could not possibly concern her.

"I don't know what you're worried about," he said. He sipped his coffee and watched her over the rim of his cup.

She twirled a lock of hair between her fingers, avoiding his eyes. "Don't you think you should do something? Stop this, or send someone to talk to the Klee . . ."

William put down his coffee cup. The tray held a boiled egg and a rasher of bacon, but he ignored them. The lighter he was today, the better for Diamond. "I am doing something," he said, buttoning his coat. He retrieved his quirt from the bureau and tucked it into his belt. "There's no need for you to trouble yourself, Constance." He walked to the door and held it open for her. "I must say, it's unlike you to take an interest in public affairs."

She said obstinately, "You should do something. You're the Duke."

He stiffened and glared at her. "I don't need a woman telling me my duty." His fingers itched for his quirt.

Her eyes flickered up to his again, then away in that maddening way she had. "My lord husband," she said, "Clarence tells me you've had a message from Prince Nicolas. It seems he's out of patience with you. Why should that be?"

It was true, of course, and Clarence would pay dearly for revealing it to anyone, much less a foolish woman with no understanding of state affairs. Nicolas had sent a message by courier—a horsemistress, of course, one of Oc's own—that William was to do everything in his power to pacify the Klee. He hadn't said anything specifically about the Fleckham School, and the issue of the winged horses, but he had implied a great deal. William had allowed Clarence to read it to him. He regretted that now, but it could not be undone. Unfortunately, the Prince had also seen fit to send a copy of his message to the Council of Lords, and the horsemistress had delivered that one first, before William could order her not to.

But he had no intention of discussing any of this with his wife.

"Go away, Constance," he snapped. "Find something to occupy your mind—if you have one—and let me get on about my work." He spun about and marched out of the room, letting the door fall shut behind him. He had no time for her nonsense this morning. In fact, he thought, when he moved to the Fleckham School to help the lads begin their own preparations to fly, he would send Constance back to her family. Barren as she was, she was useless to him, and she irritated him like a sliver under a fingernail. Thinking of her mewling on about the Prince and the Council—it made his blood burn.

But by the time he reached the stable door, he had forgotten her. The dead militiaman, the drowned horse, even the Klee and the Prince faded from his thoughts. His mind filled with anticipation until there was no room for anything else. He could already smell Diamond's essence, that sweet broth of horseflesh, straw, oats, and alfalfa.

He seized Diamond's bridle from its hook in the tack room, checked to see that the flying saddle was ready and waiting, and hurried eagerly toward her stall.

* * *

HE had meant to make his first flight with Felicity Baron and Sky Baron to monitor him, but they were nowhere to be found.

He could have ordered one of the horsemistresses assigned to the Palace to do it, he supposed, but he didn't know if he could trust any of them. It had been a shock to see how few of those at the Academy had followed his orders the day before. He had no intention of exposing himself to more betrayals. He would do this alone, as he had to do everything else.

This would solve all his problems. Once he had flown, Prince Nicolas would give way. The Council would cease challenging his every decision. Even the horsemistresses would come to heel, knowing their futures depended on accepting the new order in Oc.

That horsemistresses had no future in Oc—none at all—was a secret he would keep to himself just a little longer.

His pulse quickened when Diamond's finely cut head lifted above the half-gate of her stall. She shone like a jewel in the shadows, her great eyes gleaming, her coat bright as new satin. He approached her slowly, his boots soft in the sawdust, and held out his hand. She bent her muzzle to sniff at his palm, and her ivory forelock fell across his wrist like the silken drift of a lady's scarf. William breathed a sigh of pure pleasure and not inconsiderable relief.

It would be all right. It was going to be perfect.

He reached across the half-gate to stroke her neck, and the smooth muscles shivered beneath his hand. Gently, he slipped the bridle over her head and snugged the nosepiece lightly down over her muzzle. He thought he could not have borne it if she had shied away from him or shivered in that way she sometimes did. She tossed her head and blew through her nostrils, but she seemed eager to leave her stall.

She made no demur as he walked her down the aisle, dropped the reins, and brought the saddle from the tack room. His stableman poked his head out of one of the stalls in the connecting aisle, and said, "Do you need anything, Your Grace?"

"No, Blackley. Stay where you are."

"Aye, m'lord."

William smoothed the saddle blanket over Diamond's back and lifted the flying saddle into place. She snorted as he connected the breast strap and shied away as he tightened the cinches. "Quiet, Diamond," he said. "Quiet. We need these today." He ruffled her mane. "We're going to fly, my girl. Today. At last."

Her head went high, and white showed around her eyes. He stood back and stared at her. It was as if she understood his words, knew his intentions. Perhaps this explained why the horsemistresses were obsessed with their bondmates, why his father . . .

He picked up the reins and turned abruptly toward the paddock. His father couldn't have known this feeling. It was not possible for Frederick even to get close to a winged horse. Only he, William . . . He was the first.

His heart beat so hard he could barely hear Diamond's hoofbeats behind him. He led her to the mounting block and stepped up on it. She sidestepped, shying away from him. He had to step down and urge her close to the block again. He realized, as he did this, that he had not removed her wingclips. He hesitated, his hand on her near wing, wondering if he should wait, or release them now. He couldn't remember if Felicity Baron had said anything about it.

He closed his eyes, trying to remember. It seemed to him that when Diamond flew with Sky Baron, Mistress Baron removed her wingclips just as they went into the park. William glanced up at the windows of the horsemistresses' apartment, in the south wing of the Palace. He could, he supposed, send someone to ask them, but the idea of having to argue with them, of having to endure their sour expressions, that look of resentment at his daring to do what they did every day, was just too much.

He released the near wingclip, then stepped around Diamond's head to undo the other one. As he stepped up on the mounting block one more time, he said, "You and I, Diamond. You and I will do it our way, alone."

This time she stood still. He put his right leg over the cantle and settled into the saddle, snugging his knees beneath the thigh rolls, checking to see that Diamond's wings were free of the stirrups. The high cantle felt odd against his back. First-time flyers sometimes used leg straps, but he disdained them. If women could fly without being strapped in, it couldn't be hard.

Diamond shuddered once, then quieted.

He lifted the reins and turned her toward the park.

IT was not, he thought, what it looked like from the ground.

Diamond, of course, knew what to do. His weight did not seem to trouble her, though her balance wavered, just once, as she sped from the canter to the hand gallop, her wings outstretched, her neck beginning to reach forward. When they reached the level part of the park, where a narrow brook meandered over white stones, he felt her gather herself. It was the place Sky Baron used, launching just short of the little stream to skim the tops of the live oaks at the end of the park.

It was the launch that surprised him. He heard his own indrawn breath, even over the sound of the wind rushing past his ears and the beat of Diamond's wings. His muscles cramped beneath the thigh rolls as he gripped the saddle with all his strength. He hung on to the pommel with his right hand, only barely managing to keep the pressure out of his left, to let her have her head.

When he watched her fly from the ground, the process seemed as smooth and effortless as the flight of a bird. From a distance, she seemed to soar upward, weightlessly, as if the air caught her and lifted her almost without her volition.

Now that it came to the actual fact, the power in those silver wings stunned him. As Diamond leaped from the ground, he felt the strain across her chest as her wings caught the air. When she tucked her hooves beneath her, the movement nearly jarred him from his seat. Her wings beat once, twice, a third time, propelling them up and over the trees, and the ground fell away from them in a dizzying swirl of green and brown and remnants of white where the snow of the day before had not yet melted.

William's head swam with a sudden, vertiginous nausea, and he wished he had eaten something after all. His own muscles felt like butter in the sun compared with the hard, driving strength of this perfect, magnificent Diamond.

As she banked to the west, the usual flight path she and Sky Baron took, William remembered to sit deep in the saddle, to hold his hands low, to keep his heels down. He was startled to find tears on his cheeks and to feel a sob burst from his chest. He was terrified, and elated almost past bearing.

Flying! I'm flying. At last.

THIRTY-FIVE

PHILIPPA rose, dry-eyed and weary, after sleeping no more than three or four hours. A glance in the glass above the bureau made her groan. She poured water from the ewer into the basin resting on the marble-topped side table and splashed her face with it. She took a long time drying her face, breathing ragged sighs into the soft, thick towel. She treasured the moment of peace, of oblivion, before she put the towel down and went to the window.

Amanda Beeth had given her a room facing east. Only pastures and farmhouses lay between Beeth House and the sea. The early sun brightened the fields, emptied now of their harvests of alfalfa and timothy. The green water glittered, empty as the fields. The light from the North Tower was dimmed by the sunshine, and Philippa could just see, if she leaned very close to the glass, the tips of the masts of the Klee ship above the muddle of city buildings. There was nothing in the scene to hint at the forces set to explode into action.

But there were such forces, and she had to face them.

Amanda's housekeeper had left an assortment of brushes and creams and lotions on the bureau for Philippa's use. Philippa looked these over, but she had no idea what most of them were for. She picked up a jar of cream scented faintly with almond, which seemed safe. She smoothed some of it into her cheeks and throat. She brushed her hair and tied it in its rider's knot. It was nearly as much gray as red now. An old woman's hair, she supposed regretfully. She clicked her tongue with impatience at her vanity and turned resolutely away from the mirror. What did it matter? There was no one who cared about her appearance.

Someone had brushed her tabard and skirt and muddied boots, and laid out a set of clean smallclothes. With an inward nod of thanks to Amanda's excellent staff, Philippa put everything on, buckled her belt, and tucked her cap and gloves into it.

The main floor of the house was busy, though quietly so. Lord Beeth was going from ballroom to parlor, from dining room to morning room, giving instructions to the men in each. Maids hurried here and there with trays of coffee and sausages and baskets of fresh bread. Amanda Beeth, who Philippa doubted could have slept even half as long as she herself had, was in the foyer conferring with her housekeeper and caught sight of Philippa descending the stairs.

"Ah, Philippa," she said, as if it were any ordinary morning, and all of these people were ordinary houseguests. "Everything is in such a bustle. Won't you come to the kitchen with me for your breakfast? I swear, it will be quieter there than in any of the parlors."

"Thank you, Amanda. Good morning." She followed her hostess beneath the broad staircase and through double baize doors into an airy, high-ceilinged kitchen where three cooks were at work at a broad stone sink. Flames roared in an enormous close stove, and freshly made loaves were rising near the heat.

Amanda led Philippa to a worktable snugged under a slanting section of ceiling that was probably the underside of the main stairwell. There Philippa found Larkyn tucking into a plate of sliced bloodbeets and boiled eggs. Larkyn jumped up when she saw her.

"Oh, Mistress Winter!" she said. "'Tis such a relief to see you well!"

"Well enough," Philippa said, her tone tart to disguise her own pleasure at seeing the girl. Larkyn, at least, looked as fresh as a spring rose, the sunrise color blooming in her cheeks, her violet eyes sparkling. Her short hair sprang in vigorous curls around her face, and her tabard and skirt, like Philippa's, had been thoroughly brushed. "You certainly look well, Larkyn."

"'Tis because I've found Nick!" the girl exclaimed. "My brother Nick is here."

"Indeed," Philippa said in a dry tone. She pulled out a chair and sat down, nodding thanks for the cup of coffee Amanda handed to her. "Indeed he is, Larkyn. As you would say in the Uplands, 'tis lovely fine to see him again."

Larkyn grinned. "And as *you* would say, Mistress Winter, precisely so!"

Philippa laughed. Larkyn twinkled at her. "Take a blink at you!" she said impertinently. "You should smile a bit more often."

"Larkyn!" admonished Lady Beeth.

Larkyn sat down again, still smiling. Philippa, soothed by the exchange and the company, accepted a plate with a boiled egg and a few slices of dark red bloodbeets. One of the cooks brought a platter of rolls fresh from the oven, and Philippa took one. "Have you seen the horses yet this morning, Larkyn?"

"Oh, aye, Mistress Winter," the girl said. "Of course. I went straight there when I woke up. Both their stalls are cleaned and their water buckets full."

"Was Sunny calm?"

"Not last night, when you were away, but she knows you're back now. And there's an oc-hound with her."

"Very good, Larkyn. Thank you."

"And Mistress Winter—" The girl broke off, the color surging and receding in her cheeks.

"Yes, Larkyn?"

"They say that Caroline Rambler—well, I don't know what you call her now—survived. The patrol boat pulled her out of the water, half-drowned, but breathing."

"But Rambler . . ."

Sudden tears glimmered in the girl's eyes. "They never found him," she said. "The poor horse . . . he couldn't have . . ." Her lips trembled, and she pressed a finger to them.

Philippa touched the girl's shoulder. "Try not to think about it now, Larkyn," she said, striving for a gentle tone. "There will be time later."

"Aye," Larkyn said sadly. She dashed at her tears. "They say in the Uplands, a thousand days to grieve."

"Wise," Philippa said. "Like so many other things they say in your Uplands." She sighed, and started on her breakfast, though she would have liked to simply sit here in this bright, warm kitchen and drink cup after cup of the good black coffee. It was likely to be a long and difficult day, unless something good had happened she hadn't yet learned about.

"I suppose it's too much to hope that Amelia turned up overnight?" Philippa asked.

Francis gave a mirthless chuckle. "Yes, Philippa. Too much to hope."

They stood side by side on the front steps of Beeth House. The air had a bite to it that stung Philippa's nose and fingertips. She pulled her gloves from her belt, and shrugged into her coat. It was a good day for flying, at least.

Francis pointed to the men gathered in the oval courtyard. "We sent a patrol of our own out into the city last night, hoping for some sign of her. They found nothing. They stayed until the sun came up, to ask shopkeepers and warehousemen—those who have the fortitude to actually go to their businesses—but no one has seen her."

"She could have gone the other way," Philippa said. "To the foothills. Or even south, toward Isamar."

Francis nodded. Philippa glanced at him and saw that his eyes were as heavy-lidded as her own, his face drawn. "Francis, you look as old as I do," she said abruptly.

He managed a crooked smile. "That's not so old," he said.

She snorted. "You're being gallant. I look a hundred today, and worse, I feel it."

He said, "You know, Philippa, these men have gathered to follow my lead. And I haven't the least idea what to do next."

The men stood in squads of ten or twelve. There were a few smallswords, and not a few long pistols and muskets in evidence, but the lack of uniforms made them look ragtag and disorganized. Still, they were men who had come together out of conviction, Philippa thought. The lack of uniform should not matter, and they had proved themselves last night.

She caught sight of Larkyn flanked by her brothers. She was talking to them, gesturing, her black curls shining in the sun.

"Look, Francis. Do you see Larkyn, and Nick and Brye Hamley?"

He stepped forward a little. "Yes. Nick Hamley was lucky his captain didn't shoot him in the back."

"They are so close, the Hamleys. You and I, unfortunately, have had no occasion to understand that sort of family. But they and families like them are what's at stake here."

"I do know that, Philippa," he said. His voice was weighted with emotion. "I wish there were a wiser man to protect them."

"They're lucky to have you, Francis," she said. She put her gloved hand on his arm. "You will know what to do, when the moment comes."

"I hope you're right," he said, and patted her fingers.

"I believe," Philippa said, with as much conviction as she could muster, "that I would rather have a leader who questions himself than one who thinks everything he does is right simply because he is the one to do it."

Francis grimaced. "William was always that way, even as a boy."

"I remember that very well," she said. "And now, Francis, I am off to the stables at the Rotunda. I hope to talk some sense into Catherine Cloud and Elspeth Summer and the other horse-mistresses who have apparently taken up residence there."

Francis said, "I'm doubly sorry this rift has reached the Academy."

"I am, too, but perhaps we can at least heal our own differences. That would surely be of more help to you, to have a united flight to support you."

"Indeed. Although I hope it won't be needed."

LARK watched Mistress Winter take her leave of Lord Francis and stride across the courtyard toward the stables. She was so slender, Lark thought, her back so straight and her movements so quick, that she might have been a girl were her hair not going gray and her face weathered from flying.

Her own face would look the same before long, tanned and

lined by the wind and sun aloft. She wouldn't mind it. Such a face was a badge of office for a horsemistress.

She put a hand to the plain black fabric of her collar, where she hoped one day to pin the silver wings. If Duke William prevailed, her dream of becoming a horsemistress could vanish as swiftly as yesterday's snow had disappeared before the rising sun.

She shivered a little. Nick looked down at her, frowning. "Feeling peaky, Lark?"

She shook her head. "Nay. I'm fine."

The stable-girl met Mistress Winter, and they went into the stables together. A moment later Mistress Winter came out again, and beckoned to Lark.

Lark said, "Nick, Mistress Winter wants me. I need to go."

"Have a care, then, lass," he said, and patted her shoulder.

"'Tis you in danger, not me," she said. "Are you going off to fight the Duke's militia?"

"Only if Duke William does something—"

"Or if the Klee attack," Lark said.

Nick's cheerful features darkened. "We have no quarrel with the Klee. Their complaint is against the Duke."

"I know." Lark sighed. It was all so complicated. She saw no way out of this impasse, and no good resolution. She hugged her brother and crossed to the stables.

She paused at the door, looking east to where the sea glimmered green beneath the pale blue sky. Here and there thin streams of smoke rose from the plowed fields where farmers were burning the stalks of corn, the stubble of straw, the empty vines of peas and beans. Char was what they called that smoke, in the Uplands. They had called Tup's dam Char, because she had been the color of that smoke.

Lark touched her chest, where the icon of Kalla had hung until she gave it to Amelia. Thinking of Char always gave her a twinge of guilt, the feeling that she had failed her. And now she was Amelia's sponsor, and she had failed her, too. "Oh, Kalla," she breathed, "if only I knew where my icon is, there would be Amelia!"

She imagined she felt the faintest heat at her breastbone, where the icon had hung, the residue of its power. She had made a gift of it to Amelia when her foal was on its way. Amelia had been so frightened that the foal might not survive, or might be wingless, or might not like her, but all had gone well under Kalla's protection that day. Perhaps, even against these odds, Kalla could protect her creatures and the women who flew them.

Tup, hearing Winter Sunset preparing for flight, was hanging his head over the half-gate of his stall, whickering impatiently. As Lark passed Winter Sunset's stall, Mistress Winter said, "Saddle Seraph, will you, Larkyn? I want to get to the Rotunda right away."

"Aye, Mistress Winter." Lark started off, asking over her shoulder, "Why the Rotunda?"

"I have hopes it may not be too late to forestall another tragedy."

"Aye." Lark hurried down the aisle to Tup, just as he banged on the wall with one hind foot. "Tup! Tup! Be still," she whispered as she reached him. He tossed his head in answer and made his whimpering cry.

She let herself into the stall and made him back away so she could slip on his bridle. The stall needed mucking out again, but she would have to leave it to the Beeth staff.

She slipped the saddle blanket over Tup's back, and he sidestepped and threw his head, impatient to be moving. "Tup!" Lark said. "Not now!" She shortened the reins and made him bend his neck, snugging his head against her side. "Now, be quiet. Let me put the saddle on, then we'll be away." He blew against her tabard, but he held still. She released him, and lifted the saddle from the dividing wall.

"Larkyn! Are you ready? Let's get Seraph out of there before he does damage to the Beeths' stables!"

"Aye, Mistress. Coming!"

Lark, with her saddle already in her hands, saw that she had forgotten the saddle blanket. She set the saddle down in the straw, and spread the blanket over Tup. Winter Sunset, on her way out of the stables, whinnied.

Tup, hearing his monitor's call, began to prance. The saddle blanket slipped from his back and fell to the floor of the stall. When Lark picked it up, she saw that it was fouled with wet straw. She brushed at it with her hands, but the straw stuck to the wool. She couldn't put a wet, dirty blanket under the saddle.

"Larkyn!" Mistress Winter called again, and Lark heard the impatience in her voice.

"Wait here!" she commanded Tup. "And don't kick!" She raced down the aisle to the tack room, hoping to find a clean saddle blanket.

Just as she opened the door, she caught sight of Mistress Winter riding across the courtyard toward the ride used as a flight-and-return paddock at Beeth House. At the same moment, Tup's resounding kick against the wall of his stall made her exclaim, and whirl to see if he had broken something.

"Larkyn! Now!" An edge had come into Mistress Winter's voice.

Lark said, between her teeth, "Kalla's tail! I'm betwixt and between!" as she ran back down the aisle to Tup. She left the saddle where it was in the straw. She hastily unbuckled her old breast strap, the same she and Rosellen had made so long ago, and which she kept looped on one ring of her saddle skirt. It was the width of two fingers, and ran from one shoulder, around Tup's chest, and buckled in at the opposite shoulder. She had passed her first Airs by using this breast strap, though she had been scolded soundly when Mistress Winter discovered her subterfuge.

She slipped it around Tup's chest now, and buckled it. The leather was well used and pliable, and in a flash it was secure. She tested the handhold and leaped onto Tup's back.

"It will have to do, my Tup," she said, as she urged him out through the gate and down the aisle. "And after all, we're only flying to the Rotunda."

LARK hurried after Mistress Winter and Winter Sunset, taking Tup at a trot down through the courtyard, past the long cow byre, on toward the break in the hedgerow that opened into the ride. The men parted for her to pass and touched their caps as she rode by.

Nick called a farewell, and she flashed him a smile.

Behind Nick loomed Brye, a reassuring presence. "Be careful, Philippa," he said, his low voice rumbling across the courtyard as they reached the byre.

Lark caught up with Mistress Winter in time to see her cheeks flush pink as she inclined her head to Brye and touched the tip of her quirt to her cap.

Lark was so startled by this exchange, and especially Mistress Winter's blush, that she almost missed the turn into the ride. It was Tup who reminded her, tossing his head against the bridle, turning to the right without being bidden.

Lark recovered herself and set Tup to the canter a few paces behind Winter Sunset. Halfway down the ride, a gentle decline wide enough for two carriages to roll abreast, Tup sped to the hand gallop on the dry grass, and Lark gave him his head. At the far end, the land sloped upward again just a bit, with the bare branches of a hedgerow marking the lane beyond. Sunny ascended ahead of them, her broad wings shining like flame in the cold sunshine. Tup's haunches collected beneath him, and well before the hedgerow, he launched.

Even in the darkest and most fearful moments, the power and magic of the launch never failed to exhilarate Lark. Tup's wings caught the air with powerful downbeats, his hooves tucked tightly up against his body, reducing the drag of the air, and his neck stretched forward, as if he could swim upward from the land into his natural home, the sky. She remembered how overwhelming it had been, that first time, to feel the sheer strength of the launch, how improbable—how magical—it had been to shed the bonds of earthbound life.

The wind from the sea was sharp, buffeting Tup as he ascended. Mistress Winter led the younger flyers in a banking turn to the east, riding the wind's energy. When they reached altitude, she banked again, turning to the west where the fat wedding cake of the Council Rotunda nestled among boulevards and parks.

Lark pulled the peak of her cap down over her eyes against the glitter of sunlight reflected from the sea. Now she could see the Klee ship in the mouth of the harbor. It was long and narrow, with five masts of various shapes jutting above it, sails furled. A longboat hung in ropes at its side.

A much smaller boat was crossing the bay toward it, tossing in the choppy water. Lark squinted, trying to make it out. It wasn't one of the patrol boats, with their snapping black-and-silver pennants. This little boat bristled with poles, and she supposed it must be a fishing boat. But what was it doing there? She touched her fingers to her breastbone in the habitual gesture.

A tingle in her fingertips made her peer harder at the harbor. Something—some spark of intuition—called to her.

Her lips parted, and she narrowed her eyes. Was the spark on the Klee ship, or on the small boat? Was it possible the smaller craft was on its way to intercept the Klee ship? Why did that matter?

The sensation of a spark, like a small flame, intensified. She shaded her eyes with her hand, trying to see. Someone was on the deck of the little boat, standing among the poles. The someone was waving flags, black flags that tapered at the ends . . .

Kalla's teeth, those weren't flags! They were wings!

"Amelia!" Lark breathed. "It's Amelia—and Mahogany!" She urged Tup to a faster speed, trying to catch up with Mistress Winter. She called out, but the wind caught her voice and swirled it away. Winter Sunset was already beginning her descent toward the park across from the Rotunda. Mistress Winter didn't look back, and Lark couldn't catch her attention.

A carronade fired.

Lark gasped, and frigid air shocked her throat. Tup faltered, just for a wingbeat, enough to make them fall behind Winter Sunset.

She twisted her neck to look back at the harbor. It wasn't the Klee ship that had fired its cannon. A puff of gray smoke rose from the inner side of the harbor, and she saw that it came from a patrol boat just setting out across the water, angling toward the fishing boat. As it approached, it fired again. The ball splashed uselessly into the water, halfway between the patrol and the fishing boat, but the patrol boat was moving fast, its sails puffing in the wind.

The spark Lark sensed flared brighter, like an ember from a banked fire. She knew what it was, though Mistress Winter would have scoffed.

It was her icon, calling to her.

The Klee ship's sails began to unfurl and open. They belled majestically, each great white canvas filling with wind as it rose above the decks. The ship heeled, coming about, but its size made it slow.

A second patrol appeared from inside the docks, its sails fluttering as it sped across the bay. A battle was building even as Lark watched, and those awful cannonballs would fly right into the path of the boat carrying Amelia and Mahogany. How was it that she could see that a winged horse was on its decks, and they couldn't?

Or perhaps . . . perhaps they could. Perhaps that was the whole point.

"Kalla help me!" Lark cried into the wind. She reined Tup up away from the Rotunda park, out toward the harbor. She had to help Amelia. She didn't know what she could do, how she would stop the patrol boat before it engaged the Klee ship, catching Amelia and her colt in the middle of their battle. She didn't have an idea yet, but she would have to do something.

Lark glanced over her shoulder and saw Winter Sunset was coming to ground in the Rotunda park. She could almost feel Mistress Winter's fury when she looked up and saw that Tup was not behind her, that he and Lark were winging out toward the bay. Lark was sorry about that, regretting that once again she had caused Mistress Winter aggravation and concern.

But this was no time to think of the trouble she herself was in. She was the only one who saw what was happening. Amelia and Mahogany had no one else to help them.

"Hurry, Tup!" she cried, loosening his rein and shifting her weight a little forward so the angle of his wings could be sharper, could catch more of the clear, chill air, drive them faster toward the harbor. He responded, his wings beating harder, the flex of his muscles radiating through her thighs and her calves. As he tilted, she felt every movement, felt as if she and he were one body, one will. Praise Kalla she had no saddle to impede her!

"Oh, Tup, my lovely, fine boy! Fly as fast as you can!"

THIRTY-SIX

WILLIAM found that his teeth were chattering from excitement as much as from the chilly air aloft. Diamond flew straight toward the hills, her wings glistening an exuberant silver in the sunshine, her neck stretched, her ears pricked forward. William experimented, just a little, with his seat in the flying saddle. It seemed that the deeper his heels were in the stirrups, the more he could settle his weight against the cantle and press his thighs and calves against the stirrups, the better he could feel Diamond's movement. He was glad of the thigh rolls that helped him keep his knees down, and he tried to loosen his grip on the pommel, to trust Diamond's balance to keep him in the saddle.

The ripple of muscle across her chest caught his eye, and he looked down, past her beating wings. It was dizzying to see the ground spin by so far beneath him, the farmhouses like chess pieces on a great, uneven board of fallow fields and narrow lanes. Only the road from Osham, twisting away toward the Uplands, gave him some certainty that he knew where he was.

When he judged they had flown far enough to the west, he laid the rein gingerly on the left side of Diamond's dappled neck and pressed his left calf against her shoulder, just beneath the jointure of her wing. Obediently, as if it were a logical thing to do, she banked and turned.

William seized the pommel with both hands in a sudden spasm of terror at the change in angle, and his thighs clenched beneath the knee rolls. Diamond's body quivered in response. He struggled to relax, to keep the rein loose. Her flight evened out in a few seconds, and soon he felt secure again, heels down, head up, hands low on the reins. They were flying north now. Perhaps they could take a turn above Fleckham. Perhaps the lads there would look out their windows, stream out into the courtyard, and catch a glimpse of the glorious future that awaited them.

They flew on for perhaps ten minutes, and William's thighs began to tremble with effort, his neck to feel rigid from holding his back straight. They would, he thought, take the turn over Fleckham, then go straight back to the Palace. They still had that first landing to deal with. Mistress Baron had warned that coming to ground was more perilous than the launch. He felt a jolt of anxiety as he thought about how far down he had to go, how hard the ground would be when they got there.

But first, the slate roofs of Fleckham House beckoned ahead of them. He saw the tops of the trees of the little beech grove and the clean-swept stones of the courtyard. With a little more confidence, he reined Diamond in a big circle. As her right wing dipped, he couldn't help seizing the pommel again, leaning to the left, and he wished, after all, that he had strapped himself into the flying saddle. There might have been no shame in that.

He gripped the pommel until he thought his knuckles would split as Diamond banked through the turn, wheeling high above the park. The paddocks and gardens spun beneath them, tiny rectangles of brown and green and beige, set off by the rail fences and the hedgerows. And now they were above the house, the Fleckham School. A surge of pride flooded William's chest, making him giddy. He dared to rein Diamond around again, a smaller circle this time.

He must, he thought, give credit to Felicity Baron for her flights with his filly. Diamond's wingbeats were so smooth, her balance so perfect, that although he was quite naturally nervous for his first flight, his confidence grew with each passing moment.

And there they were! The boys of his very first class, the lucky young men who would—after William himself—be the first horsemasters, the genesis of a new breed. They came out of the house, and stood in the center of the courtyard, staring up at him, just as he had dreamed they one day would.

He wanted to wave at them. He forced himself to loosen one hand from the pommel, to lift his quirt in a salute.

And one of the boys below, the one called Frederick, no doubt, with his pale hair shining in the cold sunshine, gave an answering salute, arm lifted, white face turned up to the sky.

William's heart pounded with a burst of reckless energy. He would land here, at the Fleckham School! It was a momentous occasion, and it should be shared, celebrated, with these fine lads whose futures had just been assured.

He reined Diamond around one more time, aligning her with the lane other winged horses used to come to ground. It was raked smooth, rocks and clods picked from the surface. He pressed his knees against her shoulders, as Mistress Baron had told him to do, and he loosened the rein. She had to have perfect freedom of movement, he knew. She had done this dozens of times, following Sky Baron, gathering herself, tucking her hind legs, reaching with her forelegs. The only difference was balance.

And if the girls of the Academy could do it, he could most certainly manage. For a wingbeat, two, Diamond hesitated, as if she might refuse his direction. His heart nearly stopped until he felt her acquiesce, give in to his will. She pointed her ears forward, stretched her neck, and began to descend.

And then, abruptly, she beat her wings again, hard. She ascended, skimming along the lane, her tucked hooves nearly brushing the heads of the boys in the courtyard.

William shouted at her. "Diamond! No! No! Down!"

Her wings beat harder, rippling with effort as she drove upward, away from Fleckham House. She turned to the east, banking so sharply this time that William had to lean forward over the knee rolls, grasping desperately at the pommel to avoid sliding out of the saddle. His muscles felt like water, and he wished again that he had eaten something, anything, that would have given him strength. He dared not look back to see the boys gawping at him, watching him lose control of his filly, observing this utter humiliation.

"Diamond!" he cried. "What are you—"

And then he saw it. He saw *them*.

Beyond the rooftops of the White City, past the Old Bridge and the ironwork arches of the New Bridge, the sea flashed green and silver in the sun. The sails of the Klee ship were open, bellied with wind, and the ship was heeling about, angling across the harbor mouth toward what looked to William, at this distance, like one of the little fishing boats that moored at the Osham docks and plied the waters beyond the bay. From the inner harbor came a patrol boat, and as he watched, a puff of smoke rose from its decks, and the distant thud of the carronade sounded. He was too far away to see the splash as the ball hit the water.

But what had attracted Diamond, what had caused her to refuse his command, was a winged horse. William knew that horse, and he knew his rider.

It was the brat. And it was the little black stallion that should have been his, which had been foaled in the wrong place because Pamella had fled into the Uplands and somehow lost her mare in the process. Her mare had foaled Black Seraph at Deeping Farm, and that cursed Hamley brat had bonded with him before William had a chance to do anything about it.

And now here she was—here they both were—ruining his second chance as they had ruined his first.

Fury obliterated all caution. William lifted his quirt again, and this time he used it. He struck Diamond's sleek, dappled flank with the little braided whip, and screamed at her, "No! No! You will do as I tell you!"

She shuddered beneath him, but still she would not turn. She laid her ears back, and the muscles across her chest ridged with effort. He struck her again, and again. She squealed as tiny drops of blood flew from her delicate hide, but she would not respond. She kept on, flying faster and faster, higher and higher, driving toward the company of another winged horse.

Fear clutched him as Diamond rose so high that the copper dome of the Tower of the Seasons spun beneath her wings. They soared above the white, crenellated circle that was the roof of the Rotunda. The flags of the great houses fluttered in the wind, mocking him with their gay colors. William gritted his teeth so hard they hurt.

He tried to gather in the reins. Diamond shook her head against the pressure, and her flight wobbled so that William nearly lost his seat. He grasped the pommel with all of his failing strength. She would have to come to ground sometime, because she would tire. He would simply have to hang on, to outlast her.

In the meantime, their path brought them closer and closer to Black Seraph and Larkyn Hamley.

It was her fault, that damned Uplands chit of a girl. William kept his quirt in his hand, squeezed tightly between the pommel and his palm. He would, he swore, make them both pay.

THIRTY-SEVEN

AMELIA clung to Mahogany's neck as the little boat rocked perilously on the waters of the bay. The two of them huddled behind the cabin. The *Marinan* was turning toward them, slowly, slowly, its great sails tilting, emptying, then filling again as it swung about. They had seen her signal. But the patrol boats were smaller, faster, far more maneuverable than the *Marinan*. And they, too, must have seen her signal.

There had been no other way for her to let the *Marinan* know—to tell her father—that she was there, that she was coming. But it seemed she had made everything worse.

Mahogany had been so obliging. She had led him to the bow, spoken softly in his ear, then removed his wingclips, admonishing him all the while. He had tucked his chin, listening to her, his ears turning to the sound of her voice, his wide, wise eyes gleaming with understanding. She touched the jointure of his wings with her hand.

Mahogany had not hesitated. With heart-stopping grace, he opened his wings. They spread wide, black and glistening, great silken flags that quivered in the wind. The pinions fluttered like the wings of the gulls that flew curiously overhead, but he held them steady, as high above the deck as he could. It seemed almost that the *Ram's Head* itself might take flight.

The shout of the ship's watchman from his perch at the crossbeam of the mainmast had carried across the water. Amelia couldn't make out the words, but she could see the sailor scrambling down the mast, and moments later she saw the blue-uniformed officers come out of the captain's quarters and hurry to the stern to peer across the water.

Mahogany stood like a copper statue, his red coat burning

in the cool light, his black wings arched and still. He held his head high, his nose into the wind. His hind legs stretched in a proud line, and his tail arched, flowing like a black pennant. It was not natural for a winged horse to hold his wings thus. His muscles quivered against Amelia's shoulder as he balanced against the movement of the waves, but still he kept his wings lifted, because she had asked it of him, because whether he knew what it meant or not, he understood it was important.

Amelia's heart pounded with pride, then relief. Someone— it may even have been her father—waved an acknowledgment with a blue-and-white flag, three deliberate passes of the flag above his head. She touched Mahogany's wing points again, and he folded them as deliberately and elegantly as if he were folding a great fan. She had stood there in the prow of the dingy fishing boat, feeling at that moment as if she were the Viscount himself, standing at the head of a great procession. Success seemed within her grasp, and elation at having succeeded in her mission made her eyes sting.

And then Vinny, from behind her, shouted, "Patrol!"

Amelia looked back, toward the inner harbor, where the docks of the north and south sides of the bay angled toward each other. A patrol boat came skimming across the bay, its little sails full, carronades sprouting from its bow. Behind it came another, flitting across the water as nimbly as a seabird. She backed Mahogany as quickly as she could, out of the prow of the boat, turning him, scrambling back to the frail shelter of the cabin.

Just as they reached it, the first patrol boat fired its cannon.

The distance was too great to reach them, but it was a warning. The patrol boat meant to stop the *Ram's Head* from reaching the *Marinan*.

The Klee answered with another carronade, the ball splashing uselessly into the water.

"Can you go faster?" Amelia called to Vinny.

He shook his head. "'Tis all she's got," he shouted back.

"The *Marinan* is turning," she said. "If we can get behind her—"

But she could see it was no use. The big sloop, though the sailors were running up the sails as fast as they could, was not easily maneuverable in close quarters. She heard the slap of the sails in the wind, and saw the bow dip and rise again, plowing heavily through the choppy green water, slowed by the backwash of its own wake. The patrol boats were coming up fast. The nearest one fired again. This splash was closer, the boom of the gun louder.

Someone shouted from the deck of the *Marinan*, and Amelia buried her face in Mahogany's neck, feeling helpless. They would take her again and separate her from Mahogany. She had failed, failed her father and failed her adopted principality, to say nothing of the Academy of the Air. The Klee would attack the city, and the war would break out. There would be no stopping it.

Mahogany threw up his head, jerking his neck away from her. He whinnied, a long, loud call that pierced the sounds of the wind and the cannon and the shouting of men.

Amelia looked up at him in surprise. He craned his neck above her to look west toward the city, his ears pricked forward, his nostrils flaring wide.

Amelia spun about to peer into the pale sky. There, winging swiftly toward the bay, was a black Ocmarin with long, narrow wings.

"Seraph!" Amelia cried. "Oh, Mahogany, it's Seraph! And Lark!"

And then, from farther inland, just cresting the dome of the Tower of the Seasons and swooping high above the white circle of the Rotunda, came another winged horse.

Amelia didn't recognize the second flyer. The horse was a pale gray, with silver wings and a white, streaming tail. The rider was tall, dressed in black, but there was no ripple of skirt behind the horse's laboring wings, and there was no peaked cap to signify a horsemistress. Whoever it was hunched forward over the pommel of the flying saddle like some terrified first-level student. But no first-level girl would ever be flying over water, or flying without a monitor to watch every wingbeat, every hoof tuck, every twitch of rein and angle of boot.

A carronade ball whooshed over the prow of the boat, terrifyingly close now, and struck the water three rods to starboard. Amelia held Mahogany's head close to her, murmuring, "Don't be afraid, my dear. Don't be afraid," as much for herself as for her colt.

The *Marinan* had almost come about, its starboard carronades rocking in their webs of rope, the blue-clad sailors training them on the patrol boats. But the patrols swept on, driving themselves through the water, hurrying to put the *Ram's Head* squarely between their own craft and the Klee ship.

"Vinny!" Amelia cried. "Do you see them?"

And Vinny, her mercenary champion, struggled with his sail to bring his own little boat around, swearing and sweating in the cold wind. Spray shot over the deck and splashed Amelia's bedraggled skirt. Mahogany, too, was wet with salt water, but he stood his ground, bracing his hooves against the slippery boards. His muscled neck trembled against Amelia's shoulder as she felt him lean with the sway of the boat. Once her foot slipped, and she slid sideways. She grasped at Mahogany's mane, and he tucked his chin across her body as if to hold her in place beside him. When she had recovered her footing, she held his neck tightly and crooned endearments to him. She could think of nothing else to do.

She realized a moment later that the *Marinan* was holding its fire. She looked up, past Mahogany's streaming mane and forelock, and saw the soldiers on deck, poised behind the rank of cannon. Behind them were blue-uniformed officers, all of them frozen in a tableau of waiting.

It was because of the *Ram's Head*. She squinted, trying to make out which of the officers was her father. He would be trying to give Vinny a chance, to give the *Ram's Head* enough time to duck behind the *Marinan*, where the cannonballs could not reach it.

They were lowering a longboat, too, she saw, on the port side of the *Marinan*, but that would be of no help to her and Mahogany. It would never hold her colt, and surely her father knew she would not leave him.

Another carronade fired, with a puff of greasy smoke, and Amelia and Mahogany flinched at the same time. Amelia glanced over her left shoulder, to see how close the patrols were. She cried out again.

A third winged horse was coming across the bay, and coming fast. This horse Amelia knew. The gleaming red wings, the perfectly tucked hooves, and the elegant head of Winter Sunset were unmistakable, outlined in pale sunshine. No one had a better seat or more perfect posture in the flying saddle than Philippa Winter. She and Winter Sunset were closing on the mysterious gray, even as the gray's flight wobbled, then steadied, only to wobble again. And Lark and Black Seraph came on, flying directly at the patrol boat nearest the *Ram's Head*.

"Oh, no, Lark," Amelia sobbed. "Don't! Don't!"

It was clear that Lark and Seraph meant to distract the patrol boat, to give the *Ram's Head* a chance to get behind the *Marinan*.

"Oh, no," Amelia cried again, her voice breaking. She wanted to bury her face in Mahogany's mane, and not watch, but she couldn't. She had to face what was happening. If Lark had the courage to fly in the face of such danger, then she must, also. She was a Rys. And she would one day, Kalla willing, be a horsemistress.

Of all the Airs and Graces, Arrows was the most dangerous. Lark had listened to Mistress Dancer's lectures about it a dozen times. She and Tup had tried it only twice, and then under Mistress Dancer's careful tutelage.

But this was what Arrows was meant for. This was why it was the final test for the flyers of the third level, why it was the last of the Airs to be performed before they earned their silver wings. Every horsemistress hoped she would never have to use Arrows, but every flyer prepared for the eventuality.

And Lark was about to try it without a saddle.

She put her hand on Tup's neck. She felt his confidence and strength through the heat of his muscles, saw it in the stretch of his neck and the power of his wingbeats as he slowed just above the patrol boat. He liked her flying bareback. He liked to feel her legs wrapped securely around his barrel, her toes tucked tight beneath his wings. She firmed her hold on the handgrip, and pressed her calves hard against Tup's ribs.

The *Marinan* dipped and wallowed as it made its turn, coming about into the wind. Lark saw Amelia's white, upturned face. Mahogany stood on the deck, his red coat dark with sea spray. A man was pulling lines, running back and forth between the little open cabin and the piles of rope that dotted the deck. The patrol boats had all the advantage, full crews, narrow hulls, and a running start.

And on the first patrol boat, the carronade swung in its rope sling to point directly at the fishing boat, where a precious winged horse braced on the deck with his bondmate.

"Tup!" Lark cried, though she doubted he could hear anything over the wind. "Are you ready?" She offered a silent prayer to Kalla as she let the reins swing free, and she shouted, "Now, Tup! Now!"

His slender wings stilled for just a moment, and he hovered briefly above the leading patrol boat. Then, like a hunting seabird, he dove toward the restless water.

The men on the patrol boat froze. They were citizens of Oc. They revered the winged horses, as their fathers had, and their fathers' fathers. A winged horse had already died in the conflict, and that loss would have been a shock to every citizen.

From the corner of her eye, Lark saw the captain of the patrol boat drop his arm, ordering the carronade to fire.

But the men handling the cannon straightened and backed away from it, just as Tup's fierce dive toward the water brought him within a wing's length of the waves.

PHILIPPA'S heart lurched when she realized what Larkyn and Seraph were attempting. Larkyn had always been impetuous, but this was madness. She was wagering her life, and Seraph's, against reverence for the winged horses. Lark trusted that the patrol would not fire on another of Kalla's precious creatures, no matter what a mad Duke ordered them to do. She could not imagine how Lark had convinced herself . . . but Lark often knew things she couldn't know, that she shouldn't know. Philippa could only pray the girl's faith was not misplaced.

And Larkyn and Black Seraph were still students, still young, and Arrows was the culmination of the six years of training required of every horsemistress and every winged horse. There were good reasons it was held until the third level. Philippa had lain awake many a night at the Academy, anxious about teaching the maneuver. The speed of descent, the strength required to pull out of it, the dangers of coming too low, of employing too sharp an angle . . . More than once she had called a pair of flyers out of the pattern, fearing a fatal mistake. And now Larkyn and Seraph were about to try it, and they were too far away for her to help them.

The *Marinan* rolled from side to side as it turned, its bow dipping deep into the water and rising again as it plunged through its own wake. The patrol boats surged toward the little fishing boat, where it bobbed helplessly, struggling toward the *Marinan*.

And between Philippa and the threatening disaster was the dapple gray filly, her tail streaming in the wind like a banner of cloud, her silver wings beating more erratically every moment. William hunched over the pommel, his tension and strain exhausting his mount as she fought to compensate for his lack of balance.

Sympathy for the filly made Philippa's heart ache. The young horse had been too isolated, and even her monitor had deserted her. She was making a desperate effort to join others of her kind, hindered by an imperfect bonding and an incompetent flyer. Philippa feared there was no way to save her. If William fell, one or the other of the boats below him in the bay could fish him out. But a winged horse, with its wings extended and vulnerable, would be doomed. That had been proved only yesterday.

But there was no time for such thoughts. They would not help Larkyn, or Black Seraph, or Amelia and Mahogany, huddled there on the little fishing boat. Philippa resisted the urge to press Sunny to fly faster. Sunny was doing everything she could. Philippa felt the heat of her effort through her hands, through her calves. Foam from the juncture of her wings and chest spattered her wing membranes, and her breathing grew labored. Philippa, too, found herself gasping for breath.

Old, she thought. Winter Sunset and I are both getting old. Our battles should have been behind us by now.

She peered ahead, past the straining filly. Seraph was poised over the patrol boat, his small body hesitating in the air like a hawk plying thermal currents, wings stilled, head forward, feet tucked. And then, just like a hawk, Seraph's wings tilted and he drove toward the water. Every line of his body, every angle of his wings, was perfect. Larkyn kept her hands low, her body curled ever so slightly forward. There would be nothing to criticize in such a performance, no remonstrance about balance or tension.

The same could not be said for William. Just as Seraph, with a flash of his shining black wings, began his precipitate descent between the patrol boat and the ungainly little fishing boat, Diamond began to lose altitude. Her wings wavered as William leaned too far forward. His hands gripped her reins too hard, pulling her chin back so that she was forced to expend even more precious energy fighting the bridle.

Philippa swore. She couldn't reach Larkyn and Seraph, and she couldn't stop the patrol from firing its cannon. But perhaps she could talk William and Diamond down. Furious though she was at William for creating this situation, she couldn't abandon a winged horse, any winged horse. She would have to try.

THIRTY-EIGHT

TUP angled his wings, and dove so quickly toward the patrol boat that the men on board cried out. As they fell toward the water, the dark maw of the carronade trained on them, so close that Lark's bones ached with awareness. She could almost taste the cold tang of the seawater, feel the icy surge of it over her body. All control was Tup's. She could only cling to him, curled above his withers, her legs molded to his body. The wind burned her throat and her eyes, and her cap flew off, twirling away to land limply in the water.

And then, at what seemed the last possible moment, the tilt of Tup's wings changed. They began to beat again, hard. His body shuddered as he exerted all of his strength to level his path, to dodge the prow of the boat. He skimmed the water, his tucked hooves almost touching the waves, for one, two, three wingbeats. Lark praised Kalla that she had no saddle to deal with. Through her thighs and her calves, she sensed every movement of Tup's great wing muscles, every shift of his body weight. She never felt, for even a moment, in any danger of slipping. She straightened, leaning forward, and almost felt that her own will, her own strength, assisted Tup as he began to rise again. The men on the boat exclaimed in amazement as Tup ascended, lifting from the dangerous water. Lark became aware that gulls were circling them, flying with them, creating a formation rather like Open Columns. Their cries filled her ears, and she found a trickle of tears on her face, tears of pride and relief and even hope. She cried, "Lovely, fine boy you are, Tup! Brave boy! Well-done!" The gulls seemed to echo her praise.

Lark glanced back and down, and saw the captain of the

patrol boat gesticulating at his men. She couldn't hear what he was saying, but she could guess. His men had backed away from the carronade, letting its muzzle clatter onto the deck. Its web of ropes lay slack around it. Someone else had run down the sail, and it draped about the mast, flapping uselessly.

Beyond it, the little fishing boat darted to safety behind the bulk of the *Marinan*.

Lark hoped the *Marinan* would keep holding its fire. Surely Baron Rys would not punish the men on the patrol boat for disabling its cannon. His daughter would soon be safe in his care. He had no reason to fire again.

Tup rose more slowly now into the empty sky. Lark felt his fatigue, and she knew what Arrows had cost him. She lifted the rein, to turn him back toward the land.

DIAMOND'S wings labored, fluttering. Sunny caught up with her easily, and Philippa let her pull a little ahead, hoping the filly would match her wingbeats to the older mare's. Diamond's eyes were wild, and spittle and foam blew from her lips. Philippa's heart broke at the sight of her.

William's eyes were wild, too, black as night in his pale face. His hair had come loose from its queue to flutter around his head. He had Diamond's reins wound through his fingers, and his hands clenched the pommel of his saddle, one fist on top of the other.

He cast Philippa a sideways glance, then away, as if she were no more than an apparition, a figment of cloud and wind. She shouted, "William! It's too much for her!"

His lips were pulled back from his teeth, and he looked like a death's head, bone-thin, grimacing, cruel. His quirt hung by a loop from one wrist, and there were strips of red on the filly's flanks. What a fool he was to whip a winged horse, and on their first flight!

Philippa shouted, "William, please! Your filly! You'll kill her!"

He looked away from her, and she saw how his eyes glittered, how his legs cramped beneath Diamond's wings. He was doing everything wrong. Diamond dropped lower and lower toward the water, her hooves beginning to flail, her neck bowing against the pull of the reins.

Philippa drew breath to try again, but at that moment, Larkyn and Seraph darted out from behind the patrol boat, which bobbed crazily in the wake from the *Marinan*. Seraph was ascending. Larkyn's spine flexed beautifully with his movements, and her hands were easy on the reins. Relief rushed through Philippa as they turned inland. They, at least, should be safe.

But then William pried his left hand from the pommel of his flying saddle. He yanked on Diamond's rein, forcing her to the left, on an intercept path with Larkyn and Seraph. He twirled his quirt on its loop, deftly lodging it in his palm, and he lifted it above his head.

His shriek pierced Philippa's breast with terror. "Brat!" he screamed. "Uplands bitch!"

"Larkyn, watch out!" Philippa cried. Larkyn couldn't hear her. Seraph came on, unaware, and Philippa cringed in anticipation of the two horses colliding.

Suddenly, without warning, Diamond swerved to avoid the disaster. She tilted her wings and rolled to one side.

William slid sideways. Only the thigh rolls stopped him from falling all the way out of the saddle. Somehow he struggled back into the saddle, though he lost his right stirrup. It flapped against the struggling filly's side. He gripped her reins as if they were a lifeline, forcing her jaw open, bowing her neck.

Sunny, without being told, descended, and flew perilously close to William and Diamond.

At last Larkyn could see what was happening. William, though he was barely holding on to his own seat, still pulled on Diamond's rein, trying to force the filly into Seraph's path. Larkyn's lips parted in a cry of warning, and Seraph, already weary, tried to dodge out of Diamond's course.

Diamond began to tilt away again. William lifted his left hand and whipped Diamond's flank with his quirt, a vicious cut that made Philippa wince. She shouted, "William, no! No!"

He seemed not to hear. He slashed the silvery hide again, then again. The filly squealed, and her whole body shuddered.

She lost the rhythm of her wingbeats and dropped a rod or more in a heartbeat.

Black Seraph, as the dapple gray nearly collided with him, seemed almost to pause in midflight. It took incredible strength to stop his momentum in that way, and Philippa cried, "Seraph! Kalla's teeth!" as the little black stallion, with a visible ripple of the muscles across his chest, of the tendons of his arching neck, achieved a hover, holding at Quarters in a flurry of sweat and foam.

And still Diamond lurched toward him, William any which way in the saddle. It was beyond belief that the filly was still in the air. William had a murderous grip on her reins, and her neck twisted sideways, halfway to his knee.

Philippa could hardly bear to look as the tragedy built before her eyes.

THIRTY-NINE

WILLIAM saw the patrol boat break off its attack when the little black stallion dove toward it. He wanted to scream with fury, except he couldn't spare the breath. He could hardly believe his eyes when Seraph emerged from his dive, driving upward again, out of danger. William seized Diamond's rein, brooking no resistance, and he lashed her forward, determined to put an end to the outrage.

The cold sun glittered on the water, nearly blinding him. Diamond fought him like a demon, her wings wobbling, her neck bowing as he forced her toward Seraph. William's heart burned with grief and rage, and hatred for the Uplands brat and her crossbred stallion. His mind reeled with awareness of impending humiliation, of the possibility of defeat.

Only one thought stayed clear in the clouded agony of his mind, one goal that drew him on. Larkyn Hamley had ruined his plans and destroyed his opportunity. He wanted to see the brat and her horse tumble into the bay, sink below the water, disappear from his life forever. He imagined her black curls sodden with salt water, her cheeks going pale as she drowned. The stallion would flounder, his wing membranes soaking, dragging him down beneath the waves.

He would strike them as they ascended, where the stallion could not recover himself, and it would put paid to everything. If the brat were gone, he would no longer have to deal with her cursed family. Even if Pamella accused him, no one would believe her. The rebel force gathered around Francis would have no purpose.

The burning certainty he felt drove out any question about how these things might come about. Diamond would cease to resist him when these two were gone. She would accept him as master. She would bank and turn and hover the way the other winged horses did for their bondmates.

But for now, as she fought the rein, he whipped her. This was no time for a soft heart. His need was greater than Diamond's temper. He struck her again, forced her head around with an iron hand, and drove her toward the black stallion.

But Seraph, the devil, through some feat of agility and strength William could not fathom, pulled out of his steep ascent as if it were no more than a stroll up a gentle slope. He leveled his flight and hovered like a shining black hummingbird, as if he weighed nothing, as if the very air held him up. Only the sweat darkening his chest, the foam that flew from his wings, revealed the effort it cost him.

And the girl! The brat clung to his back as if she had grown there, swaying with the stallion's movements as if she were part of his body. She seemed not to touch the reins, but to balance with her thighs as if she, too, weighed no more than a bundle of feathers. It was unnatural. And it was grossly unfair.

William could see nothing but the pair of them. He knew Philippa Winter was coming up behind him, but he could not spare a thought for her. Sun, sea, the patrol boats beneath him, the damned Klee ship with its treacherous blue-and-white pennants snapping from its masts, all faded away. His vision narrowed to a small, vivid point with the black stallion and the black-haired girl at its very center. He raised his quirt to whip Diamond again.

He had the reins in his right hand, the quirt in his left. But the reins had grown slippery and stiff with spray and sweat, and his strength was at an end. Horrified, he saw the strips of leather slip through his nearly nerveless fingers. They swung loose in the wind of Diamond's flight, and she, her head free now, steadied and flew on.

Still she flew toward the stallion. Was this what she had wanted all along? Perhaps Diamond, too, understood what was needed, what had to be done. Perhaps their bonding was better than he had thought, and out of ignorance he had only gotten in her way.

William grinned fiercely and dropped the quirt so that it

hung by its thong from his wrist. This time he gripped his pommel with his left hand. With his right he drew his smallsword. It was mostly ceremonial, the same sword his father had carried, but it was sharp enough. First he would deal with the girl, then he would put an end to the stallion.

The smallsword glittered in his hand, the gems in the hilt afire in the sunshine. He felt a surge of fresh energy in his muscles as he raised it. Ye gods, it was almost over at last!

FORTY

LARK saw the Duke draw his sword. She screamed, "Tup! Break Quarters!"

But though Tup valiantly strove to bank away from the dapple gray's course, she tilted her wings to follow him.

Lark could see, and no doubt Tup could sense, how tired Diamond was, how she struggled to hold her altitude, how she fought against Duke William's clumsy seat. It seemed she could not possibly stay aloft, but when the reins blew free of the Duke's hand, she steadied. Relieved of that torturing pressure, she stretched her neck eagerly forward, and came on.

Diamond couldn't know her rider's intent. She was a young creature half-mad with loneliness, with longing for her kind. Lark could see she wanted only to fly with Tup, to be near him. But she brought him peril instead.

The Duke's smallsword caught the light with glimmers of ruby red and emerald green, and the dull gleam of steel. The wind of flight whipped the Duke's pale hair around his even paler face, and his eyes were as black as nightmare. Lark bent low over Tup's neck, to give him as much freedom, as little wind resistance, as she possibly could. She wrapped her arms around his neck and snugged her heels tight beneath his wings.

He made another enormous effort, dipping back and away, a maneuver she could not imagine would be possible for any other winged horse. He gained a few moments, as the laboring filly had to turn, and bank, fighting her off-balance rider.

Her determination was agony to watch. She was inexperienced, and she had everything working against her, but still she persevered, her pretty silver wings shivering with effort, her delicate nostrils flaring as she panted. If only there was a way to save her!

The filly drew closer, her rider brandishing his sword. Lark shuddered, anticipating the blow of that steel against her body. And how could she protect Tup?

And then she saw Winter Sunset coming up fast behind Diamond. Sunny's great red wings beat strongly as she surged toward Diamond. Mistress Winter, like Lark, bent forward, urging her magnificent mare right into the danger.

Lark bit her lip so hard that a trickle of blood stung her chin. Neither Diamond nor the Duke sensed Sunny's presence. They were focused on Tup, both of them. Sunny ascended above Diamond so the two horses looked like fighting birds, terrifyingly close, the stability of their flight at risk should their wings or their bodies touch. When the sorrel mare was right over the gray, Mistress Winter bent far down and to her right, left hand gripping her pommel, right hand outstretched with her own short quirt in it. Sunny deftly compensated, tilting ever so slightly to the left, and Mistress Winter, with a swift, hard motion, struck the Duke's sword from his hand.

The Duke was exhausted, Lark could see, his face as white as the sails of the *Marinan*. The sword flew out of his fist, spinning into the air, jewels flashing as it revolved. Lark gasped as its sharp point sailed past Winter Sunset's wings, barely missing her outer pinions. It spun again, and again, lazy sun-bright circles, before it fell, hilt first, toward the water.

But Duke William was not yet done. Madness had its own energy. Lark didn't watch the smallsword splash into the bay. She kept her eyes on the Duke as he stretched his mouth in a scream of rage. He grasped his quirt in his left hand and swung it above his head.

Mistress Winter could not see the quirt, that awful magicked bit of braided leather, as it slashed at Winter Sunset's belly, striking her a fierce blow just behind her tucked forehooves. The blow in itself could not have been so bad, but it jarred the mare at a precarious moment in flight, when she was striving to stay above the filly, to keep her wings free of the other horse.

Winter Sunset flinched, and her wings faltered. Mistress Winter leaned to her left, trying to see past Sunny's shoulder, and the Duke, still shouting, stood up in his remaining stirrup and whipped at her face just as it appeared above the point of her mare's left wing.

The magicked quirt caught Mistress Winter's cheek, then, on the downstroke, it struck a tearing blow at Winter Sunset's wing. Sunny was battling to stay free of the filly, to hold her altitude. Her wings were fully open and in their most vulnerable position. The membranes were stretched thin, like scarlet parchment in the sunshine, the pinions fully extended as she fought for purchase on the currents of air.

Mistress Winter, though Lark could see clearly that the quirt had broken the skin of her face, never faltered. But Winter Sunset, with a great shudder, fell out of her trajectory, her wing broken, the membrane torn, the inner pinion fractured.

Tup saw, too. He made a sound Lark had never heard before, a scream full of his own fury and power. The surge of energy that ran through him nearly unseated her as his wings drove hard against the wind.

His forefeet came out of their tuck. She would not have thought he could fly in such a position, but such was the strength of his narrow wings, the agility of his slender body, that he lunged forward through the air, propelled by mighty wingbeats, and his small, sharp hooves reached toward Diamond and her rider.

There was no time to worry about whether Tup might harm Diamond. Lark did not even dare watch Mistress Winter's desperate efforts to save her mare. Tup had no thought for his rider at that moment, or for anything except to protect Winter Sunset, the mare who had been his monitor.

Lark gripped the breast strap with all her strength, and gripped Tup's barrel with her calves. She cried out as Tup struck at the Duke. His flight carried him past Diamond in a rush of wind and a cacophony of shouts.

Tup spun, nearly in midair, a Grand Reverse at high speed. Lark slipped sideways, one hand torn free of the handhold. She seized Tup's mane to steady herself, and only just in time. She hauled herself back into her seat as he was already driving toward Diamond. Lark saw to her horror that Diamond, too, had turned. Clearly she could not last much longer. Her eyes were wild, her nostrils gone red, and her wings beat twice for every one of Tup's.

"Tup!" Lark called. "Don't hurt Diamond!"

She had no way to know if he heard her, or if he cared. She was to remember, later, that it was Duke William himself who had refused to have Tup gelded. It was a young stallion's fury that fortified him now, supplied him with a fearsome power.

William, as Tup drove back toward Diamond, raised his quirt above his head. Lark feared it would strike Tup as it had Winter Sunset, tear through his wing, its magicked, hard leather destroying everything it touched.

But she couldn't stop Tup's momentum. His will was as set as a steel blade, an answer to Duke William's own. She curled her body over his neck, clinging with hands, feet, and thighs.

Diamond struggled to hover, but she had little experience. The Duke leaned so far forward, standing in a single stirrup, that Lark marveled he didn't tumble out of the saddle. Tup, with a grunt from deep within his belly, reached with his hooves, and struck.

Duke William struck at the same time.

Lark knew well the iron-hard leather of the Duke's quirt. But magicked though it might have been, it was no match for the rock-hard hooves of a full-grown winged stallion.

It was strange, she thought, that Duke William made no sound when he fell. Perhaps he was fortunate, and the blow of Tup's hoof that caught him squarely in his left temple ended his consciousness mercifully, and immediately. Or perhaps he was simply past understanding.

However it was, the Duke fell, arms and legs sprawling, bloodied head lolling. His quirt, still tied to his wrist, fell with him. His ice-blond hair flared around his head in a bloody halo.

He fell swiftly, and silently. There was an aura of unreality about the whole event, a dreamlike quality. Lark saw his black-clad figure break the surface of the green water and disappear instantly.

The patrol boats came about to converge on the spot, and Lark was shocked at how close they were, how far Tup had descended. The water was only a few rods beneath him.

Tup regained control of himself almost at once. He leveled

his flight and banked gently to the right, from the bobbing masts of the patrol boats, giving Lark a long moment to recover. She straightened and looked frantically about for Mistress Winter and Sunny.

When she didn't see them at first, her heart clenched anew with fear. Then, as Tup began to ascend to a safer altitude, she found them. Sunny was winging crookedly, almost drunkenly, toward the nearest shore, where fishing boats moored beside the long, wooden docks. Lark could hardly see how she maintained any altitude at all, except that Mistress Winter must be coaxing her, begging her, using every skill she had to help her bondmate to ground.

Lark breathed a prayer to Kalla, and urged Tup after them. She had to think of something . . . Winter Sunset would be lost if she fell into the bay, or if she fell upon trying to land. And Mistress Winter . . . Lark couldn't bear to think of it.

"Hurry, Tup," she called. "We have to help them!" He responded without hesitation, drawing what she feared must be the last bit of strength from his small, courageous body.

In moments, they caught up with Sunny and Mistress Winter. Lark didn't realize until the last moment that Diamond was behind her. She flew below Tup, her neck stretched, her hooves wobbling in their tuck, her weary wings barely keeping her above the water. It was another thing to worry about, but Lark focused first on Winter Sunset.

The strain was evident in the ridging muscles of Sunny's chest, the bowing of her neck. Lark tried not to look at her wing, torn and bleeding. She tried to concentrate on Tup, as he took up the monitor's position. She peered ahead, looking for a safe place to come to ground. She held Tup in, with just a glance back at Sunny now and again to be certain they were not getting too far ahead.

Sunny dipped and weaved, but stayed in the air. Mistress Winter's face was rigid. She kept a reassuring hand on Sunny's neck, while with the other, she held the reins up, not loose, but level, trying to keep the mare's head steady.

Lark turned her gaze forward, searching the land for a place, a lane, a park, a street, where the wounded horse could come down. "Kalla, where? Where's our place?" she muttered.

And then, as if a beam of sunlight had suddenly illuminated it, she saw the alley that stretched between two ramshackle warehouses. It was empty of carts or wagons, empty even of any stacked barrels or other objects. The opening of the alley looked wide enough for the horses' wings, but it narrowed quickly as it led to a loading dock that blocked one end. The horses would not have long to run off the speed of their landing.

But it was all there was.

Lark reined Tup toward it, nudging him with her right knee, shifting her weight to help him bank to the left. There were men on the docks, pointing out into the bay, shading their eyes as they tried to see what was happening. She prayed they would stay out of the way, that they would see the two winged horses descending, would not step into their path. She sensed Winter Sunset behind Tup, falling into his pattern, letting his steady flight guide her faltering one.

The men on the docks fell back, leaving the mouth of the alley open. Tup slowed his wings and glided. His forefeet reached, touched, and his hind feet came down with a clatter of hooves on cobblestones. He beat his wings once for balance. And then, even as he cantered forward, he began to fold them, seeing the narrowness of the alley. He trotted the moment he could, but still the loading dock came upon them frighteningly fast. Tup skidded to a stop only a hand's breadth from its wooden platform. And then, without being told, he sidestepped, giving Winter Sunset as much of the space as he could.

Lark leaped from the saddle the moment Tup was still and braced herself to help.

Winter Sunset came soaring into the alley, off-balance, her good wing extended, her broken one flapping pitifully. Mistress Winter was in an odd position, leaning to one side in her saddle, one hand reaching forward, the other gripping the pommel. At first Lark couldn't figure it out, and then she realized that Mistress Winter was holding Sunny's fractured wing together with her own hand, giving her every chance of coming safely to ground, with no thought for her own safety.

Winter Sunset's feet touched, and her wings quivered, one

beating, the other one trying to, but giving her very little lift. For an awful moment it seemed she might fall, that the momentum of her flight was too much for her injured state. Then, just as Lark put both hands to her mouth in anticipation of the worst, the great sorrel mare found all four feet on the ground. Her good wing began to fold, and her bad one dragged horribly, but she cantered a few steps, then trotted, reaching the end of the alley a moment later, dripping sweat and blood and foam.

A movement at the end of the alley caught Lark's eye, and she cried out. "Mistress Winter! Look out!"

It was Diamond. She careened toward the alley after the other horses, her wings shivering with exhaustion, her hooves out of their tuck. Lark heard the watching men on the docks shout a warning, whether to each other or to her, she couldn't tell. The filly struck the cobblestones so hard Lark felt the jarring in her own bones. She bounced up again, her wings lifting her from the ground, then settled a little more gently. The whole routine repeated one more time before she found her balance and came galloping up the alley, wings drooping, head down.

Lark leaped to stand behind Winter Sunset, to stop the filly, somehow, from crashing into the already-wounded mare. Diamond saw her, and threw up her head, spreading her wings in a desperate effort to stop her headlong rush. She looked like a great silver swan landing on a lake, her feet sliding, her wings out, her neck stretched up and back. At the last possible moment, she skidded on her hind feet, rearing, coming so close that her wings brushed Lark's head.

And then, with a groan, Diamond settled to the ground, too tired even to fold her wings.

Lark stepped close to her and let the filly rest her forehead on her chest. She encircled her head with both arms, and breathed into her ear, "There, now. There, now, my lovely, fine girl. You're safe. You're safe here with us." The filly panted, great gasps of air that blew foam over Lark's tabard. Her legs trembled. Many minutes passed before she was able to fold her wings. When Lark released her, she stood with her head down, shivering with exhaustion.

Lark looked up to find Tup standing as close as he could to

Diamond, watching the alley as if for fresh dangers. His eyes gleamed, and his ears flicked this way and that.

" 'Tis all over, my Tup," Lark said. "All over."

But it wasn't, not yet. As Lark turned toward Winter Sunset, she found Mistress Winter gathering her bondmate's broken wing in her hands, folding it rib to rib, gently, gently pressing the pinions closed until she stood with her arms full of scarlet membrane. She looked like a dressmaker with a bolt of red silk in her arms. And she was weeping. Her tears splashed down her weathered cheeks and fell on Winter Sunset's ruined wing.

Lark said, "Oh, Mistress Winter! What can I do?"

Mistress Winter didn't look at her, but put her forehead on her bondmate's sweat-soaked shoulder, and sobbed, "Nothing, Larkyn. There's nothing anyone can do." She choked something else, something Lark couldn't hear.

Lark left Diamond standing beside Tup and went to Mistress Winter's side. She tore strips from her riding skirt to help bind the ruined wing, testing it here and there to see that it would hold. Mistress Winter sobbed silently throughout the whole operation. When they were finished, Lark stepped back, and Mistress Winter, rubbing her face with her long fingers, took one more shuddering breath.

As she lowered her hands, Lark had to bite her lip to keep from exclaiming.

Mistress Winter's tears had ceased, but her face was swollen and tear-streaked, and her eyes were dark with shock, stark in her tanned face. Her cheek bore an angry red mark left by the Duke's quirt. She looked as if she had aged twenty years in a day.

"She will never fly again," she said in a broken voice. Her arms went around Winter Sunset's neck, and she pressed her cheek against the sweat-stained sorrel coat. "My darling Sunny, my grand girl. She will never fly again."

Lark struggled for something to say, for something to offer. There was nothing.

She stepped forward, and put her own arms around Mistress Winter. Mistress Winter burst into fresh tears, weeping against Sunny's neck, and her body shook in Lark's grasp. Lark simply stood, holding her, supporting them both, until the men from the dock came up the alley, full of questions and offering to help.

Lark left Mistress Winter alone with Sunny, and went to stop the men from coming too close to the winged horses. She hardly recognized her own voice as she gave orders and instructions, and requested blankets and ropes and the largest wagon that could be found.

When it came, she was greatly relieved to see her own brother Nick was driving it. And at the head of the brace of oxen who pulled it was Brye. There was no need to explain anything to them. They stood back as she and Mistress Winter, her face strained but composed now, helped Winter Sunset into the wagon, using planks from the loading dock as a ramp.

Lark offered to drive the wagon, but Sunny was in too much pain, it seemed, to mind the scent of Nick as he climbed up onto the bench seat and took the reins. Brye walked beside the oxen, looking back from time to time to see that Winter Sunset and Mistress Winter were not jostled too much.

Lark was left with Tup and Diamond. She told the filly, "You follow Tup now, lass. We'll be safe and sound in the Academy stables by this evening." She turned Tup toward the boulevard that led past the Rotunda and west out of the city. It would be a long walk, but there would be no more flying today.

They passed the wagon just as it reached the boulevard, and Lark lifted a hand.

"I'll have Sunny's stall ready," she said.

Mistress Winter, swaying in the wagon bed next to her bondmate, only nodded. Brye said, as Lark and the horses made a wide circle around the oxen and the men who handled them, "Have a care, Lark. The news won't have spread yet."

She asked, over her shoulder, "What news, Brye?"

"The Duke is dead. Drowned."

"He's dead? He's really—are you sure that none of the boats—" Lark shook her head, unable to take in the thought. A shiver of revulsion shook her as she remembered Duke William's black-clad figure tumbling toward the bay.

"Nay," Brye said. "He went straight down, and no one could find him. But until everyone knows, the streets may not be safe. Keep a watchful eye."

"Aye." She turned forward, toward the center of the city, where the Rotunda's colorful pennants lifted in the breeze. She guided Tup and Diamond through the lanes toward the boulevard, but she barely saw the streets she passed. She relived, for the first of countless times to come, the struggle in the air above the harbor that had ended so bitterly for Winter Sunset.

As awful as that was, it was better than wondering what lay ahead for the Noble mare and her bondmate.

FORTY-ONE

PHILIPPA didn't leave Sunny's side all that night or the next. Larkyn stayed with her, and Philippa thought there could be no better help than a country girl who didn't blanch at the blood that poured from the broken veins of the wing membrane, who shrank from no task, no matter how distressing, who never shuddered or winced as she looked at the shattered pinion. Larkyn warmed and sweetened a bucket of water to tempt Sunny to drink. When it seemed the mare could no longer stay on her feet, the girl helped Philippa to coax her to lie down on her good side, to arrange the bandaged wing with gentle hands. They took turns sitting in the straw by Sunny's head, soothing her, talking to her.

The hours of the night stretched into a cold gray dawn. Philippa, with Sunny's head in her lap, dozed a little. Nightmares chased themselves through her dreams, Sunny bleeding, falling, dying, William emerging from the bay, dripping, with his quirt in his hand.

She was not exactly sure she was awake when she opened her eyes in the darkest part of the night to see Larkyn with some fetish in her hand, a little doll with a printed skirt and a thatch of improbable hair. Larkyn twirled the fetish over Sunny's wing, tracing the tear in the membrane, spinning it over the broken pinion. When she was done, she cast Philippa a furtive glance before she slipped out of the stall.

Philippa placed no faith in small magics, but it seemed to her that Sunny grew stronger from that moment. Larkyn persuaded Sunny to lip a little water while Philippa replaced her bandages. Larkyn patiently replaced the blankets over the mare's body when Sunny wriggled them off in her fever. And the girl murmured endearments to Sunny in her Uplands dialect, endearments Philippa found as comforting for herself as they were to the mare. When Sunny's fever broke, and she struggled to her feet, Larkyn was there, guiding her, protecting the broken wing, bringing the hot mash Herbert had kept simmering on the close stove.

Two days passed. Neither of them had been out of the stables for more than an hour at a time. They stood watching Sunny nibble at the mash. Though her eyelids drooped and her sides were gaunt, she was steady on her feet.

"She will live, Mistress Winter," Larkyn said hoarsely.

"Yes," Philippa said. She kept her hand on Sunny's neck, blessedly cool at last, and watched the mare drink more of Larkyn's sweetened water. "Yes, she will live." Her throat closed for a long moment, and she swallowed the pain away. She managed to say, before her voice utterly broke, "But she won't fly."

"Nay. I know that." Larkyn, leaning against the wall of the stall, turned her eyes up to Philippa. There were dark circles beneath them, and her cheeks were hollow with fatigue. "I'm so sorry," she whispered. "So terribly sorry for both of you."

Her small, work-hardened hand found Philippa's and held it. It was that, the feel of someone else's skin against her own, that undid Philippa's hard-won control yet again.

She wept great, wrenching sobs. They hurt, tearing at her chest and her throat. She cried for some time before she realized that Larkyn's arms were around her, holding her through each spasm. She hid her face in her hands, unwilling to let the girl see her wretched face. Larkyn held her and patted her, and when her tears ebbed, released her without a word.

Philippa wiped her eyes and blew her nose. She saw that Sunny's water bucket was full, and the straw on the floor of the stall was clean and dry. Larkyn was gone, leaving her alone with her bondmate.

WHEN Philippa could bear to leave Sunny for a few hours, she went to the Residence for a much-needed bath and change of clothes. It was early, and the girls were at breakfast. A light snow had fallen overnight, and the courtyard and the lane were frosted with white.

Matron fussed over Philippa, adding hot water and some fragrant soap as Philippa soaked in the claw-footed tub. Philippa rested her head against a rolled towel, and listened, with her eyes closed, while Matron chattered.

"It will be Duke Francis now," she said, pouring more water. "We know he was never meant to rule, never trained for it, but there it is! His elder brother went and got himself killed, and there's no one else, is there? Lord Francis will be invested tomorrow, at the Tower of the Seasons, but today they say he's already at the Rotunda, meeting with the Council. The Duchess, poor thing, is moving her things out of the Palace and going home to her family. My cousin works there, and she says Duchess Constance has never looked so happy. Can you imagine that? Well, I don't know if she's still the Duchess, but I suppose she is, as there is no other. And now, you know, Master Crisp has been restored as Master Breeder, because Master Jinson is dead."

Philippa opened her eyes. "Jinson is dead?"

"That he is," Matron said with a grim glance. "Poor young man. Never wanted that position in the first place, I would guess. Not suited, was he?"

"No," Philippa said faintly. "But what happened to him?"

"Well," Matron said. She glanced at the door of the bathroom to be certain it was still shut. "Well, I hear they're talking about it right now in the Rotunda, but word is that man of the late Duke's shot poor Jinson! I never liked that man. Never trusted him."

"Slater! Kalla's teeth," Philippa said. She closed her eyes and let her head fall back against the edge of the tub. "Slater," Philippa said again. "And where has he got to, now that his master's dead?"

Matron sat down on a stool near the tub, a thick towel folded in her lap. "No one knows," she said with satisfaction. "He'll never dare show his face in Osham again; that's a fact!"

"And so . . ." Philippa rubbed her face with her wet fingers. She could hardly take it all in. "So Eduard Crisp has regained his position."

"Yes," Matron said. "He's in the stables now, I believe, with Mistress Star."

Philippa sat up, lassitude falling away from her like the drops of water that splashed from her wet face over her shoulders. "Why?" she demanded.

Matron smoothed the towel. "To straighten things out, I should think. To close that silly Fleckham School, and send those boys home where they belong. To see that poor little Amelia and her colt are back where they belong, now that her father has delivered her back to the Academy. Duke Francis wasted no time making peace with the Klee, I can tell you that!" Philippa stood up, dripping, and Matron handed her the towel.

Philippa scrubbed at her hair, then held out her hand for another towel and climbed out of the tub. "Thank you, Matron." Her nerves felt stretched and raw, and her hands were unsteady as she dried herself. "Hand me my clothes, will you?"

SHE met Suzanne and Eduard in the middle of the courtyard. Suzanne's face told her everything, but she didn't speak until they were in her office with the door closed. A fire crackled with incongruous cheerfulness in the grate. Philippa stood just inside the door, braced and wary.

Eduard turned to face her, his lined face grim. "You'll have to put her down, Philippa," Eduard said. There was compassion, even pity, in his voice. "There's nothing else to be done."

"What do you mean?" she snapped. "She's through the worst already."

"You mean, because she's alive? She'll never fly again."

"I'm not a fool, Eduard," Philippa said. "I know she can't fly. But she'll walk, and run. She'll live."

"She'll be miserable. She'll be trying to fly every chance she gets."

"I'll watch out for her."

"Where?" Eduard asked. His voice was gentler than usual. "You can't keep her here, where other horses are flying every day. She'll go crazy, or she'll drive them crazy. Or both."

"She will not! I'll be with her, and I'll see to it that . . . Kalla's heels, Eduard," Philippa exclaimed. "After her long service, you would just put her down? Give up on her?"

Suzanne had gone behind her desk, but now she came across the room toward Philippa, one hand out. "Philippa," she began. "It would be the kindest—"

"Kindest for whom?" Philippa grated. "For you? For Eduard? Not for Sunny, surely, and not for me, either!"

Eduard folded his arms across his breast, and his face closed. "She's too old to breed, and she can't fly. She's useless. Where would you keep her? There's never enough room here at the Academy, and I'm not going to take the chance—"

"*You're* not going to take the chance? *You?*" Philippa's voice rose, and Suzanne put up a hand, but she ignored it. "Since when did you ever take the chance? Did you fly with her, that very first time, at the risk of your neck? Did you fight the battle of the South Tower? Did you face a madman over the bay? Have you monitored dozens of young horses, taught young flyers for years—" Her voice broke, and she turned to face the fire, gritting her teeth against a fresh wave of sorrow.

Suzanne spoke softly. "Eduard, give her time. Philippa's had a terrible shock, and she needs time to think."

Philippa whirled, her hands on her hips. "I need no time, Suzanne, though I thank you! Winter Sunset will live out her days in peace, and that's all there is to it!"

"No," Eduard said flatly. "She'll be put down, Philippa. I'll do it myself if it will make you feel better."

"If you touch her," Philippa hissed, "I'll kill you."

"Philippa!" Suzanne cried.

Eduard said, "Calm down, Philippa. Hysterics won't help."

"Hysterics!" Philippa pulled her flying gloves from her belt—the gloves she would never need again—and began to crease them between her fingers. "Eduard, don't be a fool." She slapped the gloves into one palm. "You cannot force me into this."

"I can order you," he said grimly. "By the authority vested in me by the Duke."

Philippa gave a bitter laugh. "We have no Duke."

"The investiture is tomorrow," Suzanne said softly.

"Fine. Ask the new Duke then," Philippa snapped. "But for today, don't give me orders you can't enforce."

She spun about and stalked through the door of Suzanne's office, slamming it behind her. She blundered through the foyer, so blinded by tears that she saw none of its familiar marble and glass, none of the ancient portraits of winged horses that lined the walls. She stumbled out the double doors and down the stairs. She was halfway to the stables when Suzanne caught her.

"Philippa! Stop! Listen to me, please."

Philippa stopped where she was, but she couldn't look at Suzanne. "There's nothing more to say," she said in a low tone.

"But Philippa—where will you go? Where can you go with a winged horse who is so badly injured she can barely walk? I know how you feel—"

"You couldn't possibly know how I feel."

Suzanne sighed. "No, you're right," she said sadly. "I can't know how it feels. But I know that you have a hard road ahead of you, Philippa. Even now, Winter Sunset may die."

"She may. But I'm not going to make that happen."

Suzanne said in a shaking voice, "Please, Philippa. I can stop Eduard from putting Sunny down, but I can't force him to make room in the stables for you if he won't do it."

"I'll go to Francis," Philippa said stubbornly.

"I think the new Duke will have his hands full for some time," Suzanne said. "And time is something you don't have."

Philippa was trying to think, but the effort of controlling herself was making her head ache and her thoughts muddy. Where could she go? She would never be welcome at Islington House. Meredith would blame her for the loss of his advantages with the Ducal Palace. "I could go to Beeth House," she said feebly. "They could make room."

"Perhaps so," Suzanne said. "But would Sunny be happy there, Philippa? And just as importantly, would you?"

Now Philippa lifted her head and stared at Suzanne. "Could you do it?" she asked hoarsely. "If it were Star Gazer?"

Suzanne's face reflected all of Philippa's misery. She shook her head. "I don't know. I just don't know."

"Come and see her," Philippa said suddenly. "Come see Sunny, then tell me what you would do."

Suzanne took a step back. "I can't," she said. "I have to think of the whole Academy, not just one horse—or one horse-mistress."

"And I have to think of Sunny."

"You have to take her away if you're not going to obey Eduard's order." Suzanne's voice was firm, though her mouth trembled.

"Fine," Philippa said. She had no energy for sympathy with Suzanne's plight. She turned away from her and strode carelessly on into the stables. Her shoulder struck the doorjamb as she walked past, and she half ran down the aisle, clutched by an irrational fear that Eduard could have somehow got by her, got to Winter Sunset with his lethal potion. It made no sense, of course, but her nerves were stretched to the breaking point. She staggered into Sunny's stall and found her with her head down, leaning against the wall. Blood stained the bandage over her wing, and her eyes were nearly closed. Philippa sagged to the straw, careless of her fresh skirt. She sat with her legs extended, her back against the wall. She would let Sunny sleep as long as she could, then . . . what? She had no idea what to do next.

She rested her head in her hands. It seemed she was not yet out of tears.

THE morning was half-gone when Larkyn roused her.

"Mistress Winter!" the girl said, from the aisle. "Mistress Winter. Brye is here, and he has a wagon."

"A wagon?" Philippa said. She had fallen asleep. Her tears had dried on her cheeks, and her face felt stiff and crusty.

"Aye!" Larkyn opened the gate and stepped in. She carried a halter in one hand and a pile of fresh sheets clamped under the other arm. "Aye, 'tis the same wagon that brought you here from the docks, he says. Come now, he's pulled it up right in front of the door, and the oxen are yoked and ready. He rigged a very nice ramp, and I asked Matron to pack your things."

Philippa struggled to her feet and winced at the pang in her bruised shoulder. "Larkyn, what's happening? What's this about?"

"I heard you," Larkyn said simply. "I came out for breakfast, and I heard you and Mistress Star in the courtyard. Brye came to say good-bye to me, and I told him all about it." She went to Sunny, stroking her with her small, sure hands, and slipped the halter over her head. "Come now, Winter Sunset," she said. "You and your mistress are going home to the Uplands."

"Uplands?" Philippa said. She felt sluggish and stupid. "Why the Uplands?"

Larkyn coaxed Sunny to turn, step by careful step. "I told Brye you had no place to go with Sunny," she said. "And he's going to take you to Deeping Farm." She persuaded Sunny to take another step, and then another. " 'Twill be a long ride, but we've padded the wagon with blankets, and I've put a covered bucket of water behind the seat."

Philippa stood back, allowing the girl to lead Sunny into the aisle. Sunny walked gingerly, ponderously, as if every step pained her. For one awful moment, Philippa doubted her own decision, but when Larkyn looked back at her, her eyes full of hope and trust, her doubt faded. It was an enormous relief to let the girl coax Sunny down the aisle, to follow obediently behind her. When Bramble came out of the tack room and paced beside her, that felt right, too.

Tall and broad and stable as a rock, Brye Hamley stood at the head of the brace of oxen. It was all too easy to give herself and Sunny into his hands. Between them, she and Larkyn led Sunny up into the wagon. Larkyn checked the binding of the wing herself and readjusted the blankets arranged over the sides so that they would protect Sunny from the jouncing of the cart. She murmured into Sunny's ear, and the mare lay down on her good side, well cushioned by mounds of blankets over a generous bed of straw.

Brye said, " 'Twill be a long day. You can sit there, on that cushion. Beside the mare."

And Philippa, gratefully and wearily, did just that. She could barely muster the energy to thank him, but that didn't seem to matter. He embraced his sister, then went to chirp to the oxen. Larkyn stood in the snow-dusted courtyard, waving, as the wagon pulled away.

The oxen set a steady, ponderous pace up the lane, and

Philippa put her head back against the rail of the wagon. She waved to Larkyn once, then lapsed into a sort of daze. She wondered for a wild moment if she were dreaming.

But there was Brye Hamley's strong figure up ahead. And here was her poor Sunny, her grand girl, lying in comfort on a bed of straw and blankets.

She put one hand on Sunny's neck and let the other lie idle in her lap as she watched the familiar, beloved outlines of the Academy of the Air dwindle behind her, little by little, as the oxcart carried her away into the west.

FORTY-TWO

THE snow that fell in the Uplands was different from that of Osham. It was cleaner and dryer, and its purity lasted longer, great, unbroken blankets of white filling the empty fields, mounding against the winter-dry hedgerows. It glittered under the pale sun, and under the black night sky it glistened like silver leaf. Brye said the snow would not leave until spring.

Philippa lay in the old bed under the sloping eaves, listening to the sounds of Deeping Farm waking. Everyone rose a little later in the winter. Even the crowing of the rooster was muted by the snow. The sounds of water running in from the well, of the clink of kettles in the kitchen, of doors opening and closing, were softer than she remembered.

Or perhaps it was she herself who was softer. Sadness had made her vulnerable. Grief rendered her empathetic to every emotion around her.

It was not a change Philippa welcomed. She thought, rebelliously, that she had enough emotional weight to carry without picking up everyone else's.

She had been remembering Margareth, and wondering if, when Margareth's flying career had ended, she had felt this same crushing sense of uselessness. Margareth had said to her once that every horsemistress feels old when she loses her mount. Philippa didn't feel exactly old, but she felt as if she had shed the woman she had been the way a chick sheds its shell, and a new, painfully tender creature had emerged.

It was too soon. She wasn't ready.

She rolled to her side and thrust back the thick comforter that smelled of summer sunshine. The estimable Peony must have aired it on the line behind the house, when the kitchen garden was still in bloom and the broomstraw and bloodbeets were just coming on. Philippa would have been in Marinan then, flying every day to the mountain lake, coming back to hearty country meals, breathing the scent of lavender from morning till night.

Remembering those sun-warmed days, the lazy flights she and Sunny had made, brought fresh tears to her eyes, and she rubbed them away impatiently. "Kalla's heels!" she muttered to herself, hurrying to the basin to splash water into the ewer, then onto her face. "I'm sick to death of weeping!" In her adulthood, she had cried only once, when Margareth died. She wondered if unshed tears built up in a person, like water behind a dam. If that was the case, her own dam, which she had thought impregnable, had broken to pieces.

She dried her hands and face, then pulled on her tabard and skirt. As she brushed her hair, she pondered finding some other clothes. Wearing the riding habit probably made no sense now, but she was loath to part with it. Her mother had despaired of her when she was a girl, when no one could interest her in the silks and satins that so intrigued her sisters. She had always been content with the riding habit. It felt as natural to her as her own skin, and she couldn't imagine what she would wear if she put it aside.

As she pulled her hair back, more tears threatened. She had no further need for the rider's knot, either. She stared at herself in the mirror. She undid her hair, and tried it this way and that, to see if it made any difference.

In the end, she tied it back again, clicking her tongue impatiently. She would wear the rider's knot forever. It suited her. And no one cared how she looked, in any case.

She slipped silently down the stairs and took her coat from the row of pegs by the kitchen door. Pamella and Peony were both in the kitchen, their backs turned to her. Peony was just in the act of twirling the bedraggled fetish over the teapot, which made Philippa long for Larkyn.

Philippa remembered, with aching clarity, watching the fourteen-year-old Larkyn give the teapot a spin with the Tarn the day they had first met, in this very kitchen. Philippa thought then that she knew something about the world. She had learned great and painful lessons since.

Pamella was stirring something on the close stove and humming to herself. Her little boy would be following Edmar about somewhere. Brandon adored his stepfather, and walked in his footsteps constantly whenever the big, silent man was at home. It was strange to hear Pamella singing, even so quietly. She still almost never spoke, and Philippa supposed now that she never would. It was one of many tragedies laid at William's door.

That door was now closed forever. It did no good to dwell on what was behind it.

The air was as clear and clean as the fresh snowfall, and the light, reflecting from every crystalline surface, nearly blinded Philippa. She shaded her eyes with her hand as she slipped out beneath the bare branches of the rue-tree that guarded the kitchen steps. She pulled on her coat, shivering a little, as she hurried across the yard to the barn.

It was warmer there, and the smell of straw and hay and animals comforted Philippa. Bramble rose from her bed of blankets and came to her, moving stiffly, but waving her plume of tail. Like Philippa, she would never be young again, but life at Deeping Farm seemed to agree with her. Brandon adored her, and Pamella cooked special food for her. Peony gave her treats whenever she showed up at the kitchen door.

Philippa stroked the oc-hound's silky head, then picked up a measure of grain and carried it down to the box stall. Bramble padded companionably at her side. The goats bleated from their night pen as she passed, a peaceful sound that was more greeting than complaint.

Sunny's whicker at her approach lifted her spirits. She hadn't done that in a long time. Hurrying toward her, Philippa thought Sunny's eyes were a little brighter, that she carried her head a little higher this morning. Philippa fretted over Sunny's efforts to stretch the wing that would never open again, but she was healing. And Philippa was beginning to hope.

She went into the stall and set down the grain. Sunny pressed her forehead against her chest, and Philippa stroked her neck, combed her forelock with her fingers, caressed her wide, smooth cheek.

Sunny tried to rustle her wings, the old signal to request a flight. Philippa touched the injured wing with the palm of her hand, and her voice was as broken as the wing. "It will mend, sweetheart, and then we will ride. We won't fly, but we'll ride. I promise you that."

She retrieved the oats from the floor and held the measure in her hands while Sunny nibbled them. She filled Sunny's water bucket, changed the bandage on her wing, and was about to begin mucking out the stall when Brye appeared in the doorway to the barn, keeping his distance from Sunny.

"Wish I could do that for you," he said.

"I have nothing else to do," Philippa answered. She dug the pitchfork into the damp straw and spilled it into the waiting barrow. "Did you come to get me for breakfast?"

"Aye." He leaned against the doorjamb, his solid figure limned by light from the snow-filled yard behind him.

"You can go ahead, Brye," Philippa said, lifting another forkful. "I'll be along shortly."

"Nay, no rush." He was bareheaded, and the reflected light gleamed on the silver that threaded his hair.

Philippa liked looking at him. She liked watching him work about the farm, and she liked seeing him at table with his family. It had been a long time since the crushes and infatuations of her girlhood. She remembered those feelings, but this was different. It was less exciting, but it had a sense of permanency and predictability, and she liked that, too. She would always, she thought, like looking at Brye Hamley, whatever her future might bring.

She scraped up the last of the wet straw from the floor. She scattered a little sawdust and covered it with fresh dry straw, then patted Sunny again. "I'll be back soon, sweetheart. We'll go out for a bit of a walk."

Sunny lifted her head from the hay bin to breathe in Philippa's smell. Her velvety lips just touched Philippa's cheek. Philippa closed her eyes, tasting her bondmate's scent. She couldn't fly, but she still had her beautiful girl. She was grateful.

When she stepped out of the stall and closed the half-gate,

she saw that Brye had already emptied the barrow. They walked out into the yard together. She noticed how his eyes narrowed against the glare of sun on snow as he assessed his land and his house for anything that needed doing, any branch or blade that required his attention.

As they reached the rue-tree, he stopped and gestured toward the barn. "Thought I'd enlarge it," he said, pointing. "Make Sunny's stall bigger."

"Oh," Philippa said faintly, a little uncertainly. "But—you don't need to do that, Brye. It's a little cramped for her, perhaps, but as a temporary stall, it's fine."

"Temporary?" he growled, bringing his gaze down to hers.

She felt her cheeks warm, like a girl's. "Well, yes. We can't stay here forever."

He said gruffly, "Don't see why not."

She spread her hands. "But—you do understand, don't you? Sunny could live like this for ten years or more. Fifteen."

His customary hard expression softened. "I hope she does." He tilted his head a little, as if considering what to say to her, then, surprisingly, he smiled. He had Nick's handsome smile, his teeth very white in his tanned face. She had never seen that smile before.

She stared at him. When he took her hand, and held it between his big ones, her heart fluttered so she thought he must see it beneath her tabard, and she had to drop her eyes.

"You like it here," he said. "On Deeping Farm."

"I love it." She felt as awkward as she had at sixteen. Irritated at her own foolishness, she lifted her head, and said too sharply, "But it's never really mattered what I like. My life is not my own."

He looked a little taken aback by her tone, and she gave a small shrug, careful not to dislodge her hand from his. "Sorry," she said. "It's not your fault. It's just that—I devoted my life to the winged horses, and to the Duke's service, and now—it's all in pieces. And at the moment I don't know what it was for. What it was all about." Her voice grew harsher as she tried to keep it from breaking. She turned her head, hoping he wouldn't see her weakness.

He held her hand a little tighter. She could feel the heat of his body, like a bridge connecting the two of them through the cold air. He was so—so masculine. She wasn't accustomed to this.

She had the sudden alarming thought that anyone in the kitchen could see them, standing here under the rue-tree like a pair of—of what? Not lovers. That wasn't possible.

She took her hand back, and rubbed her forehead with the back of it. "Sorry," she said again. "I just don't know what to do with the rest of my life. I always thought I would be at the Academy of the Air until—until the end."

He cleared his throat. "Well. Philippa."

She looked up at him, at his dark blue eyes so like his sister's, at his strong, steady features. "What?"

He hesitated, and his eyes shifted briefly, then came back to hers. "You can stay here," he said in his bass rumble. "With us. With—" He cleared his throat again. "With me."

For a moment she couldn't speak at all. This was not at all what she had expected, no matter how treacherous the feelings in her heart. She had never seriously considered such a thing, nor had she thought he would. At last, taking a deep breath, she blurted ungracefully, "But you know that's not possible!"

His mouth curved. "Why not?"

She shook her head, and this time it was she who put out her hand, who took his. "What would I do here, at Deeping Farm?" she asked. "I'm no farmer, and I'm certainly no cook."

"No need to do anything," he said. "Just be."

"Just be," she repeated. She squeezed his hand with her fingers, and said, "I can't do that, Brye. It's kind of you to offer . . ."

He turned his hand over to grip hers again. They stood very still for long moments, looking at each other. Philippa said, after a time, "I'm not sure what you're asking me, Brye."

He released her hand with a little, self-deprecating laugh. "I think you are."

She gave a small sigh, and he laughed again. "Been a solitary man all my life, Philippa. It suited me. But . . . I like seeing your face at my table." He looked away, out across the snow-covered fields of Deeping Farm. "I like your voice in my ear."

"And my horse in your barn?" she said, as lightly as she could.

"I know you can't be separated."

There was another pause, and Philippa heard the sounds of breakfast beginning in the kitchen behind them. She said, "You tempt me."

Something kindled in his eyes, and she bit her lip. She hadn't meant to encourage him. She searched for a way to explain. "You tempt me, yes, Brye. If I were a different sort of woman . . ." She shook her head. "I need work. I need a purpose. I'm still a horsemistress, though my bondmate . . ." She couldn't bring herself to speak it aloud, afraid she would break down again. She dropped her eyes to her boots. "My first allegiance," she said softly, "is—and must always be—to Sunny. I can't—I don't see how I could—"

"Philippa," he said. He spoke gravely, but the hint of a smile was in his voice. "You will have noticed that I am no youth burning with heat." The elegance of his phrase both surprised and moved her.

"Nor am I," she said. "Though I like seeing your face, too, Brye Hamley, and hearing your voice." She laughed a little. "Not that you speak a great deal."

His own chuckle was a bass rumble. "Nay. Nothing to say."

"I can't agree with that. When you do speak, it's always worth hearing."

"Well," he said then, and reached for the latch of the door. She sensed, rather than heard, his disappointment. "Well, Philippa. I hope you'll stay as long as you like."

She looked up into his face once again. "You are so kind. I'm grateful. For my sake, and for Sunny's."

He pulled the latch and held the door for her to go in. A wave of warm air swept out, redolent with the smell of fresh coffee, hot bread, and rashers of bacon frying on the close stove. Philippa took her seat at the table and accepted a cup of coffee. She watched the faces around her, the little boy, the younger women, silent Edmar, laughing Nick . . . and Brye.

It was good to be at this table, to eat this homely food, to feel safe, to be in amenable company. It was good to be in Brye Hamley's company, and it made her heart beat faster to know that he felt the same.

But it was not enough. It would never be enough.

FORTY-THREE

LARK had always thought the horse goddess must intervene with the weather on Ribbon Day so that her precious creatures would look their best against the pale blue of Oc's early-autumn sky. Accordingly, she was not surprised when she opened her eyes on this, her final Ribbon Day, to find the sky untroubled by clouds, the treetops barely moving in a light breeze. She shivered with anticipation.

The Academy had been uneasy during the months since the Duke's death. Mistress Rambler had come for her things, white-faced and wretched as she moved between the Residence and the Hall. Mistress Star and Mistress Moon had a bitter argument in the stairwell of the Hall while the girls cowered in the library, listening. Everyone tried to pretend afterward that the disagreement was at an end, but no one really believed it.

The students had their own problems, especially the third-levels. Beatrice, Lillian, and Beryl remained sullen and resentful. Isobel complained to Hester that neither camp accepted her efforts to make peace. Amelia, returned in quiet triumph to the Academy by Baron Rys, was more reserved than ever. Lark worried that her experiences had driven her further inside herself, but she thrilled at the sight of Amelia and Mahogany flying at last, demonstrating the same calm competency they showed in everything they undertook.

But Lark had little time to address any of this through the months of that dark winter. She had spent every free moment she had with the orphaned Diamond.

The silver filly, after losing her rider, had trotted behind Tup like a lost puppy as they wound through the streets of Osham.

News of the Duke's death had spread swiftly through the White City. The impressed militiamen threw down their muskets and swords to return to their homes. The regular militia stood about in confusion, uncertain of what to do. Lark had passed through the city unimpeded, reaching the Academy late in the evening, with Tup beside her right shoulder and Diamond, head down and ears drooping, close to Tup's right flank.

It had been a sad homecoming. Lark, having no one to advise her, put Diamond in the stall next to Tup's. The filly leaned so hard against the dividing wall, trying to be close to him, that Lark was afraid she would break it down. Lark talked to her, and stroked her, but the filly stamped and fidgeted, flexing her wings, snuffling over the wall at Tup's neck. Lark knew she couldn't put a filly and an uncut stallion in the same stall, but she was afraid to leave Diamond untended. In the end, it was Tup who solved her problem, sidling as close to the wall as he could get, nosing Diamond and whickering gently to her. Diamond settled down then, and when Lark left them at last, they were standing nose to tail, with the wall between them.

"Thank you, my Tup," Lark said wearily, as she closed the gate. He flicked an ear at her in acknowledgment as Diamond's head nodded wearily near his hindquarters.

The dapple gray showed no signs of madness, which could be expected in a winged horse after the loss of its bondmate. But she was decidedly fractious. No one but Lark could get close to her. Anyone else found the filly's teeth bared, her hooves flashing.

Twice, Master Crisp brought girls to the stables, hoping one of them might be able to bond with Diamond. The results had been disastrous, with girls fleeing and Diamond trembling in fury and confusion. The Master Breeder had not yet threatened to put her down, but as the months passed and she grew no more cooperative, Lark began to fear that pronouncement.

The only days Diamond was calm were the days she flew with Tup, wearing a flying saddle and sand weights. Cautiously at first, then adding distance and altitude and complexity, Lark and Tup monitored Diamond so she could stretch her wings, practice her launches and returns, expend her nervous energy in the air.

Lark, with two horses to care for, was spending twice as much time as any other girl in training, grooming, feeding, and mucking out. She often felt she was doing justice to neither horse. And she fretted over what would become of Diamond when she and Tup left the Academy for their first posting.

The sleeping porch was coming awake now. Nervous whispers carried between the cots as the girls began to push back their blankets and roll out of bed. Lark hurried to wash her face and dress. She was afraid that Diamond, with all the excitement brewing around her, would be at her worst today, lashing out at anyone who passed her stall. She planned to work the filly on the longue line to settle her down. If Diamond created an uproar, on this morning in particular, Lark worried Master Crisp would banish her to the Palace stables or someplace worse, where what was left of the filly's spirit would wither. She was a winged horse without a flyer, a winged horse whose bonding had failed. There was no precedent, and no one knew what to do about it.

Lark was the first into the stables that morning. She greeted Tup, and brought him his oats. Diamond hung her head over the wall, snuffling at Lark's pockets. "You're next," Lark said to her. Diamond nipped at her hand and tossed her head impatiently. Lark said, "Please, Diamond. You have to be calm today!" But the filly stamped and began to turn in her stall, around and around, making a trough in the straw.

Lark sighed. "Tup, I have to do something about Diamond. I'll be back."

Tup lifted his nose from the oat bin to look at her, his ears twitching. He understood, she thought. He always understood.

She planted a kiss directly on his shining black nose, then slipped out of his stall and into Diamond's. As she led the filly toward the dry paddock, Amelia came in, on her way to Mahogany's stall. She raised one eyebrow. "Do you have time for that, Black?"

"I have to make time," Lark said. "I'm afraid she'll raise a ruckus the whole day otherwise, and Mistress Star will be furious if she upsets the other horses. Like yours!"

"She won't upset Mahogany. Very little does. But if I could help you, I would."

"Oh, it's all right," Lark said, though in truth, she wished someone else could handle this, just for today. "In any case, you have your Airs to think of!"

Amelia's reserve softened at that. "We're ready," she said. She turned down the aisle to where Mahogany was waiting for her, his glossy neck stretched over the half-gate of his stall.

"I know you are," Lark said.

"And you are, too," Amelia said, over her shoulder.

"Oh, aye," Lark said with a little laugh. "Tup and I have already used Arrows, and in worse conditions than these! Today's trial should be no trouble at all."

A festive air settled over the Academy as the rows of chairs in the courtyard filled with ladies in jeweled caps and ropes of pearls, their silken tabards shining in the sun. The Lords of the Council, in dark jackets and trousers, stood beside their ladies' chairs as the winged horses paraded out of the stables. Every mount gleamed with brushing, and the membranes of their wings had been rubbed until they glowed. Manes and tails flowed with silver and black ribbons, and hooves were oiled and buffed. The girls were spotlessly dressed, boots cleaned, peaked caps tilted at jaunty angles above their riding knots. Every member of the Council was in the courtyard. Oc had nearly split apart over these girls and these horses, and no Council Lord wanted to miss the event.

The new Duke, flanked on either side by secretaries, stood on the steps of the Hall. His pale hair gleamed like ice in the morning light as he nodded greetings to those who came to curtsy or bow to him.

Lark reined Tup toward the flight paddock behind the rest of the third-levels. Hester led them through the gate, and everyone took off their wingclips. Their horses stamped and shook their wings. Tup danced sideways, and Lark let him be. It was best if he worked off his excess energy before the demands of the close drills ahead. Beatrice was just in front of her, and she looked back, frowning, as Tup's bridle jangled, and her own Dark Lad pranced nervously.

Lark said, "Don't worry. They're just excited. We're going to be fine."

Beatrice's brow smoothed. For the first time in months, she smiled at Lark. "I know," she said, stroking Lad's neck. "I'm so glad this day is here at last."

"Aye." Lark looked forward, at the rest of her classmates, and saw that they were all smiling, even the often-anxious Anabel. They fell into formation behind Hester and Golden Morning, every eye bright, every back straight. A rush of hope brought a flush to Lark's cheeks. Perhaps they could be a flight again after all.

She glanced back at the steps of the Hall and saw that Philippa Winter, slender and erect, and still wearing the black riding habit, had come to stand beside Duke Francis. Behind her was a tall, broad-shouldered figure, standing beside the Duke of Oc as if it was perfectly natural for him to be there. It was Brye, taking time from harvest to watch Lark win her silver wings.

"They're here, my Tup," Lark whispered. She touched his neck with her fingers, and lifted the reins for the canter down the flight paddock. "They're both here!"

PHILIPPA watched from the steps of the Hall as the girls and horses launched, then began their Airs. The miseries of the past year seemed to fall away in the joyous exhibition of skill. Their Half Reverses and Grand Reverses were as polished as anyone could wish, and their Points were precise. They flew a single Grace only, but they had chosen the most intricate of all, the horses spinning in opposite circles, a shimmering kaleidoscope pattern of bay and palomino and sorrel and black. Philippa stole a glance at Suzanne, and saw that although her hands clenched tightly together, pride glowed in her eyes.

She had every right to be proud. As the flyers assembled for Arrows, the final proof of their abilities, they rose high over the Academy almost as one. Every horse's wings were steady and strong, every ear pricked forward, all hooves tightly tucked. A slight, cooling breeze fluttered the ribbons in their manes and tales, and belled the girls' full sleeves. Hester lifted her quirt, pointed it, dropped it.

Philippa's own fingers tightened their clasp on her belt. She, like every other horsemistress, knew how difficult Arrows could be. But surely, on this crystal-clear autumn day, it had to be easier than it had been over the bay, with carronades firing and sea spray splashing. The flyers plunged toward the courtyard with nothing to distract them. Seraph's drop was the most dramatic, fast and steep, the angle of his narrow wings the sharpest of all. When they reached the height of the tree-tops, the flight leveled, skimming the roof of the stables, darting past the dry paddock, then ascending like a flock of birds swirling into the sky.

On a wave of applause from the courtyard, Hester began the return pattern, banking, descending, soaring down toward the paddock. They came to ground in order, the girls grinning, the horses' tails arching with pride.

Seraph, the last to land, made one, small dip before he came over the hedgerow, tilting his wings this way and that, no doubt just to show that he could.

Philippa covered her mouth with her hand to hide her smile.

LARK and her classmates stabled their horses and went to stand before Duke Francis and Headmistress Star, whose smile was so wide Lark thought it must hurt her cheeks. One by one, they stepped forward. They nodded to the Duke, and he bowed elegantly to each of them before he pinned the shining silver wings to their collars.

When it was Lark's turn, she stood very straight and still. She had known that she and Tup were ready, but at this moment, it hardly seemed possible they had reached their goal at last. So many things had stood in their way! But Char's sacrifice, her brothers' devotion, Mistress Winter's guidance, Hester's help, and Rosellen's, then Amelia . . . and always, Tup.

He was, indeed, one of Kalla's miracles. And this was a moment of pure magic.

Behind the Duke, Brye smiled. Mistress Winter stood at his

shoulder, her weathered features impassive, but she nodded her approval.

Duke Francis bent his head as he pinned the wings to her tabard. "Welcome to the service of the Duchy," he said. "You are now a horsemistress of Oc."

The words thundered in Lark's ears. Her voice suddenly choked in her throat. She looked helplessly at Mistress Winter, shaking her head, unable to speak her gratitude.

Duke Francis touched her hand. "It's all right," he said quietly. "It's a great moment."

Lark nodded, again and again, feeling the color surge and fade in her cheeks. She managed to stammer, "Thank you, Your Grace. Thank you!"

He gave her a boyish grin, and she suddenly remembered that he was only ten years older than she. "It is I who thank you, Horsemistress Black," he said. "And I look forward to many years of your service to the Duchy."

When Lark turned away, eyes glittering with happy tears, she found her brother at her shoulder, his strong hand under her arm. He led her away from the crowd, and the moment they were out of sight, he lifted her off her feet in a great hug. By the time he put her down, she was laughing. And Mistress Winter, following, indulged in one of her rare smiles.

PHILIPPA slipped out the side door of the dining hall, leaving the bright-eyed young flyers to their celebration. She had no part of it anymore. She missed Sunny, waiting for her in the Uplands, but she also missed the Academy with a pain that was physical, a pang beneath her breastbone she could not breathe away.

She turned toward the stables, seeking comfort in the company of winged horses. Herbert, working in the tack room, looked up as she passed the door. His glance was full of pity, and that stiffened her spine. She didn't want pity.

"Can I help you, Mistress Winter?" Herbert asked.

"No," she said shortly, then, regretting her tone, said, "I'm just going to have a look at the horses before I go to bed."

" 'Tis good to have you back," he said.

"Thank you, Herbert." She walked on into the stables. An oc-hound jumped to its feet and came to her side. She stroked it, and it followed her down the aisle.

She was patting Hester's mare when she heard a murmur at the far end of one of the aisles. She went to the corner to look past the row of sleepy horses. Amelia was just opening the half-gate to Mahogany's stall. Philippa cleared her throat to announce herself.

Amelia paused with her hand on the latch. "Good evening, Mistress Winter."

"Amelia," Philippa said. She walked down the aisle to stand outside the stall. "You've left the party, too, I see."

"Yes," she said. Mahogany Master stared across the gate at Philippa as if taking her measure. The two of them, Philippa thought, girl and colt, were as like as two peas.

"Congratulations on your promotion to the second level," Philippa said.

Amelia's lips curved. "Thank you. We're very pleased."

"Your father will be, as well." Philippa stood for a moment, letting Mahogany sniff her palm. "Are you lonely here, Amelia?"

The girl arched one slender eyebrow, which made her look startlingly like the Baron. "Lonely?" she said. "Not particularly."

"You'll miss Larkyn, I think."

"Of course," the Klee girl answered. She stroked her colt's neck, and Philippa thought that for this girl, her horse would always be her only real companion. Amelia said, "But I'm happy here, Mistress Winter."

"Are you?"

"Yes. I'm doing what I've always wanted." She straightened a strand of Mahogany's mane, then stepped away from him and came out of the stall. "Please don't worry about us."

"Very well, Amelia. I'll try not to." But Philippa felt sure that Amelia's very self-containment would always set her apart from the other girls. As if being Klee were not enough.

As they turned away from Mahogany's stall, Philippa heard a ruckus from another aisle, the rhythmic, irritated thumping of a hoof and the rattle of a stall gate.

"Who's that?" she asked Amelia. "Not Seraph, still?"

"No." Amelia cast a worried glance toward the noise. "It's Diamond," she said. "Duke William's filly. No one but Lark can do anything with her."

Philippa reached the turning of the aisle. Black Seraph's stall was halfway down, near Golden Morning and the other horses of the third level. In the neighboring stall the exquisite dapple gray filly tossed her head, then struck at the stall gate with her forefoot. Seraph whickered at her, and Diamond stopped, but she soon started again, turning, switching her tail, striking at the gate.

Amelia said, "We don't know what will become of her. It's such a waste."

"It is indeed," Philippa said. She thought of Sunny, uselessly flexing her wings, begging to fly, and her heart ached anew. "It is precisely that, Amelia. A great waste."

PHILIPPA rose late the next morning. It was odd to be in her old apartment, which Matron had refused to reassign to one of the junior horsemistresses. Philippa stood in the window to gaze out over the courtyard, just as she had done for so many years. Clouds had rolled in from the sea, turning the day as gray and dull as the day before had been glorious. The trees and hedgerows were nearly bare.

Students and horsemistresses were streaming out of the hall on their way to the stables and paddocks. Philippa sighed as she closed the curtain. She supposed she could stay here and teach. She could petition Duke Francis to rescind Eduard's order barring Sunny from the stables, and he would surely grant her request. But somehow—without flying—she had no heart for it.

She dressed, and after begging a cup of coffee from Matron, she wandered outside with the cup in her hand. She felt idle and useless. Brye would come with the oxcart later, to take her back to the Uplands. She knew it was time to decide where she and Sunny could go, a place of their own. Sunny needed the company of other horses, even if they were wingless. And for Philippa, the longer she stayed at Deeping Farm, the harder it would be to disentangle herself.

She heard someone working in the dry paddock behind the stables, and she wandered in that direction, sipping her coffee as she went.

She found Larkyn in the center of the dry paddock with the filly, Diamond, on a longue line. Diamond cantered around the perimeter of the paddock smoothly enough, but she tossed her head as she ran, and her tail switched irritably. When she saw Philippa she stopped dead in her tracks, throwing up her head and glaring at her. Larkyn gave the longue line a flip, but the filly shook her mane and stamped, refusing to move.

Larkyn glanced over her shoulder. "Mistress Winter! Good morning. I was afraid you'd leave before I had a chance to say good-bye."

"I wouldn't have done that." Philippa came to the pole fence and looked through at the silver filly. "She's a lovely thing, isn't she? Has she flown since . . . since it happened?"

"Aye. Tup and I monitor her, or at least we try. Twice she headed off on her own, as if she was looking for something. She turned around and came back soon enough, but 'twas a terrible worry."

Larkyn looped the longue line over her arm, drawing it in. Diamond took two steps, then set her feet, refusing the lead. Larkyn tugged, and clicked her tongue, and the filly stamped her forefeet and showed her teeth.

Philippa frowned. "Does she do that often?"

"Aye." Larkyn sighed. "She's a bit unpredictable."

Diamond switched her tail, and backed away, pulling on the longue line, stopping only when she felt the fence behind her.

"She's confused," Philippa said.

"Aye. I know. I don't know how to help her."

"There may be nothing you can do."

"I'm worried about that, Mistress Winter. I'm afraid Master Crisp will put her down."

Philippa couldn't deny that possibility. On an impulse, she

set her coffee cup on the ground, and moved to the gate. She let herself into the paddock, and stood just inside.

"Careful," Larkyn warned. "She bites. And she kicks, sometimes."

"So I've heard."

Philippa stood where she was, her hands hanging empty and still beside her. She looked at the silver filly's delicate muzzle, the arch of her croup and the short curve of her back, and a wave of sadness filled her. She remembered so well how Sunny had looked when she was a two-year-old. How different things had been then! She and Sunny had both been little more than babes, with the road open before them. Neither of them had had an idea of how hard a journey it could be, nor how joyous. And here was this filly, this poor damaged Diamond, with no one to help her follow her own path.

The filly stared at her, the whites showing around her dark eyes. She switched her tail, and she took a hesitant sidestep.

Larkyn started to move, but Philippa said, "Wait."

The filly lifted her hoof to paw at the ground, and Philippa murmured, "No, sweetheart. You don't need to do that."

Diamond lowered the foot and arched her neck, laying her small, perfect ears flat against her head.

Philippa said again, "No. No, Diamond. It's all right."

The filly tossed her head and backed away, pulling at the longue line. She flicked her tail back and forth, back and forth. She relaxed her ears and turned them to Philippa. She snorted once, then she stood very still, her head high, staring at Philippa.

As Philippa gazed back at her, she thought again of her girlhood. She had been a misfit in her own family, with no one who understood her, no one who knew what she cared about. Not until she was bonded had she felt she belonged to anyone or anything.

Diamond must feel just that way. She was a misfit. Abandoned.

Philippa took a step forward. Larkyn whispered, "Have a care—" just as the filly reared, snorting, flailing with her forefeet.

Philippa stood her ground. "Steady, Diamond. There's no need for all this."

Breathing hard, the filly glared at her. Philippa took another step, her hands relaxed by her sides. Diamond reared again, but this time it was halfhearted, her forefeet barely leaving the ground. She huffed, and stamped, then stood still.

"That's my girl," Philippa said gently. "You're lonely, I think. A beautiful girl, Diamond, but lonely and frightened."

Diamond took a quick look to the side, to see that Larkyn was still there, then her great eyes fixed on Philippa again. Light gleamed in their depths, the spark of spirit and intelligence. Her nostrils flared like the petals of a pink flower edged in silver. Her lashes were so dark a gray they were almost black. They fluttered down over her eyes, and she gave a long, gusty sigh.

Larkyn laid the longue line down. Diamond turned her head to watch her, and her feet shifted nervously.

"Should I—" Larkyn began.

"No," Philippa said, keeping her voice low. "Let's let her think. Let her work it out."

Distantly, she heard the sounds of the Academy, horses whickering, equipment clattering, voices raised in the stables. The wheels of a carriage rattled on the cobblestones of the courtyard, and a draft horse whinnied.

Diamond reacted to none of these things. Her eyes were fixed on Philippa, and her tail, bit by bit, ceased its anxious switching. After a long, still moment, she took a step forward, lifting her hooves high, settling them into the dirt with delicate deliberation.

Philippa waited where she was.

The filly took another step. She turned her head to Larkyn, then back to Philippa, her nostrils twitching.

Philippa didn't move, but she held out her hand. "Come to me, sweetheart," she whispered. "You poor, abandoned girl. You can come to me."

Diamond drew a shallow breath. Like a dancer, she inched closer to Philippa, each step a question and a challenge. When she was only two steps away, she lifted a forefoot as if to strike.

Philippa murmured, "No, Diamond. No, dear. This is all up to you."

A horse whinnied from the stables. Larkyn said ruefully, "Tup. He wants his breakfast."

"You can go, Larkyn."

"Oh, nay, Mistress Winter. I wouldn't miss this for anything. Tup can wait for once."

Philippa said, "We're close, I think." She turned her palm up. "Come along now, little Diamond. You can use a friend, I think."

Diamond looked at her, and at her hand. Her nostrils quivered, and she blinked uneasily. She took another step, then another, each as careful as if she were walking on ice.

At last, gingerly, hesitantly, she stretched her neck to its full length to put her nose into Philippa's palm. Her muzzle was cool and soft, and her indrawn breath tickled.

Philippa barely breathed.

Diamond took another step, bringing her close enough to sniff at Philippa's face, one cheek, then the other. Philippa tousled the filly's short fluff of mane, keeping her touch featherlight and noncommittal.

Diamond sighed, a sound that came from deep within her chest. She pulled her head back and looked into Philippa's eyes as if she could read what lay behind them.

And then, after a moment's breathless, wondering pause, she rustled her wings.

Philippa breathed again. She stroked the speckled gray satin of Diamond's shoulder. The filly lowered her head, and butted gently at her chest. She flexed her wings, the pinions stretching with the sound of silk unfolding. She took another step, so that she had to bow her neck to keep from pushing Philippa over, and she butted her again, like a child trying to get its mother's attention. A third time, her wings rippled against the wingclips. The invitation was as clear as if it had been written on parchment.

A strange, welcome sensation of warmth began to spread in Philippa's chest.

She touched Diamond's smooth cheek and breathed, "Oh, yes, my dear. Yes, indeed. I would love to fly."

EPILOGUE

On her last day as an Academy student, Lark packed up her few belongings, cleared her space on the sleeping porch, and embraced her classmates. They had spent six years together, studying, arguing, gossiping, and flying. They would see each other from time to time, but it would never be as it was now, all of them together in these familiar halls, sleeping next to each other in the Dormitory. They would go their separate ways, and there might be some who would never return to the Academy of the Air.

Hester, as expected, was assigned to the border. She would set off for the Angles this very morning to take up her duties there near her parents' summer estate. It had recently been re-deemed from the lenders by Duke Francis himself in gratitude to the Beeths. Anabel, with Beatrice and Grace, was to fly to Isamar, to be part of Prince Nicolas's palace flight. Lark had heard Mistress Star say that the cost of the royal flight had risen nicely since the troubles, and the Duke had assured her that the increased revenue would be spent on the Academy.

Lark herself would take up residence in the Ducal Palace. She was to be Duke Francis's special courier. She would be allowed to see her brothers from time to time.

But she would see Mistress Winter often.

She carried her bag downstairs. Duke Francis was sending a carriage for her things, so she left the bag just inside the door of the Dormitory and hurried across the courtyard to give Tup his breakfast. The autumn sun was bright as the twopenny coin for which Tup had been named, and it gleamed on Winter Sunset's coat where she grazed now with the yearlings in their pasture. Lark paused at the fence to call softly to her.

Sunny lifted her head and flicked her ears in greeting before she resumed grazing. There were only four yearlings with her, but next year there would be more. Master Crisp was working hard at restoring the breeding program.

Molly, the little brown goat, came trotting up to the fence to bleat at Lark.

Lark bent to stroke her. "So where is Diamond, Molly? Is she flying so early?"

Molly pressed close so Lark could scratch at her poll. Lark stroked her for a moment before she turned toward the stables. There was a lot to do before she could leave. She wanted to leave Tup's stall as clean as she had found it. And she wanted to clean Diamond's stall for Mistress Winter one more time.

The sound of Winter Sunset's whinny stopped her where she was. She looked back, and saw the sorrel mare with her head up, her ears pricked forward. Lark followed her gaze, and found Mistress Winter and Diamond just banking for their descent into the return paddock. She shaded her eyes to watch them come to ground, Diamond's silver wings wide and still, her forefeet reaching as she soared down over the hedgerow. Lark sighed with pleasure at the sight. As always, Mistress Winter's slender form was erect, flowing with the horse as if she were part of the animal, her hands easy on the reins, the sleeves of her tabard rippling in the wind.

Winter Sunset came trotting up to the fence and pressed close to the rails, stretching her neck over the top rail to watch. Lark gave her mane a gentle tug.

"Aye, sweetheart," she murmured. " 'Tis a hard thing for you to see, isn't it? You're a lovely, fine girl to share your bondmate this way."

Sunny's head turned to follow Diamond's canter up the return paddock toward the stables; and then, once Mistress Winter dismounted, she gave a deep sigh and went back to cropping the dry grass. Lark opened the gate for Molly to come through, and the little goat trotted at her heels as she walked toward the stable.

No one but Lark had believed it could work, that the orphaned filly would accept a new bondmate. When Mistress Winter had set out to fly her, that first time, Suzanne Star had begged her not to, fearful of another tragedy.

But Lark had seen Diamond's invitation to Mistress Winter. There had been not the slightest doubt in her mind that this was what Diamond wanted.

She was not surprised, either, that Mistress Winter could manage both Diamond and Winter Sunset. She stabled them side by side, and she borrowed Molly to foster the filly when she was out with Sunny. She told Eduard Crisp that her price for saving Diamond was for Sunny to remain in the stables at the Academy of the Air. His dour protests were overridden by Mistress Star and by the Duke himself, and now even Master Crisp admitted he had been wrong. The other winged horses accepted Winter Sunset's presence though she didn't fly. The yearlings loved her, trotting up to her whenever they were turned out to graze, yearning after her when she went to her stall and they to theirs. And for her part, so long as Mistress Winter rode her each day, she seemed to accept her new role.

Suzanne Star had offered to step down, to make Mistress Winter Headmistress. But Mistress Winter, with a young horse to train and an injured one to care for, refused. Lark suspected she wanted to retain a bit of freedom to visit the Uplands from time to time.

Lark smiled as she went into to Tup's stall. Six years before, Philippa Winter had allowed an unsuitable farm girl to come to the Academy of the Air. And now, Philippa spent as much time as she could on the very farm where she had first met Lark. And though Lark knew Brye hated to see her leave Deeping Farm, he was all the more glad when Philippa returned.

Lark finished her chores, saddled Tup, and tied her saddlepack behind the cantle. She brushed bits of straw from her tabard, and put on her peaked cap and her flying gloves.

Hester and Anabel and the others were also ready, gathering as a flight for the last time in the courtyard. Lark leaped up into Tup's saddle and fell in behind her classmates. Just as Hester turned Golden Morning toward the flight paddock, Amelia hurried out from the stables. She came close to Tup, and held something up to Lark.

"What's this, Amelia?" Lark asked.

"It's your icon," Amelia said breathlessly. "I almost forgot!"

"But I gave it to you. 'Tis yours now."

"And it protected me," Amelia said. She pressed it into Lark's hand. Lark turned it over in her fingers, the little carved figure of Kalla she had worn for a long time around her own neck. She hesitated, and Amelia said, "It will protect you again now, Lark. I mean—" Her lips curved, and her eyes twinkled. "I mean—Horsemistress Black."

Horsemistress Black! It was true. Kalla's miracle was complete, from Tup's birth on an Uplands farm to this shining day. "Oh, Amelia. Thank you."

Amelia stepped back and lifted her hand. "Good-bye. Good luck!"

Lark nodded farewell and lifted Tup's reins. Hester began her canter down the flight paddock, and the rest of the flight followed, one by one. Lark and Tup were last to launch into the sky, lifted on Tup's strong wings. When the whole flight was in the air, they hovered at Quarters, the girls gazing into each other's eyes one last time.

Then the formation broke apart, splitting in every direction in a sunburst of sorrel and palomino and bay and black.

Lark looked back once at the gambrel roofs of the Academy stables, at the majestic lines of the Hall and the Dormitory and the Residence, at the younger girls gathered in the courtyard to watch them leave. As Tup carried her away, the figures below her shrank until she could no longer tell them apart.

She was certain, though, that one of them was Mistress Winter, standing in the very center of the courtyard with her sorrel mare at her shoulder. She lifted one arm to wave.

Lark, her heart as light as if it had its own wings, waved back before she turned her face forward to her new life.

To read more about the winged horses of Oc,
please visit www.tobybishop.net.

Toby Bishop can be contacted at DuchyofOc@aol.com.